GLADIATORS

OF THE

NAUMACHIA

STERLING NIXON

S&J Publishing

The final approval for this literary material is granted by the author.

First printing

ISBN: 978-0-9903708-4-0 (trade paperback)

S&J Publishing

Printed in the United States of America

To my mother who inspired me;

My brothers Adam, Brandon, and Travis
who always supported me;

My sisters Lisl and Elizabeth,
who helped with the final edits.

To my wonderful wife and best friend, Julia.

And my father, whose belief in me carried
me through the most difficult of life's challenges.
Without him, there would be a very different book
in your hands than there is now.

Dear Most Admirable and Well Versed Reader,

I am proud to present this book for your enjoyment. I have gone through great lengths to ensure the historical acuity of this book as well as keep it fast paced and entertaining. Many of the gladiatorial fighting styles, techniques, diets, and weapons that are contained in this book are derived from revelating research that is being conducted in the graveyards of Ephesus. Although many of the ideas and concepts in this book are based on fact, I feel that I must qualify three important elements about the novel.

The two main characters in the book are Priscus and Verus. Although these characters are based on real people, little is known about their lives before their grandiose conflict in 80 AD. It is postulated that Priscus was a Celt and had some ties in Gaul, and that Verus was recruited to be a gladiator while he worked as a slave in a stone quarry. The monumental fight between these two warriors is, however, well documented by Marshal in *Liber de Spectaculis,* and stands as one of the few accounts of actual gladiatorial combat.

The *Naumachia* described in this book did happen, but its appearance is chronologically incorrect. Instead of occurring before the inauguration of Fluvial Colosseum, this specific *Naumachia* took place after. Little to nothing is known about the preparation for a *Naumachia*. It is known that when Julius Caesar orchestrated the first naval gladiatorial battle, slaves were the principle fighters—not trained gladiators—and they fought on boats that acted more like fixed bridges. There did, however, seem to be a trend among the emperors to surpass their predecessors; for this reason, amongst others, it seems logical that eventually trained soldiers would engage in a *Naumachia*—as presented in this book.

The last major element that is historically inaccurate is the use of modern months, dates, and years. The original Roman calendar is believed to be a lunar calendar that was supposedly invented by Romulus and began in 753 BC. Since then the calendar had several subsequent changes, including days added and months altered. Later, while in the position of *Pontifex Maximus*, Julius Caesar completely overhauled the system. What makes the calendar even more convoluted is that the Romans did not keep track of years; instead, the years were named after the Consul who was in power at the time. In the late republic, Romans finally began to keep track of the years and counted up from the founding of Rome—approximately 753 BC, but there were many discrepancies and debates over the numbers of years that had passed. Dates given by this method are numbered *ab urbe condita, which means* after the founding of the city and are abbreviated as AUC. A rough way to convert modern AD years to AUC years would be to simply add 753 to the AD years; this, however, would only give you an approximate AUC year. To convert BC years to AUC, one would take 753 and subtract the BC year. In *The Sea Kings of Rome* series, I decided to use the modern calendar instead of the Roman one to prevent an endless problematic debate, not to mention the difficulty the reader might have placing everything in context.

I hope you enjoy reading *Gladiators of the Naumachia.*

Sterling Nixon

Chapter 1

August 1, 69 AD
Verus

"If we don't cut—he'll die in a week," Tulias whispered.

Verus grimaced, "But he's only been alive seven seasons; no one that age can withstand that much pain."

Tulias folded his arms defensively. "If we don't cut, he will experience more pain as the infection spreads. And after all that pain, he'll end up dead anyway. Listen, Verus, my long time friend and neighbor, the longer we wait the less likely it is that I can save that leg. After a few days, it will be even less likely that I will be able to save the boy. We have to act quickly if we want to save his life; if we don't, you might as well use the Denarii for his funeral."

Verus wiped at the blacksmith dust on his arms—which never seemed to go away; he had tried olive oils from all parts of Italy, but no amount would take off the black hue. An old traveler once mentioned that an exotic thing called "soap" would help, but it would probably be a while before such a commodity would ever reach the small town of Pinacale, even though it was next to the thriving city of Nepet.

He rubbed his brow, "Of the four humors, which one is out of balance with the boy?"

Tulias shook his head. "Don't believe that Greek nonsense. Medicine is much more practical than that. As Celsus the Great writes, and I wholeheartedly agree: 'I am of the opinion that the art of medicine ought to be rational.' There is no humor that is out of balance that causes this, nor is it a curse from the Gods. This is a real problem that needs real action. He has an infection spreading up his leg, which will soon grip his whole body with poison." With dried sweat on his thin beard and dirt on his brow, Verus had a decision to make: Does he spend his coin on his dying son—whose life was tentative at best—or save it so his family does not starve that winter? His son was only six when he first started showing small signs of the curse, and after only three months, the boy was too weak to stand. Few ever survived the curse, fewer still could ever walk again, and those who did usually came from wealthy families that had the money to spend on exotic treatments and odd smelling remedies.

In an odd sense, Verus was fortunate to even have the ability to choose. While most of his neighbors were too poor to even consider treatment for their dying children, Verus' little blacksmith shop had been steadily increasing in business, which had allowed his family comforts the typical Roman did not have. One of those luxuries was medicine. Despite the increase in money, his son's treatment was draining any extra coin he made, and with winter already setting in, things looked bleak. The operation would cost the last of Verus' Denarii, and without anything saved, his family could easily starve. Business slowed in winter and only started picking up in the spring; by the time summer rolled around, his family might already be dead. Even without the cost of the operation, it was looking to be a difficult winter.

"This decision is not mine alone," Verus said.

Tulias gave an exasperated sigh, "You know I am doing you a favor, right? This whole procedure usually costs a lot more."

"Yes," Verus sighed, "you've mentioned it—quite a few times actually, Tulias. But this decision is not mine alone to make. I need to talk to my wife."

"Your wife?" Tulias scoffed.

"Yes," Verus said emphatically, "she runs the household."

"But this is a monetary decision—she should have no part in that…"

"She does in my house."

Verus was not tall—he was actually smaller than the common Roman—but he knew how to handle himself well. In his wild younger days he had been quite a wrestler and, consequently, his presence commanded respect. Even though his persona was soft as Persian silk, he often intimidated the people around him. If it was not for that blasted emotion called love, Verus might have joined up with a Roman Legion, where he would have been wielding swords instead of forging them. Some days—like today—he envied the carefree life of a Roman soldier.

"Fine," Tulias said with a defeated tone, "but you must tell me your decision by tomorrow. If you haven't decided by tomorrow morning, the boy will be as good as dead by the evening."

"I will know by tonight," Verus replied, "just give me a chance to talk to my wife."

Tulias shook his head, "Oh, how I miss the traditional days of Augustus, when a man made the decisions and the wife obeyed them."

Verus afforded a small smile, "I noticed that you pray to Vesta—isn't she the Goddess of... domestic well-being? Why would a traditionalist be praying for domestic well-being—you think you would have your wife under control by now."

Tulias frowned. "She's been the Goddess of my family for generations…"

"I thought they favored Aesculapius, the God of medicine," Verus said playfully. "At least, that is the God inscribed on your family crest."

Tulias shrugged his shoulders and desperately looked to change the subject. "Just let me know by tonight." He grabbed his cow stomach bag and threw it over his shoulder; with a huff and narrowed eyes, he waved a goodbye.

Verus nodded. "I will stop by the *Domus* tonight. Oh, and if you have any left, I would not say "no" to some of those raspberries, too."

Tulias nodded with a secret smile and disappeared out into the warm sun. In the new silence of the smithy, Verus felt nervous— it was usually never quiet here. He had rented out sections of the smithy to other apprentices who were usually noisily making weapons for the army, but presently all were gone for the day of Volturnus— the God of waters.

Verus stepped outside. It was brighter than he anticipated, forcing him to squint. This city was his family's home—it had been for generations. Pinacale was a simple, serene city. The town had seen it all: In the year 392, the invading Gauls passed within five miles of the city but left it untouched; in the year 217, the city was directly between Hannibal and his conquest of Rome, but the Carthaginians never mustered the courage to attack; and in the year 72 a slave revolt led by Spartacus set everything ablaze but somehow spared Pinacale. It had all the elements of a large city—such as a bathhouse and water supply—but not the problems of one. It was a secret gem that was beginning to attract a little more attention than the locals really cared to have.

The blacksmith had wheat-colored hair that turned even whiter in the summer. His body was thick around the chest and slender at the waist, with most of his muscles massed around his shoulders. By far his most distinguishing feature was his eyes, which portrayed every feeling, whether he tried to conceal them or not. They naturally slanted away from his brow, giving him the appearance that he was scrutinizing everything.

He had work to do, so he went back inside. Grabbing the metal he was working on, he examined it closely: It was a Roman *gladius*. The weapon was strong and heavy. While most of the world still struggled with metal working, the Romans had perfected it. And owing to the several civil wars that had broken out, there was an even bigger demand for well made weapons, which was good for a smithy who specialized in them.

He pumped the bellows with his leg as he turned the thick metal in the fire. Once it reached the right temperature, he pulled it out and struck it with his hammer until it began to take shape. The process went on: heating and hammering, reheating and hammering some more. It was not his best work—lately, nothing was—but it was good enough. With the weapon finished and a mist of sweat around his face, he decided to head home. The muddy path that led up to his humble house was more than just worn, having been forged by Verus' family for centuries.

Camelia and peony flowers dotted the rolling hills of Tuscany with such beauty that they seemed to have been planted by the Goddess Flora herself. Everything grew naturally in Pinacale, including the friendships; there was no politicking or campaigning— it was too small for that. If Jupiter had the ingredients for a perfect town, where civility and honor ruled, he surely used them to make this city.

After a long hard day, Verus thought it was annoying to have his house on the hilltop. Everyone else was satisfied to build houses in the valley, where the land was flat as papyrus, but whether it was foresight or stubbornness, Verus' descendants determinedly built on a hill away from the city. When he was a child it did not seem much of a climb, but after years of trekking it, the path seemed to stretch out just a little further every day.

And suddenly, as he climbed the hill, there she was—his patient wife, waiting for him at the door. Her face was drawn into tired, weary lines, which did not look as pretty, but she at least attempted a smile. Verus remembered fondly when he first met Julia: She had soft skin and round features, but now, a life of labor had hardened her face and tightened her skin. She had actually been sent to Pinacale as a punishment for not getting married quickly enough. At the old age of seventeen, most of her family had given up on the idea of her finding a man. But from the moment he saw her, he loved her in a way that was as consistent as the Tiber and as deep as the Mediterranean. Verus had a different perspective of love than most: to him it was about absolute loyalty before everything else.

"Hello, Julia," Verus said with a warm smile.

Julia ran for him, grabbed him with her arms, and pulled him in close, "Oh, Verus..."

The force of her running was a little more than the Blacksmith expected. "What's wrong, dear?"

"Hold me," Julia whispered. Verus obeyed, pulling her head into his barreled chest with his thick arms. Long moments passed before she spoke again.

"What did Tulias say?"

Verus took a deep breath before he answered. "Even though Tulias said he was doing us a favor, it was more Denarii than we thought, dear. With everything we have saved, it won't be enough; I will have to sell part of the smithy...if we decide to do it."

Julia pulled her head back, "...*if* we decide to do it? This is our son we are talking about."

"Dear, with the drought this summer, grain will be expensive this winter. We don't have enough to last us through. If we spend all of our coin on this operation—which might even kill Gaius—then we endanger the rest of the family with starvation. If it was just you and me—that would be one thing—but what about the other three children?"

"What about the free grain in Rome? They give out lots of grain, don't they?"

"Yes," Verus said with a mock laugh, "I hear they get as much as 40 million modii a year, but that is only if your family cognomen is Scipii or Brutii. It would take weeks for me to become one of their clients, and even after that, who is to say how much grain we could get. I don't want to burden you, but I do want us to decide together. If we try to save our son there is no guarantee of him living; if we spend our coin on this operation, there is the possibility that all of us will die."

Julia hugged Verus again, pulling herself deep into his powerful chest. "I love you. You've never wavered or been worn by trials of the past, and I don't see us failing now."

"I knew you would say that, dear," Verus said with a warm smile. "I just needed to hear it."

Julia leaned back and kissed her husband on his rugged hands. They embraced for a moment longer before Verus finally pulled away.

"I need to saddle up old Potter—Tulias wants to know tonight."

Chapter 2

August 1, 61 AD
Priscus

"He's a wild one," Galen laughed.

Brulic shook his head. "This one has turned in age. Let's just finish him. If you keep him, you'll have to raise him with a stick in one hand and a whip in the other."

"That's how all the Northern Gauls are—it's in his nature," Galen said. "Besides, he's only a boy."

"A boy!" Brulic mockingly replied. "He's bigger than you or me. A large lad like that will be even bigger as a man. He will be the death of you if you bring him in."

"Brulic, you old coward, have you forgotten what slaves are selling for these days? He will fetch a good amount of gold, and until then he will make a strong slave. Nero needs workers for his new palace and he will pay a high price for ones as strong as this."

"Will you sell him as a normal slave?"

"I don't care what they use him for—they could use him to clean the streets if they wanted to—as long as they pay."

"They pay more for gladiators. If they are strong enough and know a few things, you can make a decent profit. It would only be worthwhile if you trained him."

"Maybe, maybe…"

Brulic was shaking his head nervously. "But I don't trust northern blood. We've already captured enough slaves, why do you want to take this boy?"

"There is something in his eyes," Galen retorted.

"Yes, it's called sedition, and it will breed nothing but other seditious slaves."

Galen laughed and shook his head. "You forget the strength

12

of the Celts. Stand up boy—we have a long march ahead of us." He then slapped his comrade on the shoulder. "Don't worry. He probably won't even survive the trip."

Upon command, the young Gaul ambled up and clenched his jaw. His body was bleeding and bruised from fighting, but his spirit remained untouched. He hated these Celts; they were traitors to their own people. As one of them tied Priscus' hands with coarse ropes, the Gaul stared at his village, trying to make sense of everything that had just happened. In his young mind, it seemed like the whole world was destroyed—everyone he had known was dead. His mother's blood still speckled his chin and cheek, where it had splattered just moments before.

The boy had black hair and even blacker eyes. His skin was darker than most Gauls, like his mother's, and he would have been ridiculed for it if he had not been so big. Even at this young age, the boy had developed a round, barreled chest and two thick arms that were muscled from years of hard use. He had a large cut above his right eye and another on the back of his hand, but besides these two marks he was virtually unscarred.

And then the march began. Priscus had not seen them before, but as he looked around now, he could see hundreds of his people bound and tied—most of them children. With a spear point in his back, Priscus shuffled forward on his bruised legs. All the while a large grey cloud the color of mud slowly crept towards them like a stalking wolf, threatening to unload a torrent of rain. While the Celts were sweating under an abundant amount of clothing, which was a combination of their own clothing and the garments they had taken from dead Gauls, the prisoners had nothing more than thin shirts and pants, and even thinner shoes.

They were forced to move quickly through the Gallic hills; those that did not move fast enough had their throats instantly cut and their bodies tossed to the side. They marched long into the afternoon and still later into the night. By torchlight they followed deer paths through a freezing rain. Still Priscus pushed on, determined not to show any weakness. He was a Gaul, and they were known to be fierce. But the Celts were merciless as they whipped their prisoners onward. The young captives were slowly tortured by the cold until finally, one after another, they began collapsing with exhaustion. When one did fall, Priscus would see a young friend or sometimes an old neighbor slashed to pieces by the captive's whips. Sometimes the fallen would find new energy and motivation to get up, but usually they did not. When the Celts were finished slashing and cutting—when the bodies were cold from death—the Celtic dogs would have their fill, attacking the flesh as if they had not eaten for days.

Some begged for their lives, crying to the *Tiwaz* for protection, but their words seemed to be swallowed up in the mist filled land. There were five hundred prisoners in the forced-march that evening, but by the next morning, there were only sixty. By some miracle or by chance, or even maybe by some twisted fate, Priscus' closest friend had survived. He had not seen him before, but with so few survivors, he could see him now. His name was Trontian: He was short and stocky, which was uncommon for a Gaul, but it was rumored his mother had had an affair with a Ligurian.

Priscus and Trontian were like brothers from the moment they had first met, which seemed odd considering their situation. Their fathers hated each other and each boy was raised to hate the other's father, but this did not stop the two boys from becoming friends. By some ill fortune, it was actually their fathers' hatred that brought them closer. Three years before, one father was so consumed with rage he challenged the other to a duel of death. With Priscus on one side, and Trontian on the other, they watched as their fathers fought, locked in mortal combat. The crowd laughed and cheered, while the two boys watched with unflinching eyes. When the battle finally ended, both opponents lay dead—their hands frozen around the other's neck. The fight gulfed the two grieving families, but it deeply united the boys in their pain.

The Celts jealously guarded their prisoners like vultures over a meager meal. If any of the children said one word—just one word— it meant instant death; the Celts seemed to have more interest in killing and torturing than in keeping slaves. Trontian nodded slightly to Priscus, which gave him a little bit of courage. It was just them now—no one would be coming to their rescue. In the space of one day, the two boys had seen an end to the world they had known, and now they were farther than they had ever traveled and colder than they had ever been.

They had a few moments of sleep in the early hours of the morning, but these were interrupted by pricks from Celtic spears and jabs by bloodied swords. By morning there were only forty children left. The night had been so cold a few of the boys were stiff with death. The Celts rolled them down a cliff for sport and made wagers on which body would roll the quickest.

Despite the morning brutality, the Celts finally showed some sense of charity. The prisoners were finally fed and better clothed, which filled Priscus with ambivalence: He longed for the warm clothing but was repulsed by the thought that they came from one of the bodies of his murdered people. One of the tunics he was handed still had fresh blood on it. Trontian nudged his friend in the side, encouraging him to just put it on. With a whisper of vengeance, Priscus finally obeyed; it was lucky that he did too, for just at that moment, one of the Celts was eyeing him carefully.

After three grueling days of travel the Gallic prisoners were allowed to talk, which was a freedom eagerly welcomed by the miserable children.

Trontian huddled next to his friend. "What do they want with us?"

Priscus, who was known for his silence, only shook his head.

"I don't think they are trying to kill us off anymore—they seem to have had their fill of blood."

Priscus nodded. "I suppose they intend to sell the rest of us into slavery."

"Slavery?" Trontian said hoarsely, "We can't be slaves…"

"Why can't we?" Priscus retorted angrily.

"We're not slaves," Trontian said quickly. "We're freemen…"

"Do freemen have bonds around their hands?" Priscus lifted his ropes for emphasis. "Do freemen fear for their life and sleep in the mud, or eat watery soup and are whipped for talking? We were free, but now we are slaves. Now we are valued like the dust, which means we are nothing."

"Slaves?" Trontian said with only mild comprehension. "I hardly even know what a slave is."

"I heard one of them talking about it," Priscus continued. "The king of Rome is building something new—I can't quite remember what—but we are being sold to build it. We might be gladiators."

"What is a gladiator?"

Priscus shook his head, "I don't know, Trontian, but it can't be good."

Suddenly Galen yelled at the company, "Get up! We're moving out!"

Obediently, the two boys quickly stood, preparing themselves for the march; a few of the other boys moved too slowly and were whipped for it. Amid screams of pain and drips of blood, the whole company was ready to move in moments.

Despite their wretched condition, the land around them was at least warmer than it was before. While the trees were already starting to lose their leaves, the grass was still a deep green. The hills of Gaul did not look tall from afar, but when one was climbing them, they seemed to double in size. The occasional stone fence would crop up, marking the beginning of some border or the end of some boundary.

It felt like it was going to be a cold winter. This would have been fine back in their village—they had had a good harvest and a large store of food—but now their lives seemed so tentative. Now they were at the mercy of the merciless.

Chapter 3

August 2, 69 AD
Verus

"Dad!" cried Gaius.

Verus had his son by the hand and was squeezing the boy's palm. The pain was so tremendous that Gaius slipped between conscious and unconscious convulsions. When he was unconscious the doctor worked the quickest, plunging his awkward looking instruments into the flesh as quickly as he could. But when the boy was awake, he gave off sharp screams of pain, which curdled Verus' blood.

Gaius did not fully understand the purpose behind all of this pain, but he trusted his father, and that seemed to be the only thing that mattered. Instead of screaming for the doctor to stop cutting, Gaius only painfully called out for his father. It was his father's presence that helped the boy the most—not the doctor's repetitive attempts to soothe him. Verus was right there beside his son like an immobile sentry. He never flinched or looked away as the long painful hours passed by.

The sun had reached its zenith, sending powerful beams of light down on the large villa. The air turned slightly humid with the heat, which began to stifle the slaves as they hurried about with various chores. The doctor was done. But the boy's fate was still undecided.

For the first time since the treatment began two days earlier, Verus left Gaius' side at the behest of Tulias. The boy had been moved to Tulias' elaborate *Domus* where he would stay for the next couple of days. The estate was equipped with everything that made the Romans famous: large columns, two cooking areas, four fountains in the courtyard—which was sealed off by a ten-foot wall—huge rooms, silk drapes, a private bathhouse, and a separate area for the stables. One of the attributes that made Tulias such a fantastic doctor was his attention to detail, and this personality trait seemed to have transferred to the cleanliness of his house. The old man was generous and kind to his slaves, but he insisted that they clean constantly and meticulously. Even before Verus could properly drain any of the cups of wine that were given to him, he was always promptly given another.

"How do things fare?" Verus asked tentatively as they walked into the bleaching rays of light.

"Fine," Tulias replied. "I hope I removed all of the infection; we won't know for a few days. But be sure to apply the ointment three times a day and change the wound's dressing just as often. For the next couple of days he can stay here; my servants will take good care of him. But when he is at your home, make sure that Julia makes the special broth that I wrote down for you; it will give him the strength to move about."

"How bad was the infection?" Verus asked.

"It was worse than expected, but not as bad as it could have been," Tulias answered. "I saw a woodpecker this morning, which is a good *auspice*. I think the boy will live, but only Hermes can tell. Pray that Viduus does not know the boy's name."

"Who is Viduus?"

Tulias shook his head impatiently. "Surely, you know of the God that separates the body from the soul..."

"Well, thank you for doing everything you could," Verus said solemnly.

"So...how can I expect payment?"

"Oh, right," Verus said absentmindedly, "I have half now in gold Denarii and the other half will be paid...in installments."

"Installments? Installments?"

"Yes," Verus continued, "But, you know my word is good—I honor the Gods."

"You don't even *know* most of the Gods," Tulias protested.

Verus looked at his friend with pleading eyes.

"And so it is, young Verus," Tulias nodded, "but how are you planning on feeding your family during the winter?"

"It's going to be hard," Verus said with little emotion. "I

honestly don't know how we will make it, but we will be praying to *Felicitas* for success. I would ask my sisters or my brother for help, but it looks like they will be struggling as much as me."

"The Gods are busy protecting the soldiers that fight in this horrible civil war," Tulias said wisely. "My advice is that you have your wife pray to Saturn, who is the God of time; he can grant you more life, and I don't think he gets as much attention as the other Gods. But while your wife is praying, you should go to Rome. There is a family there, the Vitelli, which my family has served for years. Tell them your situation and that you're one of my patrons, and they may take you on as a client. If you can win their favor by promising them your vote, then they will take good care of you. I will even give you papers of introduction."

"Rome?"

"Yes," Tulias replied proudly. "Rome is the center of civilization—it is the city of light in this darkened world."

"I've never been there," Verus said quietly.

"Well be sure to pack your wits with you," Tulias said seriously. "Things have changed since the rule of Nero; it is now no place for the naïve. And even though Nero cut his own throat and Vittelian is the Emperor, things have not improved much."

"Who will protect my family while I'm gone?"

"Protection?" Tulias scoffed. "You'll need the protection, not them; you're the one going into the political fire."

"Who's the Emperor now?"

"Vitellius of the family of Vitelli, of course, as I just told you," Tulias said proudly. "He is of the very family that I am sending you to. He is a fine Emperor too—my family has been one of his biggest sponsors. He was the Consul in forty-eight and a Proconsul in Africa in the year sixty, where he led his troops with much success. The Germans love him."

"What about the Romans?" Verus asked.

"Well, I'm a Roman," Tulias replied. "He has done some good: He made it illegal for soldiers to bribe their Centurions to get out of guard duty, and Equites can now take imperial positions."

"I guess that's nice if you're an Equite," Verus mumbled. "Not all of us can have more Denarii than we can spend."

"Now that they are in the royal line, it will be easy for them to help their friends."

"I did not know you were so involved in politics," Verus said.

"I'm not," Tulias replied grumpily, "but my family is, and sometimes—not usually however—it pays to have family involved in politics." Tulias pulled Verus in close as if to tell him a secret: "You should work really hard in the next few weeks and make as much money as you can. Use your extra coin to pay for the trip down there, go to the house of Vitelli, get sponsorship, and come back here before the first frost."

"That would help," Verus nodded.

"Help?" Tulias laughed. "If you link your family with Vitelli you will be set for life. Even if they only give you a partial sponsorship, you will have more than enough grain to last through the winter."

Verus nodded solemnly.

"Stop being so glum," Tulias said with a slap on the Blacksmith's back. "We are Romans; we are the most advanced people in the world. As a Roman Citizen, you've never had a bad day in your life."

"Maybe I have," Verus whispered. "I've gone through some really rough things—I've had some pretty bad moments."

"Not even close," Tulias rebutted.

"Ah, what is this?" said a third voice. "Is my old friend Tulias trying to swindle some young man out of his money again?"

Tulias' body stiffened as he gave a polite laugh. "Ah, Plini, you're awake. You always seem to appear right around dinner."

"And I always shall as long as that pretty young slave of yours is cooking."

"You're going to be the financial ruin of me."

"Yes," Plini said with a wink. "I've noticed that you started watering down my wine and giving me twice as much bread as you do meat."

"It's not free you know."

Plini decidedly switched subjects. "Who is this young man? What does he bring? Let me guess: you're a blacksmith and the father of four; you have a young wife and a house just up the hill."

"Yes," Verus said with surprise. "How did you deduce all of that?"

"Tulias told me this morning."

Tulias and the old man laughed loudly, leaving Verus with a confused look on his face. This, at least, gave the Blacksmith time to study the old man. Plini the Elder—as he was called—was extremely worn and torn. If it had not been for the many conversations that Verus had with others in the town about the old man, he would have passed Plini off as a beggar. But anyone who ever talked to Plini for more than a moment quickly realized that he was no beggar. The man had dined with emperors and led vast armies in Gaul; he had been victorious in war on land and sea. But his greatest interest— much to Tulias' delight—was natural philosophy.

Tulias cleared his throat, "This is Verus. Verus, this is Plini the Elder."

"I've heard about you," Verus murmured nervously.

Tulias smiled widely. "Plini, have you come to lecture us on why Vespasian would be a better Emperor than Vitellius?"

Plini mimicked Tuilias' smile. "I don't need to lecture anyone on that... because that is already common knowledge."

"Hah," Tulias laughed, "if Vespasian is so great, why is Vitellius still the Emperor?"

"We will see..." Plini whispered.

"What brings you up this way?" Verus asked.

"Oh," Plini replied, "that would be because of the 'magnificent' Vitellius. Since taking the Emperorship he has been killing every astrologer that he can get his hands on. And since I have looked up at the stars once or twice, he thinks I'm an astrologer."

"Are you sure that is all you have been doing?" Tulias asked innocently. "You sure it wasn't because of your treatise on 'Why Vespasian is Better than Vitellius?'"

"You're too cruel to me," Plini answered.

Tulias slapped the old man on the back. "Oh, I only jest. Verus—I must tell you. This man is the wisest man I know. He has spent his life watching the world around him, trying to piece it all together."

"I've heard about some of your writings," Verus said awkwardly. "Your observations are a common conversation around here, especially since you have been staying at Tulias' *Domus*."

"Yes," Tulias said with even more excitement. "In fact, my

friend and I were just discussing how good he has it. I was telling Verus—who thinks that his life is so hard right now—that he has never had a bad day in his life. What do you think Plini?"

Plini gave a slight nod. "Let me rest my old body under that olive tree there."

"I need to get back to my son—" Verus whispered.

But Tulias quickly cut him off, "Your wife is watching over him now. Come rest for a moment." Without waiting for Verus to respond, Tulias turned towards Plini. "We want to listen to your oration 'On Happiness'—the one you gave the other day."

Plini led the way while Tulias quickly followed, leaving Verus in the rear. They did not walk far before they camped themselves under an old olive tree. With a generous gesture, Plini seated the other two. It was a warm March day, which had bronzed the tips of their noses and the puffy parts of their cheeks. There was silence for a while, but then Tulias excitedly spoke.

"Well come on now, Plini, speak up. I've never known you to enjoy silence."

Plini gave a modest laugh. "These are just the ramblings of an old man—an old Vespasian supporter, I will have you know."

Tulias smiled.

"Well," Plini began, "I'm nothing, but nature is something. Everything I know I have learned from observation." There was a long pause in the conversation, so Tulias jumped back in.

"Go on."

Plini gave a warm smile and cleared his throat. "Nature looks like it is even and balanced, but in truth, it is always in opposition to itself. While the coney looks to breed and eat, the wolf looks to eat the coney. All of them have the same objective—that is to survive— but when one meets its objective, it cancels out the other. If the wolves were so effective in hunting, as they would hope to be, they would all be able to catch their fill. But soon, the coneys would be so few that the wolves would not have food to eat. It is in this opposition that these animals find balance."

Plini looked at his two listeners for a moment, and then he continued on. "It was then that I realized that in order to find balance in our lives, we need to face opposition. To understand joy we need to feel pain; to appreciate peace we need to live through war. So many call up to the GODS and ask fruitlessly 'why me? why me?' but they don't understand. Without opposition, you would not even know the Gods; for we pray the most, when we have the least. This opposition is important for our happiness, but it does not cause it.

"Once our basic needs are met, misery is caused when we are in opposition to ourselves—when we act like animals instead of humans. And this happens in three instances: when we are selfish, when we expect more than we deserve, and when we forsake our relationships.

"Within us there is a constant struggle: Our animal flesh wants to possess everything and think individually—like the wolf and the coney—while the human soul, on the other hand, knows that by giving to others, it will receive more in return. When we are selfish, we put ourselves first, which leads to introspective thought and raises our expectations of our needs. When our expectations surpass what we need, they make us want more than what we have. It is selfishness—which has resulted in Greek individualism—that increases our expectations.

"And as our expectations increase, we judge ourselves and others more harshly and soon, we forsake our relationships—which is the core of our happiness. Happiness begins with one simple thing: charity. When we care more for others than we do ourselves, that is when we are not aware of our misery—that is what makes us happy."

"I am not sure I understand," Verus said. "Misery can be brought about by death in the family, or the lack of Denarii in your wristband."

"No," Plini said with a mischievous smile. "That is the great secret to life. While the wealthy in Rome would try to convince you that they are happy, I will swear to you they are not. I was in Rome when Nero was Emperor and I was with Galba after Nero died. With all the gold they had, and honors they were given, only one thing eluded them—happiness. My friends, let me tell you, they were never happy because they have never served anyone but themselves. True happiness comes from our relationships and those are best forged by charity."

Verus' mind flashed to the face of his son. "What if those relationships are suddenly taken? What if one in your family dies?"

"Yes," Tulias said. "That is a sad thing, but it does not mean it is the end to one's joy. If we have the expectation for someone to live forever, of course it is disappointing when they don't. The same thing happens when we expect our relationships to always be perfect when they are not. This is seen when a young couple gets married after falling madly in love with each other. But then, only a year later, they are miserable with each other. One might ask, if they were so madly in love a year before, why are they miserable now? The answer is in their expectations: They thought they had married the perfect person and they were disappointed to find out that they did not. They did not understand that it is opposition that humbles them and makes them charitable to each other. It is this charity that fills life with real happiness. Eventually, the young couple will find a union with each other, which will be stronger than before; but their union will not be born of love so much as it will be strengthened by overcoming opposition together. Their expectations will adjust, and so will they adjust to each other. And as both of them think of the other more than themselves, they will find joy.

"If someone dies it is necessary to feel sad—that just means your mind is adjusting to your expectations—but you can still choose to be happy. If you are charitable to others, your sadness will be like sand in the wind, and eventually it will drift into the distance. While if you turn selfish, acting like a victim of circumstance, that sand will never leave you, and neither will the misery or the bitterness."

"I am not sure I understand completely," Verus whispered.

Plini nodded with a distant look. "You've never lost anyone before, have you?"

"No. I haven't," Verus said. "Both my parents are well and they live in the house next to mine. I have three sisters who live just a little farther down this hill, and a brother that lives in the center of town. All of them are well. But let me ask you this: Imagine the worst possible situation, where everything has been torn from you. Let's say you lost your family, and your house burns down; you are captured and made a slave, forced into servitude. Do you think you would be happy then?"

Plini put his hands up. "Yes. If someone's basic needs of food and shelter are met, there is no difficultly that they cannot overcome. Look at me for instance; I am an exile—forced to be at the whim and mercy of Tulias." The other two gave slight laughs, and

Plini continued. "But here is the secret to true joy: If one is freely charitable, honest with their expectations, and appreciative of their relationships, then they will be happy.

"Sometimes, however, it takes a while for a person to see the benefits of those three things—to experience the happiness that I am speaking about. It can be long days and months, perhaps even years, before someone feels true joy. And during those hard years, I am convinced that the only thing that will carry a person through life is hope. If hope exists, no matter how slight or obscure—maybe it is only the hope to see the sun rise in the morning and set in the evening—then that person will not die because of misery. If you are wading through trial, the only thing that will see you through is hope—hope that what you lack today, you will find tomorrow. I have seen perfectly healthy men die because they lacked hope in the future; while on the other hand, I have seen wretchedly sick men live because they clung to hope like a newborn clings to their mother. If you apply these principles, hoping that they will lead you to true joy, you will be able to face any challenge that you come across."

Chapter 4
August 4, 61 AD
Priscus

"Watch your tongue, Sedrix, or I will cut it out," Galen spat.

Sedrix was slightly bigger than Galen and looked quite a bit more intimidating, but Galen did not flinch, not even for a moment. The two brothers stood there, staring at each other until an awkward silence fell all across the Celtic camp.

"I say what I want, when I want," Sedrix countered as he shoved Galen, who stepped back defensively, knocking over a bowl of dried beans. Galen clenched his jaw and hesitated for a moment, studying his opponent with a fire in his eyes.

A third Celt stepped between the two fighters to ease the tension. It was Maulic, the War Chief of the Cotini clan. He was tall and thin, but wore a bearskin on his back, which made him seem bulky when he had it on and oddly small when he took it off. Around his neck, bouncing proudly for all to see, he wore bear claws fastened together by leather, a symbol of position and power in the clan. With a voice like a deep river, Maulic spoke, "Ballwin was killed the other night over a foolish game of bones; I want no more bloodshed during this journey."

"He insulted me," Galen protested. "By our law I can challenge him."

"I only insulted your mindless slave," Sedrix spat. "Have you taken to your slave so quickly that you are offended so easily?"

"I can turn anything into a warrior, Sedrix," Galen hissed.

"And when you insult my slave's ability to learn, you insult my ability to teach."

"That boy would only last a few moments in a fight!"

"Come here!" Galen stepped forward while his palm swiftly

26

went for his sword. Sedrix did the same, and soon, they both had their blades out, pointing them at Maulic who was still in the middle.

"Do I have to hang your bodies over a tree and let the dogs lick your dead toes before you will learn anything?"

"He's a worthless fool!" Galen yelled.

"But he is your older brother and my son!" Maulic roared back. "And there will be no more bloodshed among us."

"Make the slaves fight," another voice suggested from the watching crowd.

"What?" Maulic questioned.

Sedrix quickly picked up on the idea. "Yes, put your slave against mine; we will see who has a better eye for talent."

"Have you not seen enough blood?" Maulic hissed.

"Its only Gallic blood," Sedrix replied, "and their blood is as poor as the mud."

Maulic sighed, "Fine, but only to first blood."

"No!" Galen grinned broadly, "If we start something, let the boys finish it. If they fight, it will need to be to the death."

"Are you so eager to lose your slave?" Sedrix mocked.

"Not only am I eager to bet my slave," Galen said roughly, "but I will wager my share of the bounty against yours."

Sedrix's smile sunk ever so slightly. He did not care about losing a young slave's life, but it was something quite different to wager his bounty. The large Celt scratched his chin thoughtfully.

"My bounty is larger than yours," Sedrix replied. "It's not a fair wager."

"Then I will match yours," Galen replied just as coolly. "If I lose I will have nothing, and if you lose you will still have something. Don't be a Roman and change your mind. Let the boys fight it out to the death."

Sedrix bit down hard on his teeth before he answered, "To the death." The two brothers watched each other carefully, keeping their swords high as they stepped forward. They locked arms, brutally sealing their wager.

Maulic sighed again with frustration, "You two boys will bring the end to your people."

The brothers stared long and hard at each other before they finally turned away to find their slaves. Priscus, who up to this point was barely paying attention, suddenly turned pale as he realized Galen was coming for him. There was a moment of panic—he considered running—but Galen was at his side before he could move.

The young Gaul understood the Celtic language well enough—their tribe often dealt with Celts—but he could barely speak it. Priscus could only say a few words in defense, "I can't fight...I can't fight..."

"I don't care if you can fight, as long as you can win," Galen said as he cut Priscus' bonds. Although Priscus was taller than Galen, he was clearly inferior, and like a rabbit being forced to its death, Priscus was shoved towards the middle of the camp.

"To the center, boy," Maulic hissed.

The rest of the Celts crowded in, forming a combat circle. Like chanting wolves they narrowed their vision at the large Priscus. The Celts laughed and hollered with excitement, sadistic smiles wickedly splitting their faces. It was almost as if they were summoning something, or someone—perhaps a demon or a demigod—to come and sanction the fight.

Then Sedrix's champion appeared. It was another boy Priscus' age. The boy was short and stocky: It was Trontian—Priscus' last and only true friend. There was no time for conversation—no time for planning. The Celts were eager to see blood, and these two boys were there to provide it.

Maulic lazily entered the circle of Celts and pulled the frightened boys together. "This is to the death. Do you two know how to use a sword?"

Priscus tried to answer, but all he could do was nod. Trontian did the same.

"Good," Maulic said with a twisted grandfatherly grin. "That will make it more entertaining. *Tiwaz* will bless the one who can strike the quickest. If neither one of you kill the other, then both of you will die—and by die, I mean horribly tortured to death. Do you two know what torture is?"

The boys nodded again.

"It is a pity one of you has to die; you seem like smart boys." With this, the old man walked away, leaving the boys with the frenzied mob.

Sedrix put a blade in Trontian's hands. Another was given to

Priscus. Now they stood: brother against brother. They had fought like this several times before, but that was when they had wooden swords; now they held metal blades that glistened with permanence. If neither of them fought they might both be killed, but if they did fight, one of them would surely have to die. Trontian tried to catch Priscus' eyes, but the large Gaul was so distracted by the zealous Celts around him that he did not seem to notice.

With an ugly grimace, Trontian rushed forward, attacking so quickly that many of the Celts took a step back; Priscus matched his friend's swing and returned his own. It turned into a battle of careful swings and reluctant attacks. As one went in, the other pulled back. The tactic seemed vicious enough, but soon the Celts realized the boys were stalling.

"Come on!" Sedrix screamed. "If you beat him, you will get your pick of meat tonight, boy! Chop his head off and I will give you a share of my spoils."

Galen looked affronted, "How can you offer a slave spoils, Sedrix; have you forgotten that he is still a Gaul!"

Trontian, angered by being called a slave, made another series of attacks, which drew the Celt's attention back to the center. The boy was smallish but quick, and his swings were impressive but ill formed. Priscus, on the other hand, had more powerful and calculated attacks. He went in for the kill, but Trontian stepped back, dodging the death blow at the last second.

Trontian whispered, "What are you doing? That almost cut me down."

"What can I do?" Priscus replied coldly. He then ducked under a swing and pushed Trontian so hard he fell to his back. With his friend down, Priscus rushed in. The fighting turned vicious as the dust was kicked up. Trontian tried to gain his feet, but he was quickly knocked down again. Dirt clouded up and caught the boy's eye, forcing him to defend himself wildly. It could have ended there, but Priscus hesitated.

"KILL HIM!" Galen yelled. "Now is your chance, slave. KILL HIM!"

Priscus went in carefully: it looked like he was being cautious, but really he was just trying to think of something he could do. But no matter how much he hesitated, no matter how much he stalled, no idea of escape came to his mind. While he paused, Trontian attempted to stand but fell back down as Priscus stepped forward.

"Get up!" Priscus said.

"FINISH HIM!" Galen yelled. The Celt's eyes had a gleam of greed in them now. He grabbed a whip and tightened it as if he was holding his destiny. This whip was different from the others the Celts used: Instead of having just strips of leather, this one had bits of bone woven into it, and when it went across someone's back, it ripped into the flesh, leaving gaping wounds behind. "Kill him or the whip will bite into your flesh!"

Priscus hesitated, giving Trontian enough time to stand up.

Galen spat and shook his head. Using all his strength he sent the whip forward, slicing Priscus in the back. The Gaul's mouth opened in pain—he had not seen the strike coming. Three gashes opened instantly, gashes so deep that it took awhile for them to start bleeding. Priscus was still gasping for breath—a shiver rippled through his body.

This gave Trontian an advantage, which he used to wipe his eyes completely clean. When he looked at his friend cringing in pain, he hesitated. A tear slipped down his cheek. Another tear came down the other cheek and pooled at the bottom of his chin. This scene was so familiar to Trontian, so haunting that all he could do was shake his head as the tears continued to drip. Just a few years ago it was Trontian who watched from the corners of the crowd as his father fought on until his death. Now, instead of seeing his father's blood slowly drain from his body, Priscus stood before him, bleeding more than either one of them ever had before.

Priscus gritted his teeth and tried to get away from Galen, who took another swing with the whip. One of the toothed leather strips sliced the back of Priscus' neck, dripping blood down the fighter's back and sending him forward into the wall of Celts. The warriors were first like a cushion that had caught him, but soon they became a wall of fists that bloodied his lip and knocked him down. Dust filled his lungs, burning his ribs. Someone's foot pounded into his side. He coughed and spurted. It was not long before Galen pulled him to his feet

"Finish him or I finish you, boy!" his owner hissed.

Priscus shivered and faced his old friend, Trontian, who was holding his sword as tentatively as if it were a snake.

With new resolve, Priscus stepped forward.

"One of us will have to die," Trontian whispered.

Priscus gritted his teeth and lunged at his friend, but Trontian was hardly fighting now. In moments, Priscus knocked him back to the ground, and in another moment Trontian's sword was hit clean from his grasp. Now the friends stared at each other—neither one able to say a word.

"Kill him," Galen ordered. "KILL HIM!"

Priscus put his sword to Trontian's throat, but he couldn't do it...

Galen cracked his whip, hitting Priscus so hard in the back it forced him down to one knee; this time the blood splashed over his body, coursing down him like red wine. The whip struck him again. And then again. The pain burned like fire, but his lungs felt like they were frozen by ice. He coughed.

"The whipping ends when you end his life!" Galen decreed.

The whip cracked again. And again. Priscus' whole body was shaking—he felt like he was about to vomit. His head was spinning. With a tear in his Gallic eye, he ended it. He ended all of it.

Chapter 5

December 18, 69 AD
Verus

After packing everything he thought he would need for the next few days and saying farewell to his wife and kids, Verus set off towards Rome. He traveled alone, which was dangerous, but Verus felt moderately safe—he was not carrying anything of value and was not anyone of importance. The Blacksmith loved to travel; everything, from the wind that filled his lungs to the insects that crawled alongside him, brought a smile to his face. And although fellow travelers were never friendly, Verus made it a point to be kind; he greeted everyone with the common phrase "Ave" as they made their way past him. He was in such good spirits that the hours and the distance went gently by. He had brought his horse, old Potter, but rarely rode him, deciding that it was better to save the beast's strength for when it was needed.

He traveled on the *Via Flaminia,* a wide road built of stones in the 3rd century BC. Despite a few wagon ruts cut into the stone, the path was smooth and efficient. At every intersection, called *Trivias,* there were signs posted that held the latest news and gossip. Verus did not bother to stop at the first few crossroads, since everything posted was already common knowledge, but as he traveled into unfamiliar territory he took interest in the little signs.

Verus stopped to look at one of the larger, more official documents. He had never learned to read, despite his wife's best attempts to teach him, but he was able to pick out a few words.

"VESPASION THE TRAITOR IS DECLARED EMPEROR IN THE EAST. The longtime champion of Jerusalem set sail for Rome a few weeks ago. It is widely rumored that he aims to unlawfully usurp the Emperor, taking power for himself, leaving the city of Rome in chaos. Can you let Vitellius be pushed aside after all the good he has brought to Rome, including the public banquets and elaborate games? We have seen Vitellius' good graces—we know what kind of Emperor he is—but what about Vespasian?

Vespasian is a ruthless leader and cruel tyrant; he has spent the last few years bloodily subduing a JEWISH revolt. And how will he subdue Rome? His skill is on the battlefield, not in an Emperor's chair. Do you not remember how...

The papyrus suddenly ended. In its place there was another, more elaborate roll of paper that demanded even more attention.

VITELLIAN'S ARMY IS SMASHED IN BEDRIACUM. The *auspices* are clear, the auguries are definite. The Gods have favored VESPASIAN. Despite the Senate's recognition of the current leader, Vitellius says he will step aside for Vespasian when the war hero arrives. Vitellius is even now en route to meet Vespasian in Mevania, where he will formally acknowledge Vespasian as the new Emperor. Vespasian promises to bring financial reforms, which will bring more wealth to Rome.

Verus looked over the writing twice but still could not make any sense of it. He recognized the name Vespasion and Vitellius, and a few other words, but the collective meaning eluded him. But this did not bother him much. He knew little of current events and cared even less about them. If there was another Hannibal riding an elephant on the hills of Tuscany he would like to know, but if not, he preferred to be ignorant. After the death of Nero, there had been three Emperors that each lasted very little time, making it all that much more difficult to remember who was in power. Politics in Rome were like dirt in a torrent of wind: just as it looks like things will settle a sudden gust musters and turns everything around. Even the position of the Emperor had been debased. After Caligula died, the godlike position was auctioned off to the highest bidder by the Praetorian Guard.

Verus smiled and nodded. *"Ignorance is the best defense."*

The Blacksmith went on his way thinking little of what he had read. He traveled long into the evening until he was finally compelled to find shelter. Being a Roman had its benefits, and instead of being forced to stay in a dirty *Tabernae*, he was allowed free stay in a *Mansione*, which was more comfortable than most houses. The *Mansiones* were built every twelve kilometers and were marked by round milestones that pointed the way. The people at the *Mansiones* were initially rude, but once he presented his papers, they let him right in, giving him a room and a bed for the night.

It took him four days to travel to Rome. As Verus drew nearer to the grand city, excitement filled him like a child who had discovered his first mud puddle. He found himself riding more and walking less; he had traveled so quickly, he actually arrived a day earlier than planned. He stabled his horse outside the city at a place that charged four times as much as a stable in the country. Reluctantly, Verus paid the gold and left faithful Potter behind.

The city was surrounded by a wall that was thicker than anything Verus had seen. It rose up suddenly, like a massive split in the earth. The stone wall was so finely crafted that it seemed to be shaped by the Gods themselves. The *Via Flaminia* led right up to a giant gate that was open wide. Droves of people swarmed in and out of the city: there were peasants in tunics and slaves in chains, large Roman soldiers and poets wrapped in togas.

Verus sighed and stopped. He looked at the cold and distant faces that came out. *"May the Gods bless my wits."* With another sigh, he pulled his cloak tighter around his back and stepped towards the crowded entrance.

The closer he drew to the wall, the tighter the crowd became. People shoved and pushed, passing Verus on all sides. He felt like an awkward child again. Every time he bumped someone, he would mumble a quick apology; but as he got closer to the city, he was bumped and pushed so much he was unable to keep up with apologies.

He felt an animal cross his path—maybe it was a dog—but his vision was so restricted he could not even see it. A whip of dust hit him in the right eye, forcing it closed. Finally, after wading through more people than he had ever met in his life, he passed through the entrance. The gate itself was something to marvel at, and Verus would have stopped to examine it had he not been pushed forward. The walls were a symbol of immense power. These walls separated the civility of Rome with the barbarity of the world. It had been over three hundred years since Rome had been occupied by a foreign power, and to Romans, that had been three hundred years too soon. Since then, Romans had done everything to secure their position of power by taking over anything they set their eyes upon.

Verus did not like his first impression of Rome as he was driven forward like a sheep into a pen, but as he freed himself from the crowd and checked his papers with some guards, he could see why Rome was called "the center of the world." The city attracted people and entertainers from all over: There were musicians to his right and jugglers to his left; a group of merchants that wore turbans and sold curved blades, another that peddled salt and spices; a troop of little children that were bending their bodies in ways that the Blacksmith had never seen before. The city was as filthy as it was loud. Between all the beggars and rats, old women chasing their husbands and guards marching through the streets, Verus could hardly focus on anything in the distance. Merchants yelled so loudly that they constantly startled the Blacksmith, who recoiled from them as if they were assailants.

There were statues and figurines glistening with white marble, great obelisks of grey granite, and banners that decked the streets and climbed along the rows of homes. Since he was still in a poor sector most houses were constructed with a coarse wood that seemed to be collected at random. A fountain that was positioned close to the gate shot water out of the mouth of a big fish and collected in a basin down below.

The smells of the city changed as quickly as a winter wind: one moment, as a chef roasted exotic meat with sizzling spices, it smelled divine; the next moment the sweet smell would disappear only to be replaced by something that was akin to a rotting fish. Despite it all—despite the roads being crooked, small, and confusing—the city had a power that emanated through the streets and rose up from the roofs of the buildings.

"Excuse me, sir," Verus said to one man as he tapped his shoulder.

The man looked affronted as he grumpily turned around. "What?"

Verus was thrown off a little by the man's rudeness—people

did not talk that way in the country—but the Blacksmith continued, "…I am lookin' for lodging."

"And I'm lookin' for people to buy my grain," the man gruffed. "I don't have time for questions."

"Will you answer me if I buy some grain?" Verus said quickly.

"Hmm…how much do you need?" the man asked.

"Enough for a few days."

The man scrutinized Verus, "A few days, huh. It will be cheaper if you buy a week's worth."

"I just need four days…"

"You're not an assassin are you?"

Verus shook his head quickly, "NO! Why would you think that?"

"That is exactly who would stay for only four days," the shopkeeper whispered.

"Well," Verus said with a faint smile, "I'm a blacksmith."

"And I'm busy," the other man replied. "How much gold do you have?"

"Here's five *dupondius*."

"Are you insane?" the man replied quickly. "The bags I pack the grain in are worth more than that."

"Here then," Verus said shyly. "Two *sestertius*. Will that be enough?"

The shrewd shopkeeper shook his head, "It will be enough for three days worth, and not a kernel more."

"Fine," Verus said with a defeated tone.

"Here," the shopkeeper handed him a pitifully small bag and turned to go.

"Wait," Verus said weakly. "You were going to tell me where I could find lodging."

The shopkeeper grumbled and sighed, acting as if this was the greatest inconvenience. "Go down there, take a left, pass a fountain and turn right. On that street you should find decent lodging."

"Ave," Verus said as headed off.

But the directions turned out to be as wretched as the shopkeeper. Verus ended up in a street with a broken lead pipe, which filled the air with a nauseating stench. He wandered some more, looking carefully for signs of lodging, but nothing looked promising. The city was infinitely impractical and complicated; not only were the signs worn, but the people were completely rude.

After an hour of his feet pounding the cobblestone, when the sun reached its zenith, Verus came across a square building that seemed promising. There were a few people at the door, but they were too busy to stop Verus, who somehow looked like he belonged. The Blacksmith passed a strong smelling tree, which Verus recognized as a stone pine, and walked through the front doors. The entrance led down a wide passage that again opened to the outside. The site would have been impressive to just about anyone, but it was even more so to a man who had only seen little villas his whole life.

It was built for one purpose: to entertain the many by the death of a few. Verus had never seen a gladiatorial pit before—his wife would have never let him go—but as he looked at it now, it filled him with new energy which flowed through him like a fresh breeze. It brought warmth to his arms and focus to his eyes.

Despite the warm day, fighters were in the middle of the arena practicing with wooden swords and odd shaped armor. They were not going at full speed, and their movements were constantly being corrected by men on either side, but each one had a look of surreal determination. It was so captivating that Verus could not look away. These men were training to kill: The harder they trained, the longer they would live. The fighters seemed even more dedicated than the Roman Legions Verus had seen before. While Roman soldiers depended on a collective force, gladiators focused on their individual strength; whether they won or lost was solely up to the discipline of the lone fighter.

"Do you see someone you like?" a voice called from behind.

Verus turned quickly. He did not realize someone was watching him. "I'm sorry…I am lost…"

"Sit down stranger," the other man replied. "As long as you're not from an opposing gladiatorial school you're welcome here."

"No, I'm not," Verus awkwardly answered.

"I did not think you were—" the man smiled. "I'm Horace. I own those gladiators you see in the pit."

"I'm Verus Flaminius of Pinacale, son of Gaius Flaminius."

"Any relation to Gaius Flaminius the Consul that led Rome's

Legions against Hannibal?"

"Maybe," Verus admitted humbly.

Horace gestured towards the warriors. "Do you like what you see?"

"They all seem well trained. You must own hundreds."

"Yes, but not more than six hundred and forty."

"Why no more than that?"

"A private individual can only have that many." The old man laughed and leaned in. "If someone has more than that, the Senate gets worried that you are starting a coup."

"How many fight for you?"

Horace shook his head. "Oh, don't make that mistake, boy. They don't fight for me—they fight for their lives. I only purchased half of them—the other half joined up themselves."

"They joined up? I thought only slaves were gladiators."

Horace took a seat next to Verus. "They were free before, most of them Citizens of Rome, but now they are gladiators."

"Isn't that a death sentence?"

"No," Horace replied, "it has its rewards. A fighter can become as well known as a senator and more popular than the Emperor. Those that have the skill can gain wealth and power, making them akin to the Equites of Rome. Most sign up with a three- to five-year contract. You are mistaking gladiators for the Damnati—those are the ones that are forced to fight to the death. There are some gladiators that have gained great fame in the pit. Have you not heard of Hermes, Spiculus, and Eutyches? Spiculus was so favored by Nero that he was showered with gifts; and Eutyches was paid over two million sestertius for his skill in the arena."

Verus shook his head shyly. "My wife never lets me...I mean...to say...I've never had much interest in the games."

Horace slapped Verus on the back. "Too bad. You have the look of a gladiator yourself."

This time it was Verus' turn to laugh, "A gladiator?"

"You've got the strength for it. Are you a lumber-miner?"

"No, a blacksmith—just like my father, and his father."

"What do you specialize in?"

"Weaponry."

Horace scratched his head for a second. "Well, I could use another good blacksmith. Vitellius has us running so many games we hardly have time to repair our weapons."

"I could use some work in the winter."

"Of course I would need to see if you are any good."

"And I would have to find out how much you pay," Verus replied just as quickly.

"Excellent. What can you show me of your craftsmanship?"

Verus shook his head. "I don't have anything to show you, but I could make something—that is, if you have the right tools."

"Of course I do, boy. Do you have time now?"

Verus was about to say "yes," but then another thought struck him. "I need to talk to the family of Vitelli as soon as possible, but after that I can stop by."

"Oh, do you?" Horace said as he raised his eyebrows. "If I were you I would avoid that family."

"I have urgent business with them: One of my friends sent me to seek their counsel."

"I don't meddle in the affairs of others," Horace whispered, "but you better conduct your business before sundown. After that, there will be blood in the streets."

"Can you show me how to get to the house of Vitelli?"

Horace nodded. "Yes, but you must promise me one thing: If they offer you a room to sleep in, don't take it. I will make a room for you here in the gladiatorial pit."

"Fair enough," Verus nodded.

Chapter 6
December 18, 66 AD
Priscus

It had been five long years. Five years since Priscus was made a slave; five years of back-breaking servitude; five years since his only friend was murdered. Even though the Gaul was already big when he was a boy, he grew taller as he became a man. His height was received with a mixture of caution and admiration amongst the Celts, who cherished him for his skill in fighting, but mistrusted him for the threat he might become. Slavery had taught Priscus three important things: Don't argue with your master; don't move slowly when you're told to go; and no matter how much it kills you inside, don't look your master in the eyes—or he will see your unquenchable thirst to kill him.

Most slaves eventually adjusted, but Priscus never did. He wanted them all dead—every last one of them.

The Gaul looked up into the sun, praying for the patience to last another day. This time he had been sent to hunt for deer. His master walked with him, armed with a sword at his side and a bow in his hands.

"What's wrong, Priscus?" Galen asked. "Are you upset from killing another slave last night?"

"No, master," Priscus simply answered.

They had only just begun their march up a hill away from their Celtic city of Cotini. It was a large but simple city: The houses were built of clay and wood, while the roofs were sodden with grass. The whole thing was surrounded by a large palisade that offered protection from wind and sudden attacks. Around the spiked wooden walls, there was a creek bed that was usually muddy and slick, which was meant to slow the progress of invading armies. The city had initially been a circle, but after generations of improvements and changes, its design was more random and spread out, like spilt milk on a table. In the center was an artificial hill that ran up to the base of the largest and most permanent building, a keep made of thick logs and large wooden doors. At the moment Sedrix and his clan of lazy friends were in the keep, dining on food that was prepared by the efforts of others.

"You've not given me any trouble in the last few months," Galen smirked. "Are you starting to like it with the Celts?"

"Yes, master," Priscus whispered.

"You lie. You hate it here."

"No master."

Galen ran forward, pushing Priscus to the ground. "Don't lie to me, boy! You've wanted to slice off my head ever since you set eyes upon me."

Priscus was careful to not look up at his master; things would have turned deadly if he did.

"Why do you hate it here? Do I not feed you and clothe you? Have I not trained and protected you?"

Priscus did not respond.

"Answer me!" Galen struck Priscus across the cheek but still the large Gaul did not react. Priscus would have loved to grab a sword and rush at the Celt, but he knew it would accomplish little; not only were there a dozen more Celts within a few feet of him, but they would have brought others to fight as well. It was not that he feared death—he actually looked forward to it—but he wanted to cause the Celts as much pain as they had caused him, and now did not seem the time. With this one hope in mind, he patiently waited.

"Yes, you have my Lord, and I am grateful for everything that you do," Priscus whispered. He hoped his voice sounded humble, but he doubted that it did.

"Your pride will one day be the death of you," Galen replied. "Now get up. We have deer to hunt."

Priscus pulled himself up and went to follow his master but, suddenly, a cluster of arrows came whistling through the trees. Two of the closest Celts took shafts in the chest, a third was hit in the calf.

Galen drew his sword. "AMBUSH! Back to the city!" More arrows came after them, skewering another Celt in the eye.

41

"Come on Priscus!" Galen yelled. "Protect Cotini!"

The large Gaul gathered himself and ran, leaving the others behind. As the Celts fled, the attackers emerged like swarming ants from the forest line; they were wearing mismatched clothing, rugged pants, and wielding large swords.

Priscus happened to glance back and see them. "*Celts?*" he questioned. He was the first to reach the village and pass through the wooden defenses; but he did not stop there—he needed a weapon. From somewhere behind him a Celt shouted.

"WE'RE UNDER ATTACK!"

After years of living precarious lives, the Celts had learned the benefit of efficiency; the men armed themselves quickly, grabbing bows and arrows from their homes. The women gathered their children and headed for the keep, while still others took time to saddle horses to make themselves mobile.

After Galen reached the gate, two large doors swung closed, trapping a few of the remaining wounded Celts on the outside; they screamed in protest, but to no avail. Galen instantly took command of the men that had already assembled, organizing them into rows.

"Brulic!" Galen ordered, "Put men up in the towers—I need to know the enemy's position!"

"They're one hundred cubits from the gate!" Brulic replied.

Galen grinned. "Good. Just within range. Archers ready! Full bow! LOOSE!" A barrage of the defenders' arrows was released; they sailed up quickly and whistled down deadly, ravaging the ranks of the attackers. More defenders gathered, and Galen lined them up with the rest.

"FULL BOW! LOOSE!"

The arrows rained down on the attackers again, hammering into their ranks as they tried to reform their lines. They were not nearly as organized as the defenders, but twice as numerous. The Celts were able to shower the attackers with arrows two more times before they had a battle line formulated.

Now it was the attackers' turn to fire. The arrows were so numerous they stuck everything from the buildings to the defenders' bodies. It became a battle of attrition: both sides firing in turn. While the defenders had more ample cover, the attackers were able to spread their archer ranks out. As the Celts were distracted by the archers, a wall of ladders reached the wooden walls. The first attacker that appeared over the palisade was shot in the throat, the second was hit in the eye, but soon, there were so many that they could not be stopped.

* * *

Priscus was clear on the other side of the city before the fight had really begun; he was heading for his master's house. Galen's frightened wife was there, shaking as if she were cold. She had always treated Priscus like a dog.

"Are we under attack?" she asked quickly.

Priscus smiled. "Yes." Without another word, he clubbed her with a chair, breaking it into pieces. She collapsed to the ground in a heap. Wasting no time, Priscus finished her.

Galen's house was large and elaborate; it was made and designed by Roman engineers who had been captured a few years before. The furniture was foreign and elegantly crafted. Most of it had been stolen from neighboring tribes or misfortunate merchants, but in any case, none of it was truly his master's.

Priscus went to the back, smashing everything along his way; he toppled tables and dropped vases. He scattered pottery pieces like weeds in spring. He kicked dishes that had carefully been set on the kitchen table and smashed a washing bowl. Tapestries were torn down and doors were kicked open. In moments the house was shredded into pieces. The last door was locked, but this only slowed the large Gaul down for a moment.

Light burst in as the door broke open. Priscus grinned. Galen's collection of shiny weapons grinned back. The Celt had collected every weapon from every warrior he had ever killed; over the years, the storage room had filled up until it was seeping at the sides. Priscus armed himself with leather armor, strapping it around his chest and thighs; on his head he mounted a Roman helmet, which still had the scent of blood about it. He put a bow on his back, a *gladius* sword at his side, a Hoplite shield on his left arm. With his right hand he picked up a long-lost possession—his father's sword.

His mother was wielding it when Galen killed her; she had been butchered so badly that blood had splattered on Priscus' face, turning it a red hue that never seemed to fade. The memories were still so fresh in the Gaul's mind that it felt like it could have happened only days before.

Now, it was his turn to make the memories.

* * *

Galen squinted and pointed his sword towards the enemy. "Drive them back over the wall!" He had just been reinforced by a unit of spear-wielding Celts, which he sent forward into the massing attackers. The first wave of invaders had successfully gained some ground, but now that the defenders had regrouped into formation, the combat turned into a bloody stalemate. Arrows from both sides flew haphazardly through the air, striking victims from either force.

The attackers made a strong push for the gate but were met by a lesser but more determined Celtic unit; the fighting turned fierce and the air was speckled with red. What was dirt before now became a reddish mud.

Galen moved faster and was more determined than the rest. He ducked under the swing of a blade and returned his own attack, slicing a man's belly and spilling his insides like a broken bottle. The man screamed and fell; Galen did him the favor of finishing him quickly. He then jumped back from another attack, sidestepped, and kicked a warrior in the gut while slicing another man in the ear. A spear came at him, its point looked like an eagle, but Galen parried it and broke the shaft. The eagle point became the Celt's new weapon and he used it to great effect, skewering one man in the eye and another through the belly.

From outside of the fortress the attackers released another volley of arrows; they did not seem to care whether they hit foe or friend, and they killed as many of the attackers as they did the defenders. Galen used an enemy's body for a shield, which caught three of the arrow shafts. He then tossed the body like a sack of wheat at some unfortunate warrior, who looked too young to know what he was doing.

With a horn blown in the distance the attackers were reinforced by a new wave of men that climbed the ladders and leaped into the palisade. These warriors were more seasoned—at least their armor seemed more complete. They formed battle lines as they hit the ground, locking their shields into a mini-phalanx that was constantly being reinforced.

Galen studied them for a moment. *"Celts don't march like that. Who are they?"* But the large Celt did not have much time to ponder the dilemma before he was forced back into the fighting. He tried to call his own troops back into formation, but they had scattered. Everything had turned chaotic.

He thought for a moment as he scanned the area. Toward the top of the keep there was a grouping of carts that were used for transporting oil through the village. Presently they were not tied to any horses, but they were still full of oil. With the outline of some wild plan in his mind, he made a run for the oil carts.

He stopped quickly to grab a Celt by the shoulder, "BRULIC! Reform our battle lines at the base of the keep. Fall back to the base of the keep!"

"What if we lose the gate?"

"We need to regroup first!" Galen said as he continued towards the oil carts. The keep was not far, but it was still uphill. He reached it with little time to spare—the attackers were almost at the gate. If the attackers reached the gate and were able to open it, it would allow them to be reinforced by the rest of their army that was waiting outside. After that, it would be impossible to push the enemy back. Using a flame from a nearby fire, he lit the hay that was put there for the horses. The fire caught instantly, voraciously burning up whatever was close.

"I hope this works," Galen prayed. Using his legs to brace against the keep, the Celt pushed with his might, rolling the cart slowly forward. It was quick to pick up speed, even quicker to be engulfed with flame. With the wind feeding the fire, the cart haphazardly rolled straight for the enemy phalanx. It bumped once and then twice, sending it slightly off target, but it still steamed forward like a raging bull. The next few moments were tense. The attackers who saw it coming stepped sideways, leaving the middle of

the formation open.

Then suddenly, the cart rammed right into the middle of the enemy, shattering the vases of oil as it did. The cart exploded, sending a ball of flame that quickly engulfed the closest soldiers. Writhing in pain, the oil-soaked men panicked and twisted while the others pushed them away. This sudden change forced the phalanx to stop and regroup.

With a grin on his face and blood dripping from his chin, Galen faced Brulic, who had managed to regroup a sizeable force of Celts. "Let's give them hell!" The Celts poured down the hill screaming wildly. The attackers were disorganized and disheveled, and they had little time to prepare themselves before the Celts were upon them, slashing them with their long swords.

In the distance a Celtic horn sounded. While Galen had been inside defending the walls, Sedrix had rounded up a small cavalry unit and slipped out a side gate. It took some time to flank the enemy but now it had proved worthwhile. The cavalry unit pushed full-on into the attacker's flank. The collision of horse and soldier rang like an avalanche in a valley. The attackers were now cut off from their troops, making reinforcements an impossibility for the men that were already inside. The battle turned bloody. After moments of intense fighting, the attackers finally broke and ran, fleeing before the enemy.

The rest of the attackers who were now trapped inside the fortress found that death awaited them on either side of the defensive wall. It was a bitter struggle, but eventually, the Celts cleared the field of attackers. A few of the attackers tried to surrender, but the Cotini clan had no mercy for them.

With a mix of blood and sweat dripping down, Galen gave a victory yelp that echoed through the village. The rest of the defenders soon followed suit, making so much noise that it was impossible to hear the enemy that was moving in position behind them. Their victory was short-lived. What the Celts thought was the main attack was really only a distraction for the larger, more powerful force, which had now positioned itself on the opposite side of the fortress.

A lone Celt gave off a cry that only the closest few heard, "Romans!" The next moment, the man was skewered by a bolt so powerful that it pinned his body against a house. The victory cries soon turned into shrieks of terror as the air filled with thousands of burning arrows, which made the very sky seem like it was on fire.

Behind the town of the Celts, the Romans suddenly appeared as if they came from the rivers of Hades. They were perfectly lined and ordered; their armor was ornately made, and shined like the teeth of a saberwolf. The Roman artillery decimated the Celts, flying completely through the houses like they were nothing more than cloth. The air smelled like burning flesh. It was absolute confusion. A baby was crying in the distance.

One of the Celts screamed, "TO THE KEEP!" But no one seemed to be listening. There was no honor now—no stories of bravery to be retold around the fire. The Celts fought each other as much as they had fought the attackers before; they ran for cover, pushing past their brothers for better protection. The keep did offer defense from the thick artillery bolts of the Romans, but it was soon locked up and secured from the inside, leaving the rest of the Celts to die at its gate.

Wave after wave of arrows dropped in, slaughtering everything that had stood before them. Then the Roman's siege engines were loosed upon the city, sending rocks smashing into the Celtic homes. After a few of these gigantic stones whistled through the air, hitting the outer wall with perfect precision, they made a gap big enough for a Roman Century to charge in. Like blood from a wound, the Romans gushed out of the forest and into the city, killing everything in their path.

Priscus had seen the Romans coming before any of the Celts; and now, with a grin on his face, he realized that this was his time to strike. The Gaul barreled out of Galen's house, carrying his long sword with him.

"Priscus?" a Celt asked.

The Gaul turned his head slightly and vaguely recognized one of his captors. Before the Celt could ask another question, Priscus sliced the warrior's head clean off his body.

Once the Romans had broken through the city, the Celts panicked and retreated to higher ground—straight toward Priscus. He sheathed his sword and grabbed his bow. He was an excellent shot and as rapidly as he could, he unloaded on the Celts, catching dozens of them in the throat or chest. None of them could get past the

Gaul. He kept firing until the ground was covered in wounded Celts and his quiver ran low on arrows. Finally, he fired his last arrow and stuck the forehead of a confused, older warrior.

Again he hefted his shield and drew out his sword, staring straight at a group of Celts who were charging forward. With a cry he barreled down the hill towards them. Just before impact he lowered his stance, putting his weight behind his shield; the collision was so horrific it sent the Celts to either side, while Priscus stood boldly in the middle.

"What are you doing, Priscus?" one of the Celts asked.

The Gaul answered the question by stabbing the man through the throat, and then another in the chest. The men were either too wearied or wounded to last very long. He finished them off and continued running down the hill, killing everything that he passed. Body after body fell before him—hardly any of them saw it coming. As he reached the bottom of the hill, and after killing dozens of surprised Celts, Priscus ran into the one he was looking for— Galen.

"What are you doing?" Galen cried. "Are you mad? Why turn on us now when we need you the most!"

Priscus' blood-red eyes narrowed. "How can you ask me to stand with you after how you dealt with my family? How can you even expect me to protect you when you would not do the same for me?"

"You're my slave, boy."

"Do slaves carry weapons and steal their master's possessions?" Priscus countered. "Do they break into their master's house and kill their master's wife?"

"If you touched her—," Galen's face turned tight.

"I murdered her. It was easy; she was so trusting. She thought you had sent me to protect her."

"How could you have done this? We practically raised you!"

"You fed me from a bowl on the floor! You gave me nothing but the dirt to sleep on and torn clothing for warmth; you killed my family and forced me to murder my own people. You spent years insulting and hitting me when I was young, abusing me with every torture your mind could conceive. But now—master—your people die just as easily as mine did before."

Galen clenched his jaw. "I may die this day, but I will kill you first." The large Celt lunged forward, swinging his sword so quickly Priscus barely had time to raise his shield. The blow took a chunk of wood from the top of it and sent it flying through the air. Despite Galen being wearied from battle, he went on the offensive, throwing attack after attack at the waiting Gaul.

Priscus defended each blow easily; it was hardly even a competition. All these years, Galen was so full of pride he thought he was superior with the sword to everyone around him—but now, as he was learning, he was inferior to his own slave.

There was a pause in the fighting: Galen was gasping for air while Priscus barely even breathed.

"What are you waiting for?" Galen spat.

Priscus laughed. "Are you so anxious to die?"

"You coward!" Galen countered.

Priscus' face turned into an ugly image of hate—it was now his turn to take the offensive. The Gaul dropped his shield and drew a smaller Roman sword, which seemed oddly clean compared to the bloody mess all around him. Priscus charged in, swinging so viciously that Galen could only step back in defense. The Celt tripped over a body, and fell backwards; it took him a few moments to scramble up, but as he did, he picked up another sword. The two stared at each other, circling each other in hate, both of them now holding two swords.

Priscus rushed in, but he was met by the determined Celt. It was a stalemate for a while, but eventually Priscus' attacks forced Galen against a wall. The Celt could sense he was losing. He could feel his attacks becoming more desperate, feel himself relying too much on his lead arm, until finally, Priscus sliced it clean off.

Galen dropped his other sword and reeled back in pain; his face went pale with disbelief. He looked at his bloody stump, and then fell to his knees. "Spare me...and help me protect our city..."

Priscus kneeled down in front of his master. "Know this: this was never my city, and you were never my master. For the life you stole from me, I now take yours. For the years of slavery your people put me through, I now pledge to make them slaves. After you die, you should know, I will do everything in my power to destroy your city..."

49

"Why—" Galen began, but Priscus' sword cut him off.

"Now you die, demon." the Gaul hissed.

The Celt's body fell like a rock to the ground. He was dead in moments.

He had not realized it before, but as Priscus turned his back on Galen's lifeless body, he had a crowd of people around him—not Gauls or Celts but a troop of Romans that suddenly appeared.

"Who are you?" a Roman asked. "Whose side are you on?"

Priscus did not answer.

"I asked you a question!"

An older man, who must have been some sort of leader, leaned forward. "Let him alone Romulian; he just killed his master, can't you tell, and now he is a free man. He doesn't know what to do with his freedom yet."

Priscus narrowed his eyes and studied the leader: The Roman was wearing the classical decorative Roman armor, he was balding and rugged, but in his eyes there was something different. Those eyes had seen war and death—as anyone born in Gaul—but they had also seen something more.

"Who are you?" Priscus asked.

"Fabius Valens," the man said with some pride. "And now let me ask you two questions: First, where did you learn to use a sword?"

Chapter 7

December 22, 69 AD
Verus

"ONE LINE!" a fiery Roman shouted.

Verus had just arrived outside the house of Vitelli when he found himself assaulted with instructions. The house was filled with screaming people who were all convinced that their issues were of the utmost importance. The crowd consisted of all kinds of people, from beggar to senator, from soldier to house wife.

"ONE LINE! Write your name down! And your request!"

Verus—like a little boy on his first day of orator school—quickly followed the instructions. He put his name down, then his family name, and then his home village. And then he included—almost as an afterthought—the letter of introduction that Tulias had given him.

The Emperor's home was less of a building but more of a palatial mountain. The Palatine Hill seemed to grow suddenly from the ground and encompassed a huge section of Rome. Outside of this massive structure, several long lines of people stretched out in every direction, completely clogging up nearby streets. Verus had to wait over an hour before he could pass through a massive set of pillars and enter into the courtyard. It was large and pillared, like the typical Roman building, but not large enough to accommodate the mass of people. Verus found himself pushed aside by old people, who burrowed their way through the crowd like grubs. Several times he was pushed so hard he fell to his side, and on two occasions he was yelled at for no apparent reason. He felt as uncomfortable as a priest in a brothel. After another hour of standing in line, the Blacksmith had barely made any progress. Every time the line moved a step forward, a group of people would push their way in, forcing

Verus to take a step back. The whole place was mad—absolutely mad.

If Verus had been there on his own accord—maybe even if it had just been him and his wife—he would have forgotten about the whole thing, but he was there on behalf of his children, who might starve if he did not find help. His position as a father gave him more precedence: The next time an old senator pushed past him, Verus shoved him back against a stone statue, taking him by the throat.

"Wait your turn," Verus hissed.

The senator went pale-faced and gulped. The old man nodded and fell back into line. Another person tried to pass, but Verus put his arm in the man's path, knocking him in the head.

"WAIT YOUR TURN!"

The large framed Blacksmith finally made some real headway, and by his effort alone, the line became what it was supposed to be—efficient and orderly. It still took another hour before he reached two long tables, which seemed to be everyone's objective.

The man across the table looked disheveled and tired; he was furiously writing with a quill on some papyrus as Verus approached. "What is your business?" the man asked without looking. "What account do you want me to transfer?"

"Account?" Verus asked.

The accountant looked up in frustration. "Yes, what do you want me to transfer or change? What do you want me to blot out?"

"Blot out?" Verus asked stupidly.

The accountant took a deep breath. "How long have you been in line?"

"A few hours," Verus replied.

"And after you had all that time, you could not think of what you wanted to do when you got up here?"

"I…" Verus was perplexed.

The accountant shook his head, "Forget it. NEXT!"

"WAIT!" Verus said with a commanding voice. "Here are my papers: They include a letter of introduction by Tulias Scipio and my census information. I was sent here to request grain. My son had an operation, which depleted all my Denarii, and I don't think we will last the winter without more grain."

The accountant frowned wickedly. "Are you saying you want

the help of the house of Vitelli?"

"Yes, of course."

The accountant's voice took on a honey-coated tone that made Verus feel uncomfortable. "Interesting. Well, I think we can help; the family of Vitelli is always willing to do what it can. But you must promise us a few things in return."

Priscus nodded. "Just tell me how I can be of service."

"First," the accountant said, "come with me into the back of the palace; I can't hear with all this noise."

"Yes," Verus replied.

The accountant stood and gestured to Verus, who went around the tables and followed. They passed underneath gigantic pillars and walked through two wooden doors, which were shut behind them by some hidden servants. The inside of the home was ornate and smooth, full of gold trimming and exotic smells; there were decorative pots and metallic sculptures that filled it with perfect precision. Curtains hung from everywhere and pillows were stacked high on every couch, giving them a very comfortable appearance. It was the biggest and most elaborate room Verus had ever seen. He suddenly felt embarrassed by his muddy sandals and sweaty back.

"Wait here," the accountant whispered.

Verus gulped and nodded.

"Please," the accountant said as he gestured to the couches, "take a seat."

Verus nodded again but did not sit. He felt too intimidated to acknowledge his desire to rest. His entire house could have fit in this room—almost his entire property. The Palatine Hill had far surpassed every seemingly surreal story that he had ever heard.

Verus did not have to wait long before another man entered the room. The man was round and plump like a grape. He had rings of fat around his neck that jiggled when he walked and vibrated when he talked. He looked like a very lazy man—and indeed he was—but presently, he was worked up into a sweat that dripped down him like wax from a candle.

"Ah," the fat man began, "Verus Flaminius of Pinacale. It is more than a pleasure to meet you. Please have a seat. Are you hungry? thirsty?" Without waiting for an answer the plump man clapped his hands. "Servants, bring me food and drink."

Verus finally sat down. "I...I...am..."

"Not very articulate," the fat man suggested. "Verus, do you know who I am?"

"I do not," Verus croaked.

"I am Vitelli Germanicus—the Emperor of Rome."

Verus felt a shock run all over his body. It was like someone had unexpectedly doused him with freezing water on an extremely hot day. He fell to his knees. "Caesar."

"Oh," Vitellius said quickly, "get up, get up. You're embarrassing me. And don't call me Caesar—that is a name I have never taken—I prefer Germanicus."

"I thought you went to Mevania to meet Vespasian."

"I only sent some servants there. I was just testing the temper of Vespasian. But never mind that; tell me, what can I do for you?"

"Well..." Verus gulped, "thank you for seeing me...I had not expected to talk to you directly. But I do need help. My oldest boy just went through an operation, he is recovering quickly, but I spent all of my Denarii paying for medicine, and I don't know if we will make it through winter."

Vitellius looked lazily at one of his dirty fingernails. "What do you need?"

"Grain..." Verus squeaked. "Not much of course...my Emperor...just enough to get us through."

"What about gold?"

Verus shrugged his shoulders, "That would help too but I don't want to ask for too much."

"Hah." Vitellius laughed, "You're too modest my friend. You must remember that I take care of the people of Rome; by my great leadership, Romans have been entertained by many good games and filled by many banquets."

The accountant suddenly emerged carrying documents and quills.

"Ah," Vitellius said with a smile, "Lucius, my loyal accountant, do you have everything ready for Verus to sign?"

"Yes," Lucius answered. "Everything is ready."

Verus felt a little nausea sweep over him; for some reason, he did not feel good about this whole situation.

Vitellius slapped the paperwork in front of Verus. "Just fill in your census information, your family name, and the date you would like to begin receiving grain shipments. Everything else will be arranged."

The Blacksmith began looking over the documents, which seemed normal enough.

"I need to go Verus," Vitellius said quickly, "and I need those documents signed before I do."

"Yes, Germanicus," Verus nodded. With held breath, he grabbed a quill. Everything was going so quickly. A few tense moments passed. But then finally, almost as if he was giving up his freedom, Verus signed the documents.

"Good," the accountant said. "Here are your copies. Please keep them on you for the next few days as you may be required to present them later."

"Excellent," Vitellius said. "Unfortunately, I must be leaving. Verus, it was a real pleasure to meet you; please, stop in next time you are in Rome." Just then a few servants entered into the room carrying fruit trays. Vitellius waved them off, "No, no, you've already taken too long; I don't have time to eat anymore."

"Thank you, Caesar...I mean Germanicus," Verus said reverently as he pounded his chest.

"Well then," Vitellius said with a smile, "with this little business done, I will be on my way." The fat man heaved as he tried to stand but then fell back down again. Verus came to his aid.

"Let me help you, Germanicus."

Between the two of them, Vitellius was able to shimmy up until he could get to his legs. "Thank you my boy."

"Yes, of course," Verus whispered.

"Oh," Vitellius added, "and I expect you to stay here as my guest tonight."

"Great Germanicus," Verus whispered, "I've already made other arrangements."

"Nonsense. Have you ever stayed at the Palatine Hill before?"

"No," Verus shook his head.

"Well, you do tonight," Vitellius said with a wink. "This is a rare opportunity my friend, and as the Emperor of Rome, I will not accept 'no' for an answer."

Verus nodded. "Yes...but I will have to go get my things."

"Very good. Very good." With these last words, Vitellius disappeared out of the room with the accountant following quickly after, leaving Verus in the palace by himself.

The Blacksmith's head was spinning. Not only was it amazing that he had just met the Emperor, but Verus' request was so easily granted. It was almost like Vitellius was convincing Verus to take the grain and gold. The young father had no mind for politics—he had always strived earnestly to avoid entangling himself in them—but now he knew just how ignorant he was. *"Why was it so easy to secure grain? Maybe it is because they gave me so little grain it did not matter."*

Until now, Verus had not thought about the amount of grain he was being given—that did not seem to be important. If Vitellius was only going to give him one bag of grain he would have taken it, and he would have been grateful to get it. At this point, anything would be helpful.

Verus studied the paper for a while. He was only able to pick out a few words.

"One ton?" Verus questioned. "That is more than enough for the winter—is that just for my family?" As he continued to look over the document, he recognized a word that startled him. *"Daily? Does that mean that I will receive a ton of grain daily? How is that possible?"* He scanned the rest of the document, his veins now pulsing with adrenaline. He then recognized another phrase that shook him to the core. "Five hundred Aureus. That can't be for me." Never had he regretted not learning to read as much as he did now. His eyes retraced the words again and again, trying to make sense of anything else.

Five hundred Aureus of gold was more money than he made in a year. It was more gold than he would make his entire life as a blacksmith. If he was only to receive one shipment of gold in this amount, he would have enough coin to buy the entire city of Pinacale.

He scratched his head. "For what? Why? That can't be right, can it?" In the space of a few moments, he had become the wealthiest man that he knew. A huge grin spread across his face, "Amazing. Hah! How is this possible?" A sudden rush of energy overcame Verus. He began to run for the door but then slowed before he reached it. "Perhaps this was a mistake. And if it was, I would hate to anger a Caesar." Doubt crept over Verus like a chill. "It is too much."

Decidedly, he turned the other direction and headed after the Emperor. He searched from room to room, scanning each one for signs of the Emperor, but he was not in any of them. The palace was almost deserted except for a few slaves that were scattered about. Verus stopped one of them.

"Where is Vitellius? Where did he go?"

The slave was dumbstruck, "Vitellius?"

"Yes, the Emperor…"

"He fled…of course."

Verus frowned. "He fled? Where to?"

"I don't know," replied the slave with a twinkle of gossip in her voice, "but I imagine he won't get too far."

Verus nodded. "How can I find him?"

The slave offered little help but her advice did not have to be great. Once Verus was outside he found himself swarmed by a crowd of people that was so forceful, he was compelled to move with the mob or be trampled by them.

"Where are we going?" Verus yelled to one of the Romans that crowded around him.

"Gemonian Stairs!"

"Why?"

"VITELLIUS is yielding up his Caesarship to Vespasian."

Verus nodded with only mild comprehension. "Why would he be yielding it up?" But the other man did not have time to answer before he was swept away with the mob. The Gemonian Stairs were crowded, as could be expected, but Verus was able to fight his way through and come out ahead of the group. His large muscles forced people to one side, and if someone turned to push Verus back, they suddenly changed their mind upon seeing the size of the Blacksmith's massive arms.

Verus was tired of being pushed around by tiny shopkeepers and wizened old men; now it was his turn to push through to the front. Before long, Verus was the closest anyone could come to Vitellius, who was now only ten feet in front of him. The Emperor was sweaty and out of breath; he was speaking but the crowd was hardly listening.

Verus smiled broadly and waved stupidly to Vitellius.

While everyone was completely ignoring Vitellius, they were enamored with the man who stood next to him. All eyes were on Vespasian—the great subduer of the Jews. He had a large nose, big ears, and a balding head. His eyes were narrow and sharp, like the eyes of a cat, and his face was wrinkled from excessive laughter. His looks were rather simple, but his presence was divine. All around him were a host of loyal soldiers, armed with glistening swords; and that, it seemed, to be the source of all of Vespasian's authority. The crowd quieted down.

"MY FRIENDS! Listen well to my voice and hear my plea," Vespasian screamed. "Before us we have a traitor. A born *proditor* who has spent his time defiling his holy position with gluttonous gorging and callow conversation. He saved little and did even less; his manners were vile with our allies and dishonorable before our enemies."

The crowd booed at Vitellius.

Vespasian continued. "I am a soldier—one who is paid to spill another's blood—but I do not enjoy the color of Roman red. As I look at this sweaty hog wrapped in the toga of Rome, I can't help but think of the lives he has cost. In Jerusalem, I did what was needed, and in Egypt also, being forced to fight against Romans, but it was this man who brought me to it—it was Vitellius who let the sons of Rome fight each other. While I fought to protect the freedoms of Roman Citizens, *he* wanted to protect himself. At the battle of Bedriacum—a battle which cost many Roman lives—the Gods favored us. And of course they did; I've honored them all my life, while Vitellius has spat in their faces. He took office on the anniversary of the battle of Avia, which was the lowest time in Roman history; what more of an *auspice* can you ask for?"

Someone threw a tomato, striking Vitellius in the head.

Vespasian drew his sword. "We are at the tip of a knife—the pinnacle of Roman power—but we need a mighty leader to rule a mighty empire. For we are Romans—rulers of the world!"

The mob roared with approval.

"WHEN HANNIBAL CROSSED THE APPENINES, forcing Rome into war, did we falter? did we faint? After we had lost at the battles of Trebias, Trasimene, and Cannae were we beaten?

were we lost? And let me answer with a resounding 'NO' that rings through Rome. We will never be wrong if our leaders are right. And before you now is our leader—our great Emperor—who has done everything wrong. Kneel, Vitellius, and let your neck be bare! Kneel before the Roman people, whose sons you have killed through civil war."

Verus was still smiling at Vitellius as if this was some sort of theatrical spectacle.

Vitellius stuck out his hands, pleading with the crowd, "I WAS ONCE YOUR EMPEROR! Am I not still your friend? Do you remember the games we saw, and the banquets we held? I was already your Emperor when Vespasian began the civil war. How could I start a civil war if I was already Emperor? He began it all. The Senate had already proclaimed me Germanicus."

"KNEEL!" Vespasian ordered.

The fat man knelt, but his eyes locked on Vespasian, "Yet, I was once your Emperor. How can you ask me to kneel? I have given you the seat of the Emperor, what am I guilty of?"

Vespasian laughed. "That is my point, Vitellius; you are guilty of nothing, for you have done nothing. Inaction may be suitable for the Greeks, but Romans demand action. If you had nothing to fear, why were you hiding away in a doorkeeper's lodge when I found you?"

"I have given you a list of traitors," Vitellius replied. "Even now you hold it in your hands. Is this the reward I get for my service?"

"I will deal with these traitors as well," Vespasian said as he waved a stack of papers in front of Vitellius. "They will die for their corruption, but you...my friend, not Charon, will be the one that leads them across the river Styx."

"Yet, I was once your Emperor..." Vitellius began to say, but he was cut off—and so was his head. The crowd roared its approval, screaming so loudly that it filled the whole of Rome.

The Blacksmith was horrified.

Besides the chanting of the crowd, and the raised head of Vitellius, Verus saw one more thing that turned his stomach. Vespasian had turned his attention to his generals that were behind him and had given one of them the stack of papers of which had been Vitellius' last attempt to save his life. The names on those lists now had become the *proscription*—the public enemies of Rome—and anyone whose name was on them would probably not last the night. On the top of the pile, in larger print than all the rest, sat one that was familiar to Verus. He could clearly see it from where he was, and even though he could not read the lettering, Verus recognized the handwriting—for it was his own. On the papyrus was Verus' name, written in bold and large print. Just below that, was the name of his family, and just below that, was the name of Pinacale.

It was his death warrant, and Verus had been the one to sign it.

Chapter 8

December 20, 66 AD

Priscus

"What is your name?"

Priscus squinted in the morning light, trying to make out the figure before him. "Give me yours first."

"Hah. You must be a Gaul. My name is Generix; I am from the Germanic tribes of the North."

Priscus crossed his arms and narrowed his eyes. "And what is your interest in me?"

"I've been put in charge of you; I was told I should watch over you," Generix answered.

"Guard me?"

"No, not guard you, but show you around. I don't know if you've noticed by now, but you're not in chains. You've had more freedom in the last two days than I think you probably have had most your life."

"Why? Why aren't they worried that I will escape?"

"Because," Generix said with a smile, "Romans believe that Rome is the center of the world. Thousands of people would rather be slaves in Rome than princes outside of her. They are too prideful to believe you would leave. And…in your case…I think they're right."

"Priscus. My name is Priscus."

"Have you always been so mistrusting?"

The large Gaul did not answer. Instead he clenched his jaw a little tighter and narrowed his eyes.

Generix swallowed. "Come here, let me show you around."

Again Priscus was silent, but obedient. He stood up from the dirt and followed after the squat man. Generix was hairy. All sorts of rope-like hair sprouted out every dirty dimple in his cheeks and every wrinkle in his body. From a distance, he might have been mistaken for a bear. His unwashed beard was braided with a mix of his own hair and colorful sheets of cloth, which gave it the look of a foreign textile. He was dressed like a Celt but had the shoes and armbands of a Roman.

The morning was hazy. There was a slight fog that tentatively covered the ground and shifted as they walked. Despite the early hour, the Romans were awake. There was a group of them gambling to Priscus' right, another group huddled around a fire to Priscus' left.

As Generix stepped into the center of the road, he gestured impressively to the walls and large tents around him. "This is a Roman *Castra.*"

"This isn't that fantastic," Priscus said as he stopped in front of Generix. "The Celts build palisades that are twice this size."

Generix laughed. "Yes, but it takes them years to do it. The famous Roman *Castras* are built in only a few hours, and that is after a twenty mile march. Every piece of timber you see stuck in the ground around us is a piece of timber that was carted here on the backs of one of these Romans. Every time these demented Romans camp, they dig a trench around themselves—sometimes as deep as ten feet—and then they stick posts in the ground that are six feet high. They've got specialists—I think they call them *architecti* or something—whose sole job is to make sure the exact same fort is built every time. No matter what the conditions, if Romans are in enemy territory, they don't rest until they have a fort around them."

To the left and right of them were dozens of tents, lined up perfectly in rows. Half-armored soldiers scurried in and out of them with a purpose in their eyes and pride in their chests.

Priscus was slightly disappointed in the average Roman soldier. All his life with the Celts, and even before with the Gauls, he had heard story after story of the mighty Roman soldiers; but as he looked at each one individually he realized they weren't so mighty. In fact, to Priscus, they seemed rather smallish. The biggest one of them came up to his chin, while the rest of them were far smaller. Priscus was used to being bigger than everyone else amongst the Celts, but compared to the Romans, he was a giant. Despite Priscus' size, the Romans never flinched when they saw him coming; they never turned back and stared when he walked by; they never even fumbled when they talked to him, as most others did. Even the most common Roman soldier had more confidence and presence than the bravest of the Celts.

Generix pointed to the front gate. "That is the *Porta Praetoria*—the main gate. It is through that gate that they go to conquer."

"How many soldiers are camped here?"

"Two Legions—ten thousand men."

As they approached the front gate, to their right was an open area where soldiers drilled with wood lances and shields. Each lance had a ball of padding on the end that the soldiers used to knock down their opponents. When the combat was too crowded for lances, the Romans drew out wooden swords that were about the length of a forearm. With their shields crowded together they formed a line; occasionally one of the soldiers would stab at the enemy with his wooden sword and strike the enemy in the leg or gut.

Priscus had never seen combat like this before. Instead of fighting individually, like the Gauls and Celts, these Romans fought together as a single body. They had strength in unity, protection in numbers. As long as these little-bodied Romans marched together, they proved to be an impenetrable mass of men.

"Come," Generix said as he grabbed Priscus' shoulder, "there is still more to see."

Priscus watched the soldiers for a few moments longer before he followed. Farther down the path, there was a small blacksmith and a canteen, a tent designated as a brothel and another for a healer. At the edge of camp a foul stench hit their noses.

"If you need to piss, now is the time," Generix said.

"No," Priscus answered.

"In a typical Roman *Castra*, the *Principia* is in the center," Generix said as he pointed at where they had come from, "but that is now where the slaves are being kept—like yourself. A few nights back, some wild Celts shot arrows into the center of the *Castra* and wounded a few of the commanders, so they moved the *Principia* over to the side, just for an added measure of protection."

"Is this where you are taking me?" Priscus asked.

"Yes," Generix replied, "but be on your guard. That room is full of pompous Romans."

"What do they want from me?"

"I'm not sure. It is hard to say what they see in you. They've all heard how many Celts you've killed, so they know you are a fighter. They might ask you to be in the army, or they could try to conscript you as a spy, or hire you as a porter." Generix smiled and pointed at a large tent. "But now is the time to find out. Go there and state your name to the guards."

"Where are you going?"

"I will be in the tent—the same place you slept last night," Generix said as he stepped away from Priscus, "Farewell Gaul. May the Gallic Gods protect you—whoever they may be."

Priscus nodded ever so slightly and turned his attention back to the large tent. There were two guards at the entrance, standing at attention. As the Gaul drew closer, they put their hands on the hilts of their swords.

"Halt," one of them growled. "What is your business?"

"I'm Priscus…and…I was summoned here—"

"The Gaul," the other guard chimed in. "I've heard about you. They said that you put down over fifty Celts in the raid."

"I heard it was closer to eighty," the other guard replied.

Priscus did not know how to respond, so he held his tongue.

One of the soldiers broke the silence. "Wait here." One of the guards turned and entered the tent, leaving Priscus and the other soldier out in the open air.

"So how many was it really?" the guard asked.

"Whatever it was," Priscus hissed, "I wish it was more."

"Were you a slave there?"

Priscus narrowed his eyes; he did not like idle chatter. "How long have you Romans been here?"

"A week… or so. Not long."

"And what are you doing here?"

This time it was the Roman's turn to feel uncomfortable. "If you don't know, then you're not meant to."

"I know that Romans love to steal things that aren't theirs."

"Watch your tongue, Gaul—your life is not worth much in this camp."

Priscus heaved a deep breath, which made his chest more barreled than normal, but this normal gesture of intimidation did not work on the Roman. Instead the Roman glared back at Priscus, daring him to do something.

Just then the tent flapped open, "Enter Gaul..."

Slowly, but obediently, the large Gaul stepped out from the light and into the tent, which was much warmer than outside. The tent was large and well built: It was held up by several thick poles that were sunk deep into the earth. Upon these poles the soldiers draped armor and swords, packs of food and sandals. Priscus realized that the floor was not dirt, as he had expected, but a series of animal skins which tickled the tips of his bare toes as he walked. To Priscus' left and right were Roman soldiers, dressed in full battle gear. They looked fierce, albeit bored. For the first time in his life, the Gaul actually felt small.

"Ah, Priscus," said one of the soldiers to his right. "This is the warrior everyone has been talking about."

Priscus spoke only a few words of Latin so he was surprised that he understood the Roman so perfectly. It took him a while, but after a few moments, he realized that the soldier was speaking Celt, not Latin.

"How do so many of you speak my language?" Priscus asked.

"Why would that surprise you? Do you think that it is impossible for an elevated being to learn your crass language, or did you think that your crass language would be of no interest to an elevated being?"

Priscus did not know how to respond.

"Priscus," the soldier said with a great gesture of his hands, "we are Romans—conquerors of the world. We've taken control over everything from Britannia to the far reaches of Egypt, and by the Gods, I assure you we are more than capable of conquering your language with our tongues."

"What are you telling him?" asked an older, sterner man. "Why are you pestering the Gaul?" This older man was the only Roman Priscus recognized—Fabius Valens.

In broken Celt, Valens spoke, "Do you...recognize...me?"

Priscus nodded ever so slightly.

"Answer him!" another soldier yelled.

"Caecina, calm yourself," replied Valens. "He did answer with a nod of his head."

"He's a Gaul," Caecina yelled. "A scoundrel that should be kicked in the teeth and used as a stepping stool, not treated well and catered to!"

"Caecina," Valens said as he stood up, "I will have order in my presence or…"

Caecina tightened up. "Yes, sir…"

The Romans spoke mostly Latin and so Priscus was unsure what was being said. After a few moments, Valens continued to speak. This time an interpreter translated.

"Now, let's make this business quick. Why were you killing Celts when we found you, Priscus?"

"I hated them. All of them."

"Did they kill your family?"

Priscus shifted uncomfortably. "Yes, what was left of it."

"And now, by Fortuna's hand, you find yourself in a Roman camp. What are your plans?"

Priscus relaxed slightly, "Plans? I planned on being dead right now; I thought my body would be amongst the Celts. I was not fighting to cheat death; I was fighting to escape from life…"

"Then you have nothing left living for. You must not have children of your own."

"No…"

Valens massaged his brow. "Well, that is interesting. After this conversation, Priscus, I am setting you free; you are no longer a slave, chained down to the whims of another, but a free man."

Priscus held still.

"You don't seem too enthused about the prospect of freedom."

"I…I…just did not think you would grant me freedom so quickly."

"What?" Valens gave a rich laugh. "Did you think that Romans were so beyond reason that we would not grant you freedom?"

The large Gaul shook his head slightly.

"But what will you do with your freedom?" Valens continued. "What does any man do that is set free in the wild terrain? I imagine that for protection, you will join up with a neighboring faction— perhaps the Gauls or Germans. A warrior such as yourself will be readily accepted. They will give you a little section in their palisades, where you'll be able to build a wooden hut. In the winter you will come close to starving; in the summer you will most assuredly be at war. You will eat gruel your whole life, except for the occasional meat, which will be from the unwanted portion of your new master."

Priscus stayed silent.

"That is one life you could live, Gaul, but I have another proposition for you." Valens furled his brow. "Join me. Not as a slave, but as a Roman soldier. Join me and I will grant you Citizenship."

Caecina stepped forward. "He's a Gaul! A Celtic slave. If you grant him Citizenship just for serving you, you cheapen the value of Citizenship all together."

"I'm not the first to have a Gaul in my army, nor the last," Valens replied.

"But those Gauls are in the ranks of Auxilia—they aren't Roman Citizens. He is from a conquered people; he is weak in every way."

"I saw him fight," Valens yelled back, "and I know that weakness is not within him. He slew twenty-seven Celts."

"They thought he was one of them. He betrayed his masters, and eventually he will betray you."

"If you were not the son of a senator, Caecina, I swear by the brow of Neptune, that I would have you whipped from this camp. That is the problem with you *patricians*. You believe that the blood that runs through your veins is somehow worth more than everyone else's. But let me tell you boy, I've killed me many o' nobles, and they bleed just as much as the *populi*."

Caecina tried to restrain his temper but his flushed cheeks were too difficult to hide. "Valens, you go too far. I am only suggesting that this man's loyalty is in question. How can you grant Citizenship so easily to this Gaul when it takes other foreigners years of service in the army? How do we know he is not a spy, sent to infiltrate our ranks?"

"Spy for whom?" Valens countered. "We found him attacking the Celts. He has not had any contact with the Gauls for years—you pompous fool. You would have the whole world segregated between the rich and the poor if you could."

Caecina went for his sword, but he was stopped by Priscus'

67

large hand before the Roman could pull it out.

Priscus laughed—a deep belly laugh that was so forceful that it startled the closest of Romans. "I know what freedom is, but I never wanted it—never cared for it. You speak of freedom and loyalty as if they're as good as a hot meal or a warm bed. When one does not have food to eat or a place to sleep, freedom is as worthless as the effort it takes to say the word. I have been a slave, but it was not to a man, only to misfortune. I wish to be a slave of misfortune no more; I wish to join the ranks of your army. Feed me. Clothe me. Put a sword in my hand, and you will see how well I can serve Rome."

Chapter 9

December 22, 69 AD
Verus

With Vitellius dead, the crowd stood there, waiting for Vespasian's next move. After a long while, Vespasian approached the crowd with a stack of papers in his hands. "Here are the enemies of Rome! Bring their heads to me and receive your reward!"

He threw the papers in the air, sending them fluttering like birds. The crowd quickly turned into a mob. Despite his muscular frame, Verus found himself constantly pushed to either side as people grabbed at the fluttering pieces of paper. Out of the corner of his eye, the Blacksmith saw an old woman fall under the weight of the crowd; but before she was trampled to death, Verus pulled her back to her feet. After awhile of fighting and pushing, he and the old lady were able to reach the safety of an empty alley.

The old lady sat down on a discarded wood box. "You saved me. I thought I would die in there. Thank you. What is your name?"

The Blacksmith breathed deep as he raked his fingers through his hair. "My name is Verus. And this is madness. What has possessed these people?"

"You've never been here during a *proscription* before, have you?"

"Lady, I've never been to Rome before…"

"Look at this," the old woman whispered, "I was able to grab one of these when I fell to the ground; it about killed me, but I got it."

Verus snatched the piece of paper and read it quickly: It was a list of Roman *patricians* and generals who supported Vitellius. Verus' name was right on top.

The old lady had a grin on her face and a twinkle in her eye.

"Just look at how much money they are offering for these traitors."

To the left of each name was an amount that had been hastily penned in; next to Verus' name, was an amount so high that he could barely believe it, "Two million sestertius."

"Oh," the old lady whispered excitedly, "that's a good one. I would love to catch one for that amount. Who is it? Maybe I know where they live. Come on—we can go together if we hurry." She tried to snap the list back, but Verus held it just out of her reach.

He shook his head. "This is wrong. This is all wrong."

The old lady was confused for a moment as she studied Verus' weighty eyes, but then slowly, ever so slowly, a grin crept up on her face. The Blacksmith was so absorbed in the list that he did not realize the woman was reaching for something within her robes.

"What did you say your name was again?"

"Verus…"

Just then the lady moved so quickly that she seemed twenty years younger. A little blade, the size of a finger, pierced Verus in the arm. It did not go deep—most of it was caught in his heavy garb— but it was enough to stain his robe with a dot of red blood.

Verus stepped back. "Are you insane? I saved you from the crowd."

She began to pull another blade from her robes—this one was twice as big as the one before. "Tell me your name!" She leaped off a discarded box and came flying towards Verus; this time, however, he was prepared and sidestepped, letting her fall to the ground unhindered. Her face was the first thing to hit the stone beneath, knocking her out completely. And there she lay— motionless.

The Blacksmith bent on his knees and listened to her mouth. She was still breathing. "You'll be fine—as fine as a crazy lady can be."

Verus was not a thief; in fact, he could not remember stealing anything in his life. So the first time he thought about taking the old lady's knife, he ignored the impulse; but the more he thought about it, the more he knew he needed it.

"She tried to kill me," he justified. He picked up the dagger, looked at it, and then looked at the old lady, "I'm sorry, whoever you are, but I need this. If everyone is as crazy as you…then this will be the first of several things I need."

He shoved the bigger of the two daggers into the folds of his tunic and walked away, whispering apologies as he went.

Horace had been right—the streets ran with blood that night. Verus saw his first two dead bodies as he walked out of the alley; they did not appear to be stabbed but trampled by the crowd. Blood trickled from their heads and filled the crevices of the stones below. Verus clenched his jaw and pushed on. Every street he passed seemed more chaotic than the last: there were fires burning, people fighting, guards marching, and children screaming. There were shouts in the distance and metallic clashes down almost every street. Verus tried to find a sword, but the dead bodies had already been picked clean. In the shadows of every house were golden eyes that stared out hungrily, like a pack of scavengers, waiting for the next victim to fall to the ground.

He went down one road where a full-scale battle had taken place. A large estate had been besieged by Roman soldiers. The defenders, who wore armor similar to the Roman soldiers but different colored tunics, had put up a fight, but it was all in vain. Eventually, they gave way to the onslaught.

Verus wandered aimlessly through the streets, trying to avoid the mobs that ran up and down them. He was doing quite well until, in the distance, a mob appeared out of nowhere and spotted him; even though they had no idea who he was, they came charging. Verus outdistanced them by pulling himself into another alley.

He hid behind a box that had something rotting inside. The mob passed a few moments later. Just as they disappeared, a large hand grabbed Verus by the shoulder.

"Who are you?" a man hissed.

Verus grabbed his dagger and spun around; the hilt got caught on his tunic and, despite his frantic effort, he could not get it free. Instead, it looked like he was enthusiastically rubbing his belly.

"Calm yourself," the voice replied. "If both of us are hiding from the mob, then that means that we have nothing to fear from each other. I am Fabius Valens, commander of the tenth Legion—or I was until a few days ago."

"Valens? The tenth Legion? I thought you were up in Gaul."

Valens stepped into a crack of light, revealing the face of a bloody and bruised man. His face was round and balding—he seemed so harmless, especially with the dried blood stuck to his cheek. "We were in Gaul, that is, until Vitellius sent for me. I arrived too late for the battle but just in time to be labeled a traitor."

"So you are on the *proscription?*"

With some hesitation Valens answered, "Yes. But you must be too if you're hiding."

Verus looked down and away. The memory of the old lady in the alley was still so fresh in his mind that he hesitated to answer. "Maybe."

"Maybe?"

"Well, yes my name is on it, but it's a mistake."

"Hah," Valens growled, "so is mine. So is everyone's. We just happened to put our lots in with the wrong side. But who could have known that Vitellius was such a coward."

"Where is your Legion?"

"A major part of my forces switched sides, while the remainder is in *Pisa*, awaiting my arrival. We still have a chance to win this war if I can sail back to Gaul and raise a strong enough army."

"Why weren't you there at the battle of Bedrianumb?"

Valens stared at Verus for a moment. "It's pronounced Bedriacum, and I was sick." In a mock voice, Valens repeated Verus' question, "Why weren't *you* at the battle?"

"Me?" Verus pointed at himself. "I'm a poor blacksmith— I'm not on anyone's side."

Valens narrowed his eyes. "If you are not on anyone's side, then why are you hiding in the dark from one of them?"

"I don't know. I was trying to get some grain for my family this winter—my son had an operation that drained all of our Denarii— and all of a sudden I'm on the top of the *proscription*."

Valens paused for a moment. "You're on the top of the list?"

"Yes," Verus said as he pulled out the *proscription*. "That's me—number one."

"So you're Verus Flaminius of Pinacale, son of Gaius Flaminius."

"Yes. And I need to get out of Rome to protect my family."

"I might be able to help," Valens whispered quickly, "do you have a weapon on you?"

"Just a dagger."

"Give it to me then," Valens ordered. "I think I know how to get out of here."

Verus complied quickly, giving Valens the dagger. As soon as Valens had it, he turned the point toward Verus' throat.

"What are you doing?"

"I'm getting out of here," Valens hissed. "Now do what I say or I will cut a hole in your throat that is as big as your mouth." The old Roman general gestured with the knife toward the entrance of the alley. "Put your hands on your head and move."

Verus obeyed but he could not help but speak, "Why are you doing this?"

"Because," Valens replied, "you're a blacksmith—your life means little—while I am a Roman general who is destined to rule Rome. Now, be silent."

With Verus in the lead, and a dagger pointed in his back, they walked to the edge of the alley and waited.

"What are we waiting for?" Verus asked.

"Silence!" Valens hissed. "Or you will die tonight."

They did not have to wait long before a small group of Roman soldiers appeared down the road. As they passed, Valens hailed them. "Halt, good Romans."

The soldiers suddenly stopped and placed their hands on the hilts of their swords. One of them spoke, "Who goes there?"

"Peace," Valens replied. "I have here, with me, the number one public enemy—Verus of Pinacale."

"Hand him over then," the Centurion commanded, "and you shall receive your reward." He began to step forward, acting like Valens had already agreed.

"Halt or I slit his throat here and now; you and I both know that he is worth more alive than he is dead."

"How dare you interfere with Roman law—"

"I don't want the reward—you soldiers can keep it. All I want is safe passage out of the city."

The Roman Centurion laughed. "If you are so eager to leave the city, you must be on the *proscription* yourself."

"I am," Valens admitted. "But I'm not as high on the list as Verus."

"What is your name?"

Valens' arms tightened around Verus' throat. "My name is my business—and your business is hunting rebels. I will give you this rebel but let me keep my name to myself. Swear to me safe passage out of this city and I will deliver Verus to you unharmed."

Just as Valens finished speaking, a mob of people came around another corner looking for public enemies. They were a mixed group, ranging in ages from ten to forty. Their bloodied faces seemed to provide ample evidence that they had already killed a few people and were eager for more.

The Centurion hissed at Valens, "Why don't I take both of you in and collect twice the reward?"

Instead of passing by, the crowd made a circle around the soldiers.

"On your way," the Centurion yelled at the crowd. "Be on your way."

"Who've you got there?" asked one of the Citizens.

The Centurion drew his sword and pointed it at the closest Citizen's throat. "On your way!" The rest of the soldiers followed suit, drawing their blades and pointing them at various members of the mob.

"Who do you have there?" shouted another one in the mob.

Verus did not know if it was instinct that made him speak, or perhaps good fortune, but something inspired him with an idea. "It's Fabius Valens, the commander of the tenth Legion!"

"You fool," whispered Valens in Verus' ear.

"Fabius," said one in the crowd, "he is worth more than a million sestertius. I have the *proscription* right here; he is third from the top!"

"BACK!" the Centurion yelled. "The next one who speaks gets their throat slit. You Citizens continue on your way!"

"We want some of the reward," said one in the mob.

The Centurion was not sure who had said it, but he was true to his word; he turned on the Citizens, stabbing one clear through the throat. "Be on your way!"

His actions, bold as they were, did not have the effect that he was hoping for. Instead of retreating, the Citizens rushed in; pulling sticks and swords from their clothes, they came at the soldiers from all directions. One of the Roman soldiers was cut across the throat; another was stabbed in the eye.

"Get Fabius Valens!" yelled someone in the mob. "Get him—" But before the Citizen could finish his sentence, a soldier had stabbed the man clear through the stomach. The fighting turned fierce. Blood ran like wine.

Before Valens could slit Verus' throat, a Citizen charged at them, forcing the old general to defend himself. Verus was thrown to the side, landing on a mound of old chicken cages that cracked under his weight. The Blacksmith only had time to turn around before another soldier stood over him, brandishing a bloody sword; but before the death blow could be struck, the Roman took an arrow in the arm. The soldier reeled back, dazed by the sudden wound. Verus had just enough time to find his feet and tackle his opponent. The soldier went for a dagger at his side, but Verus twisted the arrow in the man's arm, sending pain throughout the soldier's body.

The Blacksmith knocked the man in the face with an elbow—breaking his nose—and then picked up a fallen sword. Verus brandished the blade, waving it threateningly as he took a step back. Within a few moments, the Roman soldiers were all dead or unconscious, subdued by the mob. Once they were done with them, they turned an anxious eye to Verus, who had backed himself into a corner.

"There goes Fabius Valens," Verus pointed towards an empty alley. "Get him! He's worth over one million sestertius!" With this the mob cheered and went on pursuit, leaving Verus with the dead Roman soldiers. The Blacksmith only had seconds to scrounge whatever money he could from the dead before another troop of soldiers entered from the opposite side of the street.

"Halt!" one of them yelled.

Verus looked up, as if his name had been "halt." The soldiers drew their swords and came running at the Blacksmith, who had begun to run the opposite way. He was not a fast runner, but with all the confusion, he did not have to be. Soon he outdistanced the soldiers and took refuge behind a tree.

The soldiers passed, their voices still echoing in the distance long after they were gone. Verus stayed there, waiting. Waiting for some idea to pop into his head; waiting for the city to regain its wits;

waiting for a chance to escape—but none came. He was forced to lay low next to the tree, which smelled twice as potent as it should have. He spent most of the night lying in the grass, tensing up whenever someone passed. Toward midnight, as another mob was passing Verus' hiding spot, the Blacksmith was hit with sudden inspiration: *"This is a stone pine tree."*

"That is why it smells so potent. This is the same tree they plant in front of every gladiatorial pit." Verus looked behind him. "I've been here. This is Horace's gladiatorial pit!" Verus jumped up so suddenly that he attracted a little too much attention.

"There's one!"

"Get him!"

Verus swallowed and ran to the front door; he reached it in moments and threw his body into it. It was locked. Using one hand to hold his sword, he used the other to bang on the door. Slowly the mob crowded around him.

"Who are you? What is your name?"

Verus scrambled for an answer. "My name is…Sajanus."

"No you're not," shouted one of them. "Let's see your papers."

"I am," Verus said with more confidence, "And…I'm a gladiator, just returning from…the tavern."

"Who do you fight for?" asked one of them.

"Horace…"

Suddenly the door opened up slightly, leaving just enough room for Verus to slip through. The Blacksmith took his chance and sidestepped into the building just as the mob charged in.

Horace was on the other side of the door. "Help me lock it, boy." Verus rammed the door with his body, just as Horace slid the bolt to lock it into place. A second later, the mob rammed the entrance, hitting it with their collective force.

"Who do you have in there? Who are you hiding?"

Horace slid open a small hole in the door. "What are you doing?"

"Let him out—he is on the *proscription*."

Horace looked back at Verus with a sly expression and studied him, "Is he now?"

"Let him out—he is on the *proscription*!"

The old gladiator laughed. "This is a gladiator of mine, just come back from doing an errand for me. His name is Qualic."

"He said his name was Sajanus."

"It is," Horace said forcefully, "Sajanus Qualic."

"Let us in. Show us his papers."

"There is no way that I am going to let a mob into my arena."

"We will bust down your door and take him by force."

Horace's face turned red with anger. "Then do it quick. It will give my gladiators some live practice. You start busting down the door, and I will go rouse 'em. They will be in a fit of rage to be woken up in the night, but quite happy when they get to cut down the likes of you."

There was a moment of silence.

"Come on then," Horace yelled, "start banging the door down."

Verus could hear whispers on the other side of the door.

"Have you lost your wits," Horace yelled through the hole, "or just your mind? If you would charge into a gladiatorial pit armed with sticks and daggers, thinking that you can make an army of gladiators do what you want, then I say you've lost both."

Silence ensued.

"Be gone then," Horace yelled, "if you don't have the balls to go forward."

There was a longer pause and more whispers, until finally, like a group of dismayed children, the mob walked off into the night.

"Fools," Horace whispered to himself. "Frenzied fools. I can't believe that even for a second they thought they were going to come into a gladiatorial pit and tell me what to do." Horace turned toward his new guest, "Verus, you're as much a fool as them. What have you gotten yourself into?"

Chapter 10
December 23, 69 AD
Priscus

Priscus stood before his reflection in his Roman tent. Scars new and old covered his body like the exposed roots of a tree. He was so scarred that it was difficult to tell where normal skin began and where the scars seemed to end. He shook his head as he put on a shirt-like padding over his naked shoulders and tied a red scarf around his neck. He hated asking for help but this next part he could not do himself. "Orderly."

A few moments later a servant appeared and saluted by pounding his chest.

"My armor."

"Yes, Lord." The orderly walked over to Priscus' side and picked up a large shelled breastplate. Because of the Gaul's enormous size, it took three times the normal metal to complete the armor. It was shelled like most Roman armor but, by command of Priscus, an extra length of protection was added on the right arm. The Gaul did not prefer to use lances, although he did so with the utmost skill; he preferred face-to-face combat, where he could smell fear on his opponent's body. The armor was banged and dented—there were at least two spots that had been repaired completely—but it was his armor, paid in full.

After the armor was on and situated, the orderly busily tied the front.

"An old friend has come to talk to you, my Lord."

"Old friend?" the Gaul asked. "I don't have old friends. What is his name?"

"Generix, sir. He is with the tenth Legion."

"The tenth? Generix?" Priscus scratched his head. "What is

he doing here? I haven't seen that hairy mongrel for years. Send him in when you leave."

"Yes, Lord."

After tying the armor into place, the orderly handed Priscus his sword. The sword itself had been modified from the Roman design: Instead of a straight short blade, it was a little longer and slightly curved so that it could slice clean through limbs. Then, with the help of his orderly, Priscus attached a long sword to his back, which was more in the tradition of the Gauls. After this, a leather belt with studded metal was put around his waist. Then arm guards were fastened on, followed by leg guards. Most Romans did not put on their full array of armor unless they were going to battle, but Priscus preferred it, even in the warmer months.

"Do you want your helmet, my Lord?"

"No, not now. Send Generix in; I'm ready to receive him."

With this the orderly saluted and bowed out of the tent. Moments later Generix came in.

"Priscus," Generix said with open arms.

The Gaul awkwardly nodded.

"What, no warm receipt for an old friend?"

Priscus frowned. "Have a seat. Orderly, come back in here and pour us some wine."

Generix smiled. "You're everything I remember and more. How long has it been since I saw you last—two years? Ever since you were transferred out of the tenth Legion, you've been the center of the most fantastical stories. Almost every conversation I hear is about how 'Priscus did this,' or how 'Priscus took over that.' Is any of it true?"

Priscus gave a loud scoff, "Depends on what you've heard."

"They say that your one Century took over the entire city of Copua in a fortnight."

"Well," Priscus replied, "that's true."

"How? Most of the generals thought it would take a whole Legion to conquer."

Priscus frowned—he was tired of having to retell the story. "They had a river in the middle of the city; we simply floated past the walls."

"What about the bars in the river?"

"They were corroded."

"Amazing," Generix whispered. "Truly, amazing. What about the battle of Hurn?"

"Yes, I was there."

"They say you slaughtered over a hundred men."

The Gaul nodded. "They insulted me the night before by sending a slave to negotiate the terms of peace."

Generix took a sip of his wine. "And at the battle of Bedriacum?"

Priscus' jaw tightened. "I was there, but I fought on the side of Vespasian. If the Tenth Legion would have made it on time, I'm sure you would have fought for Vitellius."

"Most of the Tenth has defected to Vespasian," Generix replied. "We are all on the same side now. But, they say you fought like a demon, trampling every opposing Roman in your way. They say you, alone, captured the Eagle of the Fourth Legion."

Priscus shook his head slightly. "That wasn't the battle of Bedriacum; that was in a skirmish a little after. I did take their Eagle, the pride of the fourth, but by some blunder of one of the leaders—may Mars castrate him—they were able to get it back. I swear…generals are the army's greatest vice; they very rarely make a smart move, but when they do, they expect more than just praise for it. It is the Centurions, the leaders in the middle—the ones who are not born *patricians*—that should be leading the army."

"That reminds me," Generix said with a small grunt that was intended to be a laugh, "did you hear what happened to Caecina?"

"Caecina? I remember that peacock. That man filed the most vehement grievance when I rose to the rank of Centurion."

"Yes, that's the one. He was looking to meet up at Bedriacum and then, at the last moment, switch sides. His men, however, wouldn't have it; they captured Caecina and put him in chains. He died shortly after."

Priscus nodded, "That's good news. That pompous fool thought that he was the son of Jupiter. His favorite time was spent in front of a mirror, admiring the pale face that looked back at him. He lacked boldness and brutality—those are the traits that get a man power these days."

Generix nodded. "He was weak and now he is dead because

of it."

"One less nobleman to give orders is one more reason to stay in the army. The fewer *patricians* there are in the world, the better off we will all be."

Generix nodded but he was careful not to agree out loud. "So what are your plans? Where are you going?"

Priscus scratched his chin. "That sounds like you are prying into military matters? You know better than to ask a Centurion his orders."

"Sorry…"

Priscus interrupted. "But…since you asked I might as well tell you. We don't have orders right now, besides camping here, outside the walls of Rome. Supposedly there are secret orders coming—from Vespasian himself—but I will believe them when I see them in my hands."

"Orders of a secret nature?"

Priscus rubbed his eyes with the back of his hand. "I would guess that they—"

Suddenly the muffled voice of the orderly interrupted. "My Lord, an urgent message has just arrived. May I come in?"

"Pass."

The young boy appeared through the flaps, brandishing a roll of papyrus.

Generix raised his eyebrows, "That is a fancy roll of *vellum*. That certainly must have come from someone important."

Priscus ignored the hairy man and grabbed the message. He opened it and stared at the words; it was all a farce, however, because Priscus had never learned to read Latin—or anything for that matter.

Generix cleared his throat. "What does it say?"

"Routine orders," the Gaul lied. "Now if you will excuse me, I must attend to them."

"Come on," Generix coaxed, "you can tell an old friend what your orders are."

Priscus' jaw turned taut. "That is the second time you have asked me to break military regulations; you do it again, and I will report you. Now, leave my tent. I have work to do."

"Yes, of course. Please, forgive me. I did not mean—."

Priscus gestured to the door, "Away with you."

Generix did one more awkward nod and left.

"Here," Priscus growled, "what does it say…and be sure to read it in a low voice."

The orderly cleared his throat:

From the valiant Emperor Titus Flavius Vespasian, the first of the Fluvial Dynasty.

A disloyal group of Vitelli supporters have taken refuge in the city of Pinacale. You must march there at once, taking only enough provisions to get there in the greatest of haste. Once there, detain all Citizens with shackles or ropes—at your discretion—making sure that none escape. Then wait there for the Legionnaire commander Antonius, who will relieve you and question the rebels.

Vespasian

Priscus sighed, "Rebel hunting."

"I think that's the Emperor's real stamp," the orderly said.

"Sure," Priscus waved away the suggestion with his hand. "I imagine he personally marks every document that passes through his house, especially seeing how busy he is with the government being taken over."

"Well," the orderly replied, "aren't you excited to receive orders that came directly from the Emperor?"

Priscus heaved a deep sigh. "What is your name?"

"Samuel."

"Samuel?" Priscus whispered, "That is an odd name. Is that why you have such an odd accent? Where are you from?"

"Jerusalem."

"And how long have you been my orderly?"

Samuel thought for a moment, counting the months on his hand as he did. "Six months."

Priscus tipped back his chair. "Six months is a long time. In the last six months, how many rebel hunts have we been on? How many little villages have we slaughtered?"

"I don't think he wants you to slaughter this one."

Priscus laughed. "Do you think that you know the Roman mind better than me? I started out as a simple Hastati and now I've been promoted to a Centurion in the space of three years. The mind of the Roman general is simple: when they say capture, they mean kill; when they say kill, they mean slaughter; when they say slaughter, they mean absolute destruction. Let me tell you a story about the Roman mind. When Rome invaded Carthage in the year 146 BC, they sent an army so massive that it made the sand on the beach seem like nothing. The Carthagians were so terrified that they vied for a peace treaty. The Romans accepted, with the simple condition that the Carthagians must give up all their weapons. Carthage agreed, and the next day—after the Carthagians gave up their weapons—the Romans made another demand: that three hundred of the sons and daughters of the aristocracy be sent off to Rome. Carthage complied, giving up their most precious children. The next day the Romans asked for all the gold in the city—the Carthagians gave it. And do you know what happened next, orderly, after Rome took all of the weapons, children, and gold from the city? The Romans then demanded the city herself; the inhabitants were supposed to walk away from everything they knew. The Carthagians refused, and Scipio, the great commander of the Romans, ordered the decimation of Carthage. The Senate sent Scipio to take the city, but instead he decimated it, leaving no stone on top of another. After that, Scipio had the earth salted so that nothing more could be grown. Instead of the Senate accusing him of disobeying orders, he was hailed and praised as a hero."

"It's different when we are dealing with Roman Citizens. You're used to dealing with worthless Gauls and Celts—Rome does not care for their lives…"

"Silence," Priscus yelled. He stood and grabbed his orderly by the shoulders, hitting him across the cheek. "I'm a Gaul! And I'm also your commander; I will decide who gets killed."

Samuel's eyes lit up. "Mark my words Priscus: If you kill Romans on Roman soil, it will be the end of your pitiful life. Rome will not spare their pet Gaul."

Priscus grabbed his sword from his side. "Watch your tongue, you spineless dog, or I will color my sword red with your blood."

The orderly stood up straight. "You were once a slave, born to misfortune. You hated being conquered, but now you have let Rome conquer your heart. You've become what you hated most. You've gone mad with power—"

"Silence."

But the orderly could not contain his rage. For the last six months, the Gaul had beaten and abused him, forced him to make a fool of himself everywhere they went. It was not until now—only when the orderly began to question the Gaul—that Priscus finally asked him his name. "You're a curse to everyone around you. If only you knew and could hear the dissenters' voices among your men—"

Priscus plunged his sword through Samuel's heart, killing the orderly instantly.

The Gaul stared at the boy's eyes as the light slowly drained out. "You are too weak to be alive in this world, boy; you would have never made it far in the army." With this he wiped the blood on the boy's tunic. Priscus shook his head and swore. "Now I've got to find myself another orderly."

With an ugly grimace, the Gaul left his tent. "Soldiers! Prepare to march; we leave within the hour. We have a city to destroy!"

Chapter 11

December 23, 69 AD
Verus

"Why did you help me?" Verus asked.

Horace shrugged. "Wouldn't you have done the same?"

Verus looked down at the steaming bowl of porridge in front of him; he was using the bowl more as a heater for his hands than a source of food. "I would've done the same, but I think there are few people in Rome that would."

"It was a mob—a ramble of drunken Romans. They were no real threat."

"They would have killed me."

"Well," Horace said, "they were no real threat to me. All you have to do is cut a few of them and the rest will go running." The old gladiator had a round but stern face; his features had hardened in his early years but softened as he grew older. He reminded Verus of his grandfather—the one who was always stealing treats from the children. The old man would always give the treats back, of course, but only after he had taken taxes. Horace was nimble for his age, although his bones did creak when he bent over to stoke the fire. Scars, purpled and faded with time, decorated his body like a neglected and graffitied temple. Now instead of golden—as Verus had imagined—white hair hung from the sides of his head and drooped to his shoulders.

"I've never been trained with a sword. How can I fight against a mob?"

"And I've never been trained to run from a fight."

"What do you mean?"

"I mean, it is all a state of mind," Horace said as he pulled out a chair and sat down. "When someone goes to grab your throat,

85

you can either flinch or try to block it. There is no such thing as a born coward, or a natural sword fighter. Men can either choose to act cowardly or gather their courage and act bravely."

"What about natural skill?"

Horace scoffed. "It's overrated. I've seen plenty of good gladiators get killed by terrible fighters. It all depends on the calm one can keep in the face of battle. A fighter, in essence, chooses his level of skill. If I knew all the sword techniques in the world, but I was not brave enough to use them, they would do nothing for me."

"Why do gladiators train then?"

"Let me show you why: If I go for your eye, you're going to try to block it; if I swing at your legs you're going to jump. But just because that is your immediate response, it doesn't mean that is your best one. All training does is teach you the techniques that are the best—or at least the most effective—but it is up to the fighter to execute them. For example, if you went for my throat…in fact…come at my throat…like you're going to strangle me… no…come at me like you mean it…" Verus awkwardly moved towards Horace like he was going to strangle the old man, but before he could even reach the gladiator, Verus found himself on the floor, writhing in pain.

"See that," Horace boasted, "instead of going on the defensive, I kept my head and saw an opportunity to go on the offensive. Fighting requires more than brute strength, more than simple skill with the blade; it requires you to have a clear-thinking mind that can adapt to the danger around you."

"How did you do that?"

"It was your thumb." Horace grabbed Verus' arm to demonstrate. "If you lock someone's thumb—almost like a handshake—you can control the rest of their body. It is like the rudder of a ship: It's small, but where it is pointed the ship will follow."

"Well, I appreciate the lesson; the Gods know I could use tips for fighting."

Horace squinted. "I've always had a good eye at picking out the best fighters, and I can see a lot of potential in you."

Now it was Verus' turn to scoff, "Why do you say that?"

"Because," Horace winked, "you've got an even head on your

shoulders. You've got ability to stay calm even if things look bad. When you are in the arena and a three-hundred pound Britannian is charging at you with flaring nostrils and blue dyed skin, staying calm is the only thing that will keep you alive. The worst thing you can do is flinch; the best thing you can do is let things happen."

"And what makes you think I'm calm?"

Horace laughed, shaking his belly. "You just made the top of the *proscription*, which is the most prestigious death list in the world. In short, you are the most wanted alive, and yet, you sit here talking about fighting technique."

Verus looked down, as if he was ashamed. "I didn't know you knew. How did you know I was on the list?"

Horace pulled out a copy of the death list and slammed it on the table. "It's been put on every wood post from here to the end of Tuscany."

"Then," Verus said with a clenched jaw, "if you knew all this time, why did you not report me?"

Horace looked at his palm for a second; a memory seemed to be coming back to him. "No, I didn't report you; you're safe here. I have discovered that there are things more important than money and fame. If you would have met me fifteen years ago, however, that would've been a different tale. I was the same kind of gladiator as I was a person—ruthless."

"Were you good as a gladiator?" Verus asked.

"I was the best, as they say," Horace said as he dusted his hands, "and by the best, yes, I mean I was the most vicious. I was a killer and would kill every man that stood against me, even when I did not have to kill to win."

"What changed?"

"Family," Horace whispered. "I had a daughter and then a son. I don't know why that changed me, but all of a sudden I lost the edge. I was still a gladiator, a real good one too, but I became merciful. Gladiators no longer feared to fight me because they knew I would not go for the kill, and I wouldn't. It's funny though, even though everyone thought I was not fighting my best, I was actually fighting a lot better."

Horace suddenly stopped speaking as he spotted something out of the corner of his eye, a wide smile spread across his face.

"Arria...I can see you hiding there. What are you doing out of bed?"

Verus followed Horace's gaze until he spotted a girl peeking around the arched doorway. She was young—probably no more than ten or eleven. She smiled shyly and batted her big eyes as she spotted Verus in the room. "I heard noises Daddy."

"I told you there would be; the whole town is alive with parties."

Arria slowly stepped out from behind the doorway and tentatively walked towards her father. "But I heard someone screaming. I think someone was in trouble." She finally reached the wizened gladiator and pulled him into a deep hug.

Horace laughed ever so slightly. "Oh, my dear. It's all right. People sometimes yell like that when they are having too much fun."

"Who is this?" Arria said quickly. Without waiting for a response, the young girl ran up to Verus and prodded him in the arms. "Are you a new gladiator?"

"It's not polite to poke," Horace said quickly. "This is Verus—and he is not a new gladiator, but an old friend."

"How come I've never seen him before? Does he live in Rome? Judging by the dust on your shoes, you must have come from somewhere far. The only time I've ever had so much dust on my feet was when I traveled up to Silica. We had horses, but I preferred to walk, and by the time I made it there and back, mother said I looked like a walking dust cloud..."

Verus laughed. "That does sound like fun. I love to travel."

"Me too," Arria admitted, "although, I never travel as often as I prefer. Usually I don't get to go anywhere besides the bath house, and that's only with my Mother."

"It can be dangerous in a big city."

The little girl rolled her eyes. "Mom always says that. But, I can take care of myself; I know how to use a sword. I practice with sticks and stuff."

"Sweet dear," Horace interrupted gently. "Mom was telling me how frightened she was of the noises tonight—you know how scared she gets."

"Really?" Arria said with a large sigh. "I thought she might; that is why I came down here—to see if she was all right."

"Can you go check on her for me?" Horace asked. "Just go

cuddle with her until I get back—I won't be long."

"Yes, Father," Arria whispered. "Maybe it was her screaming."

"I don't think it was," Horace said, "but go check on her just in case."

Arria squeezed her father in one last warm embrace. "Don't be too long Father; I can't console her all night."

The old man laughed as she squeezed him a little harder than he expected. "I won't."

As the little girl was shuffling out of the room she waved to Verus. "Nice to meet you. I hope you do become a gladiator so we can talk more."

"I'll think about it," Verus said.

With this she smiled broadly and exited the room.

Horace chuckled. "Nothing compares to the joy of having a set of children, eh. I'd trade my best day as a gladiator for the worst as a parent—well maybe not the worst day. What about you Blacksmith, do you have a family?"

Verus shifted silently, "Yes, I do…"

"Is your family on the *proscription?*"

"Yes," Verus replied quickly.

"We need to get you out of here, Verus. Where is your home?"

"Pinacale. It's about 100 kilometros from here."

"Since they are in a remote location, it might take anywhere between a few days to several weeks before the Emperor dispatches an army up there. Getting out won't be easy: The gates will be heavily guarded for at least a week—maybe longer."

Verus pulled his hands through his hair. "I don't have a week. For all I know, there's a Roman Century marching there now."

"I," Horace said as he lowered his voice, "know of ways to escape."

"How? I will do anything for you if you can get me out of the city."

"They're as dangerous as I am old, but they still work," Horace went to a cupboard and pulled out an old roll of papyrus. "When I was young, before I had become a gladiator, I was involved in smuggling."

"What did you smuggle?"

"Humans, mostly." Horace rolled the papyrus out on a table. It was a map, as far as Verus could tell, but it was different than any sort of map he had seen. Instead of containing roads and streets, it was marked with the paths and patterns of the aqueducts and sewers. "Every time a *proscription* comes out, there are always hundreds of people that want to escape."

Verus stood up and crossed his arms. "I don't have money to pay you right now."

"I'm not looking for money," Horace replied. "If you want out, I can help you."

Verus swallowed. "We are in the largest city in the world, guarded by the most experienced soldiers who have the best training and weapons. How, in all the ages of time, can we sneak through dozens of streets, passing thousands of soldiers as we do?"

* * *

Between all the torches in the streets and bonfires along the way, it hardly seemed like night. It had been two bloody days since the beginning of the *proscription*. The stocky Blacksmith spent his time hiding in the gladiatorial metal shop working off the hours on dented gladiator's armor. He thought it was the least he could do for Horace. He worked fast, feverishly at times, trying hard not to think of his family. Finally, after the noise of the killing and the mobs had subsided, Horace decided that it was safe enough to make an attempt. Verus had been so impatient to leave before, but now, after venturing out into the city, he wondered if he was trying too soon.

The city was ravaged from the roads up: market wagons were tipped over; bodies were piled on the corners of streets; stale blood stained whole portions of the road. It was a gruesome scene—one that Verus did not care to see. The darkness made things seem worse as the flickering lights from the fires cast grotesque shadows on the walls. Worse than the shadows was the smell, which seemed to come from random places in the road. The Blacksmith had smelled death before but that was either soon before a body was buried or long after a person had died.

One time, when Verus was young, one of his neighbors in

Pinacale had a whole herd of cattle that was stricken with a curse. The cows died slowly, leaving the farm with a mound of ruptured bodies that were like broken dams of pus. Maggots came out next; flies soon followed. The smell was so horrendous that eventually the Governor ordered the property burned. Verus' friends dared each other to get as close to the farm as they could. The Blacksmith not only surpassed all of them in his tolerability of the smell, but he took it a step further and ate his lunch in the middle of the field—just to prove he could do it. Verus did not know what it was about this smell, but now, as he passed through winding streets and order less roads, he could not help but gag with every step.

At the junction of each major street, soldiers stopped Horace and Verus, ordering them to present their passports. For Verus, Horace had prepared a false set of papers that carried the name Lucius Critus, a man who had been a gladiator a few months before but had died after too many of his wounds turned green. They passed another set of guards and two more streets before Horace pulled Verus into a dark building, which had the warmth and smell of a wool-dying factory.

Horace stepped closer to the Blacksmith. "That was the easy part my boy. It's going to get a little more risky from here on out."

"All right. What do we do next?"

Horace grinned and pulled out a hidden dagger from the folds of his clothes. "If you are going to save your family tomorrow, you might have to kill someone tonight."

"Kill?"

"It's your passport," Horace said. "At the next guard post you will be discovered. I've sold that passport six times now, and the last one to use it somehow got noticed by the Government. The guards before were just looking for those on the *proscription*, but this group we're approaching will be looking for every enemy of the state."

"You mean to say that Lucius Titus is a wanted man?"

Horace slapped Verus. "Don't make that mistake, boy: Your name is Lucius Critus—not Lucius Titus. And yes, he is a wanted man. We are going to have to do this the old Sulla way."

"What is that?"

"With a sword in our hands and Fortuna at our backs."

The old gladiator handed Verus the knife.

91

"I'm not very good with a dagger."

Horace scoffed and pulled out another blade. "There is no special trick. A dagger is not used for fighting but for pressure." The old gladiator stepped forward and grabbed Verus' shoulder, pushing him into a hold that he could not escape. "Soldiers can feel inexperience. If they feel weakness, they will exploit it. There are three important techniques to know about a dagger: Use the tip of the dagger to get their attention—just poke them in the skin with it; slice the side of the neck if they become obstinate; and if you need to dispatch them quickly, cut one way with the blade, while you twist the head the other—that will stop them from making noise. The more firm you are in the beginning, the less likely we will have to kill them in the end."

"If we are going to have to fight some guards, why don't we try to make it through one of the gates? The aqueducts will be cold this time of year."

Horace shook his head. "The gates will have ten times as many soldiers as the aqueducts."

Verus gritted his teeth. "All right, what is your plan?"

Horace walked a few feet away, "When we come up to the guards, act respectful, almost weak—that will lower their guard. When I distract them with the papers, you seize one of the guards around the neck—just how I showed you—and I will take care of the rest."

"Are you going to kill them?"

"I hope not," Horace said with a frown. "It will all depend on how determined they are to stay at their post. When we get past the guards, you will have seconds to climb the aqueduct before you will be spotted."

"Why do they care if I am climbing the aqueduct?"

"Because," Horace said briskly, "they think you might be a Vitelli supporter trying to poison the water. Over two hundred thousand Romans depend on the Aqua Marcia."

"Once I get to the top, where do I go?"

"Horace stuck out his palm and cupped his fingers. "There will be a bowl shape at the top of the aqueduct, filled with over 5,000 *litre* of water. Fresh water flows in one side and older water flows out the other. You want to dive in the water and find the gap where the fresh water flows in—there should be a hole just big enough to fit your body through. Once through the hole, the aqueduct will open up slightly, giving you a little more room. It will be pitch black because it is covered from the elements; at that point, at least, you won't have to worry about the soldiers."

"Won't the tunnel be flooded with water?"

"Yes and no," Horace answered. "At night, other cities along the Aqua Marcia are scheduled to use the water. The water level will be extremely low, and, hopefully, will stay that way for a good portion of the night. It will be tight, however; you will only have space enough to crawl."

"What happens if the cities aren't using the water this night?"

"They will be. You have about two hours to crawl in the aqueduct—maybe less; after that, the other cities will stop funneling off the water and send it straight for you. Even if you could hang on to the walls, you would drown in seconds. There will be little water in there, but it will still be cold; so it's important to keep moving or your muscles will freeze up. When you start to lose sensation in your body, keep flexing your stomach muscles—it will keep you warm. Once you are in, there will be no turning back; not only is there no room to, but it will be so cramped that moving backwards will be almost impossible."

Verus did not realize it before, but he found himself holding his breath. "This seems hard. Is this the best way?"

Horace gave a half-hearted smile. "Son, it is the only way— now pay attention. After you travel for a while in the aqueduct, your head will hit a rope. It will be dark, so you will have to trust your hands, but the rope will lead you to a loose stone. Push it open—it may be a little hard because it has not been used in a while."

"What if it has been repaired?"

Horace clenched his jaw. "Pray to the Gods that it hasn't. Once the water is being channeled back into the aqueduct, you will be able to hear it coming. It will take twenty minutes to reach you, maybe less—so make sure you hurry."

Verus swallowed.

"Keep thinking of your family and you will make it—I promise."

"Thank you, you've been more than fair to me; may Jupiter

bless you and all of your house."

Horace nodded. "Save that blessing for yourself. Keep calm and you'll make it through. Now, let's go." With that they both left the wool mill and headed for the base of the Aqua Marcia. Two streets later, they ran into another group of guards. There were five of them—four more than Verus was hoping.

"Halt," the lead Centurion barked. "What is your business at this hour?"

Horace smiled humbly. "This is the only safe hour to travel; we are just heading to the other side of town."

"What kind of business do you conduct?"

"I have a gladiator here—Critus is his name. He is to be part of a special entertainment for Vespasian."

"I was not told that you would be coming through here."

"Well," Horace said as he nodded towards Verus. "It's an important affair."

Verus frowned. "*Was that a sign? Was he telling me to grab one of the soldiers?*"

The Centurion furled his brow. "What do you mean 'important?' Are you saying they wouldn't tell me because I'm not important enough? Speak up old man."

Again Horace gave Verus another hard look. "Oh no, Centurion, don't think that I meant that. I was simply saying that perhaps the information was lost in confusion; perhaps, no one thought it was important enough to let you know. We have our passports, and they are in order, so there should be no problem for us to walk through Rome."

"This is a protected sector," the Centurion hissed. "I have orders to detain anyone of suspicion, and you my friend, are quickly rising in suspicion. Let me see your papers."

The old gladiator looked at Verus a third time, clearly communicating something.

Verus tightened his grip on his dagger, which helped him build up his nerves. Before Verus could react, however, the Centurion made a last and fatal mistake—he read Horace's name out loud as he looked at the passports.

Suddenly, and simultaneously, Horace and Verus went for their daggers. Verus had one of the guards by the throat, while the old gladiator worked on the other four.

The lead Centurion had his throat cut, the second was stabbed in the belly with the Centurion's sword, the third had his eye gouged, and the fourth, who had tried desperately to free his sword, was punched in the throat and then finished off when he was crawling on the ground. Horace had moved so quickly that even Verus—who knew it was coming—was amazed.

The Blacksmith tightened his grip on the last of the Roman soldiers. "Don't move or we'll finish you."

Without hesitation, Horace slit the throat of the last guard.

Blood squirted onto Verus' face. "What happened? I thought you said you weren't going to kill them."

Horace shook his head. "I wasn't, that is, until they read my name aloud. You were supposed to jump in before then while I was distracting them. Once the Centurion read my name aloud, it was like a death sentence for the other four. Why for all the souls in Hades did you hesitate?"

"I…" Verus stammered.

Horace cursed. "This is bad. They wouldn't have cared much if we just forced past them, but now with five dead soldiers…"

"Halt!" A voice came from the other end of the street.

"GO!" Horace yelled. "Run for the aqueduct, boy!"

Verus nodded and ran. Adrenaline was working in his body now, pushing him faster. He sprinted down one street, made a left, and was half way down another before he crashed into a wagon of clay bottles. The Blacksmith flipped inside, smashing at least a dozen different trinkets as he did. He sat up and looked out to his right: the guards were only moments away. He stood up and leaped back out of the wagon, throwing a bottle as he went.

The studded Roman sandals pounded the ground just behind him. Verus was the first to reach the aqueduct, but before he could climb it, the soldiers caught up to him. He drew out his little dagger, waving it threateningly in the air. Two soldiers stood before him— eyeing Verus with laughter.

"Come on, urchin, do you think that little dagger will stop a Roman gladius?"

Verus shook his head. "You've got the wrong man. I don't know why you're chasing me."

"Then why were you running?"

"There are five Roman bodies back there, freshly stabbed."

"We know," answered one of them as he drew his sword.

"We saw them," said the other as he mimicked his companion.

"I only saw the killing," Verus pointed to himself. "I did not do it."

"Sure you didn't," the guard said doubtfully, "that is why there is a stream of blood running down your dagger."

Verus studied the blade for a second, giving the guards the perfect time to strike. One of them swung for Verus' head, missing him by a thumb's length, the other leaped for Verus' feet. The Blacksmith took two large sidesteps before he found himself trapped. He had walked right into the edge of a large fountain. The guards leaped forward with their swords just as Verus jumped backwards, sending him splashing into the water behind. The fountain was not deep—it only came up to Verus' chest—but the water was freezing. The guards hesitated as they watched Verus shiver in the water.

"That's it, urchin," jeered one of the Romans. "Take a nice swim—it will be the last bath you will ever have. Segundus, go get us some bows. Let's have some sport with this one."

Verus drifted to the middle of the fountain where his head bumped something: It was a statue of Neptune, powerfully riding a herd of some type of creature. The statue was large—bigger than anything Verus had ever seen. Water, by some fantastical force, was somehow coming out of the mouth of the mighty God. The statue was so large that the top of it was only a few feet from one of the columns of the aqueduct.

"I can make it," Verus whispered to himself. "I have to make it." Using the base of the statue, he pulled himself out of the water.

"Halt," the guard yelled. "Don't get out just yet; we haven't even begun."

Verus scrambled around the sea God, scraping for holds as he went. The wet marble and was so slick with water, he could barely hold on. By the time Segundus had come back, the Blacksmith had made it to the top of the statue.

"I'm sorry for this disrespect," Verus whispered into

Neptune's ear.

"He's getting away!" Segundus yelled.

"He's got nowhere to go," the other guard answered. "Give me a bow."

Along with Segundus came another dozen guards—all of which had swords in their hands and bows on their backs.

"Ten sestertius to the man who can hit him first," Segundus yelled. "We will take it in turns."

With a scream of acclamation the Romans took to the game, notching arrows in their bows as they bragged about their marksmanship. The first arrow was over Verus' head and to the right. The second was much closer but still too high. The third arrow would have been a direct hit, but Verus ducked behind Neptune's head; the arrow harmlessly bounced off the sea God's stone eye.

"That's bad luck," one of the Romans jeered. "You will have to make a sacrifice in Neptune's temple to make up for that."

Verus sighed. He was safe from the arrows while he hid behind Neptune's head, but now he would have to expose himself by jumping to the aqueduct. The distance between the statue and the aqueduct seemed so much closer from the base of the statue than it did now.

The Blacksmith closed his eyes and focused his mind: he first thought of Julia—his beautiful wife; then Gaius his adventurous son; then Octovis his rebellious boy, who loved to tease his brothers; Helenica, his sweet daughter who was beginning to string sentences together; and finally Crassian, his newly-born son.

Verus' eyes snapped open. As a passing arrow whipped towards him, he leapt into the air. Time floated for a moment as he scrambled to grab the stone. He caught it, struggling wildly to find a foot-hold. Finally, his foot landed on something, which gave him a base enough to kick himself up.

"He's getting away!" one of the Romans yelled.

"He's going for the aqueduct!"

Although the aqueduct was not wet like the statue, Verus still had a ways to climb before he could get to the top. An arrow came at him and hit to his right, missing him by the length of a palm, another scraped the side of his calf.

Pain shot adrenaline through his body. He leapt for the next hold and scrambled with his legs, kicking loose dirt and moss to either side. Another arrow came but Verus moved out of its path just as it passed.

More soldiers joined in the sport.

"He's almost to the top!" one of the Romans yelled. "You men there...get to the top of those buildings and shoot him if he makes it."

Verus daringly leapt for the top of the aqueduct and caught it with the tips of his fingers. He shifted and readjusted until he could pull himself up. He had half of his body over the top, when suddenly, streaking through the air, an arrow hit Verus—right in the pit of the left leg. The arrow hit bone and slid to the side, poking through the skin. The Blacksmith hefted his leg up and out of sight, clenching his jaw as he did. A shock rippled through his body, sending bumps all over his arms. Instantly he felt nauseous, like his head was spinning.

"There he is!"

A group of Romans had made it to the top of a neighboring building, which put them at eye level with Verus.

"Shoot him!"

Just before they fired, Verus rolled off the wall and into the water retainer that Horace said was there. Arrows came after him, hitting the water just as he disappeared.

"Wait till he comes up!"

Moments passed, but Verus never emerged. He kicked with his one good leg until he found the opening. It was a tight squeeze, but he was able to get most of his body through, despite having an arrow in his leg. But halfway in, he found himself stuck—unable to breath or move in either direction. It took a few bitter seconds of struggle before he was able to pull his head up for air.

He wiped the water out of his eyes and blinked twice, but nothing changed. It was so dark he could not see anything. Everything looked the same to him—black as the darkest night. As he pulled his wounded leg through, the arrow bumped the walls and sent waves of pain up his body.

"Come on," Verus whispered to himself. He reached for the arrow and broke off the tip. With the point gone, he began to slowly slide the arrow shaft out. Each time he pulled on the arrow, a shocking pain rippled through his body and sent his head spinning. He almost vomited. After long painful moments, he finally freed the arrow, which sent a trickle of warm blood down his numb legs. Using a torn piece of his shirt, he bandaged the wound.

The water was too cold to stay still for long, so, with his leg bandaged, he began a long shuffle into the black unknown.

Chapter 12
December 26, 69 AD
Priscus

"Sir, I see no signs of resistance, no signs that these are the rebels that we are after."

Priscus narrowed his eyes around the city of Pinacale. "And what if it is a trap? What if that is the one thing they want us to believe?"

"If it is, it is not much of a trap," the scout replied. "There are no tracks of cavalry, no evidence of foot soldiers, and no scent of sedition. It's a simple town filled with simple people. If there were Vitelli supporters here, they must have moved on. This city is not trying to start a resistance—they barely even know there is a civil war. It takes months for these backwoods huts to get any news, and even longer still to understand it."

The wind grabbed up and flicked out the red cloaks of the soldiers, making the cloth look more alive than the men that wore them. It was a clear day with a blue sky and no sign of clouds.

Priscus tightened his hand around the hilt of his sword and raised himself up on his horse. He whiffed the air and sat back down. "Interesting."

"What is, sir?"

"There are no cows. Where are the cows?"

"Sir?"

Priscus looked at his second in command, "Unas, my old friend, how does a small city like this survive?"

"With livestock?"

"Yes," Priscus growled, "and, how is this city surviving, if they don't have any?"

"They might be involved in other professions—like

medicine."

"If they practice medicine, who do they practice it on? How do they make money if the only clients in the city are their neighbors?" Priscus put his head in his hands and rubbed his brow. "There are no cows because they have been taken to feed a rebel army—an army that isn't supposed to be here."

"Is it a trap then?"

"I don't think so," Priscus said as he tightened the reins in his hand. "The scout is right: with no trace of an army, the army must not be here. But since there have been no reports of anyone stealing cows in this region, it means the cows must have been given to the traitorous army. We will find our information in the city—after we've burned it to the ground."

Unas hesitated slightly before he spoke. "Are those our orders, sir?"

With lowered eyes the Gaul faced Unas. "Your orders are to follow me, and my orders are to slaughter rebels."

"Sir, I doubt all of those children in Pinacale are rebels..."

"Rebels breed rebels," Priscus replied. "If you kill the mother, and not the son, then you raise up a generation of enemies."

"Yes, sir."

"Form battle lines," Priscus said.

"Form battle lines!"

Immediately the soldiers began moving from a column formation to three distinct squares. The metal shimmered in the sunlight, giving off a threatening glare.

Priscus took his helmet from his new orderly. "Bring the skirmishers up."

"Skirmishers, front line!"

"Unas," Priscus growled, "no one escapes. Spare only ten of the men—no one else lives, including the women and the children. I want you to come from the west side—with the sun in your eyes—while I hit them from the east. It will take you about an hour of marching for you to get in a flanking position. Once you are in position, I want you to initiate the combat by shooting arrows into the city. If you can, light the homes on fire so they come running out. Shoot five volleys of arrows and then raise your battle standards. I will come in and take out any resistance from behind. Once I crash with the enemy, I want you to charge in, but not before or that will ruin the surprise. Are there any questions?"

Unas did have a question on his mind—it was obvious to anyone that knew him well—but eventually, he shook it off. "It is as clear as victory, sir."

"Good," Priscus said. "Begin your march, and I will meet you in the city in one hour."

* * *

The sun began to lower itself when Unas was finally in position. It was a bright evening that was just becoming more beautiful as the setting sun turned orange and then crimson red. The invasion began simply; it was almost too imaginary to be real. No one saw the first volley of arrows that whistled through the air. It killed three people—two of them instantly. The third person writhed in pain long enough to attract some attention. The confused villagers came running out of their homes. That is when the second volley of arrows came whistling down.

"We're under attack! We're under..." a villager began to yell, but then, suddenly, he was silenced by an arrow that pierced his throat. The next wave of arrows was lit with fire. The arrows snaked up through the air, seemingly burning the sky as they did. Two houses caught fire with the first wall of flaming arrows, four more with the second. The last volley of flames set a dozen more homes on fire.

The villagers ran in all directions, carrying children and weapons as they did. The confusion was only eclipsed by the screams of panic that carried throughout the village.

"Invaders from the west," one of the villagers yelled. "Form battle lines!" Despite the confusion, a scanty three dozen men lined up, armed with what they could find in the last few moments. A few of the army veterans had swords, while the rest had incomplete shields and blacksmith hammers. Unas ordered his men to start marching forward—not at a run, but a gentle walk. Tense moments of anticipation passed; the defenders girded up their courage.

"The sun is in their eyes, boys. The advantage is ours…"

Suddenly, Priscus and his men rammed the rear flanks of the villagers, killing dozens of them instantly. The large Gaul was in the middle, using his infamous long sword and shield. He chopped an old veteran in the head and another in the gut. A third one he stabbed clear through the chest. The defenders' lines broke and scattered, but as they retreated, Unas' men cut them off.

The plan worked so flawlessly and was executed so perfectly that none escaped. A few tried, but all died with arrows in their back or a slice across their neck.

Unas approached Priscus, who had a splash of blood on his face. "Sir, there are a few homes up the hill that we did not see before."

Priscus growled, "You stay here and clean up. I will finish up over there." He pointed at a few men to his left. "You men follow me." With this, the large Gaul began a run up a muddy path towards the top of a shallow hill, followed by a dozen or so Romans. Under their feet, they crushed the little camellia and peony flowers that were scattered along their way. It took only moments for the soldiers to reach the homes, moments longer for them to surround them.

They approached carefully, as if the slightest sound would give them away. There were three houses grouped together. Each of them had a garden in the back with a statue of a God in the middle.

A Roman soldier approached the first door and readied himself to kick it in; but, just as he kicked with his foot, the door opened, sending the soldier off balance. A woman was there, brandishing a knife. She grabbed the soldier and pointed the knife at his throat.

"Call your men off," she yelled, "or I will finish this one before the rest of you can take another breath."

Priscus smiled and laughed. "Go ahead and finish him! Slice his throat; he deserves to die."

"Do not mock me!" she replied. "I will kill him."

Priscus stepped closer, a grin on his brutish face. "I do not doubt it, and I am not trying to stop you. The fool let himself get captured by a woman—he deserves to die."

"What are you doing here? Why are you attacking us?"

The Gaul took another step forward; he was within arm's

length of her now. "By command of Vespasian this city is condemned...to die."

"Let us be! The city is in ruins and certainly you have your victory."

Slowly the Gaul reached for the woman's knife; she did not flinch. He closed his big hand around her smaller delicate one.

"Now," Priscus whispered so softly that the other soldiers could not hear, "this is how easy it is to take a life." He jerked her hand so forcefully that the knife sliced the neck of the Roman soldier, sending blood cascading down. The soldier fell to the floor, convulsing with the last few moments of life.

The Gaul casually stepped away from the home. "She killed a Roman soldier. Finish her."

"It wasn't me," cried the woman. "Please, I have children."

But no one could hear her now. With screams of fury, the other Romans rushed in with their swords, slicing everything that moved. Vases were smashed, dishes were thrown, and furniture was tossed aside.

Suddenly, from the back of the house, a young boy escaped out a window. He rolled across the grass until he could get to his feet. Although the boy was limping he was made good time across the hill and towards the beginning of a forest. The large Gaul was the only one that saw him.

Priscus scowled. "Can't these fools do anything right?" He took off after the boy, running with his sword drawn. The boy disappeared into the woods. The large Gaul was only moments behind. The trees and brush thrashed for some time. Finally, Priscus emerged. He sheathed his sword and walked back towards the city of Pinacale.

Unas was waiting for him. "Sir, complete victory."

"What are our casualties?"

"None, sir. Just a few scratches and cuts."

Priscus pointed towards the three houses on the hill. "We lost one. A lady slit his throat before I could stop her. How many did you take prisoner?"

"Thirteen."

Priscus raised his hand as if to hit Unas. "Did I not instruct you to only keep ten?"

"Yes, sir," Unas whispered. "But I thought—"

"No," Priscus hissed, "you do not think. If I wanted thirteen then I would've asked for thirteen. I want you personally to dispatch the other three."

"Yes, sir."

"Tell the men to leave the bodies where they are; these traitors do not deserve a proper burial."

"Yes, sir."

Priscus walked down the hill, flanked by a few of his soldiers. Half of the homes were on fire, the other half were spotted with blood. The Gaul's soldiers were all there, eagerly waiting the next command. Priscus stood up on a pile of wood and shouted out to his men, "Keep all the loot you find! Once you're done with the town, burn it—burn all of it. Kill every fowl; slaughter every beast. Tonight we dine on the food of traitors!"

A cheer went up from the soldiers.

Priscus jumped off the woodpile and slapped a few of his men on the back. He walked down and out of the city towards the prisoners that were being held. Six guards stood over them. Priscus grabbed the first prisoner he saw and pulled him to his feet. "What is your name old man?"

"Tulias."

"That is a simple name," Priscus mocked. "You Romans usually have a long list of names that you love to sling out."

"What are you doing here?"

Priscus hit the old man in the head. "I will ask the questions. Where are all of the cattle? Where are all the sheep?"

"What do you mean?"

"Where are all the livestock!"

"I have a large estate not far from here with a few chickens…"

Priscus hit the old man again. "Chickens don't provide an income. How does a backwoods city survive without livestock? What is your profession?"

"I'm a doctor."

"A doctor?" Priscus laughed. "And what about everyone else?"

"Everyone else is dead," Tulias spat from a bleeding lip.

Priscus hit the old man. "Don't you disrespect me." He hit him again. And then again. "What does everyone do in the city? How does everyone survive? Are you not cattle ranchers or goat herders?"

Tulias' face was more red now than it had ever been white. "Blacksmiths…almost everyone is a blacksmith."

"Blacksmiths?"

From where he was, Tulias could see the city of Pinacale burning in the distance; he could see the Roman soldiers ravaging each home. Tulias had been in each of these buildings, visiting residents when they were sick; he had built much of the city with his own two hands—from the heating system of the bathhouse to the main forum in the middle. The old man knew the position of every pavestone that had been placed in the ground, every fence post that had been sunk in the earth. Now, instead of neighbors, he could only see the lifeless faces of everyone that he had ever cared for.

Tulias' voice was weak but resonated with the edge of experience. "May Jupiter curse you with a lasting guilt that sears your soul with racking pain. In the years to come, may you suffer for the blood you have spilled. You've killed innocent men and women today, butchered children and infants, but their pain now will not compare to the pain that later will come to you. As you've dealt out this portion of suffering to the sons of Pinacale, one day—Centurion—a son of Pinacale will come for you, causing you so much suffering that it will far eclipse what you have done…"

Priscus drew back his fist again, ready to hit the old man, but there was no need. Tulias' body turned lifeless on its own. The Gaul dropped him like a rusted tool that had worn past its usefulness.

He turned around and stared at the burning city. "*They are all blacksmiths?*"

Chapter 13

December 25, 69 AD
Verus

Verus had no way to track time—no way of figuring out how much longer he had before the water flooded. The water had been so cold at first, but now, after inching through it for so long, he could barely feel anything. The aqueduct had a clean smell, like oil cooked in the sun. He kept pushing himself on and on; it felt like he had been crawling for endless hours. His thoughts were a mix of emotions and ideas: Sometimes he would worry that he had already passed the rope; other times he would wonder if he had even gone very far at all; mostly, however, he thought of his family. With every sliding crawl, he swore an oath to the Gods that if he could save his family, he would honor them all of his life. He promised the Gods everything: fresh sacrifices, generous offerings, and a concerted effort to learn the name and hobby of every single one of them.

In the distance, like a sudden storm, the noise of the water changed. It sounded like the waves of the ocean crashing against the rocks.

Verus swore and picked up his speed. *"What if there is no rope?"*

Minutes passed. The noise of the water was growing stronger. He scrambled on and on, recklessly scratching his body as he went.

"Where is it?"

Verus' head hit something. He grabbed at it quickly: it was thick and rough like the tanned hide of a sheep. It led to a stone tablet above; Verus prayed he could set it free. He gave it a push with his hands—it didn't budge. He pushed again, but still it did not move.

The water was growing louder and louder all the time. Verus tried to shift the stone one way and then the other. He noticed it gave ever so slightly as he twisted it. He began to work at it, twisting it

107

back and forth. The more he did, the looser it became. He worked at it for a few moments until finally he was able to push it completely free. The open air and moonlight greeted his most prominent features.

Verus heard a voice in the distance. Someone was coming.

He ducked back into the aqueduct and slid the stone back over the hole. He could hear two men talking; they sounded like soldiers. He put his ear against the aqueduct, holding his breath so he could hear the conversation. As each second passed the noise of the rising water made it increasingly more difficult to hear.

"*Move on,*" Verus pleaded in his mind. "*Please, move on.*"

The water was so loud that Verus could not even tell if the guards were still there.

"There is no time for this!" Verus shouted. Just as the water came crashing towards him, he pushed the stone off and exploded out of the aqueduct. Water erupted out with him like a sudden fountain.

Verus only had moments to scan his surroundings: He was at the edge of a hill, just before the aqueduct went underground. Two guards were standing there, staring at the dark figure before them. Verus had emerged so quickly that neither of the soldiers knew what to make of him. They were stunned, unable to move.

"Who are you—" one of them ventured.

Verus charged at them, swinging the rope that had the stone tablet attached. He hit one of them in the chest with the tablet and grabbed the sword from the other. The next thing came so naturally to Verus, he was surprised he had done it: he knocked one out with the sword butt and wrestled the other to the ground. It was a vicious struggle, but soon Verus had choked the soldier until he passed out.

Verus turned his back on the soldiers and scanned the area for more enemies. He could see the city of Rome in the distance: its large thick walls glared ominously with unstoppable power. The Blacksmith closed his eyes and breathed deeply. For the last few days he had nothing but the foul air of Rome for his lungs; but now, he was free of Rome and her politics—free of the foul stench of an overgrown city and her populous.

Verus spat.

He then set to work putting the stone tablet back in the

aqueduct and dragging the guards' bodies into some bushes. Moving as quickly as he could, he swapped his wet clothes with the dry ones of the soldiers. He did not don the breastplate, but he did latch the sword around his waist. Then he took one of the soldiers red cloaks and threw it over his shoulders. As he was tying it, Verus noticed that the soldiers were wearing money bracelets. He hesitated. *"How can I steal their gold from them? But I need all the money I can get. I've lost all my Denarii because of the incompetence of Rome, and now my children's lives are at stake. But what if they have children? What if they have poor wives?"* After he finished tying the cloak, he left the money and ran off.

Nearby the two Roman soldiers had their horses tied to a tree. He glanced around, looking for any more signs of Romans; when he was sure there were none, he made a dash for the steeds.

He reached Via Flaminia in less time than he expected and then turned north towards Pinacale. Jumping between horses, he was able to maintain a rigorous speed that would have outdistanced any courier. The sun came up and still Verus rode all day, kicking the horses for more speed. The beasts were exhausted; spittle as thick as cream dripped down their mouths and against their necks. It was not until noon before Verus gave them much of a break. He found a little food in the Roman's pack: grain for the horses, old porridge for himself. He did not feel hungry, but he forced himself to eat. After feeding and watering the horses, he saddled them again.

This time he pushed the horses even harder, whipping them if they laxed their speed. Just as the sun was coming down, one of the horses collapsed. The beast's side was shaking like it had been caught in the cold. Verus patted the beast sorrowfully and pushed on. A few hours later, the other beast collapsed and died instantly. Verus took to the street running. The arrow wound in his leg burned each time he stepped, but despite it, he pushed himself harder and harder. Every time he wanted to give up, he made himself go faster. Faster and faster he ran. He started to recognize things around him: a broken down tavern; a turned over wagon cart; an old river that he explored when he was a child.

Finally, towards the middle of the night, through the darkness, Verus could see hundreds of fires in the distance—right where Pinacale should have been. Then suddenly, looming before him, Verus saw the distinct outline of a Roman *Castra.*

He rubbed his eyes to make sure of what he saw. "A *Castra?* Why is there a Roman *Castra* on Tuscany soil?" A sick feeling trickled down Verus' chest and settled in his heart, stinging him to the core. It was right then that he knew...

"*No. No, they're not. They can't be.*"

He picked up his pace again, being careful to avoid the *Castra.* It took some time—which seemed an eternity to Verus—but finally, he made it to his home. The structure was half burned and red with embers; smoke rose through the air in sharp angles as the wind whipped it back and forth. Verus could see the outline of a body in the doorway.

"No," Verus whispered. His steps became slow and pensive, almost as if his body was now twice its weight. He stepped closer and closer. A gust of wind picked up and stoked the fire, sending extra light through the house. He could tell it was the body of a woman.

"Julia!" Verus screamed. He cautiously stepped forward, like a guilty child does when approaching an angry father. Tears came to his eyes but he refused to let them fall.

"Julia?" he whispered. He was only five feet from the body now, but he still could not see her face.

"Julia," Verus stepped over the body and looked down: the eyes of his wife stared blankly back. Instantly, he felt the taste of vomit in his throat that spiraled up and burned his nostrils. With huge gasping breaths, he knelt down and tenderly grabbed her hand. Slowly, ever so slowly, he gently pulled her body into his arms, coddling her like a child. Time passed.

When they were first married, he had carried her, much like he held her now, through that very doorway. She was laughing at his feigned strained expression. Verus had worked all summer on that house, perfecting it with each long day. His father had given him the stone for a wedding gift; the wood inside had come from a brother. It took hours for him to figure out how to mix the mortar—even more time to figure out how to stack the stones—but he was determined to have a place for his Julia, and for the family they both looked forward to making. It was bigger than the standard home, being equipped with two fireplaces, one in the kitchen, the other between the two bedrooms.

Everything Verus had, including his favorite memories, were

110

all contained in this little home. The Blacksmith remembered the birth of his first child. It was on a day that rained so much, it flooded the main river that ran through town. The baby came so suddenly that Tulias did not have time to make it up the soggy hill. The little wrinkly thing was as purple as a grape when he came out—which made Verus' sister so worried she started pacing the room—but after a few deep breaths, the boy turned as perfectly peach as any new father could hope.

Then they were blessed with more children. Each birth was as easy as the first. Verus did not take these good moments for granted either; instead, he ritually made offerings to the Gods, thanking them for all of his good fortune. Despite it all—all of the burnt offerings and the sprinkled flowers—his good luck did not last. Despite it all, his wife now lay dead.

Verus slowly put his wife down and went to look for the children. He found them scattered across the house. They all held so still, like they were playfully hiding from their father. Verus touched them on the arms, but he felt no warmth. He found them all—all except Gaius.

Verus felt a rush across his body. "Gaius isn't here." He began to tear through the house, looking for a trace of his oldest son. He flipped over the table and tossed open cupboards, pulled off blankets and rifled through pots, but he was not there. At the end of the house, just above Gaius' bed, a window had been left unlatched. It was mostly burnt, but the latch still worked and should have held the window fast. "He must have jumped out this window when the guards came in; I bet he was trying to lead them away from the house." He looked out the window, forcing his mind to recreate the horrific scene. Acting like the boy, Verus jumped out of the window, recovered himself, and looked around him. "If soldiers were attacking the homes… he would've headed straight for the…woods."

The Blacksmith stood and ran towards his last hope in the world. "Please be alive Gaius. *Please,* be alive."

"In the name of Caesar, halt!"

Verus glanced to his right just in time to see four Roman soldiers, mounted on brilliantly white steeds coming at him. Instead of stopping, the Blacksmith picked up his speed and crashed through the woods. Verus only had seconds to look for his son. "Gaius!

Gaius!"

The horsemen were right behind. "Halt!"

Verus ran from side to side, making it all the more difficult for the horsemen to gain any speed. The trees weren't thick but the branches were low. Two of the soldiers dismounted and drew their swords, the third one struggled on top of his horse, while the fourth disappeared completely.

The Blacksmith scrambled through one of the bigger bushes. "Gaius! Gaius!" Still, there was no trace of his son—no response from the forest. "Where are you Gaius!"

One of the Romans ran faster than the rest and was only paces away. Just before he could tackle Verus, the Blacksmith suddenly whirled around and drew his own blade. The soldier was so surprised he tripped over himself and skidded to the ground—his own sword slicing him in the belly.

The soldier screamed with pain, "I'm stabbed!"

The other two soldiers arrived.

Although Verus spoke calmly, he spoke with a level of bitterness that he had never used before. "I'm a Roman Citizen, born and raised in Pinacale—the city which your Legion has just destroyed. My wife and all but one of my children are dead. There is a chance—as small as it may be—that he escaped and is in these woods. I am only looking for my son and as soon as I find him, I promise you, I will be gone."

"Soldier—are you injured?"

"It's my...stomach, sir...he stabbed me."

Verus shook his head. "That's a lie. He tripped and fell on his own sword."

"What is your name?" asked the Roman that was still on his horse.

The Blacksmith hesitated, knowing that if he said "Verus" he would be dead before he finished his sentence, but if used someone else's name, he would not have a passport to prove it. "*Why didn't I take Horace's passport?*"

"Put down your weapon!"

Verus felt a boldness rising through his body. "I warn you: this is not a good day to contend with me, friend. I've just lost my beautiful wife and innocent children, my old father and loving mother, my small pathetic little home and every friend that I have ever known. By the mercy of all the Gods combined, let me look for my son in peace."

"Just as you have a duty to your son, you nameless dog, I have a duty to Caesar; just as you are willing to lay down your life for your family, I will gladly do the same for Rome. Now, either you put down your weapon, or I will chop it from your hand."

"There is a little difference, Centurion, between the life of my son and your loyalty to Rome. My son will die without me—he might not even live through the night—but Rome will not lose a second of its glory with you gone."

Verus was so distracted by the Romans in front of him, he did not notice the fourth soldier that was coming in from behind. As Verus finished, the Roman rushed in, hitting the Blacksmith on the head with the butt of his sword. The world blurred then faded. Verus had one word on his lips before he slipped completely unconscious: "Gaius."

* * *

"Wake this fool up," a voice drifted into Verus' ear. "I want to deal with this one before we deal with the Gaul. There was more noise that followed: the running of soldiers, the burning of a fire, and the sound of idle chatter all around him. Suddenly, water was splashed on him, sending him into reality. He opened his eyes slightly, taking it all in. He was in a tent of some kind, surrounded by Roman soldiers. Everything from their dirty helmets to their dented armor suggested that these soldiers had seen recent combat.

"On your feet."

Verus found himself completely lifted in the air and then set on the ground; he teetered but did not fall. His vision was blurry, like when one first wakes up. As he looked around, he noticed that someone had expertly bandaged the arrow wound in his leg. He tried to rub his face with his shirt but one of the guards hit him in the gut.

"Leave your hands at your side."

Verus bent over with pain. He regained himself and stood his full height; now he could see everyone's face clearly.

"What are you doing here?" asked the Roman in the center.

Verus clenched his jaw, "I live here. This is my home, where I was raised from a boy to a man. This is where I married my wife and fostered my first child. I've worked for ten years here as a blacksmith, making weapons for the army. I've been here my whole life, so the real question is, what are *you* doing here?"

"Watch your tongue, dog..." one of the Romans began, but then another one interrupted.

"It's all right. It's obvious this man is in a lot of pain right now. My name is Antonius—conqueror of the Vitelli armies at Bedriacum. I am second only to the Emperor himself. But to answer your question, Blacksmith, we are here because we are hunting rebels."

"MY WIFE WAS NOT A REBEL! Nor am I, or my children. Pinacale was a simple town—one in which I knew everyone by their first name. Most of us were blacksmiths, trained in the art of weaponry. There's a metal mine not far, where we harvest what we need. We supplied the northern Legions with weapons. We were not traitors—but we were killed as if we were."

"Just because I let you speak," Antonius answered coldly, "does not mean you are free to speak your mind. You're full of emotions right now but don't give into them. Your fate is at the whim of my desire. You've already proved your disloyalty by cutting one of my soldiers; pray that you don't do it with your words."

"Are you saying," Verus asked slowly, "that there is a possibility that you will let me free?" Antonius flinched ever so slightly.

Verus continued. "Well then, ask me whatever you will; punish me however you like; banish me to wherever you seem fit, but do not kill me, for I think I have a son still alive. For your mercy, I will raise him to be a Roman Citizen that pays more than his share of taxes and is twice as faithful as the next man."

"Flattering words from a blacksmith."

"The love for my boy gives me eloquence."

"Well spoken, Blacksmith," Antonius replied, "but we still have the small matter of you stabbing one of my guards."

"He fell on his sword."

Antonius stood, spilling wine to the floor. "Are you telling me that one of my men—men that I personally trained—fell on his sword? I spent years in their training, sending them on the toughest hikes over the roughest terrain, carrying their swords in their hands. How can you say that this young Legionnaire cut himself?"

Verus did not flinch. "My Lord, it can happen. I know this because I saw it happen before my eyes."

"It did not happen," Antonius said. "No matter what you say, the other three soldiers witness against you—not to mention the poor soldier himself."

"The wound would have been deep if it was a stab, but a scrape across the belly would have needed just a simple bandage. If I would have stabbed him, it would have been the end of him; I could have just as easily killed him as he lay on the ground, as when he was on his feet. Why would I stab him but then be afraid to finish him?"

Antonius began to pace around the room with his hands behind his back. "No, that does not make sense. You knew that if he was wounded, he would have been more difficult to carry back than if he was dead. You were trying to slow my soldier's progression just as much as you were trying to speed up yours."

Verus thought hard for a second. "*What gain does he have at framing me? Why would he care about the life of a blacksmith? What is he hiding?*"

Antonius continued, "If it wasn't for the valiant work of one of my soldiers, you would still be out there, looking for your 'supposed son.' What is your name?"

"Blacksmith is what they call me…"

"Do not prattle with my time!"

Suddenly inspiration hit Verus, "And you don't prattle with mine. I am a Roman Citizen, born with certain rights. Pinacale was a peaceful village, full of individuals that were as loyal to Rome as the Emperor himself. This is not a trial—it's a sentence. You've had my death on your mind from the beginning. This is all a show for those that are in the room around me. What happened here is simple: Vespasian's troops smashed a Roman city, killing everyone who was there; it would be easy to cover it up, saying that it was a city of rebels—that is, unless you had a witness. And I am that witness."

"Seize him!" Antonius yelled. "Silence him."

"Take your hands off him," someone else shouted. "If he speaks the truth, then Rome must be held accountable."

"He obviously lies, Titus," Antonius said with a hiss. "Look at him, caught in the middle of a battle site; he doesn't know what to believe."

A young man came forward, dressed in the most magnificent armor. "You might be the Consul, Antonius, but I have a feeling the Emperor will side with me on this. No matter what this blacksmith believes, I want to hear it."

Verus puffed out his chest. "If you investigate it further, you will find a weak connection between Vitellius and Pinacale. There will be a few documents supporting this claim, but the rest of them will wholly be devoid of evidence. Destroying Pinacale was a sin against the Gods—and that sin, cannot be ignored."

Antonius smiled wickedly. "What are you willing to wager?"

"My life."

"Then, let's make a deal," Antonius replied quickly. "You tell me your name and promise to stay here in Pinacale, and I'll investigate the matter closely; if things are how you say, then you will be made free, along with a regal compensation, of course."

Verus hesitated. "My name is my own business—"

"Well," Antonius smirked, "if you don't agree, then I have a new offer for you. How about I kill you here and now—Verus Flaminius."

Verus swallowed.

Antonius laughed. "Yes, I've known your name this whole time—it was actually Titus who figured it all out. There was only one name on the *proscription* that was from Pinacale—Verus Flaminius, the son of Gaius Flaminius—and then all of a sudden, you show up, searching for your son Gaius. It's not hard to see how this happened. You were in Rome pledging your support to Vitellius when Vespasian marched in. Naturally the *proscription* was issued, you escaped by some miracle, and came as quickly as you could to start a rebellion—but, instead, you ended up here in my camp."

"I am Verus Flaminius—that is true—but I was only in Rome to get grain, not to ally myself with Vitellius. He tricked me into signing my own death warrant. I needed grain to save my family and Vitellius said Rome would provide it."

"It sounds like a bribe," Antonius jeered.

Titus sighed. "It's a simple mistake, committed by a simple metal worker."

Antonius scoffed. "This is the number one person on the *proscription*—this is no simple farmer. Guards, seize him."

Titus put his hand in the air. "Wait, what do you plan to do with him?"

"Execute him, of course."

"He might be innocent," Titus contended.

"Yes," Antonius replied, "but he might be guilty too."

"I forbid you from killing him."

"As Consul, and on a military expedition, my command overrules yours."

Titus exploded with rage. "You fool! Can you possibly think that your command has more sway to my father's ears than his loyal son? When we arrive in Rome I will have your body torn to pieces by horses."

Antonius slacked his shoulders. "I'm sorry...I did not mean to offend you. But something must be done with him."

"Let him go then."

Now it was Antonius' turn to be angry. "Let him go! He's the number one enemy of the state right now. Do you know what our opposition would say if we granted him mercy? They would say that Vespasian is weak."

"Unless he's innocent; then they would hail him for his mercy."

Antonius leaned in on his next question. "Are you willing to bet your father's emperorship on the whim of a blacksmith? Wait until we find him innocent before you set him free. That way you will look even more benevolent when you do."

"Fine," Titus spat, "but I want you to head up the investigation personally."

Antonius pounded his fat chest. "It will be done."

"Where do we put him for now?"

Antonius' voice turned shrill. "There is a rock quarry not far from here; his skill as a blacksmith would be a valued commodity up there."

Titus waved his hand. "Let it be done."

"Thank you," Verus said. "Thank you for your mercy."

With a wave of Titus' hands, Verus was escorted out of the tent.

Antonius sat down on his chair and sipped at a fresh cup of wine. "Now bring in the Centurion—I hope to be done with this before breakfast."

Chapter 14
December 27, 69 AD
Priscus

Priscus had been forced into a small tent and shackled to a curved stake that was sunk five feet in the ground. He still had his Roman breastplate on, but he had been stripped of his swords and arm bracelets. He tried to massage his wrists but the shackles were too tight. It had been a long time since he had been bound like a slave. Here he was now, chained by his master, like a cow waiting for slaughter.

A group of Romans suddenly stepped into the tent—all of them had their swords out as if Priscus was a captured barbarian. "Come on Gaul," one of them said, "it's your turn now."

Priscus looked up. He had not been called a Gaul for a long time—now that he heard it, he wasn't sure that he liked it. One of the Romans unlocked the shackles while the rest held their blades at Priscus' throat.

"I am one of you," Priscus cursed. "I am a Roman Citizen, protected by the laws of Rome."

"By the order of Antonius, you've been placed under arrest and removed of your command. You are now to appear before a military court for sentencing."

Priscus turned red with rage. "Sentencing! I was following orders—orders that came directly from Vespasian."

A Roman pushed the Gaul outside the tent. "Tell it to Antonius."

Priscus turned around, looking for the one that shoved him, but he was greeted by five swords that quickly persuaded him to move on.

"Priscus," one of soldiers said, "talk to Antonius and see if he grants you mercy. You are a Centurion, and a good one at that."

He scanned the faces around him and saw a few that he knew: Some of them were friends, most were enemies. Priscus narrowed his eyes at all of them—like a wolf staring down his prey. After a few tense moments, the Gaul turned away. He stepped out of the morning air and into the commander's tent.

Antonius sat there, fat and weak, sipping on some wine. Priscus had heard of this leader, heard about his great leadership in the battle of Bedriacum, but now, as he stared the Roman in the face, the Gaul could hardly believe a word that he had heard. To the right of Antonius sat another man Priscus recognized: Titus Flavius. He was a little overweight too, and his chin jiggled when he talked, but there was a sense of fairness in his eyes and regalness in his presence.

Antonius was the first to speak. "Do you know why you are here?"

Priscus stared unflinching at the fat leader. "I am here because I followed orders."

"Orders?" Titus scoffed. "Orders are the things your leaders tell you to do; orders are the things that a soldier should do; orders are the exact things you did not do!" By the time Titus finished, he was standing up—his eyes blazing. "When you were ordered to detain and capture, you tortured and killed. How do you defend yourself?"

"They were traitors—they deserved to die."

"A few of them, yes, but now where Pinacale once stood, there is nothing!"

"Easy," Antonius said with a hint of amusement in his voice. "Let the Centurion defend himself."

Priscus cleared his throat. "My orders were to capture and contain, but when we got here we found no trace of livestock—no cows for substance—which is odd for a small city. I believed that the cows had been taken by a rebel army that would not be too far distant. In order to ascertain the truth as quickly as I could, I ordered the town burned. The people resisted—so yes—they were killed. I thought that since the cows were not reported stolen, the Citizens must have been in league with Vitellius supporters; when they put up a resistance, this seemed to confirm my suspicions."

Titus clenched his jaw. "You shot arrows into their city and you think that just because they are Roman Citizens, they wouldn't try to defend themselves?"

"They're traitors…"

Titus took another step forward, "They were blacksmiths!"

"I am a Roman Centurion, which is the base of the army, and I made a decision in the midst of battle that resulted in the death of possible traitors."

"You unrepentant dog! You will die for your pride."

"Wait," Antonius said as he touched Titus' shoulder. "This is Priscus—the great soldier from Gaul. Not only has he served the Roman Empire faithfully for the last several years, he also is considered the consummate Roman soldier." The fat General turned from Titus and looked at Priscus. "How many marches are the Roman Centuries required to do in a month?"

"Two," Priscus answered.

Antonius continued. "And how many do your soldiers do?"

"Six."

"Was it not you, alone, that stole the Eagle of the fourth Legion?"

"Yes."

"How long are Romans required to train each day?"

"Three hours."

"And how long do your soldiers train each day?"

"Five."

Titus threw up his hands in exacerbation. "Yes, I see your point Antonius. He is an excellent soldier. But just because he is good at enforcing Roman law does not mean he is above it. I had an excellent hunting dog once, which had no equal, but when the dog started biting people I had to kill it."

"This is not a dog," Antonius said with a mocking tone, "this is a Centurion—one that can be punished for the mistake he made. Punish him, but don't kill him. He will learn."

"He's blood hungry," Titus replied. "I've seen it in the eyes of soldiers before, where their desire to kill overrules their wits. They love to kill—they are fed by it. If you set him free, it will only get worse. This time it was a town of Roman Citizens; next time it might be the assassination of a general. He is uncontrollable—unmanageable—and, consequently, a danger to the principles of

Rome. He must be executed at once."

Roman soldiers stepped in and flanked Priscus.

"Stop," Antonius said lazily, "this is a Roman Centurion, and therefore subject to my control—not yours Titus. He will not be executed." The fat general took a long lethargic drink of his wine. "Nor will he be banished from Tuscany."

Titus' cheeks sunk low. "Fine. But, if that is the game you play, then I want you to link his fate to Verus'. If Verus is found innocent, then Priscus must live out his life in the quarries, mining out stone for the rest of his miserable life. If Verus is found guilty, then Priscus will receive his commission again. Until that time, however, I want that Gaul working in the quarries."

"Fair enough, Titus," Antonius conceded.

"I can't be sent to the quarries," Priscus growled. "I'm a free soldier—a Citizen of Rome. I have fought and bled in the army; I've killed and been wounded in Rome's defense. I don't deserve to be tossed off like some rag, or to be shuffled under a dirty rug. I've struggled too hard and come too far to be disowned. Rescind your punishment and let me join the ranks of your soldiers; let me die at the front of some battlefield, fighting for Rome, instead of at the mercy of a rock quarry."

"Take him away," Titus ordered.

Priscus took a deep breath. "You will regret this. Mark my face, for I've marked yours. You will see me again, Roman."

Priscus was taken by four strong men and stripped of his breastplate. A sack that smelled of urine was put over his head and then he was roughly thrown into the back of a cart. Another person was already there, waiting to be shipped off to the quarries. Priscus kicked at him, bruising him until the prisoner made room enough for the Gaul. Priscus slumped down against the wagon and waited, cursing himself as he did. Every once in a while, one of the other prisoner's legs would accidentally brush against Priscus, which would send the Gaul in a flurry of kicking until the other prisoner scooted away.

"If you dogs speak," a voice said through the sacks, "you will get beaten. If you try to escape, I will have the guards beat you twice as hard. But if you don't give us any troubles, I will give you plenty of water along the way. Agreed?"

The prisoners did not know if they should nod or not, but either way, the driver seemed satisfied; he whipped the horses and the wagon started rocking forward through the road.

Priscus had taken up almost all the room in the wagon, leaving only a small section against the back for the other prisoner. Despite it all, the Gaul felt squished, and lashed out with long streams of curses. He must have cursed half the people in Rome before their escort finally punched the Gaul in the face.

It was a bitter, long ride—one in which Priscus was beaten twice more for attempting an escape. The Gaul took the beatings considerably well: He did not cry out for them to stop or moan with pain; he seemed so disconnected from his body that no matter how much he was beaten, it did not rattle his resolve. Each time the Gaul was roughed up he was twice as territorial as before and, consequently, he ended up trying to completely kick the other prisoner out of the wagon. After several hours of this abuse, however, the other prisoner became infinitely more aggressive than Priscus, kicking so hard and with so much speed that eventually it led to an unspoken truce between the two men.

At noon, the sacks were removed from the prisoners one at a time. Priscus was first to get a drink of water, which he sucked down as quickly as it was given to him. He looked at the other prisoner: he was short but had a broad chest and thick arms. He looked like he could handle himself well, but he was definitely no soldier. The Gaul finished his drink and the sack was put back over his head. Then it was the other prisoner's turn for water. Priscus could feel the stares of the other prisoner; he could feel the sudden fear that had come over the other man. This prisoner—whoever he was—was scared of Priscus.

The wagon continued all day, pushing splinters and blisters into their backs. It was not until night that they reached the outer part of the quarries.

"Halt. What do you have there?"

"Prisoners from Antonius."

"That's a mighty big one you have back there—what is he, Decian? Goth?"

"He's a Gaul."

"A Gaul, huh. How long is he sentenced for?"

"Till death, I think, or so the orders make it seem."

"How would you like to make some extra money? How would all of you soldiers like to earn some extra money?"

The other man hesitated. "We have strict orders to drop these men off at the quarries—"

"And you have succeeded. But, we have some scouts in the quarries right now, looking for gladiators. A large Gaul like that will fetch a killing—especially if he knows how to hold a sword."

"He does."

"Then pull him out and let's see what they will pay."

"I...don't—"

"Come on," the man shrilled. "He's a condemned man."

"All right, we can take a look. Boys, bring the Gaul out, but make sure he doesn't kick the blacksmith—I'm not sure how much more of a beating that little one can take."

Priscus felt fingers under his armpits as he was dragged out; he tried to bite one of the hands but someone slapped his mouth away. They struggled with the Gaul, forcing him to stand on his feet. He knocked one of the Romans in the jaw and pushed another one of them down, but three more Romans jumped in, restraining the large warrior.

"Yes, he will fetch a good price, won't he? Bring him through the gate."

There was a large creak as the door swung wide, then a slam as it hit the outside wall. Even though Priscus could not see through the sack, he could smell the scent of slave labor. All around him was the distant sound of stone chipping and chiseling, carts being pushed and people being whipped. The thick marble dust permeated the sack that should have protected the Gaul's face. The rest of the soldiers around the Gaul coughed uncontrollably.

He waited for a while, then was shuffled a few steps forward, and then waited some more. This process repeated itself again and again until finally, Priscus became the center of attention. The sack came off and the light pierced his eyes, making him squint. The dust did not affect the large Gaul like it did the soldiers around him; instead, he stood up, straightening to his full height, daring any man to cross him.

"Bring him forward. Yes, yes. This is a big brute. Looks like he can take a beating too. Does he have any experience with the sword?"

"He's a master at it—I've seen him fight."

Priscus recognized that voice—it was his second in command. "Unas? What are you doing here?"

The young soldier stepped forward and whispered in the Gaul's ear, "I'm saving your miserable life from the stone quarry. I should have chopped off your vile head as we traveled—it would have been easy to explain—but I feel sorry for a brute that is too stupid to know what is good for him."

The Gaul stiffened: He would have killed the soldier for his insolence—killed him and skinned him in front of his troops had it not been for his wretched shackles.

"Will he fight?"

Unas looked at his former leader. "Priscus was born to fight. He is the toughest and strongest man I have ever met. If you put him in the arena—no matter how many men he faces—I would wager my life and more that he would win. He is unstoppable—unbeatable. But you will have to pay a high price to get him."

"One thousand sestertius."

"Hah," Unas laughed. "That might be a good rate for a gladiator who has no thumbs. This one, however, is worth far more than that. In the battle of Bedriacum he killed over thirty Roman soldiers and then stole the Eagle from the fourth Legion. He is a war hero in Gaul, and a legend in Rome. If you put this man in the arena, I promise you, no man within five hundred miles could stand toe to toe with him."

"Four thousand sestertius."

"Come on," Unas encouraged, "I've seen prostitutes go for more than that."

"Ten thousand sestertius."

Unas considered it, scratching his jaw as he did. "Twenty thousand sestertius, and I will even let you keep his sword."

"Fifteen thousand sestertius and not a single coin more; no man is worth more than that, not even the senators of Rome."

"Fine."

Priscus' veins were surging all along his neck. He wanted to kill everyone around him—especially his old "friend" Unas. "I warn you, Unas. If I am ever freed from here, I'm going to slice your belly, pull out your bowels, and hang you with them."

"Easy old boy." Unas patted him on the back. "Watch that attitude, or I will have to beat you again—"

Priscus snapped. He dove for Unas, snatching at him with his mouth. Three guards were holding the Gaul's chains, but the attack came so quickly, none of them had time to pull him back. Priscus clamped down with his teeth and bit through Unas' ear.

"Beat him!" Unas yelled. "Beat him!"

The blows quickly came. There were so many and so misaimed that Unas took a hit to the head, knocking him unconscious. Moments later one of the soldiers struck the Gaul across the head, spilling blood down his back. Slowly, his muscles relaxed and his vision faded...

Chapter 15

December 27, 69 AD
Verus

Brutally—treating him almost as if he was obstinate—the guards dragged Verus out of the wagon. He was forced to walk quickly down the stone trail, where he stubbed his toes twice on large discarded rocks. He was then thrown to the ground. No one spoke to him; no one seemed to believe that he was smart enough to understand. He wanted to look around, but the sack still covered his head. A thick dust seeped through the sack, gagging the Blacksmith. All around him he could hear chisels and hammers, huge boulders being moved, and slaves being whipped. Not too far from where he was, Verus could hear a man pleading for mercy.

The sack was suddenly removed from Verus' head. He pulled away and squinted in the new light—an ugly man squinted back. The brute was big and round, like a misshapen potato. His whole face spilled out to one side, and when he spoke, it all moved together. "Your name is 2297. Remember it if you want to live."

"2297, I've got it—."

As Verus spoke, four slaves stepped in, each one grabbing a separate limb. "What are you doing?"

The bulbous man kicked Verus in the side. "Don't speak. No slave speaks in the quarry."

The men half dragged, half carried the Blacksmith to a set of burning fires that was only a short distance away. There were other men there, waiting in line, held captive by other faceless slaves. Each time the line moved up, there was a scream of pain and an odd sizzling that sounded like water thrown onto a fire. The closer Verus got, the more daunting the situation became. He looked around and, finally, with a sudden inspiration that sent a shock down his body, he realized that each of the slaves around him had a number burned into their arm.

Verus swallowed as his turn came up; he was determined not to scream in pain. He could feel the heat from the fire as he was placed near it; the flames danced wildly as a toothless man stoked it. From the fire another man pulled out a long piece of metal that had four numbers on the end of it.

"What number is he?"

"2297."

"Good. That's what I have ready. Bring him closer. Stretch his arm out on the board."

The red-hot poker was now a hand's length from Verus' arm; its heat was already starting to curl the hairs on his shoulder.

"Hold him tight."

Verus bit down hard but did not let out a yell of pain. The poker came down on the skin, melting the flesh instantly so that the skin hung off to the side. Despite himself, Verus gasped for air and grunted. The pain was over in an instant.

The Blacksmith was carried to the side and dropped on the ground. The potato-looking guard returned. "You're assigned to chain 74. Now up on your feet."

Verus nodded again and pulled himself up. While he was standing, he noticed that he had stubbed one of his big toes so hard that the toenail was barely hanging on. The blood had already been sopped up by the dust, making it look like a mix of red clay. The toe hurt when he stepped but, wisely, he kept it to himself.

Without the sack to cover his face, the dust swam in on Verus, choking him with its thick vapors. He coughed once, and then again. Soon he was coughing two times for every step he took. The bulbous guard responded with a few grunts but nothing more.

The quarry was huge, stretching out for hundreds of yards in every direction. Despite its size, it seemed overrun with slaves; there were two slaves for every yard of the quarry. Among the slaves that were sweating off years of their lives, were women dressed in rags, carrying clay jugs full of water to all the slaves that cried out. Verus noticed that the slaves would exchange small wooden tokens to get the privilege to drink: The more tokens a slave had, the longer they could drink.

The quarry was shaped like a horseshoe. The natural stone walls provided a perfect prison for the workers below. Despite this natural barrier, the Romans had built a fifteen foot palisade around the edge of the rock face, just in case one of the slaves somehow managed to climb out of the quarry. A few Roman soldiers were posted on wooden towers that ran along the wall.

There were no old slaves, nor ones that were disabled—as the Blacksmith thought there would be. Besides the whip cuts on their backs, the slaves looked rather healthy, considering the conditions they were in. Despite the dangerous work and the mass of people that dotted the landscape, none of the slaves nursed old wounds, or limped with injured legs, or had broken arms.

A few moments later, the Blacksmith found out why.

To his right, only twenty-five yards away, a line broke, sending a huge stone crashing down. It headed straight towards one slave that stood in the way. The slave leaped, closely dodging the rock, but as it rolled by, it slapped the man's right arm, breaking it in two. The workers around him stopped and stared, waiting to see if the man was injured. At first Verus thought that everyone had stopped working out of concern; but as the slaves began to encircle the wounded man—with yellow gleams in their eyes—he realized they were drawn in by something else.

The man stood up, his arm flapping. "It's not broken! It's not broken!"

This in turn attracted more attention from the surrounding slaves. Slowly, like coyotes around their prey, the slaves came in on the wounded man.

"It's not broken!" the man yelled.

Suddenly, one of the slaves rushed forward, brandishing a hammer in his hands. Then another. Soon dozens of slaves ran in, swinging their random weapons in the air. In a last attempt to save himself the slave's voice rang out, echoing through the valley, "Have mercy! Have mercy..." His cries did not last long before they were cut short.

Verus looked away.

Six or seven guards joined the crowd, relentlessly whipping every slave they came across. "Get back to work. Get back to work!" Gradually, the crowd began to disperse, leaving the body of the slave behind—or what was left of him.

Verus shook his head. "Why—"

The bulbous guard whipped Verus across the back. "No one speaks in the quarry!"

The pain ripped through Verus' body, tightening all the muscles in his back. He turned and glared at the guard with fire in his eyes.

The thick-headed guard had his hand in the air, ready to swing another blow, but as he looked in Verus' eyes—burning with action—the man faltered. Instead he slowly lowered his whip and whispered, "When a slave breaks a bone, they are doomed to die. Slaves and guards alike will kill him for his water tokens and, sometimes, if they are desperately hungry, they take portions of him for food. Now, watch your tongue, or we will suffer the same."

For the first time Verus realized that this guard was as much a prisoner as anyone else in the quarry. The bulbous man was a slave, destined to waste away here, but instead of cutting stone himself, he had been forced to make sure that others did. All of the guards in the quarry were condemned men, forced to cruelly beat the slaves around them or be beaten themselves; for their service they received more food, more water tokens, and occasionally, the company of a woman.

They climbed steadily upwards until they were near the top, where gigantic boulders were being cut from the side of the mountain. Slaves with sullen eyes studied the Blacksmith like he was some curious relic. Verus tightened his jaw and walked on, refusing to look directly into anyone's eyes. As they walked, they passed a discarded body on their right.

The guard finally led Verus up to a part of the quarry that was covered by a shadow of rock. It was there that Verus saw a group of five men, feverishly working on a large boulder. A long chain stretched between each of their shackled ankles. The bulbous man wasted no time in shackling Verus' leg and then attaching him to the chain.

"I think this is a mistake," Verus protested. "I was sent here to work as a blacksmith, not a stone cutter. I don't know anything about stone cutting."

"We already have too many blacksmiths," the man replied. "You'll figure out how to cut stone—everyone does."

Verus clenched his jaw, but he did not protest further. The bulbous man handed Verus two water tokens and walked away without saying another word.

Anger rose up Verus' neck like heat from a boiling pot. "What do I do now!"

"Be quiet you fool."

Verus looked away from the fading sight of the guard and turned his attention to a prisoner who was only a few feet away.

"Get up. Get to work," the man commanded. "The rest of the guards are not as nice as Chawn."

"Chawn?"

"Get up," the man persisted. "Take this chisel and let's get to work."

Verus felt anger flushing over his body again—it was getting harder to control his emotions all the time—but he finally obeyed, dusting himself off as he did.

"Leave the dust on you," the slave said. "It will make it so you don't attract so much attention from the guards. The less they see you the better."

"The guards are just slaves," Verus replied.

"Yes, but they are twice as cruel as the Roman soldiers that surround this camp. Now come here."

With the heavy chisel Verus walked forward, sliding it on the thick stone below as he did. They climbed up a crumbling rock, where the rest of their chained group was waiting for them. The Blacksmith nodded at a few of them, but they did not nod back; they seemed too focused on what they were doing to notice the newcomer.

"You hold the chisel," the slave ordered, "and I will hit it with the hammer. After each time I hit it, you need to spin it one quarter turn."

Verus swallowed, "What happens if you miss?"

"Then move your hand."

"How steady are your hands?"

"Usually, pretty good."

Verus looked around him, trying to stall for time. "What happened to your last partner? How come there was an odd number on your chain?"

"Just hold the rod," the man whispered. "Hurry before a guard spots us."

"Just tell me your name," Verus whispered back just as forcefully. "Tell me if you have any children."

The man looked around him, obviously confused by Verus' question. "Why do you want my name?"

"Tell me!" Verus ordered. "What is your name?"

"I'm 1729."

Verus narrowed his eyes, "What did they call you before you came here? Give me a name or I don't work; give me a name or both of us will get beaten together."

Panic spread through the man's face, "You fool. They will beat us so bad that we won't stop bleeding for days."

Verus stepped up closer to the man. "I would be a fool to let you swing that hammer above my head without knowing anything about you. I saw what they do to the wounded; I know what will happen if your aim fails."

The man stared long and hard at Verus, but finally, he answered, "David. My name is David."

"Do you have children?"

"I have two: one of them died before I came here, the other is in Greece."

Verus gave a half-smile. "David. My name is Verus Flaminius. I have one child left alive, whom I am planning to see when I get out of here. But if you break my hand with the hammer, be sure that before anyone else can finish me off, I will be coming to finish you. Aim well, and hope that both of us will live."

* * *

It was two more hours of sweaty work before the slaves were locked up in cages that had been carved into the very rock itself. The Blacksmith did not speak to anyone; he did not care if anyone to spoke to him. After a long sweaty day in the sun, all of them had so little energy they could barely scratch at the mosquitoes that bit their legs, let alone greet the new slave. They formed pillows with the shredded clothes from their backs and shifted on the rock as best they could. With the new addition of Verus, they could barely all lay down. If any one of them shifted suddenly, it would send a chain reaction down the line that affected everyone in turn. All six of them had to share a large winter blanket that was just big enough to cover them all.

Moments passed before finally, one of them poked Verus in the side. "Verus."

The stout Blacksmith did not answer—his mind had wandered somewhere else.

"Verus," the voice repeated.

Still there was no answer.

It was David who spoke. "Where do you come from?"

The Blacksmith rolled over slightly. "Pinacale."

"I've never been there. What's it like?"

The Blacksmith hesitated before answering. "It's gone."

"Is that how you got all those bruises on your legs? It looks like someone beat you across the shins with a rod."

Verus shook his head slightly, "There was a Gaul in the wagon with me; he kept kicking me until I started kicking him back."

"Gauls," David said as he attempted a laugh, "they're the wildest creatures I've ever seen—and that includes lions."

There was an awkward silence.

"I'm sorry," David whispered. "Sorry for being so brisk."

A long moment passed before Verus answered, "Why?"

"Why was I so brisk?" David asked. He shrugged his shoulders and continued. "I don't know, really. I've changed from when I first came here."

Tears welled up in Verus' eyes. "Why?"

David shrugged his shoulders again. "Well, I think you start to lose touch with everything—everything that had meaning before. I've only been here six months—"

"Why…"

Suddenly, David realized that Verus was not asking him "why" but someone or something else.

David stared at the Blacksmith for a while, summing him up. "You look worse than I did when I got here. What happened?"

Verus shook his head. "None of that matters now. My son is alive and alone in this wicked world." The Blacksmith quickly wiped at his eyes and turned his attention back to David. "I won't be here very long. I was only sent here for a while—just long enough for them to investigate my crime and find out the truth."

David shook his head. "I'm sorry to tell you this: No one leaves here—not unless they are dead. Death is the only way to escape this place…"

Verus narrowed his eyes. "I've been put here only temporarily, maybe just a few weeks, maybe just a few days."

David frowned. "Did anyone write your name down when you came in? Do you have any documentation to prove who you are, eh? Even if you are proven innocent, how will they find you in the midst of all these grey looking slaves? Do you think they will shout out, 'Verus, where are you, your freedom has been granted?' And how many slaves would leap up, shouting at the top of their lungs that they were 'Verus?' Without documentation, each one is just as likely to be 'Verus' as you are."

"They could question each prisoner individually, asking them details that only I know."

"And how long would that take? an hour? half a day? Trust me—they would not waste a moment to look for you. People don't get sent here to be found innocent; they are sent here because they have already been proven guilty. For the first two months, I hung on to the notion that I would be set free—that I would be found innocent—but that never happened." David looked bitterly down at the shackle around his ankle. "You've been misplaced, folded into a crack of Tuscany that most people don't know exists. The sooner you can accept that, the longer you will survive."

Anger flashed over Verus, throbbing up and out of his throat, "I will leave this place along with you and everyone else that is here. This quarry may be your tomb, but it is not mine. I am innocent."

"Of course you are," David replied as he shifted into a more comfortable position. "If you were guilty, you would've already been dead."

* * *

Just before the sun rose, a guard appeared, banging a metal

rod against the cell bars as he walked.

Verus opened his eyes and stirred quickly—he was not really sleeping anyway. The other slaves followed suit, stretching and yawning as they did. Moments later, a guard was at their cell unlocking the gate. They stepped out into the morning air, which felt chilly for everyone but Verus whose clothes had not been worn with holes yet.

"If you get whipped," David whispered to Verus, "make sure you lift up your shirt. It is better for them to shred your skin than it is for them to shred your clothes."

The Blacksmith nodded.

The prisoners formed a long line that stretched throughout the quarry. At the end of the line, which was at the bottom of the valley, dozens of pots were boiling with soup. Despite the mass of slaves, the line moved forward quickly, and soon Verus found himself with a bowl of hot soup in one hand and a piece of flatbread in the other. Despite the soup's foul appearance, it was not too bad—it even had a small chunk of meat in the middle. In addition to the food, each slave was also given three water tokens. If they wanted, the slaves could opt to trade their bread for another token.

Verus studied the faces around him: There was no hope amongst them, no purpose behind their sullen expressions. Even the guards, who were fatter than most, looked pale and broken—like a dog who had been beaten its whole life. They were all condemned men, sentenced to slowly work themselves until death.

And then the day began much like it ended the day before. Verus started out with the hammer and David with the chisel. The Blacksmith was used to the hard labor of the smithy. His aim with the hammer was precise, his endurance outdid all the others, and his strength sent chips of stone in every direction. Before lunch, he and his chain of slaves had split a large chunk of stone and sent it rolling down the mountain, where another group of workers attacked it with more precise tools. After dinner, Verus and his chain freed another large stone from the mountain.

As the stone went rolling down, a large contingent of guards was walking by. One of them, whose clothes were almost spotless, looked up at the slaves. "Good work you dogs; that is your second one today." The man pointed at Verus. "What is your name?"

"Ver..." he began to say but caught himself, "I'm 2297."

"Well 2297, you just earned your chain extra water tokens." The lead guard gestured with his head. "Give two extra water tokens to all of them—all of them except the Jew. Give the Jew something special instead."

The guards came up the rock face, giving water tokens to everyone except David. When they got to David, the first guard punched him across the face, sending him to his side. Two more guards came in and held the Jew fast while a third one readied a whip.

"Wait!" Verus yelled out. "He held the rod for me as I chipped off the stone. He deserves water just as much as me." The Blacksmith grabbed one of the guards' arms. "Let him go."

"He's a Jew," the lead guard hissed, "a religious fanatic with a frenzied mind. I reward you with water and him with a beating."

The Blacksmith swallowed. "Take my water tokens and spare the Jew his whipping. I need his strength to chip out this rock. If you want me to free more of this rock, I need him whole."

The lead guard laughed. "Have you gotten attached to him already? Is he your friend? Hah! You need to learn 2297 that you can't trust anyone down here. Every one of these slaves would kill you if it meant an extra sip of soup or trickle of water. My name is Brotean—and I am the God of this underworld, and when you question a God in his own kingdom—blood is always spilt." The man stepped up slowly towards Verus, tightening his grip on a wicked looking whip. "Hold them both fast."

Two guards snatched Verus' arms and shoved his face into the dirt. The Blacksmith resisted, but then two more guards grabbed him and held him fast. With his chest flat on the ground, his shirt was shoved up, revealing Verus' unscarred back. Brotean waved the whip dramatically, letting it flip back in the air before he brought it forward.

The whip tightened against Verus' back, bruising it instantly. Again it came at him. And then again. The valley echoed with each crack. On the sixth, the skin ruptured and blood trickled down. Verus tried to hold it in—he tried to hide the pain, but it shook his body like nothing he had ever felt before. Again the whip cracked and then again. Verus was only slightly aware that David, who was still just a few feet away from him, was being whipped as well.

After twenty lashes, Verus' head was spinning. He wasn't sure if he had gone unconscious or not, but the next thing he knew the guards had gone. David crawled over to Verus' side, whispering through the corner of his mouth, "Can you get up?"

The Blacksmith opened his eyes slightly and lifted his head—a patch of dust stuck to his face.

"They're gone now," David continued, "but Brotean will be back if we don't start to work."

Verus' breath came in large gasps. "I…I…can barely move…"

"I know," David got up on one knee, "It's always the worst the first few whippings. Once your skin is scarred up, it doesn't hurt as badly. Come on now, we need to get up."

Every time Verus shifted a flash of pain streaked through his body. He shuffled up with his knees, trying to keep his back as straight as possible. He grabbed the hammer but his arms had little strength.

"Why does he hate Jews?"

"Because he is one—one that has fallen away. He has long since turned from the principles of our people."

"And why does he hate you?"

David stood up. "He knows me from before. It always makes a wicked Jew nervous when there is a righteous one nearby. I imagine he is afraid that if I am ever freed, I will go back and spread rumors about how ruthless he is, which I might actually do if I ever am. I know where his family lives—or at least, used to live."

Verus teetered on his feet but could not lift the hammer.

"Let me hammer for a while," David said.

They went back to work, setting a pace that was quick enough to avoid being in trouble, but slow enough that they did not get much done. David's hammer strokes were half the strength they were before. Each time the Jew raised the hammer in the air, Verus prayed that he would not miss.

It was another two hours of torture: David kept at the hammer the whole time. The extra movement tore at the Jew's back, making it bleed twice as much as it did when he was being whipped. Just as thick as other slaves had sweat on their bodies, David had a trail of blood that dripped down his back and soaked his clothes.

That night, after they had been put in their cramped cell, the other four slaves that were attached to the chain surrounded Verus and David. One of them had used his extra water tokens to buy enough water to soak a portion of his clothes, which he then ripped in half to make two small rags, and then placed them on the backs of the two wounded men. The rags singed at first, sending a prickly pain through their bodies, but soon it soothed their wounds. Another slave had traded his water tokens to the guards for a small ointment that he used to dab on the whip cuts. The last two slaves had somehow smuggled in a small cup of water, which they carefully poured into the parched mouths of Verus and David.

"Thank you," Verus whispered.

"You'll be fine," one of them answered. "Tomorrow is Monday; there is no work on that day."

* * *

The next day they only left their cells for an hour in the morning for breakfast and another hour at night for dinner. During the day, the other slaves gathered around their tight cell, talking about their lives of the past. Verus listened quietly as the others spoke.

One of them was named Alejandro. He was a small, fat-nosed man from the Iberian Peninsula who was easily excitable. His ears were also considerably too big for his head and they stuck out like leaves from a tree. The little Latin that he spoke was so heavy laden with an accent that no one could understand what he said the first time around and often the second. The smallest things would send Alejandro into a fit of excitement—like a guard making an unscheduled patrol past their cell. He would work himself into such a fit that he would mix Latin words with his native language, making such an incomprehensible mess of words that most of the other slaves ignored him completely. He was constantly shifting and moving during the day and fidgeting uncontrollably in the night— much to the complaint of all the others around him.

Alejandro was paired up with an older, calmer man. This random assignment proved to be a stroke of providence for

Alejandro as no one else would have been able to put up with the Iberian for very long. The man's name was Mathias and he was Christian—as he called it. Verus had heard two main things about Christians: One, that they were responsible for a huge fire in Rome that had burned half of the city; and two, that they lived underground and fed on the flesh of babies. Mathias, however, did not seem to fit either of these, nor any other pejorative description Verus had heard. The man seemed completely... simple. He was a man that knew his lot in life and was satisfied to be living it. His favorite phrase, which he said almost every time he spoke, was "blessed are the meek."

Next came Golias—a young upstart boy who was blessed with a quick wit, but cursed with a body that was too weak to defend itself. The boy had the ability to string together a list of insults that sounded as smooth as music. He was an orphan that had been taken in by a struggling poet. By shear merit alone—or so he said—Golias put himself through orator school, offering his services as a speaker to pay for tuition. But he had the awful tendency to speak more, when he should have spoken less. It was this gift—the gift of words—that finally led him to work in the stone quarry. He never said who or what he had insulted, but it had been something important enough to turn his life upside down. Golias had an odd way about him: whenever he talked, he would dramatically gesture with his hands, almost as if there was more of an audience than just the slaves around him.

Golias was paired with Cazeem—a skinny, black Egyptian. Cazeem was a stargazer by trade, and according to him, the stars were like a mirror that reflected the world's history and future. If one studied them long enough, the stars would begin to reveal their secrets. Every day Cazeem would roll out on his knees, gaze up at the heavens, and prophetically tell everyone what they were going to eat that day—which seemed an easy feat because it was the same every day. He also used the information from the stars to provide daily news: He told everyone how Egypt had recently revolted from Rome; how Rome's new Emperor was named Achillian; and how a new weapon had been invented by the Persians that shot out the power of lightning. Both Alejandro and Golias were quite taken with him. One day, Cazeem predicted that the end of the world would occur that evening. When the sun set as normally as it always did, Cazeem still persisted that the end of the world did come—it just was not what everyone had expected.

Finally there was David the Jew. He was the son of a prosperous trader. His family had an extensive trading network that spread all the way to Iberia, where he traded spices for steel swords. But then Nero came to power. The dramatic Emperor rounded up many of the Jews and arrayed them with spurious charges. They were quickly prosecuted and sold into slavery. David had to watch as his family was sent in every different direction until, finally, he had the misfortune to be sent to Rome. He worked for a *patrician* for a while, teaching his children various principles in mathematics, but then eight months ago, David was accused of impregnating one of his master's daughters, which was a blatant lie—David assured. For punishment, his master had meant to send David to a man in Vonago named Sillex, who was a vicious teacher of slaves, but unfortunately, the master's penmanship was so horrible that the guards thought he was being sent to Silex Vorago. Next thing he knew, he was here, in the stone pits of Vorago, sweating away his youth in the blistering sun.

After dinner the little group gathered in a circle and, with the encouragement of Mathias, shared some of their deeper thoughts. Some of them talked of their hope in the afterlife; others shared experiences of God; and still others cried about their past. It turned emotional at times, when an individual was recalling his lowest moment. Finally, when the sun had fallen, David sang a low song that resonated off the walls of the cave.

Adon olam, asher malach,
b'terem kol y'tzir nivra.
L'et na'asah v'cheftzo kol,
azai melech sh'mo nikra.

V'acharey kichlot hakol,
l'vado yimloch nora.
V'hu haya, v'hu hoveh,
v'hu yih'yeh b'tifara.

V'hu echad, v'eyn sheni

l'hamshil lo, l'hachbira.
B'li reishit, b'li tachlit,
v'lo ha'oz v'hamisrah.

V'hu Eli, v'chai go'ali,
v'tzur chevli b'et tzarah.
V'hu nisi umanos li,
m'nat kosi b'yom ekra.

B'yado afkid ruchi
b'et ishan v'a'irah.
V'im ruchi g'viyati,
Adonai li v'lo ira.

The other five prisoners sat in silence, pondering the resonating lyrics. Finally the Egyptian spoke.

"What does it mean?"

"G-d is the master of the universe," David replied, "The L-rd who has reigned before all else was created. His power made the world, and even after it is gone, he alone shall still reign. To him I commit my spirit. If G-d is with me, I shall not fear."

"Singa anodder one," Alejandro interjected.

David shook his head. "I've been singing and talking all night; my voice is too tired to sing another. Why don't you let the Blacksmith talk for a while; he's been as silent as a stone, sitting over there against the wall."

"Yes, you have been, Verus," Mathias said quickly, picking up on the idea. "Why have you been so quiet this evening? Is it your disposition to be so silent, or is there something on your mind?"

The Blacksmith folded his large arms, shifting back as he did. "My son is out there, alive but alone. I need to escape."

All of them cast their eyes to the floor, awkwardly picking at their hair or sandals as they did.

Mathias was the first to break the silence, "There is no way out—no way except death."

Verus closed his eyes. "I can't stay. My son will die if I don't escape."

"Have you no family to take care of the boy?"

141

Verus bit down on his jaw—a tear began to fill his right eye. "They are gone now—everyone is gone. The boy has no one except me, no one to protect him. I must escape."

"There is no way to avoid this dread," Golias said in his eloquent voice. "A few people try every day, and they all end up dead."

"Then I will die and be free of this place," Verus said bitterly. "I would rather die with an arrow in my heart, than a whip at my back; I would rather live free for a few moments, than to be a captive for all eternity. If it is my destiny to die in this grave, then why should I stall my fortune? Tell me, how can I escape?"

"It's impossible," Mathias whispered. "We've all thought about it; we've all considered it. Even if we could break through our cell, we would have to climb the rock face in the dark—which is hard enough in the day—but then we would be faced with a fifteen foot wooden wall that is guarded by Roman soldiers. If we got past all of that—which would be near impossible because we are all chained together—we would be hunted down by a hundred men on horseback. Our tattooed arms and ragged clothes would gives us away and anyone that was loyal to Rome would report us. There is no way we would get far."

"There is," David said firmly. "Mind you, it is not a complete escape, but it is a way out of here."

"That is hardly an escape," Mathias interjected.

Verus leaned in closer. "Tell me."

David continued, "Every few months gladiator scouts come here and pick out a dozen or so men. If you can impress them, then they will take you out of here."

Golias scoffed. "They have a thousand choices and they only pick a few. Don't encourage him with that garbage you foolish Jew. I've seen those scouts before and they never buy any of the slaves; they are more interested in purchasing the guards than pulling us from our graves."

"They were just here," Verus answered. "When I was coming in, they purchased the large Gaul that was responsible for all the bruises on my legs."

"See," David said with a rushed voice. "They do purchase slaves."

"You would ztill be trapped," Cazeem hummed in his rhythmic voice. "By the fates zat you zeek to avoid, you would become your fate."

Everyone looked at the Egyptian.

"What?" Alejandro asked.

Cazeem cleared his throat. "Instead of waiting for death zhere, he would be dealing death out zthere. He would still be a slave, governed by a master; but now he would be forced to deal out death, instead of being subject to it."

"Yes," David said quickly, "but gladiators have freedoms that normal slaves do not: They can earn money and fame and, if you're talented, you can eventually earn your freedom."

"They can also be brutally killed, like a sheep that has outlived its usefulness," Mathias asserted.

"All I want is a chance to save my son," Verus said as he narrowed his eyes. "And whatever it takes—whether I have to walk through Hades to sell my soul—I will do it."

David leaned forward. "Become a gladiator and then it will be up to you to save yourself."

"How?"

"Make the scouts see how much promise you have—make them see how much of a fighter you can become."

Chapter 16
January 1, 70 AD
Priscus

"My name is Spiculus Arelias and I'm the *Magistri* responsible for you lot," said a large, hairy man in front of them. "I am your *Magistri;* I am your master. My title means that whatever I say, you will do. Make no mistake; this is not a common title that is given to even the best *Primus Palus* fighters, but one that is reserved for the Gods of the Arena. I earned this title with every scar on my body—with every opponent that I filleted in combat. While most of you were still sucking on your mother's tit, I was making myself a legend in the arena.

"Your lives are worth little now and much less if you don't obey my every word. You are part of a *collegia,* an elite group of fighters called the *familia gladiatorial,* and you will be trained to fight with honor and glory—even if it means your death. Right now you are slaves, sold by masters who did not care for you, but soon you will be given the chance to become gladiators—to take the sacred oath and enter a new society of warriors. There are over two-thousand people in this school who are training to be gladiators, only half of them will be up for the challenge. This school is an extension of the *Ludus Dacicus,* which is known to put out the greatest *Murmillo* fighters; you are all lucky to be here, lucky to be trained by the best."

The slaves were stringed out in a long procession of chains and shackles that were clamped around their wrists and ankles. Their march was slow and methodical. They were brought through three large arches and into a building that had two fires burning on a sandy floor.

The air was thick and heavy with heat, which wafted up from the sand below. Just as the last slave entered, they were commanded to stop. Priscus looked around, taking it all in. The compound was thickly walled and barred, making escape almost an impossibility. Even if one escaped out of the building, there was a series of walls that had a thick set of wooden spikes at the top that pointed every which way. Along the inside of the building was a series of wooden planks that were fastened together to make benches.

Spiculus turned and faced the grim slaves. "For those that have skill, being a gladiator can bring you wealth and fame, power and glory. The better fighter you are now, the more valuable you are to me; the more valuable you are, the better you will be treated. Once you become a gladiator you will have a large, single room, daily baths, oil massages, double the rations, and the occasional companionship of a woman, while the rest of you pukes have to scramble about for whatever you can find. If you can prove your skill to me now, I will skip your training and have you take the oath."

He pointed to one side. "I want all of the experienced fighters on this side. The rest of you maggots take a seat on the benches."

Another slave—a young boy no older than ten—came into the sandy circle dangling a thick set of keys; the slave went from prisoner to prisoner, unlocking each shackle and removing the long chain that held them all together. Once free, Priscus rubbed his wrist where the shackles had scraped his skin raw.

The Gaul quickly bounded towards the side for the experienced fighters, bumping past a few of the other slaves as he did.

"Are you anxious to prove yourself?" asked Spiculus.

Priscus clenched his jaw but did not answer.

"What is your name, slave?"

Still, the Gaul did not answer.

"You are a monstrous brute, aren't you?" Spiculus said as he eyed the Gaul. "But, don't mistake size for skill. Just because you're big, does not mean you're good. If you've never held a sword before, you better go to the other side."

The Gaul's only response was a set of narrowed eyes.

Spiculus flared his nostrils. "If any of you whelps come to this side—just so you can get treated better—and I find out that you can't wield a sword, then you better pray for the strength to live through the beating I am going to give you. For each of you must prove yourselves in combat by facing me."

Most of the slaves were stymied by this, unsure where they should go. Still, the largest contingent of slaves gathered themselves behind Priscus, determined to impress Spiculus with their skill.

"There is no shame in misjudging—only shame in showing so much hubris that you don't know your own skill," Spiculus yelled. "For those that can't pass this test, you will be known as *Novicius*, and there is no dishonor with this title. If after watching me decimate the first few, and you realize that you are not as good as you thought you were, you are free to join the slaves on the benches. If, however, you face me and lose, prepare yourself to be carried out of here—for there is no glory in this defeat. Now, who will prove themselves a son of Mars? Who is brave enough to fight me!"

Priscus gave out a loud laugh, which echoed through the circular arena. The laugh continued on for a few awkward moments; it rang through the sandy arena, reaching the ears of everyone that was there. Everyone else turned silent, including the small boy who was piling the shackles to one side.

Spiculus narrowed his eyes and screamed, "YOU! Brute, what are you laughing at!"

"It's you I am laughing at," Priscus replied. "You make it sound like your skill is legendary—you puffed up maggot. You really believe you're a son of Mars. You might have skill wielding a wooden sword and sliding along a sandy pit, but when it comes to battle, you're just a babe in the world of war. I step forward to challenge you. I will be the first to shatter your sword and bloody your armor."

Spiculus turned red with anger. Never, not once during his gladiatorial career, had anyone laughed at him, especially a slave. The gladiator stiffened his back and raised himself to his full height. "Yes, I will face you, but you will come last. That way you will have enough time to change your mind and sit on the benches. For I am SPICULUS ARELIUS and I was given a wooden sword by Nero himself; I proved my worth, rising through the ranks of gladiators, killing many o' fool along my way. Never have I been defeated in a game; never have I lost a match. Ten years I fought in the arena, dealing death to all those that stood in my way, and now a slave comes to me, thinking that he is my better."

"It is good you put me last," Priscus replied, "for once I'm done with you, you won't have the strength to stand—let alone fight anyone else."

Spiculus spat in Priscus' face, but the Gaul did not flinch or falter; he simply let the spit slide down his cheek until it finally dripped off.

"You fool," Spiculus hissed. The two stared at each other for a moment longer before Spiculus grabbed a man to Priscus' right. "You there. You're first. Grab a wooden sword and shield from the pile over there."

The stout *Magistri* turned his back to Priscus and stepped to the other side of the sandy pit, where another young slave boy was waiting. With the help of the slave, Spiculus put on a thick leathered sleeve over his right arm and a large helmet over his head. The *Magistri* looked even fiercer than he did before. He took up a Hoplite shield and a wooden sword.

The two opponents faced off in the middle.

A third gladiator, who until now had not spoken before, came to the center and barked instructions to the rest, "When I call halt, the fight is over. Are you ready? Begin!"

Spiculus immediately went on the offensive, charging the slave so quickly that the man could only step back in defense. Their swords struck three times in succession and then Spiculus barreled in with his shield, knocking the man off balance. It gave Spiculus just enough time to strike the man in the leg, sending the slave sprawling in pain across the ground. Using his shield, the slave was able to stave off a few more hits, but finally Spiculus broke through, hitting the man twice: once in the head, another time in the ribs. Blood squirted from the man's cheek.

"Halt!" The other gladiator called.

Spiculus pulled back. "Put him with the inexperienced fools; he can barely hold a sword." With this, the large *Magistri* spat and laughed, staring at Priscus as he did.

The next fighter was picked and pushed forward. Spiculus beat this slave just as quickly as the last; the slave limped away, covering a bruise on his arm.

"Inexperienced!" Spiculus screamed. "Next."

This third fighter was definitely more capable with a sword;

he lasted twice as long as the other two but, eventually, he was struck on the side of the neck, which knocked him out completely.

"This one has some skill," Spiculus ordered. "Drag his body down into the pit and lock him in one of the cells."

The next fighter went and then the next. Each one was brutally beaten until they were bloodied or bruised. Only a few were selected as experienced fighters, while the rest proved themselves wholly inadequate. None could stand before the *Magistri*. Finally, when the sun had reached its zenith, Priscus was the only one left.

"Are you ready for me, brute?" Spiculus jeered.

The large Gaul nodded and went to retrieve a wooden sword.

"Halt!" Spiculus yelled, "I need a drink. Guards, watch the brute—make sure he stays by one of the fires." With this, the large *Magistri* left the arena and headed to a lower level until he disappeared.

Priscus stood there waiting, his legs already sore from the march. The fire made him sweat so much that it was already dripping down his face and pooling in the center of his chest. The rest of the slaves watched him from the comfort of the benches, waiting to see if the Gaul would faint from the heat of the flames. Long moments passed, and then an hour. Still Spiculus did not appear.

Priscus wiped his brow and narrowed his eyes. Only one thought pulsed through his head: kill Spiculus. The longer he waited the more clear the thought became; soon he was chanting it to himself under his breath. Sweat now dripped freely from his brow, filling the air with the smell of his body. With each passing moment, hate burned in his stomach and filled his chest. His rage almost got the better of him, but before it could, Spiculus finally walked out. He was looking clean and fresh, almost as if he had taken a bath while he was gone. The *Magistri* took his time putting his armor back on and grabbing his weapon.

When he was all done, Spiculus finally laughed. "Now I'm ready."

Priscus wiped the sweat from his eyes and picked up a wooden sword and shield. The Gaul had a wicked smile on his face, almost as if he somehow knew how this fight would end.

"You arrogant worm," Spiculus said. "Keep that smile as long as you can, because it won't be long before I bust the teeth that are

148

behind it."

They both came to the center, staring at each other.

Another gladiator came over and put his hand in the middle, looking at the two fighters separately. With a dramatic wave of his hand he shouted, "BEGIN!"

While Spiculus had been fighting, Priscus had been watching the *Magistri*, watching every move that he made. He was good—there was no doubt about that—but the Gaul had seen this style before. The *Magistri* would always rush in, putting the other person on the defensive, until finally he finished the warrior off, but this often left Spiculus exposed to counterattack.

Spiculus barreled in, but so did Priscus. The two clashed shields. Priscus ducked behind his shield and swung at Spiculus' legs, hitting the *Magistri* across the calf and sending him reeling to one side. If they had been fighting with real blades, Spiculus' leg would have been chopped clean off.

The Gaul did not hesitate; he went in with a rain of swings. Spiculus stepped away, blocking the hits with his shield until he could recover. It took another few moments before Spiculus could swing back, but finally he did, nearly catching the Gaul's chin.

Priscus blocked two swings and then again went on the offensive, knocking Spiculus in the face with his shield. Infuriated, the *Magistri* came at the Gaul with full force, using his speed to send out a flurry of attacks. It went back and forth for a while—neither one could gain an advantage over the other.

Still Priscus grinned.

"I will smash your teeth down your throat and force you to choke on the pieces!" Spiculus yelled. With this the *Magistri* left the center, still watching the Gaul as he did, and exchanged his wooden sword for a metal one. "How about I use this instead?"

"No," one of the other gladiators protested, "Tresias paid a fortune for this one."

"Silence!" Spiculus yelled back. "This dog needs to learn obedience."

Priscus only laughed. "Even if you had a pick of weapons, with a lifetime to prepare with each one, you would never beat me—you waste of arrogant flesh. Fools at least know when they are beaten."

"DIE!" Spiculus screamed as he ran forward, swinging his shining sword furiously. Each swing took chunks from Priscus' shield or sword, but none of them could get past the Gaul's defense.

The Gaul ducked under a swing and struck Spiculus' leg with his shield. The shield was so frayed now, that when it hit Spiculus' leg, large splinters broke off and stabbed into the flesh, sending a stream of blood that dripped down. The *Magistri* limped back in pain and tentatively stared at Priscus, who simply stared back.

The two came at each other again—both of them swinging. Spiculus attacked and ducked, madly screaming when he came up. He found himself being driven back against the wall. With a large yell, he blocked and rolled away, just before he would have been pinned against one of the walls. Priscus lunged forward, hitting Spiculus in the back before he could escape entirely. The wooden sword thudded hard and knocked the wind from the man's chest.

The *Magistri* moaned in pain but refused to concede. "You've had all this time to watch me fight, Priscus—you vile maggot—and now you've used it against me. But now I've seen you fight—now I know your weakness."

"Then share it with me," Priscus growled, "I would love to find out if I had one." The Gaul went forward and lunged with his shield, knocking Spiculus back a step. They were in close quarters now, which put Spiculus in a desperate situation. Both swords thudded wildly against each other.

The *Magistri* swung quickly but he could not stave off all the attacks. Priscus hit him across the head, sending a pinging sound through the air. He was hit again. And then again. The helmet took several more hits until one of the eye holes was completely blocked.

Spiculus ducked behind his shield and slipped his helmet off, kicking it away as he did.

"Halt!" another gladiator yelled.

"NO!" Spiculus replied. "Let us be!" With this, the large *Magistri* ran in and stabbed for the legs, but hit nothing but dust. He went in again, but this time the Gaul blocked the attack with his sword.

Then suddenly, Priscus swung hard and true, hitting Spiculus in the face, spraying blood across the ground. But the Gaul gave no quarter. Spiculus was hit two more times in the face before he could even take another breath.

Another gladiator came from the side, hefting a wooden sword. "HALT!"

Priscus leveled this new man with his shield, and then went back to work on Spiculus, striking him until blood covered his face.

More gladiators joined in, rushing Priscus as he worked on Spiculus. The Gaul took them on, hitting one of them in the side and another across the cheek. A few of them wore armor, making it more than difficult to slow them down. More guards were called in—more wooden swords joined the arena. The Gaul now was backed against a wall, facing a dozen skilled opponents. He sidestepped and dodged an attack, and then kicked one of the guards in the chin; he broke the sword hand of a third and threw his shield at a fourth.

The gladiators then swarmed in, pinning Priscus' sword hand against his body. He was helpless to stop the beating that ensued. Through the pain his mind drifted off, until finally, his eyes closed and he felt no more.

* * *

Priscus was not sure if it was night or day when he awoke. He blinked twice, but still his vision did not come back to him. His body was sore and broken; blood had dripped from his right ear and dried on his neck. He lifted his hand and felt the side of his head—most of his ear was gone. When he touched it, a sharp pain shot through his body and tightened his chest.

His vision finally came to him: He found himself in a plush room that was seasoned with spices and filled with pillows. He thought he was alone at first but then a voice spoke. The noise made Priscus wince.

"You should have stayed unconscious. The healer has not seen you yet, and it will be painful when he does."

Priscus squinted his eyes. "What do you want?"

"I've got all I want," the voice replied. "Although you busted up three of my fighters and almost killed one of my instructors, I think it was worth the price of finding you."

"Who are you?"

"My name is Tresias. I am the *Lanista* of this gladiatorial *Ludi*." The man stepped out of the darkness and into the Gaul's field of vision. He was an older man with grey eyes and a narrow face that was tough as stone. "What is your name?"

"Priscus."

"Priscus? Where are you from?"

His head pounded as he talked. "Gaul."

The healer finally arrived. He wasted no time in rushing towards Priscus and examining his wounds. Tilting the Gaul's head to the left and right, he was able to gauge the depth and scope of each cut across the brute's face. "Not as bad as some of the others. His ear is useless—it will have to be cauterized. I'm going to have to clean these out before I stitch them."

"Go on," Tresias replied.

"Yes, sir," the healer answered. He gestured to an assistant who was standing a short distance away. "Bring me a basin of hot water." The healer began pulling out dirt and debris from Priscus' wound. While the man worked, Tresias continued to talk.

"In the year 46 BC, Julius Caesar—may the Gods bless his memory—staged a series of gladiatorial combats that far exceeded all precedence of the past. They were called *Naumachia*. Across the river Tiber, he had thousands of slaves carve out a lake and fill it with water. It took weeks to build, even longer to fill. Then Caesar, that unconquerable general, built ships—dozens of them: Biremes, with their double deck of oars; Triremes, with their heavy deck and three levels of oars; and finally Quinqueremes—the juggernaut of the sea. He then took 2,000 combatants and 4,000 rowers—all of them prisoners of war—and forced them to fight each other in an epic naval battle. The event went on for hours as they waged war on each other. Beneath the stars of the night, and screams of death, the soldiers pushed on, lighting the enemy ships with fire."

"Ah," Priscus grunted as the healer scrubbed at his wounds.

Tresias looked back at the Gaul and continued in a solemn voice. "The event was so popular that people have been talking about it ever since. Augustus replicated the experience in the year 2 BC, and Claudius did it again in 52 AD."

Priscus gritted his teeth as the doctor worked. "Why does this matter?"

The gaunt-looking man stepped closer to the Gaul, staring him straight in the eyes. "There are whispers that Vespasian is planning to do the same." He waited for a reaction, but Priscus did not give any.

Tresias threw his hands up and stepped away. "To the victors go fame and fortune. There are gladiatorial fights every day in Rome—there are so many good fighters nowadays it is hard to keep track of them all—but if one becomes a gladiator of the sea, that is something different entirely. These epic battles are rarely staged because of their enormous expense. But if you are in one, and you bring your side to victory, your name shall be in the ears and on the tongue of every *patrician* from Sicily to the Rubicon."

"Will I be paid?"

"Paid!" Tresias laughed. "If you are the champion of the *Naumachia* you will be as wealthy as a king. Not only will you receive a generous bounty for winning the fight, but you will become an instant legend. People will pay you to dine with them; they will pay you to appear at public rallies; they will even pay you to teach their children to fight. Your name will be shouted with glory and admiration. You will have more wealth than you will ever be able to spend in three lifetimes."

"And what of my freedom? Will I be free?"

"Maybe," Tresias said as he glanced down. "It will depend on the master that I sell you to. Some might want to sell you, while others might want to keep you; either way though, you should have enough money to buy your freedom."

"What do you want from me?"

"The gladiatorial battles are always replicated from historical battles and, consequently, both sides are led by a King. I want to train you to be one of the Kings of the *Naumachia*. You have no fear of death—no fear of life. I have never seen another man beat Spiculus; I have never even seen another man take on so many other gladiators. You are a gift, sent from the Gods."

Priscus looked down in thought.

"But in order to train you, I need you to obey," Tresias' voice dropped its excitement. "You can't hit another one of my *Doctores* again—you can't beat people mercilessly. The more teachable you are the quicker you will learn. The *Naumachia* is scheduled to take place a few years from now, and I need you to be ready. Even though you have skill with the sword, being a gladiator of the sea is completely different than fighting on land. You have to be trained to use the rocking of the ship to your advantage, trained on where to place your footing, trained on how to order your men to row and steer. If you can humble yourself, and be teachable, I promise you that you will be chosen to be a King. I promise you that you will make more coin than you ever knew existed. What say you, Priscus of Gaul?"

Priscus sat there for a moment before he finally stood and pushed the healer away. "I will learn as long as Spiculus is not the one to teach."

"I can arrange that."

"If you feed me meat instead of soup, give me room instead of a cell, and if you promise me wealth instead of poverty, then I will meet your challenge—I will be your Sea King."

"Yes! You will have to prove yourself amongst the other candidates for the spot of King, but I am sure you will beat them all. That is your destiny, Priscus of Gaul, to ride on the tides of battle, gripping your sword in one hand and fortune in the other, leading your men to victory. That is your fate: to become one of the Sea Kings of Rome."

Chapter 17

March 1, 70 AD
Verus

Clank. The hammer hit the chisel. Clank. It rang again.

"I need a break," Verus whispered. "I still have a few water tokens from yesterday."

It had been three months in the stone quarry and still no release came for Verus. He melded into the group of slaves and had become no different than any one of them. His clothes had become white, stained by the marble dust and rocks around him; his back had become hardened and calloused from the whip; and, like everyone there, his hope of release was fading like a setting sun.

David grabbed two of Verus' water tokens and held them high for the water maids to see. They were in the most dangerous part of the quarry, where the main rock is chiseled off and sent down. Already Verus had seen dozens of slaves crushed by stone, their bodies mangled and crippled by the unforgiving rock. Golias had been killed. It happened so suddenly that no one could shout out a warning or push him out of the way. A rock broke loose from the mountain, bounced once, and rolled right over him. Then the other slaves rushed in, stealing anything they could find. The body sat there for a while—still chained to the rest of them, stinking up the hillside—until finally the lethargic guards carted it off before it could spread disease.

The one benefit to working in the upper part of the quarry was that it took a lot longer for the water maids to reach them, which gave them a much longer break.

"That new slave," David whispered to Verus, "that came in to replace Golias, said that this stone is all going to Rome to build a gladiatorial arena."

"They already have a dozen of those in Rome," Verus replied.

"No. He says this one is bigger, a lot bigger. He heard Vespasian talking about it. He says that it will have room for over ninety thousand people."

"That is a lot of people. They say that there are twenty-thousand in this quarry; I can hardly imagine more people than that, let alone in an arena."

The slaves were sitting on the highest point in the stone valley; they could see half of the rock prison in the light of the day, while the other half was concealed by a large jutting rock. Thousands of faces dotted the land, toiling and suffering with exertion. The clanging of rock was so regular that it seemed like one constant sound. Verus and David were working close to the edge of a cliff that had a forty cubit drop-off that ended with rock and debris below. Besides the constant danger, it was an ideal spot to be working. Hardly any guards went up there, and even if they did, it was hard to see what the slaves were doing. Consequently, they took longer breaks and more of them.

David grinned excitedly. "Oh, good. It's Lucretia carrying the water—she takes twice as long as the rest of them. We can almost take a nap before she will make it."

"You should be eating more," Verus whispered. "I won't eat your food anymore."

David shook his head. "You'll need all the strength you can get when the scouts come, and I only give you a little more than what you already have. Don't worry about it."

"What if they don't come for another five months? What if they already have enough gladiators for now, and they don't come for a year?"

"Then I will give you some of my food for that year."

Verus shook his head. "You need your strength just as I do. You need to stay healthy enough so that I can rescue you."

Anger filled David's chest. "We've already talked about this. When you get sold as a gladiator, then you won't be around and I will eat my full portion again." The man took a deep breath and dropped the angry tone from his voice. "Listen, if you get tired out too quickly when we are fighting, they won't take you on. If you are too weak to stand, they won't buy you to be a fighter. We only have one chance at this, so we better make it a good one."

Verus rubbed his worn leg under the shackle. "Fine. You're right. Do you remember the plan?"

David nodded his head impatiently. "Yes, yes. We've gone over it a dozen times."

"I know, but you're right, we won't have a second chance at this. If the gladiatorial scouts don't buy me this time, who's to say that we'll even be alive for the next time."

David shifted. "All right. The plan is simple: When either one of us sees them, we are going to start shouting at each other. The shouting turns to pushing, and the pushing to punching. Soon, we will be wildly punching and kicking each other with so much ferocity that they won't want to turn away. You get the better of me and end up pushing my face into the dirt."

"Remember. Don't start pushing until they see us. If we start fighting too early, I don't think we will have much strength to keep it up. The shouting has to be loud or else they won't come."

"Just don't punch my face too hard," David said as he massaged his jaw. "Brotean really hit me hard the other day, and it hasn't felt right since."

There was a long pause in their conversation before Verus finally spoke.

"Why are you helping me? If I was with any of the others, I don't think they would even try."

David sighed deeply. "The gladiatorial scouts might buy both of us; maybe I'm just helping myself."

"They won't buy both of us if I get the better of you," Verus countered.

David shifted silently on the hard rock, thinking of a way to express himself. "I know that if you were out there and I was in here, you would try to get me out. I am not as strong as you, nor as built, so there is no way they would buy me. If you can get out, maybe you can save me somehow—maybe you can help save my family."

"Just hold on," Verus said. "Hold on and I will come back—I swear it. Once I have my son safe, I will get you out of here; whether I have to buy or break you out, I will make sure you are free."

David shook his head sadly, almost as if he did not believe Verus. "That would only be the beginning for me. After that I have to free my family. My father and mother, Jacob and Sariah, were sold to an Egyptian; my sister, Marian, was sold to an Iberian; my brother, Jarom, was sold to a fat Decian; my oldest brother, who's also named Jacob, was sent to Sicily."

"I swear by the sacred brow of Zeus that I will do all I can do to help you reclaim them."

David swallowed. "Our estate is still intact, locked away by a steward, or at least it was before I was sent here. The steward said he would take good records of where everyone went. His name is Simion Bar Sassom, and he is a good man, best one I have ever known."

"Here comes Lucretia."

A formerly plump lady heaved herself up the last bit of the path, sweating under the exertion of the heavy water skin. Lucretia had been a house slave and was accustomed to a plush life, but then her host family was slaughtered by the Emperor Galba and eventually she found herself in the quarry.

The slaves whispered warm greetings as she handed both of them cups of warm water. They drank it slowly, savoring every drop as it trickled down their parched throats.

Lucretia was still trying to catch her breath. "They're here…they're here."

Shock whipped through Verus' body, "Who's here?"

Lucretia took another deep breath, "The scouts…the gladiator scouts. Wasn't it you…who was asking…me to tell you…when they—"

"Yes," Verus interrupted. "But where are they? I don't see them."

"They will be coming…around the corner…here…soon."

Verus suddenly sprang to his feet and looked around, kicking up dust as he did.

"Easy," David said. "They will be coming to us; we don't have to go to them. Thank you for the water, Lucretia."

The water maiden nodded, turned around, and walked back down quarry towards another group of slaves that were waving their water tokens.

"We better get back to work," Verus said.

David nodded but sat there for a few moments longer. He

finally sighed deeply and started to stand, but before he could move, a whip slashed him in the back. It was Brotean. He had snuck up behind the other two while they were talking. The wicked-looking guard was flanked by two others who had whips in their hands and wood clubs at their sides.

"Get up!" Verus hissed.

David scrambled to find his feet but before he could, he was whipped again; his flesh ripped open and bled down his back.

Brotean was red with rage. "No one rests in my quarry! If you don't work, then you are useless to me."

"We were on a water break!" Verus said.

"You hold your tongue, slave! I saw him sitting there with my own eyes."

David tried to stand, turning around as he did; at the same time, Brotean flipped the whip for David's face, catching him in the eye. The Jew reeled back in pain and lost his footing. He found himself falling through the air—his arms flailing as he went. Verus dove for the chain that linked them together and held it tightly. The force of David's body jerked the chain taut and a sudden snap echoed through the valley. The Jew screamed. His body was swinging a few yards down from the forty-cubit ledge—his chained leg his only link to living.

Brotean laughed. "I heard his leg break! Come on men, give these other slaves some room to crowd in. They will have some business with the Jew."

"Hold on, David," Verus screamed over the edge. "Matthias, Cazeem, Alejandro—help me pull him up."

Cazeem screamed back, "He'z a dead man!"

"We are all dead men if we don't get him up!" Matthias retorted.

With this, the others came running. They crowded in, grabbing the chain. Between them all, they were able to pull him up slowly. Link by link the chain slid towards to the top.

David was still screaming. "Stop! Don't pull it anymore! Please!"

Still the others persisted.

Verus used his barreled arms and pulled harder than the rest. "Get him up here! Pull!" The Blacksmith could see the Jew's leg clearly—it had snapped right above the ankle. The foot was at a sickly angle and was already a blackish hue. When they finally pulled him up, Alejandro gasped at the sight of the David's wound; the little Iberian pulled back and looked away, speaking rapidly in his native language.

Bone had exploded out of the side of David's leg and was dripping with blood. He was slipping in and out of consciousness; there was vomit on the corner of his lip and down one side of his face. His body was so much whiter than before, except for the drops of blood that sprinkled down his legs and on his chin.

Mathias shook his head. "He's finished Blacksmith. Leave him here; the slaves are coming."

Verus looked up in time to confirm what the Christian had said: Dozens of slaves were on the move towards David, carrying whatever weapons they could find. They were screaming with vigor and excitement, almost as if this was some sort of athletic game.

Brotean encouraged them on. "There is a JEW up there with a broken leg. I saw him fall. To the one that strikes the killing blow, I will give him twenty water tokens and the rest of the day free of labor! Kill him! Strike him down and reap your reward!"

"Go along the chain and get as far away as you can," Verus yelled to the others.

"They will kill you just as well as him," Mathias protested.

"Run!" Verus replied. "My fate is linked with David's."

Mathias stared for a moment longer than he should have, but finally, with Alejandro tugging at his arm, he turned and went, running down the length of the chain, the sound of the links clanking as he did. The others quickly disappeared into the thick crowd of slaves that were closing in. Within moments, the mob was only feet away from Verus, greed shining in all of their eyes.

The Blacksmith grabbed his hammer and whipped it around in the faces of the slaves. "I am Verus Flaminius of Pinacale, son of Gaius Flaminius, who was a blacksmith as his father was before him, even as I am now. I've wielded a hammer my whole life, turning steel into swords and bronze into the hilts of daggers. Let it be known: There is no skull I will not crush, nor back I won't break with this hammer to protect my friend. You want water tokens! Take my tokens, but leave my friend behind! Take my tokens, and let your conscience be clear." Verus threw out three water tokens to the mob, but still the crowd pushed forward.

As one slave would venture too far forward, Verus would threateningly whip around his hammer, sending the slaves cowering back. Verus' eyes were so full of fire that no one dared to get too close. The stalemate drew on longer, neither side willing to yield.

Brotean was enraged. Vile spit flew from his mouth as he spoke. "FREEDOM! I will grant FREEDOM to the man that ends the Jew's life! Charge in and push the Blacksmith off the cliff; chop out the JEW'S heart and slice off his head! End his life and be rewarded with a life of your own!" Brotean drew a sword from his side and rushed forward until he was at the rear of the mob. In the still of the day, the slave driver's promise echoed across the quarry. Everyone, from the guards to the slaves, dropped their tools and looked up at the cliff face, straining to catch sight of Verus.

"I am one of you," Verus yelled. "Look at me! Hath I not eyes! Hath I not hands! Am I not fed by the same soup, hurt by the same whips, and subject to the same brutal slave driver as you? If you do not want to be killed like this, surrounded by screaming demons, how can you kill another? If freedom is what you seek, then step forward and I will use my hammer to set you free from this life; step forward and I will imprison you with death!"

A man to Verus' right did just that, stepping forward with a rock in his hand. The Blacksmith moved so quickly and struck so precisely, that the other man had no time to react. The slave's foot was crushed under Verus' hammer. Another slave leaped forward and Verus knocked the man in the face with the hammer, shattering the slave's jaw into pieces.

"BACK!" Verus yelled. "Or I will kill all of you!"

The crowd turned on itself and, instead of attacking Verus, went for the other two men who were wounded. But the Blacksmith would not have it. He charged in and punched a man in the face and kicked another, elbowed a third, and jabbed a forth in the throat. A fist came out of nowhere, but Verus ducked under it and returned his own. The fighting went on, but none could stop Verus in his rage. The Blacksmith stood over the men he had wounded, his large hammer bouncing in his hands. "No one dies this day—not by the hands of slaves."

The slaves who were able broke and fled down the mountain, dragging their wounded companions with them if they could. A half dozen or so were still dazed and confused; they painfully sat there as they gathered themselves.

Brotean breathed deeply as he watched with narrow eyes. With sword in hand he climbed up towards Verus, stepping over the bodies of some of the discarded slaves. "The Jew will be dead by the morning and you along with him."

"It will be on his terms then, not theirs," Verus replied. "You've made these slaves into murderers, forced them to kill to survive. Hades will not be pleasant for you, nor for those that follow your will."

"Guards, get him!" Brotean said to the soldiers at his side. But the soldiers did not move; they did not even respond.

Verus shook his head. "Come up here Brotean; come fight me yourself."

"Guards!" Brotean screamed.

"They've abandoned you, and so will the Romans when they find that you cannot maintain order."

"Surrender David to me and I will spare your life."

"Hah!" Verus laughed. "You *do* know him. In a place where everyone has a number, you know David's name. You coward! You can't live up to what you truly are. You traitor! Come restore order, then; come take my life before I take yours."

Brotean rushed forward with his sword raised—Verus met him, deflecting the first swing with a tremendous clash of metal. The guard went on the offensive, coming down on Verus with a series of quick attacks. The Blacksmith took two steps back and shifted position, putting the guard's back towards the edge of the cliff. They exchanged hit for hit. Verus ducked under and swung for the guard's feet, but the guard moved back just at the last moment.

No one in the quarry worked now; all hammers lay forgotten on the ground. It was strangely silent—only the clash of metal from the fighters echoed through the valley. The dust rose and shifted with a wind that suddenly rippled through and passed all the slaves' faces. Sweat beaded on everyone's brow as they looked out with a myriad of expressions.

The captain of the guards was now in the fight for his life, swinging madly at a man who was supposedly a simple slave. They locked weapons and tested each other's strength. The hammer grazed past Brotean's chest and then nicked one of his knuckles. Blood dripped down and splattered on his whitened sandals.

Brontean took another step back and then another; soon, he was dangerously close to the edge, but even closer to David, who sat there quietly moaning in pain. Verus had the guard cornered, trapped by the quarry that he had made himself. He had given Verus the better position so easily, so quickly.

"You're trapped," Verus said. "One more step and you fall to your death."

"Am I?" Brotean grinned wickedly. With this he lashed out his sword—not at Verus, but at David's exposed body. The blow struck perfectly, killing the Jew instantly.

The Blacksmith gasped, disbelief rolled over him like a sickening tide.

Brotean shook his head. "He was a beast that deserved to die." He hefted his sword up, and threw it with his might at Verus. The blade flew straight and true, but just as it was about to stick in Verus' chest, the Blacksmith deflected it with his hammer. The sword skidded across the rock until it disappeared over the cliff's edge.

Verus looked up to find that he now stood alone; while Verus was distracted with the sword, Brotean had fled. The coward was running madly, pushing past slaves and guards alike to escape from the Blacksmith. He had run a good distance until he hit a crowd of slaves that were meshed together. He pushed and bumped, shouting madly, "OUT of my way! A thousand lashings for everyone that does not move out of my way!"

But they did not budge, nor did they acknowledge he was even there. He was like forgotten debris that had blown into the quarry. He seemed to matter so little now.

Verus narrowed his gaze on the slave driver and clenched his jaw. He moved his chain to a jagged part in the rock and cleared the loose dirt around it. Then he brought his hammer down on the chain, sending a ringing through the valley that touched everyone's ears. Clang, the hammer resonated. Clang, it rang again. The Blacksmith worked faster and harder than he had ever before. With each strike, the chain rippled and bent, a small cut slowly spread wider in the metal. His forehead beaded with sweat, dripping down his face and stinging his eyes. The metal clanged and stretched, until finally, it snapped completely, setting Verus free.

Across the quiet quarry, Verus' stoic steps echoed through the valley. He walked past the other guards and slaves, who stared blankly at him. His hammer bounced dangerously in his hands. Brotean was petrified when he saw the Blacksmith coming; the once prideful captain of the guards now resembled a rabbit caught in a snare.

Slaves parted like waves before the Blacksmith. It took a few moments before he reached the cowardly guard, who was now on his knees, whispering prayers to his Jewish God.

"You've killed a good man."

"It was my right to kill him," Brotean hissed. "He's a slave, just as you, just as any of you."

"AND just as you are," Verus' said as his eyes flared. "AND so are the guards around you. You've been trapped here, buried amongst these dying slaves and sentenced to die. Instead of using your power to suckle the surviving, you've cursed your own people and whipped them until they died. I am not here to kill you, that was never my desire, for I will not have your foul blood on my hands, but I am here to exact payment for my friend. As you broke his leg, I will break yours."

"Please," Brotean whispered. "I will grant you freedom."

"Hah. You have no more power to grant freedom than you do to grant life. These Romans have never let you free a slave or else you would have freed yourself a long time ago. I may die this day, but I will live knowing that you—you cursed creature—can whip these people no more, that you can drive them to their deaths no more. Your promise is as empty as your heart, you worthless slave."

"Please!"

Verus brought the hammer down on the guard, breaking his leg exactly where David's had broken. Instantly, the captain of the guards screamed in a flurry of anger and anguish, his body writhing like a sun-scorched worm, twisting violently to either side.

Verus raised his voice across the crowd. "I leave it up to the rest of you whether he should live or die." The Blacksmith then turned around and walked away, leaving the man thrashing in pain.

"I WILL HAVE YOU KILLED!" was the last thing that Brotean ever said. The slaves came in and finished him quickly; water tokens were taken and flung out, flipping through the air like birds in the sky. Hundreds of thirsty hands grabbed them and waved them triumphantly.

Verus did not get very far before he spotted a Roman Century that had started marching through the front gate; they were armed with shining blades and blood-red shields that shimmered as they walked. Instead of fleeing before them, Verus went towards them; after what he had done, he knew it was him that they wanted. The Blacksmith and the soldiers met halfway, stopping only a few paces in front of each other.

"YOU! Slave," one of the Romans yelled, "what is your number?"

"My name is Verus Flaminius, and I am a slave no more. Brotean killed an innocent man, and his life was forfeit because of it. I only exacted the justice that FORTUNA would have demanded from me; my conscience is clear of guilt, just as my soul is pure. Take me. Bind me. Kill me if that is what you are here to do."

Another voice rang out from Verus' right. "Bind you? Hah! Kill you? There is no way I would do that after I have seen what you can do, nor after the price I have paid for you to live."

The Blacksmith looked to his right and saw a Citizen dressed like the wealthy Equites of Rome. He was atop a perfectly white horse that much reflected the color of the rock around them. The man was old, had a lean body, and white hair that flowed like silk in the wind. "These soldiers have come to your rescue, not to end your life—to free you, not bind you. Your life has been paid for in full, and now, you are mine. A better fate than death in a rock quarry awaits you."

"Who are you?" Verus asked simply. "What do you want from me?"

"I am Tresias of Nepet, the most famous gladiatorial *Lanistas* of the north."

Verus approached slowly, dropping his hammer as he went, and kneeled before the man. "I'm yours, as you say. And I will serve you until the last breath of my chest, but grant me one favor before I do."

Tresias frowned slightly.

"Give me leave to bury my friend, who lost his life for an evil cause. Allow me this and I will serve you better than your best warrior serves you now."

Chapter 18

January 2, 70 AD
Priscus

Priscus awoke, his eyes squinting in the faint light. It had been a long night, one in which he was constantly jerking awake with the throbbing pain in his bruised face and mutilated ear. He had been given a large cell—Tresias said that it was the biggest one he had. At one side he had a table and chair, on the other there was a straw mattress with a thick blanket. The room was heavily stoned and barred, with a door that was a finger's length in thickness. Next to his head, where he slept, there was a small grate that allowed him to barely see the other cell next to him. There was no prisoner in there now—from what he could tell—and it looked like there had not been for some time.

He stretched out his sore legs and put his feet firmly on the ground; then he scrubbed his face vigorously with his hands, accidentally bumping his bloody stump of an ear, which sent a shock of pain through his body. He sighed, breathing in the stale air. The cell smelled moist but not moldy.

"Gladiators, get up!" shouted a voice down a distant hall. The man screamed again, this time he was closer. "Gladiators!"

Priscus shuffled up out of bed, arching his back as he did. The door before him was suddenly unlocked and opened a small crack. The Gaul ducked under the small doorway and stepped into a mass of men who were heading down the hallway. All the slaves that were coming out now were experienced warriors—Priscus could tell. They all stood narrow-eyed and ready; scars of past wounds consecrated their bodies.

The hallway was long and narrow. The only source of light came from small torches and dim sunlight. The hallway finally opened up into a room that was surrounded by tall, old columns and arches. Some of the stone was new and bright, but most of it was cracked and worn. There were three or four guards in the room, their hands on the hilts of shining swords; they looked completely uninterested in the slaves that crowded in around them. The men filed out into a line, shoving past each other as they did. One person bumped Priscus' shoulder as he squeezed past; the Gaul frowned but did not react. The crowd became a line, and Priscus was at the end of it.

With a shake of his head, the Gaul stepped out of line and bounded forward, attracting the gaze of everyone he passed. He went to the front of the line and shoved the person who was supposedly first.

"Wait," the man protested, "there is a line here."

Priscus ignored the man as he grabbed a bowl from a stack that was off to the side.

"Hey!" another man yelled. "Get in line."

Priscus laughed. "I am in line—right in the front. This is where I will be from this morning out, and if one of you fools wants to challenge me for it, step forward—I would love to see the man who thinks he can best me." The Gaul's neck still had a trail of dried blood from his mutilated ear. He was so much bigger than the others, so much stronger looking that no one dared look him directly in his blood-lusting eyes.

"There is a group of us here," a third answered, "and all of us trained as gladiators. Don't be so foolish to think that you can beat us all. Just get in the back of the line."

The Gaul put down his bowl. "Then step forward, all of you; let's see if your talk is worth more than the air it took to say it."

They all hesitated for a moment, until one man—who was larger than the rest—began to step forward. Before his foot could even touch the ground, Priscus punched him in the jaw, sending the unprepared man flying backwards. The hit was so perfect, so quick and powerful, that the man instantly turned into a wet rag of muscle and flesh, his right leg twisting under him as he collapsed.

The guards drew a set of wooden clubs, but did not move from their posts; instead, they watched with interested grins that wickedly spread across their faces.

"Is that it!" Priscus laughed at the group of gladiators. "You cowards, all of you! You've been trained for combat but when it comes to it, you're useless."

"Put a sword in my hand—then we will see if you can stand against me," one of the other gladiators yelled.

"Hah!" Priscus jeered. "Ask Spiculus about that. Ask Spiculus if a sword in his hand did him any good."

Another man, one who had witnessed Spiculus getting thrashed the day before, whispered to the others around him. "I saw it: the Gaul just about killed Spiculus. He beat him so badly that he had to be carried from the arena. The old gladiator might've even died from his wounds last night."

The whispering spread like a ripple in a pond, sprawling out from ear to ear as the gladiators glared at the Gaul. The air was thick with tension; each side measuring up the other, trying to decide what to do.

One of the older fighters finally spoke. "Take your food, Gaul. We won't fight you."

Priscus still had his jaw clenched and his eyes narrowed but, finally, he turned away, grabbed his bowl, and walked over to a large cooking pot. Three or four slaves stood there, staring at the large Gaul with eyes as wide as the ladle they used. Priscus took in an impatient breath.

"Sorry, sir," one of them said as he slopped a thick soup, which was a mixture of beans and barley, into Priscus' bowl. The Gaul was also given a large piece of bread and cup of olive oil to dip it in. He did not take the oil but, instead, he took another piece of bread.

"You're only allowed one…" one of the slaves began, but before she could finish, another slave elbowed her into silence.

With another lethal glance at the warriors behind him, Priscus went and sat down at a small table that was made for four. The rest of the gladiators followed through the line, taking their soup and sitting at other tables. One of them gathered his courage, took a deep breath, and sat down across from the Gaul.

"Are you sure you want to sit here, boy?"

"I saw you yesterday," the other one whispered. "I saw how good you are with the sword."

"I already know that, but you did not answer my question: Are you sure you want to sit here—boy." Priscus' voice was as harsh and cold as winter wind.

"I just saw this open chair," the man asserted. "I thought...that...that you wouldn't mind."

Priscus narrowed his eyes.

"My name is..."

"I don't care about your name, nor do I care where you're from; this is my table—no one else's. Be gone before I split your lip and drip blood into your soup."

The gladiator swallowed and began to stand. "I'm sorry."

Before he could leave, Priscus stuck out his hand. "Wait." The Gaul grabbed the other man's soup and poured half of it into his bowl, which overflowed slightly and dripped down the sides. He then slammed the man's bowl onto the table. "Now you can go."

The gladiator was trembling slightly. He tried to speak but no words came out; instead, he began vigorously nodding his head. The shaking man turned and went away, looking for another seat. After seeing that there were no chairs left, he ended up leaning against one of the pillars and awkwardly holding his bowl with one hand, while shoveling food into his mouth with the other.

Breakfast was strangely quiet that day, almost as if the men were paying homage to a God. In truth, however, each gladiator was whispering about the Gaul: They talked about his size and bloody face; they guessed at his skill with the sword and shield; but mostly, they talked about how fun it would be to end the brute's life.

After breakfast, the gladiators were shuffled into the same indoor sandy arena as the day before and split into groups of two.

Another gladiator, dressed in the armor of a Roman Legionnaire, stepped forward. "All of you have talent with the sword, and that is why you are here; but it will still be to your benefit, and mine as well, if we drill the basics. For the next several weeks the schedule will be the same as today: You will eat breakfast and then come drill on the arena grounds until lunch."

"What happened to Spiculus?" one of the gladiators asked.

The man looked straight at Priscus, staring at him harshly, "He caught a nasty blow to the head. I will be teaching you in his place. Now, all of you have talent, otherwise you would have been grouped with the hundreds of others that are only beginning to learn the sword, but that does not mean you are above my instructions. If one of you does not obey my word, you will be punished harshly and quickly. I will turn you into the best gladiators in the world but you must be willing to become so. Pride will slow your progress. If anyone questions my will, or moans when I give an order, he will be whipped until his back is bleeding. I don't care who you are—whether you are the son of Jupiter himself—you will obey me. There is only one voice that matters when we are together—that is mine. Listen to no one else, including your fellow gladiators. I am your teacher, not they; I will punish you if you do not obey, not them. Now line up and grab a sword."

They were each given a sword and shield and were set about doing a series of basic lunges and blocks. The building was hot in the morning, and scorching by noon; each of them was sweating like melting candles. A few of them asked for water and they were whipped for it; the rest fell into a deep silence.

After these basic drills they had another meal, where they were served flatbread and a soup that was a mix of vegetables and barley. They were then sent to the heated indoor pools that were next to the bathhouse. The pool was long and wide, and divided by nets that stretched out into the distance.

One of the gladiators stood before them. "Most of you do not know, but because of your skills, you gladiators have been set apart for special training. Apart from your gladiatorial skill, you will also be trained in naval combat. You have been selected as *Naumachians*—the gladiators of the sea. While one portion of your training will cover your gladiatorial sword play, the other portion will train you on how to man and command a ship."

A few stirred in surprise.

"Each one of you has the potential and the skill to master the seas, each one of you has the skill to lead men into combat, but now we will see who has the determination. There are almost forty of you here, which means that only half of you will become *Naumachian* commanders; the other half will serve in lesser positions. To the commanders go fame and wealth, power and glory. One among you will be selected to be the Sea King and will lead the entire naval army into victory or defeat."

"This gladiatorial school is only one of four other schools that are competing to produce the two gladiators that will be the Kings of the *Naumachia*. As for the commanders, if you are selected, then you will be assigned two hundred men. You will be responsible to organize them, train them, and ultimately, lead them into the *Naumachia*. That is what is at stake now—that is why you are here. Now, strip down and get into the water."

Obediently, they began taking off their clothes and tucking them away into shelves that were along the walls. Priscus was the second into the water, which felt cool at first, but then quickly became inviting. Careful to keep their distance from Priscus, the rest waded in and crowded around their instructor.

When everyone was in the water, the instructor went over a few basic strokes, speaking slowly as he did. Once in a while, he would call on volunteers to demonstrate a stroke or technique. "I will be watching you to make sure you are doing it correctly. The better your technique, the less fatigued you will be. Now, I want you to swim from here to the other end of the pool and back using the first stroke that we went over."

With this, the gladiators kicked off and swam. Some had a little experience with swimming, most had none. It looked pitiful as the first few kicked and spluttered in the water, thrashing about in panic. Priscus was able to kick out further than the rest and stay ahead of them, but he had completely neglected the stroke he was supposed to do. Instead he trudged through the water, paddling like a frightened dog.

Only one of them was experienced enough with swimming to know what he was doing; he broke from the rest, doing a perfect example of the correct stroke. Priscus swallowed a little water in the wake of the fast swimmer and swore under his breath.

Their instructor was now walking along the edge of the pool, madly shouting out instructions to the thrashing individuals in the water. "You! The big brute in front! Lay on your side and use big long kicks or you will wear yourself thin! You, the one with golden hair: Stop trying to keep your head dry. Look at the one in lead; see how quick he goes because of his technique!"

This went on and on as the struggling gladiators swam. A few of the gladiators were so tired their heads slipped under water; each time this happened, the instructor would jump in and rescue the men from drowning.

Priscus was one of the first to finish the lap, but he was winded by the end of it. He had worked so hard just keep himself afloat that his progress had been painfully slow.

The instructor helped the last few swimmers in and then splashed into the water himself. "Wasn't that tiring? Only one of you was doing it right. I want you to swim it again—this time, practice the stroke; it may seem awkward at first, but it will save you energy in the end. Now, swim!"

Again they swam out; this time Priscus found himself being passed up.

The instructor turned red with rage. "Brute! Change your position! Change your position! Do the stroke!"

Priscus growled and pretended like he did not hear. Instead, he kept on doggedly treading water until he was halfway. More of the gladiators swam past him, kicking water in his face as they went.

"Change position! You're doing it wrong!"

Eventually, the gladiators finished up the lap; this time, Priscus was towards the rear. His chest was seething for breath and his eyes were bloodshot from the water. His once thick and wild hair now stuck to his skin like a leech.

The instructor had his whip out and waved it threateningly in the air. "Some of you must not be able to hear me. I want you to do the stroke that I showed you—the one that we practiced." He then turned his head towards Priscus. "Where are you from?"

"Gaul."

"Hmm...so you're the one that everyone is talking about; you're the one that blinded Spiculus in his right eye. You might be Mars with a sword, but you're no Neptune in the sea. Listen to me: Shelve your pride or you will not live to see the next day. If you ignore me when I instruct you, I will ignore you when you're drowning. All of you will swim another lap, and then another, and another after that, until this Gaul finally learns to swim it right. Now, swim."

Again the gladiators began to swim the lap. This time, Priscus was passed up by everyone, including several smaller, weaker swimmers; the Gaul persisted in his thrashing style, which took twice as long as everyone else. By the time that he made it halfway, everyone else had made it back.

The moment Priscus finished, the instructor told them to swim it again; and then again. Four more times they swam it—each time Priscus swam it slower.

"I'm sure," the instructor whispered to Priscus, "that if you don't swim it right this time, you won't have the energy to swim back, and I won't jump in to save you, unless you finally start doing it right."

But the instructor was wrong. Priscus was able to swim back, and then again, but after a third lap the Gaul was too exhausted to continue. His arms were so tired and his breathing so labored that he almost wished to drown in the water. The Gaul's head sank beneath the surface, *"I just need to rest."*

True to his word, the instructor did not jump in after him, nor did anyone come to his aid. He was all alone as he sank deeper and deeper beneath the water. Memories filtered through his mind: First, he remembered his father, and then Trontian—his long ago friend; finally, his thoughts rested on the brutish face of Sedrix the Celt.

"It can't end here..." Something tugged at his heart, which gave him new resolve; he kicked out of the water, shooting up like a piece of driftwood. He changed his position and began the stroke the instructor had taught. It was awkward, but doable. Between mighty breaths of air, and an occasional rest beneath the water, Priscus slowly made his way back.

The instructor shook his head in disbelief. "You wretched Gaul. I almost have to let you drown before you will let yourself be taught. Dry off, get dressed, and follow me. We have a little march we have to make."

After dressing, and a short rest, the group of gladiators followed the instructor to another building—Priscus brought up the rear. They were then sent with another troop of guards that marched them out of the compound and towards a lake that was some distance away. Without a word to each other, they ran on and on over the grassy terrain. To Priscus the hike was simple and short, but to most of the others, who were now gasping for breath, they could not wait to stop. They finally did stop at a building that extended out into a wide lake.

The structure was like an extension of the gladiatorial pit that they had just left, having several thick walls and spikes that poked out of the top of them. It was, however, simpler in design and construction. Most of it was made from logs that were piled on top of each other. After resting for a while, the *Doctore* led them out and away from the building. They walked a little distance along the shore of the lake until they reached an enormous stack of wood. "Take a seat where you can find one," the instructor said. He waited a moment before he continued. "Rome gained its independence from the Etruscans in the year 410 BC. It then spent the next hundred years engaging in a war with its former masters for domination of Tuscany. After winning this war, Rome took over city after city, conquering everyone they came into contact with. Nothing could stop them. Rome's power and influence spread from the southern tip of Italy to the northern Alps. The Romans seemed unstoppable, that is, until they were challenged by the navy of Carthage. While Rome had spent all of its time perfecting the art of land war, Carthage was spending its time perfecting fighting on ships. Never had the Romans engaged in a naval battle. The only ships they had built were for merchants and traders.

"But Rome was not beat. They eagerly fitted their merchant ships for war, arming them with flaming arrows and catapults; these, however, were quickly crushed by the more powerful Carthagian ships. Then Fortuna blessed the shores of Tuscany and caused a storm to blow one of the enemy ships aground. It was broken in two and impossible to repair, but the Romans studied it extensively until they were sure they could replicate it. Using this new design, Rome built hundreds of these ships and sent them out to sea. It was not many years later that the Carthagians were suing for peace.

"In order to understand a ship's weakness, you will be building one yourselves. You will see where the thickest and thinnest timbers are used, where a ship is most likely to sink if hit. You will see where the oars go, how strong they are, and how to best use them. In essence, you will be learning how to win."

175

Chapter 19

March 5, 70 AD
Verus

"I am Spiculus and I will be judging your skills," said a large, but extremely hairy man. The gladiator had a patch over one eye and a huge scar that draped down his face. The marks were purpled and red, almost as if they were only a few weeks old. Despite this wound across his face, he seemed capable enough to hold his own; he pulled a sword out and pointed it at the slaves before him.

The air was cool and windy since spring was still clinging to the precipice of winter. The walls and guards around them seemed as cold as the air and twice as unforgiving. There were dozens of guards, all of them hefting large swords at their sides and wooden clubs in their hands.

Spiculus turned and faced the slaves. "If you are a skilled fighter, you will be treated differently. If you can fend off one of these gladiators—these ones that are at my side—then you will be made a gladiator yourself, here and now. If you can't pass this test, then you will be called a *Novicius*—a gladiator that has not yet proved themselves to the *Lanista*. The rest of you will be fed and given little until you can prove yourself. For those that have skill, being a gladiator can bring you wealth and fame. The more apt a fighter you are, the greater your value. Prove yourself to me and you will be rewarded. I want all those that have experience to sit down on the seats behind you, while the rest of you follow Turthius so you can to begin your training. If you don't have skill with the sword, then don't think about trying to become a gladiator now; but for those that do, may the Gods bless you with strength this day."

Verus took a second or two to decide where to go. He was tempted to try to pass the gladiatorial test now, but he finally shook the idea off, deciding that even if he did pass the test, he would need the training later. He was the first to join Turthius, who was a smaller, thinner fighter. Soon others joined them until half of the slaves ended up following Turthius down a long stony pathway that sunk deeper into the earth. They made a few turns, passing small cells on either side, until they arrived at a large arena that already had twenty or so men there.

Turthius turned and faced them. "Always take off your sandals before you step out into the arena; bare feet will give you a better grip on the sand. All of you were chosen for your strength or your speed; but just because you were chosen, does not mean you will pass. The training of a gladiator is tough and ruthless; it will far surpass any of the labor you have done in the past. Some of you are here on your own accord, contracted to serve for three or five years or until your death in the arena, while others of you are here as slaves. Whether you are the son of a beggar or the bastard boy of a senator, you will find equality here in the arena. Only your skill matters now. You will be trained for three to six months before you are put to a test: If you pass, you will take the oath as a gladiator and begin your climb to glory; if you don't, you will repeat the training.

"All of you will be trained with multiple weapons but most of you will specialize with only one weapon. You will be selected for your skill during the next few weeks and then divided into specific types of gladiators. Before you now are the eleven classes of gladiators; across the empire, there are many more classes of gladiators, but only these types are trained here. First, and one of the most popular, is the Murmillo. He carries a square Legionnaire shield, a leather arm guard, a high crested and finned helmet, and is armed with the gladius. His armor is similar to a Roman Legionnaire, but his fighting style is drastically different."

Turthius moved on to the next man. "Next is a Thraex, who was modeled after the warriors of Thrace. He carries a small square shield that is used like a ram and a short but sharp, curved blade that is excellent at getting around a defender's shield and slicing their skin.

"This next man is a Secutor, the juggernaut of the arena. He, by far, carries the heaviest armor, from his ten-pound helmet to his body-length shield. His helmet is slick and rounded—so that netted weapons slip off him—and he has small eye holes to protect him from the trident of a Retiarius.

"This slave is a Retiarius and is considered the least important of the all gladiators. He is armored with a high shoulder guard and sometimes a leather sleeve for his lead arm. He is given a trident, a dagger, and a net for combat. The Retiarius and the Secutor are often paired together in combat. The Retiarius depends solely on his speed and maneuverability to survive the onslaught of the heavily guarded opponent.

"This next man here is a Hoplomachus, and he uses a strategy and fighting style similar to a Greek warrior. He has a small but heavy, round shield that is used as a weapon just as much as his light spear. He often is given a dagger or sword in case his spear is thrown or busted.

"Next to him is a Dimachaerus. And like his name implies, he carries two swords instead of a shield. Although initially these frantic warriors are given little armor, as their skill increases they often are better equipped.

"Next is the Laqueriarius, which is similar to the Retiarius, but instead of a trident, he uses a spear and lasso. He usually is not given any armor and, consequently, must depend on his skill with his lasso and spear to keep other fighters away from him.

"This next fighter is a Samnite—which is the oldest of gladiatorial styles still around today. His armor, specifically his helmet, comes from the army of the long-conquered Samnium. It is rare to see these fighters in the arena—especially since Augustus saw these gladiators as an insult to his then allies the Samnium—but recently they are becoming steadily more popular. They have square shields, but no arm guards. Their helmets are plumed with feathers and they are armed with the gladius.

"Next is the Quadrant, which is a new gladiator that is rising in popularity. He is so named for his weapon, which consists of four bars that are shaped in a square. The weapon is excellent for catching an opponent's sword and flicking it away. These gladiators take on various arrays of armor.

"Next to him is a Galli—or a Gaul. He is armed with lance, helmet and a small shield.

"This next warrior is a Provocatores, and is the only fighter that has a breastplate. He is one of the most versatile fighters since he uses different armor every time. The most distinguishing thing about him is the flat-brimmed helmet—which has a large feathered plume on the top—and the breastplate he wears. He often is equipped with a square Legionary shield, and a gladius. He usually has only one leg guard and no arm guards.

"These are the gladiators we train here. If you have the strength and skill, you will be trained to specialize in one of these weapons. Now, grab a wooden sword—which is called a *rudis*—and a shield. Let's begin."

They drilled on for a time, stabbing and slashing with various attacks and jabs. They were steadily joined by more gladiators that were coming from dinner. The arena filled up until there were over three hundred of them that trained in the sand. Despite the various levels of skill, none of the slaves that trained were gladiators yet. Turthius drilled them long and hard, until their legs were sore and their skin glistened with sweat. Finally, as the sun set, Turthius led his small group back down into the *Ludi*.

As they walked, the little warrior started assigning slaves to cells. Even though Verus was first in line, Turthius selected two others to go into the first cell and two more in the next. Soon, Verus found himself alone with little Turthius.

"Are you the Blacksmith?"

"Yes," Verus answered.

"Good. I thought you were. By Tresias' order your cell is over here." They walked on, both of their sandals flapping on the hard rock. They made a few more turns until they finally reached a door that was bigger than all the others they had passed.

"You don't share your cell with anyone, which is a treatment that I have never seen a slave receive—usually only gladiators get a private cell."

"Tell Tresias that I am grateful."

The little gladiator nodded and unlocked the door. "He already knows that you are."

"My name is…"

Turthius shook his head. "Never tell other gladiators your name until you are sure that you will never meet in combat. One day you might have to kill each other and it would be that much harder if you knew their name. It's best to be known as 'the Blacksmith'."

Verus swallowed and nodded.

"Rest for now. You will be eating supper soon."

Verus nodded again and entered his cell. It was larger than he expected but darker than he cared for. A small shaft of light came from a heavily barred grate high above. There was a straw mattress on the right side of the room, which Verus moved to the left, and a chair that looked like it was going to break. There must have been more furniture before because the cell seemed too expansive for just a bed.

The Blacksmith lay down on the mat, thoughts rolling over his mind as he did. It was not long before he was thinking about his wife and children; the memories were so fresh that it seemed laughable that they had been killed a few months before. Their deaths were finally becoming real to him. They were gone—he knew that now—but it did not make it easier. In the heat of the quarry he at least had his work to keep him busy, but now, as he lay there alone—having no one to talk to—tears welled up. The tears did not come in wrenching sobs that tore at his chest—like they did the first night he discovered his family murdered—but they dripped out of his eyes like a misty rain.

He must have dozed off, for in the next second, someone was shouting at him.

"Hey!"

Verus kicked awake and looked around—he was still alone.

"You there—stop screaming!"

Verus tried to find the origin of the voice. It seemed like it was coming from the very wall itself. "*Ave?* Who's there?"

"I am. And stop screaming or I'll cut out your tongue."

The Blacksmith finally realized that the voice was not coming from outside his cell door, but through one of the walls; he felt around and found a small drainage hole on the floor. He looked in it just in time to see a blood-red eye looking back.

Verus waited for a moment before he answered. "Was I screaming?"

"Yes."

"I'm sorry. I must have of dozed off, I haven't had…"

"I don't care," the voiced hissed. "There's already enough noise in this place without you yelling through the drain pipe next to me."

"Who are you? Are you a gladiator?"

"Yes, of course."

"How did you get here?" Verus asked. "Were you a slave?"

"Who are you to be asking me questions?"

"I'm nothing—no one. I was a...a..." Verus was about to say he was a blacksmith, but then for some reason he became suddenly cautious. "I was a... lumber-miner before this, and somehow—I am not exactly sure—I ended up here."

"Will you stop talking!"

"Why are you so hostile? Who are you?"

"I swear by the blood of *Tiwaz*, if you were before me right now, I would chop your head off."

"Well you can't," Verus answered. "There is a thick wall separating your foul stench and me, and unless you can tear it down, that wall is going to stay."

"What is your name?"

Verus shook his head, "What's yours?"

The voice took a moment to respond. "I'm the Gaul."

"THE Gaul," Verus mocked. "THE Gaul. I was scared that you were just another Gaul, but I am glad to meet THE one and only Gaul."

"If you don't know me now, lumber-miner, you soon will. I am the *Primus Palus*. Do you even know what that means, you ignorant waste of flesh? I've defeated every gladiator they have set before me, breaking their bones with my will. Don't let pride swell you up just because you're training with a wooden sword. Now stop moving your mouth or I will separate your jaw from your head the moment I see you."

Verus thought for a moment before he answered. "I just lost a close friend; I saw him writhe in pain before he was finally cut across the throat. I was thinking about how—"

"Is that what your nightmares are about?" Priscus jeered. "One man out of millions is killed, and all of a sudden, you can't sleep at night? Well, lumber-miner, you're training to be a gladiator, and in case no one has told you yet, let me be the first: You're being trained to be a killer."

Verus narrowed his eyes. "This man was a friend of mine—

he was a Jew."

"That doesn't make a bit of difference. If he's human, he can die like the rest of us. I've lost many men who I trusted most in battle, but you don't see me kicking around screaming at night."

"Were they your friends or family?"

The Gaul hesitated a moment, straining the corners of his mind for a response. "What does friendship mean? What is family? Those are just random words that describe relationships. These men were my subordinates; they were entrusted to me, and by my command, they met their glorious end."

"That's not the point," Verus shifted his position on the straw mat. "And I doubt any of them meant more to you than a set of tools."

"You can't let them mean anything more than that; if you do, then you open yourself up for pain. I've seen it hundreds of times, where two friends would join a Legion just to have one of them killed later in battle. The other would mourn and cry for days, pining for his dead friend. The soldier was useless for weeks after, and sometimes forever. Why would anyone put themselves through that again and again?"

Verus rubbed a hand through his hair. "I once spoke to a man who told me that happiness comes from our relationships. He believed that when we are charitable to others and forge these relationships, we will find meaning in life."

"What was this man's name?"

"Plini the Elder."

"Well, Plini was never a soldier."

"Yes, he was. He was a great leader and commander in Gaul, where he led many campaigns to victory."

"He must have been a distraught man when you met him."

"No. In fact, I've never seen another man more charitable, more in tune with the world around him. When I met him, he had been exiled by Vittelian, stripped of his power and position. He would've been on the brink of starvation had it not been for the relationships that he had forged earlier in life. It was these relationships that sustained him."

"And what if those relationships are taken from you by the point of a sword?"

Verus felt his throat knot up and his eyes become misty; he did not answer for a long while—he couldn't. He took a breath and forced down the emotion, making sure that the sadness was not evident in his voice when he answered. "That can happen. And I am sure that Plini had seen it happen; but he believed that if one makes meaningful relationships wherever one goes, building upon those relationships with charity, then he will be happy—no matter what befalls him."

Priscus laughed hard, scorning every word that Verus had uttered. "CHARITY? Hah! Friendships? That is not what makes a man happy, that is not what makes anyone happy. This Plini figure is a fool—a thief who was trying to get your money—"

Anger rippled through Verus. "He *gave* me money. He was the one that helped me when I was struggling, not the other way around. And don't try to convince me that you are happy, or that you have ever been; you're an embittered man who copes with his fears by coercing others. I imagine your men did serve you well, but only out of fear; I bet that when you were sold as a slave that all of them reveled in the idea. I bet they were thrilled at the prospect of ridding themselves of you."

The Gaul did not answer for a while. "What is your name? WHAT IS YOUR NAME!" The Gaul kicked at the wall and threw a table across the room, sending it thudding against the wooden door. "I will kill you, you and everyone who stands around you! How would you know what life is about? You don't know anything about the cruelty of the world. What is your name?"

The Gaul continued to scream for a long time, but finally, as Verus was released for supper, the large Gaul's voice began to fade. The Blacksmith was taken to a large room that was filled with other nervous men who did not seem to quite belong. No one seemed confident or bold in their speech. After receiving a small bowl of soup and a chunk of a flatbread, Verus sat down next to the doorway. A guard stood nearby, his eyes darting to each of the amateur fighters before him. It was Turthius.

Verus cautiously looked around while he built up his confidence. Finally, when he had already finished half his bowl, Verus leaned over to the guard and whispered, "What do you know about the Gaul?"

Chapter 20

April 6, 70 AD

Priscus

For the first three months, the gladiators spent their time drilling with the sword, sharpening and reinforcing the skills they already had. Many of the men had served as soldiers at one point—either for Rome or one of its allies.

After that, their routine changed sharply; instead of drilling in the morning, they were assailed by the same task: building the Trireme. After a few hours, they ate a noon meal, swam laps for however long their *Doctore* wanted, lifted weights, and then trained with their various specialized weapons. The *Doctores* treated the gladiators with more respect now than they did before. The training was brutal—but not in the sense that they were whipped for every mistake they made; instead, they were forced to run additional laps or do additional drills. In the evenings, they were relatively free to wander through the compound, as long as they did not leave it.

By far the most favorite spot of all the gladiators was the bathhouse, which had three separate rooms, all of them a different temperature. The gladiators would bathe with olive oil, washing the dirt from the day's training. Then slaves would give them a massage, rubbing their sore muscles until the tension disappeared.

By order of Tresias, Priscus had been made the *Praefecti* and was put in charge of the building of the ship. Despite everyone's disbelief, including the guards', the Gaul proved more than capable at organizing everyone and delegating responsibilities. He divided everyone into two large groups and assigned a leader over each; he then broke each of those larger groups into two smaller groups, again appointing a leader. Finally, he broke the groups down even smaller, leaving three or four individuals in each core. This, as Priscus explained, gave a perfect level of accountability for each individual.

The results of Priscus' organization were immediate: there was no confusion or delays on the construction; there was no question of authority; and there was little or no disobedience. The ship construction went twice as fast as anyone could have hoped. It rose from the ground like some gigantic titan coming to life.

The organization was so defined that no one was allowed to talk to anyone except their direct supervisor, who in turn had to talk to his supervisor. Priscus flatly refused to listen to anyone except two or three other men who worked directly with him. One of these men was a shipbuilder by trade. He had years of experience building ships and proved invaluable to the operation. The ship they were building was called a Trireme, and it was as complicated as it was big. It was so named for the three different banks of rowers: The *Thranites* sat on the deck and wielded the longest oars; the *Zygites* were seated in the middle; and the *Thalamites* were cramped in the damp bottom.

The Gaul's voice rang out over laboring gladiators as he barked out orders. "Tighten that rope or I will tighten it around your throat! Come on, you slug—put your back into it."

At least once a day, Priscus would become so infuriated with one of his subordinates, he would drag the unfortunate man out and hold his head under the water, swearing all the while. Sometimes he would hold the man under water so long that his limbs would become weak and slow. The Gaul knew just how long he could do it before it would kill the man completely.

Almost twice a day, as the ship was rising from the ground, one of the gladiators would accidentally let one of the main supports slip, or fail to hold a beam tight, or drop a tool in the mud. If Priscus saw the whelp, he would curse the man out with a stream of swear words that would have offended the most vile of *Damnati*. The Gaul would then stick his nose in the other man's face, spit flicking out of his lips as he did, and berate the unfortunate fool until the man would put up his hands and crumple to the floor like a child.

The whole building process was filled with the Gaul's general insults. "You aren't gladiators, but actors, pretending to be tougher than you are. You've got more place as a thespian in the streets than you do with a sword in the arena! Cowards, all of you! The next time Tresias is looking for gladiators, I will tell him that he will have better luck with a street full of orphans than the likes of you." Everything Priscus said—even if it was benign—had such an undertone of insult that it made the other men flinch.

To begin construction, Priscus ordered that several large pine logs be cut, stripped of their bark, and stuck in the mud parallel to the lake shore. This would allow the ship to roll off the pine logs when it was completed. Construction began with a board being fastened to either side of a triangular-shaped piece of pine or fir. These boards were secured by round tenons that were driven through corresponding holes that had been drilled into the wood. Once the bottom was secure, plank after plank was set on the protruding dowels of the previous tier. The whole thing cinched together as more circular tenons were hammered through their corresponding holes. The internal ribs of the ship were not added now, as it would have only slowed their progress; instead the ship's shape was held together by long cords that were wrapped around the vessel.

The front of the ship was reinforced again and again, so as to protect it when it rammed. By far the weakest point of the ship was just in front of or just behind the main sail. Multiple pieces of wood were used to reinforce the mast at its base, while only minimal amount of wood was used to reinforce either side. Reinforcing certain parts of the ship was a tradeoff: While it did provide greater protection from ramming, it also greatly slowed it down. The best place to ram a Trireme was between the bow and the mast, where the planks were not typically reinforced.

After they worked on the ship for the first part of each day, the men would finish up by training with the sword. Priscus' skill in the arena had become as renowned as it was feared. No one, not even the best of *Doctores* cared to go up against him; he was so brutal with his attacks, so merciless in combat, that even in practice his opponents would always walk away with a limp or a bruised limb. The Gaul was armed and trained as a Murmillo, which was so named for the fish-like crest on top of the helmet. The *Doctore* had initially selected him as a *Secutor*—the heavy titan of the arena—but Priscus hated the ten-pound helmet he was given to wear. When he drilled in the square, or sometimes in the circle arena at the *Ludi*, he would don an arm guard and a gladius in one hand, a curved square shield in the other, a *manica* for his lead leg, and a belt that protected his groin.

This belt, called a *balteus*, was where a gladiator's rank and position was recorded, as well as his triumphs and successes. Already, Priscus had beaten enough challengers with wooden swords to be ranked a Murmillo *Fourth Palus*, which was unheard of for a combatant who had never been in a real arena.

One day, after the noon meal, the *Doctore* gathered the *Naumachians* around the bathing houses in the main *Ludi*. "You've made good progress on the ship—I wouldn't be surprised if it's finished long before its due—so for the next few days, instead of building the ship, we will be using the heated pools to train you on how to take your armor off when you are under water.

"You will also be honing your skills of balance and speed while we train you at naval hand-to-hand combat. We will begin this lesson by pitting two fighters against each other on two small ships tied to the pool floor. These little boats are less steady than a Trireme will be in combat, especially with only one person in them, but it will give you an excellent sense of balance. Who will go first?"

Immediately Priscus stood up.

"All right. And who will face the Gaul?"

Immediately everyone looked away, pretending to be more interested in their sandals or the dirt on their hands than they were in the challenge before them.

"Lenidus," the *Doctore* ordered, "come up here; you'll fight the Gaul first."

Obediently but slowly, Lenidus—who had been the toughest gladiator before Priscus arrived—stood up and dragged his feet to the boat opposite the Gaul.

"Grab the wooden *rudis* and square shields. Lenidus, I want you to grab a helmet too. Priscus, you won't be wearing armor for this exercise. And Priscus, if you knock another one of my gladiators unconscious, you will be the one that has to fish him out of the water."

The two fighters jumped out onto the rocking boats, sending them bouncing into each other—Lenidus just about fell over as they did.

They stabilized themselves in the boats and lifted up their shields and swords as they faced each other. With both fighters in position, the *Doctore* walked around the edge of the pool until he was at the side of one of the boats. "Naval combat takes a mix of skill and balance that is so melded together that neither one is more important than the other. In the next several weeks, we will be drilling your normal sword routines, but now we will be doing them on the water. It takes more than brute skill, more than a mass of muscle to fight on boats. Those that might be the best in the arena often prove the worst on the boats. During these first few fights, watch how each fighter positions his weight. Are you two ready?"

Priscus nodded and Lenidus swallowed.

"Fight!"

Priscus waited for his opponent to make his first move, but so did Lenidus. They stood there staring at each other, summing up their opponent. Finally Priscus went in, raining blows on the large Lenidus until he became so unbalanced that he had to put his foot on the edge of the boat to stabilize himself. Priscus took the opportunity and slapped the man right in the shin with his wooden sword. Lenidus became too unstable to stand and fell backwards into the water.

The *Doctore* swore. Before the man could emerge, he was being assaulted by the *Doctore's* tongue. "You fool Lenidus. You did not even last more than a few moments. Months of training and you can't even block a blow to the shins!" The instructor went on and on, laying into the man while he climbed out of the pool using a nearby rope ladder.

"Next fighter!" the *Doctore* growled.

This time more people volunteered, standing up as they did. They seemed encouraged by the possibility of defeating Priscus at this new form of combat. Next was a small Ligurian who was known for his speed, but Priscus proved faster by knocking the man so hard in the head that he flew off the boat.

Next came a dark-haired Greek. The Greek was an expert with a shield and used it as much as a weapon as anyone did their sword. But the man was just as unstable as the previous two fighters and took a hit to the ribs that instantly bruised. He recovered from the blow and was able to stabilize himself; but as impossible as it seemed on the shaking boats, Priscus lifted up his leg and kicked his opponent square in the chest, knocking the Greek into the water.

After this, volunteers were no longer lining up to face Priscus like they did before. The *Doctore* had to pull them up by the arms, threatening to whip them if they faltered. Fighter after fighter came at the Gaul, but he was just as adept on the water as he was in the arena. Finally, after almost all the fighters were sopped with water, the *Doctore* stepped forward.

"Where did you learn to fight on a boat, Gaul?"

"I was a Roman Centurion; I had my men train on boats to increase their balance."

The *Doctore* shook his head in disbelief. "You truly believe you are the consummate warrior don't you—you prideful miscreant. Is there not one among you that hates this Gaul more than I? Until now, none of you has known my name, but hear it now: For I am Valious Octor and I was a Centurion on the seas. While you fought for practice on boats, I was on the high seas spilling the blood of pirates."

"Then come up here; let's see if your skill matches your ability to brag."

The *Doctore* grabbed up a *rudis* and a square shield. He leaped out to the boat effortlessly, putting a helmet on his head while he did. Slowly, he rose in the boat, steadying himself with perfect balance. "You still have a lesson or two to learn, Gaul, and I will be the one to teach it to you."

The instructor came at Priscus swinging his sword and shield in wild succession. He put his foot on the rim of the boat, drawing out Priscus' attack with his sword, but then lifted his leg quickly and kicked Priscus in the chin.

The Gaul took a half step back and grinned, "Hah. You weren't lying when you spoke. You do have some skill on the water."

Priscus then went on the offensive but quickly found himself evenly matched blow for blow. The instructor clearly had better balance on the boat, which he used to shift his body from side to side, but Priscus still had superior skill with the sword.

The *Doctore* had studied the Gaul's attacks and knew when they were coming; just before Priscus could swing in, the instructor would step back and send his boat bumping into the other, knocking his opponent off balance. It made it impossible for the Gaul to fully commit to the powerful swing that had made him so feared. This evened out the skill of the two fighters, or it did, that is, until Priscus jumped onto the *Doctore's* boat and took away the instructor's advantage.

Valious tried to jump back to the other boat, but the Gaul used his shield to hit the man before he could. Now, with the *Doctore's* advantage gone, Priscus moved in for the kill, attacking so viciously that the instructor could only move back in defense. The Gaul was everywhere at once. It seemed all but over now, but somehow—by the luck of Fortuna—Valious threw a wild swing that struck Priscus right across the chin. The Gaul twisted and turned, trying to catch his balance, but the *Doctore* charged in with his shield and knocked the Gaul off his feet and into the water.

The other gladiators cheered until their voices echoed through the bathhouse. They screamed wildly, yelling so loudly that Priscus could hear their shouts below the water. Everyone was still cheering long after the Gaul climbed out of the pool.

Valious took off his helmet, revealing a grin that was as wide as his face. "That's how it is done. We will end it here for today. I want all of you to take a hot bath and a massage tonight; those that have wounds are to see the doctor. Tomorrow, all of you will need to be in the best of shape."

The Gaul stood there with narrowed eyes; his chest was barreled and threatening. He cursed to himself silently as his hair continued to drip with his defeat.

* * *

Priscus returned to his cell and smashed his chair against the table, sending pieces of wood exploding everywhere. He picked up the pieces and swung them at the walls. He imagined the *Doctore's* smiling face just before him, smugly gloating with victory. The Gaul screamed so loud and so fierce that it echoed out the cell and startled a slave that was carrying a load of weapons. Priscus screamed on, shouting every curse word he knew in three different languages.

"Hey, hey," shouted Verus through the drain on the floor. "What's wrong?"

The Gaul ignored the man and kept up his screaming until he

was red in the face. Sweat beaded and dripped down the Gaul's scarred and coarse body, like a fish newly pulled from water. His screams were so angry, so wild that that Blacksmith was scared to even speak—despite the fact that a stonewall separated them.

After more time and still more cursing, the Gaul's voice began to give out; finally, the brute slumped against the wall and fell to the floor, sucking air long and hard through his nostrils.

"What happened?" Verus asked through the drain.

Priscus swore again and then laughed—a long chilling laugh that echoed through the cell. "I am surrounded by a mob of fools that believe that each one is just as important as the last. The whelps can't even put a ship together, let alone stand toe-to-toe in a fight."

"What do you mean?"

"I need to get out of here, to breathe fresh air and see my opponents in the sun. This damp cell is sucking the life out of me; I am like a plant withering away in this place, dying without the light of day. I swear that time passes twice as slow here as it does out there. Every day, I drill from sunrise to sunset and prove myself capable in every way, but they keep me here—drilling with these infernal wooden swords. I've killed them all in practice five times over now."

"I've heard of you Gaul; everyone has. I saw you the other day passing me as you went to the arena."

"What is your name?" Priscus asked sharply.

Verus ignored him, "They say you are so brutal that even the instructors fear to face you in combat. What makes you that way?"

Priscus laughed again. "No one has ever asked me that."

"Well I'm asking you now."

"That's life," Priscus replied simply. "Kill or be killed; strike or be struck. It was Athenogoras of Syracuse who said, 'If a man does not strike first, he will be the first struck.' There is no point in befriending anyone here—that is like an open invitation for death. The less others know about you the more they have to fear you; and fear, not friendship—as your fool philosopher taught you—is the true currency in this underworld. We are living in a hell, a place where demons are king and foul serpents rule. The rules are simple in this life: The more brutal one is, the more powerful they will become. It was Rome's own Emperor Caligula who said, 'Let them hate us as long as they fear us.'"

Verus scoffed. "And do you know how Caligula's life ended? He ended up being killed by the very people that feared him. You know nothing of this world or the people that are around you."

"Hah!" Priscus laughed. "Fine words from a man that has accomplished little and done even less. What were you before you came here—a lumber-miner? And how was it to be on the brink of starvation every winter? I'm sure you had plenty of friends, but what about food?"

"Yes," Verus replied, "I did have a simple life before, but it was...fulfilling."

"And after a few seasons of good times," Priscus said, "you've ended up here—cast aside like a pair of loaded dice."

"It's not our circumstances that determine our disposition in life, it is the way we face those challenges. As Horace wrote: 'Adversity reveals the genius of a person; good fortune conceals it.'"

"Let me tell you, lumber-miner," the Gaul hissed, "I was born into a world of poverty and starvation. As a young boy my father was killed and I alone had to do a man's labor to support my family. Then one day they were all slaughtered—killed by an invading army of Celts. I was raised as a slave, forced to kill my only friend in combat. Then again and again I was chosen to entertain the wealthy Celts by killing my own people—one by one in a circle of death. I did rise to the challenge and I did overcome all; but it was the brutality of my sword that got me here, not the sympathy of some onlooker."

Priscus threw a piece of wood across the room. "To the merciless and the brave goes fame and fortune. It was Terence, that great warlord of Rome, that said: 'Fortune favors the brave.'"

"Well let me be blunt with you, Gaul, as you are with everyone else: Everyone hates you for it. Instead of rallying around you like a champion, your name has become a hiss and a curse in these halls. There is no fortune you will gain by making enemies along the way. Even the greatest Emperors of Rome cannot avoid making enemies with their brutality; even they know they are not above death. Time is against you, and eventually you will be killed—whether it is by a poison that burns a hole in your stomach or a blade that is stabbed in your back."

"Yes," the Gaul agreed. "Death will be my end but it will be yours as well—and everyone else's. None can escape it, not even the friendliest of lumber-miners."

Verus sighed. "Yes, death is the end of all of us, but there is a large difference between your death and mine."

"Yes there is a difference," the Gaul replied. "People will remember me when I die."

Chapter 21

April 8, 70 AD
Verus

Verus' small group, along with several other groups, was aroused before any of the sleeping gladiators. They were rushed out and handed cold beans to eat. Most were not even finished eating before they were paraded off into a sandy arena, where they spent a good amount of time running around the edge of it. Verus was not used to running and instantly he disliked it. The only thing that kept his mind from the thought of his burning lungs and his vomit-tasting mouth was the sight of the clear blue sky above, which seemed to drift lazily out of sight. They ran faster and faster until a group of gladiators called them in. The slaves gathered around quickly, eager to stop the brutal regimen of running. The slaves slunk over their knees or hoisted their hands above their head as they sucked down air.

One of the *Doctores* cleared his throat and spoke, "Every day you will gather swiftly and silently; talking in the arena is a privilege which you slaves have not earned. You will begin and end the day with running. Strength and skill are important, but what is more important is endurance and speed. Gladiatorial fights can be as quick as a few moments but usually they stretch out much longer; whether you live or die will solely depend on your endurance. After your run, you will be given strength training until noon. Then you will have a quick meal—and mind you, it will be quick—before you'll start your sword training. All gladiators will start training with the sword, but after a few weeks, some of you will be selected and trained with other weapons. The quicker you learn, the quicker you will be selected to take the gladiatorial oath. Now grab a sword and shield; we will begin your strength training."

From the sides of the arenas, the instructors dragged out

various stands that had large chunks of wood chained to them. The wood rounds hung in all sorts of positions and angles that required a myriad of different attacks to hit them.

Verus hefted a wooden sword and shield—both of them felt much heavier than the ones they were using the day before. With these weapons in hand, the slaves were sent through a maze of swinging wood pieces, which they had to strike quickly and accurately before the instructors started yelling at them. Each of the wood blocks required a certain stroke or technique to hit it square on. As the slaves came at each one, they were required to yell the technique they were going to use before they could attack. The first few slaves to shuffle through messed up so badly that the instructors yelled at them the whole way. The obstacle course was so long and windy that by the time the slaves finished, it was their turn to do it again. Between the heavy swords and shields they wielded, and the difficult angles of attack, their arms soon began to droop with exhaustion. When one of them was going too slow, the instructors would dramatically pull out a whip to encourage them on. The whip was rarely used, and only on those that had fallen to the ground and refused to get back up.

The day was long and difficult, but Verus, who was used to a lifetime of wielding the blacksmith's hammer, kept his weapons high, much to the praise of the instructors around him. He was yelled at only twice: once when he mistakenly used the wrong technique to attack a wood round, and once when he was caught staring up at the blue sky.

After strength training they ate a quick lunch of barley and vegetables, and then returned to the arena to begin sword drills. This section of the training was taken over by a different group of gladiators that wore metal belts around their waists that were laden with symbols of recognition and rank.

They paired off and began drilling the basic blocking technique. It was certainly easier than the strength training, but infinitely more technical. Everything from the way they gripped their weapons to their stance was scrutinized by the gladiators before them. After training basic moves, the slaves were then taught a specialty move, which took a little more skill to master but seemed more effective.

196

After hours of hefting the sword, they were given a long break for dinner. They were allowed to talk, which was a welcome freedom for most men, especially for Verus, whose only source of conversation for the last little while was the bloodthirsty Gaul.

Verus found himself sitting with the same three people every day. He always sat next to a man named Docinias, who was *Veneti* from eastern Italy. He had a thick head of hair, which he braided into a long tail. His skin was white and spotted with freckles that seemed to congregate just below his eyes. Despite his scarred arms and a crooked jaw, he was surprisingly friendly. After the third day of training, Docinias went into a lengthy tale of how he was a thriving businessman who sold the best slaves—or so he enthusiastically claimed—when suddenly his slaves were stricken with a plague, killing all of them down to the last boy. Despite the tale involving a friend committing adultery with his wife, his father disowning him, and his house catching on fire, the man was still in good spirits. While some men would be pining and plotting revenge, he simply laughed and repeated the phrase, "The world is mad."

Across the table was another man named Archamay, the most lust-loving Greek that Verus had ever met. When Docinias went into details of his life, Archamay kept asking for a detailed description of every woman in the story—including Docinias's wife. But it did not stop there. Archamay lusted after everyone he could readily identify as a woman, from the old cooking ladies who looked as if they could die at any moment to the young girls that cleaned the cells.

Next to him sat a more serene and serious man, Tyre. He did everything as slowly as he could, including eating his food. When one of the others asked him his name, he slowly stirred his soup, took a sip, put his spoon down, took a drink, licked his lips, and—finally—answered. Every time he was asked a question he would repeat the process, almost as if it was a ceremony.

"What is your name?" Docinias finally asked Verus.

"Call me 'Blacksmith.' I don't want you all to know my name as much as I don't want to remember yours—no offense. One day I might be called to fight one of you and I would not want to know your name when I did."

"Fair enough," Archamay answered. "But if I were you, I would change my name to something that would appeal more to the ladies, like Bull Rider."

"Yes," Docinias joined in, "or Denarii."

"Denarii?" Verus asked.

"That's all my wife ever wanted," Docinias replied.

Archamay kicked back in his chair, giving off a laugh that carried through the hall. Even Verus had to laugh a little—which might not have been so much at Docinias' joke, but at Archamay's exaggerated laughter.

As the laughter slowed, Verus gave a slight smile. "It is good to speak to you; I thought you all would be as insane as the Gaul."

Tyre shifted suddenly and slowly stirred his soup, took a sip, put his spoon down, took a drink, licked his lips, and—finally—asked, "Who is the Gaul?"

"You don't know?" Archamay said excitedly. "I've heard talk about him down every corridor that I turn; it's not just other gladiators that are talking about him either, but all the *Doctores* as well. They curse him and praise him all in the same breath, like he is the son of Pluto or something."

"Well," Verus lifted up his mug of water like he was toasting with fate, "I happened to be put in the cell right next to him with nothing but a wall and a drainage pipe between us. If he is half as brutal as he makes himself out to be, the *Doctores* have their hands full."

"I heard that he beat one of the *Doctores* so badly that the guard lost his vision in one eye," Archamay said. "He's an unstoppable brute—no one here can stand up to him. But that is all going to change, right Docinias."

Docinias shuffled awkwardly as he lowered his voice. "Yes…yes."

"Tell him what you were telling me before."

Docinias narrowed his eyes and leaned in. "Quiet your tongue; lower your voice. This is not something that I should know, nor any of you for that matter."

"What is it?" Verus asked plainly.

"Well my cell is on the other side of the compound, right next to yours Blacksmith, right next to all the gladiators that have already taken the oath. I was up last night massaging my aching muscles and staring up at the moonlight, when I heard a voice from one of the cells. It is crowded in my cell since I share it with two others, so I couldn't move—I had to listen."

"What did you hear?" Verus demanded.

"They are going to kill him," Docinias replied with a nod of his head. "Everyone has been talking about it for weeks, but these two men swore an oath that they would attempt it, or die trying. I heard everything: how they are going to do it, when they are going to try it—everything."

"How and when?" Verus asked.

"Now don't you seem as anxious as a man on his wedding night," Archamay said with a wink.

Verus ignored the other man. "Tell me."

"They are building a Trireme, or so they said, by the edge of the lake a few miles from here. The Gaul is in charge of building it and he runs all of them ragged with work. Of course, the ship is being built quick..."

Verus interrupted, "How are they going to kill him?"

"Well, tomorrow, they are putting in a brass ram. It will pass over the head of the Gaul just as it is being moved to the front of the ship, and when it does, they are going to sever the rope and crush the tyrant's skull. If they miss, they've both sworn to come at the brute with knives."

"Amazing," Verus shook his head. "I can't believe they are going to try to kill him. What are the names of the men?"

"One of them is named Scipian, the other I don't know."

Archamay smiled with a toothless grin, "I can't wait 'till he'z gone. With a hefty fighter like that, he will be stealing all the womanly attention from me."

* * *

After supper, they went back to the arena where they finished up with a few more drills. The sun had long since set and still they pushed on through the torchlight, heaving huge breaths through their burning throats. If they faltered, *Doctores* would threaten them with whips. Finally, they were released and sent to their cells.

Verus collapsed on his mattress, still breathing hard from the exertion. He looked up through the small window above him, straining at the few stars he could see. The Gaul was there—Verus could feel his heavy presence.

"How did you fair today?" Verus whispered through the grate in the wall.

The brute did not answer.

Verus continued as if the Gaul had responded. "We spent more time with sword technique and then ran around, just like the last few days. I've never run so much in my life. What about you Gaul?"

Priscus took a deep breath and rolled over on his side. "I ran over thirty miles a day when I marched in the army. The pathetic running you are doing now compares little to the rough terrain that a Legionnaire has to cover every day."

"Still," Verus asserted, "it's more running than what a lumber-miner is used to."

"How is your sword technique?"

Verus was surprised by the Gaul's question. "Fine, I think, better than most, but it has only been a week. I'm used to using a hammer—I mean an ax—so the weight does not wear on me like it does the others. Our instructors have some real skill though."

Priscus laughed. "They're only skilled at taking a fall. You know I've beaten all of them in turn—none of them can stand before me. Let me give you some real advice: Take two breaths before you step into the ring and look them directly into their eyes. If they stare at you dead on, that means they are coming for you, so let them come forward and tire themselves out. It takes twice as much energy to attack than it does to defend. The best fighter is not always the one that strikes first.

"If they try to stare you down, but blink when they do, that means they will wait to see what sort of fighter you are before they charge, but charge they will. If they glance at you only once or twice, that means they are afraid—so don't worry about those ones. The only ones that you need to fear are the ones that look into the distance—almost as if you are not really there. Those are the fighters who are capable of doing just about anything—those are the fighters who fear nothing."

"How did you learn all of this?"

"I was a slave for five years of my life; whether I would be beaten every night or not, completely depended on my ability to read my master's mood. Reading your opponent is far more important than possessing more skill than him—although that greatly helps. The best thing you can do is observe every fighter you see, taking careful note of their facial expressions and body position as they engage you in combat. Their faces and bodies are a window to their next move. For example, if a fighter leads heavily with one foot, he is almost always looking to come in with a powerful hook aimed for your head; when a fighter has his rear foot elevated that means he is going to either rush in or kick at you when he attacks."

Verus shook his head in disbelief. "That is how you do it. That is how you have beaten them all. Have any of the *Doctores* ever beaten you?"

The Gaul was silent for a while. "No—none of them."

"What about the one that knocked you in the water?"

Priscus tightened his fists. "So you heard about that?"

Verus nodded even though the Gaul could not see it. "Yes. I've heard a lot of things about you Gaul. The more I hear from others, the more wretched you seem. They say that there is not a throat that you would hesitate to slit if their blood meant you could have a second more of freedom."

"You would profit much by doing the same," Priscus replied. "Your idealism will not get you far as a gladiator. Wake up to the world around you: It's full of death and decay, not life and love."

"How far do you think that philosophy will carry you—two more years, maybe four, maybe just till the end of tomorrow?"

"It doesn't matter when my life ends; it just matters how good it is until it ends."

Verus stretched out his legs. "And how good is it? Tell me how much joy do you feel every day or have you ever felt?"

Priscus was silent for a long time before he answered. "It's as good as any..."

"It's not, Gaul. I swear to you by the sacred head of Jupiter that there is more to life than always getting what you want."

"Hah. That is funny: One slave telling another how to be happy. Life may not be 'fulfilling' now, but it will be when I gain fame and fortune in the arena. After I've won the hearts and money of Rome—by the sheer force of my brutality—I will have what I deserve. What more is there to life than that?"

Verus remained silent for a while. His mind was splitting with thought—stuck between two options. He struggled with a decision that most other men would have laughed to scorn. He hated the Gaul—there was no doubt about it—just as anyone would, but as Verus lay there, listening to the devilish barbarian breath, something stirred within his heart. Finally, he spoke. "Gaul, there is something I need to tell you, something about tomorrow that you need to hear..."

Chapter 22

May 15, 70 AD

Priscus

Priscus was in a particularly nasty mood the next morning; he shoved the other workers to the side, knocking some of them so hard that they fell completely flat on their backs. He shouted so loudly that everyone around the ship could hear his crisp orders, which seemed to sizzle into the ears of those closest. Every command he gave came with a list of insults and curses that acted like a whip on everyone's back. Like all the days before this one, the Gaul had everyone working so hard that they accomplished twice the work that they were scheduled to do. The gladiators were like ants, scurrying around the edge of the ship carrying hammers and wood planks to either side.

Even though the work was quick, it was also precise. If a plank was only slightly too short or even a hair too long, Priscus would whip the gladiator with his tongue until it was perfectly cut.

At mid-morning the bronze ram arrived, glittering brilliantly in the bright sun of the cold day. A smile percolated on the Gaul's face. The ram was so heavy that it had to be wheeled to the side of the Trireme where a crane was waiting to lift it to the front. While the ram was being moved, the rest of the men were busy at the other end of the ship, securing the rudder into place. It took only a few moments before a few of the gladiators had loaded the ram on the crane and hefted it up into the air.

Suddenly a soldier grabbed Priscus' attention. "Sir, I've got a problem to show you."

Priscus turned around, a smile fixed to his face. "Oh, really? Where?"

The soldier walked a little ways down the side of the ship

before he stopped and pointed. "Right here, sir. I don't know how we missed it, but there is a gaping hole in the side of this plank—almost as if a chunk of the wood has rotted away."

"Well," Priscus laughed joyfully, "that is a problem. But first, I noticed that you forgot your thick winter tunic. You must be cold out here. Take my red one—it was given to me as a reward for winning a bout against one of the *Doctores*. I am the only one that has a red tunic. Here, put it on."

In the distance the sound of the crane could be heard as it creaked, lifting the ram high into the air. Once it reached the apex, the crane was slowly pulled towards the front of the ship.

The man swallowed. "Sir, I'm fine; I put mine down just on the other side of the ship."

Priscus narrowed his eyes. "Put it on or I will tie it around your neck."

The man nodded and obeyed. "Yes, sir."

"See, isn't that warmer? Now, show me the leak."

"It's just right here. I can almost fit one of my fingers in it."

Priscus examined the hole. "You're right, my friend. What is your name?" As Priscus spoke the crane was pulled closer and closer towards them; it was almost above them when the man answered.

"Scipian."

Priscus' eyes narrowed even more. "That is a fine name, but I wonder if it is too big to fit on the small tombstone you will have..." The Gaul grabbed Scipian by the shoulders and knocked the man's head into the side of the boat just as the ram from above was cut loose. Priscus leapt to the side, diving behind a large tree trunk. The Gaul's red tunic, along with the man that was wearing it, partially disappeared under the ram. It gave a loud crash as it hit the ground.

A lone man armed with a dagger came around the boat towards the wreckage. As he reached the ram and saw a pair of legs sticking out from Priscus' red tunic, the man gave out a wail of acclamation that attracted the attention of all others around him.

He raised his hands in the air, screaming with all of his voice. "I killed him! I killed the beast! I am Carbonel, and I have killed the Gaul!" The others gathered around, gawking at the scene. When they recognized the red tunic and saw the blood-splattered legs beneath, they slapped the man on the back, praising him for his brilliance.

Everyone came in with jovial shouts of praise.

Carbonel wanted to share his triumph with his co-conspirator, so he began shouting out to the crowd, "Scipian! Scipian! Where are you? We've crushed the tyrant's head!"

Using the logs for cover, Priscus was able to crawl away from the wreckage without detection. When he was a distance away, he joined the group, stepping right up to the man who was in the middle.

Carbonel shouted out even louder than before. "Scipian! Scipian! We've killed him!" The unfortunate man looked for his friend to the left and then to the right before he finally turned around completely and found himself staring straight into the fiery eyes of Priscus the Gaul.

Carbonel screamed suddenly—almost as if he saw the hands of death reaching for his throat. His skin became as pale as the whites in his eyes; his lips quivered uncontrollably. Despite all of his training, he disgraced himself by spending his last few moments of life pissing down his leg and onto his sandal. Slowly, almost as if his arms barely worked, he raised the dagger in his defense.

Without a word, Priscus finished Carbonel with a slivered piece of wood. The Gaul grabbed the dagger from Carbonel's hands, and let the body drop to the ground like the ram had only moments before. Silence ensued as all men watched Carbonel—their short-lived hero—bleeding before them.

With the dagger in his hands, no man, not even the biggest or the bravest gladiator dared to cross Priscus, who now had a stream of blood dripping down the tips of his fingers.

The Gaul barreled his chest and laughed. "A few of you throw the body into the lake; the rest of you get back to work—we have a ship to build."

* * *

The news of the assassination attempt spread throughout the school as quickly as the eastern wind. Everyone, even the *Doctores,* stopped their training to listen as others told and retold the Gaul's miraculous escape. Rumors spread and gained strength, like a stream that collects water as it comes down a mountain. By the time it spread entirely through the school everyone—except Verus—was utterly convinced that Priscus was a demon, sent by Viduus himself to claim the lives of living.

That night, as Priscus and Verus lay down to sleep, the Gaul's growling voice came through the grate. "Why did you tell me?"

Verus did not answer.

"Are you asleep lumber-miner?"

"No—I was just thinking how I could answer your question." They sat in an awkward silence until Verus finally spoke. "I couldn't let you die, not after I knew who you were. No man is beyond mercy."

"They had it planned perfectly; they knew exactly what I would do. I would've been dead."

"Everyone in the school thinks you're a demon now, sent as a plague amongst the living. They say you killed both men. Is that true?"

"Yes," Priscus said, "one of them was smashed under the ram, the other I stabbed with a chunk of wood."

Verus shook his head—almost as if he was regretting that he ever told the Gaul anything.

The Gaul's voice took on its razor edge again. "Don't think for a second that this means I owe you. It's every man for himself in here, and I don't want you to think that I am going to watch out for you or do any favors in the future."

The Blacksmith did not answer.

"I can't be spending my time watching over you just because you shared a little bit of gossip with me. Do you hear me, lumber-miner?"

Again, there was no answer.

The Gaul decided to switch subjects. "I can't wait to get out of here—out in the free air. What do you plan to do once you win your freedom and fortune?"

Verus took a deep breath. "I'm going to go back home…"

"That's it?" Priscus laughed. "I've heard eunuchs with bigger dreams than that. What are you going to spend your fortune on? a bigger house? lots of beautiful slaves?"

Verus gave a small smile. "I'm married already, and I don't think my wife will allow me to have any beautiful slaves around the house. I think she would prefer the idea of hiring servants rather than buying slaves. But as far as a bigger house, I think that is a good idea. I would start a...a...lumber-miner school that would have all of the newest equipment; people would come for miles to learn the trade from me."

"You're married?" Priscus mocked. "Why would you limit yourself like that?"

"I love being married. I love coming home to a wonderful woman who somehow thinks I am more special than I really am. She rubs the soreness out of my muscles and kisses me when I'm depressed. Do you ever get that feeling around other people that you have to impress them? Well, when I am with her, I can be exactly who I am, and instead of judging me, she loves me for it. Being married is like having a loyal friend who supports you, despite your flaws, despite your shortcomings."

Priscus growled. "Every man I know who gets married immediately regrets it."

"No, not every man you know," Verus replied quickly, "for you know me, and I don't regret it."

"Well, one out of a few hundred."

"What about you, Gaul? What do you plan to do once you win your fame and fortune?"

A thick smile spread across the Gaul's face. "That's easy. I plan to do everything that anyone has ever told me that I couldn't do. I'm going to buy a large estate, build a huge house in the middle, and fill it with the most beautiful slaves that were ever put on this earth. I will have meat cooked during the day and exotic fishes at night. There will be music, wild entertainers, and a whole slew of servants that obey my every whim and word. I won't have to do anything but sit on fluffy pillows and order everyone else around."

"I don't think that even you could win that much money, Gaul."

"Well, lumber-miner, I will also open a training resort on my property, where I will train private guards for the senators and Equites. They will pay a fortune to be trained by the infamous Gaul—the greatest gladiator of all time."

"What about children?"

"What do I need those litl' brats for—I've already got servants."

Verus again shook his head; his eyes had clouded up with memory. "I've got four children myself and, besides my wife, they are the source of all of my joy. Just to see them grow up, discovering the world as they do, puts a smile on my face. Each one is so different than the last. My oldest son is so adventurous that every time I come home he always has a new bruise to show me and a story to go along with it. My second child is a little troublemaker—like me when I was young. One afternoon he somehow figured out how to lock people in their homes by jamming the outside door with chunks of wood. He locked thirteen families in their own homes before he was finally caught. Of course I had to punish him, but it was sure hard to keep a straight face when I did. My third child is a sweet daughter who is so dependent on me that she cries every time I leave the house; her first sentence she put together was 'were'z daddee'. My final child is just a baby—but what a sweet baby he is. None of my children was as easy as the youngest: He's so simple and quiet that sometimes I barely know he is there."

Priscus swallowed. "Don't tell me you are going to start talking about them every night from now on."

Verus gave a little laugh.

Chapter 23
June 1, 70 AD
Verus

Using the advice from the Gaul, Verus quickly began to recognize general patterns with the gladiators. He would watch and study the body posture and the reactions of each fighter as they engaged in combat. Despite Verus ignoring everything else the Gaul had ever said, this one bit of advice was like a golden nugget that quickly proved its worth. The Blacksmith was already a novelty since he was a left-handed fighter, but he became even more renowned for his skill in the arena. Verus quickly beat every challenger he was put against, including ones that had several more months of experience. One thing coupled with another and soon, everyone assumed that he knew a lot more about technique than he really did. Even the *Doctores* started praising him daily for his ability and skill. Often, Verus was selected to teach entire groups of slaves a certain technique.

Verus was dual trained as a Provocatores and a Hoplomachus, which was an odd mix because they both used two completely different fighting styles: while the Hoplomachus tried to maintain his distance from his opponent, the Provocatores attempted to get as close as possible. The Blacksmith was not only able to handle the diverse training techniques, he mastered both. He was hungry for all the training that was available and took every opportunity to learn as many different fighting styles as he could—which seemed to act as a catalyst for his skill.

After a month, the training regimen shifted slightly and focused more on mock fights and wrestling than on strength or endurance training. It was still long and hard, but after three months, Verus could feel his body adapting to the strain. He no longer wheezed with short burning breaths as he ran around the arena, nor did he want to collapse onto his hay-filled mattress at the end of each day. He was stronger and quicker than he had ever been before. As he walked around the *Ludi* with confidence, friend and foe alike treated him with the utmost respect. He was given privileges that were reserved mainly for gladiators, including access to the bathhouse and freedom to roam around in the evening.

It was during this time that Tresias often called Verus into his private room to ask the Blacksmith for advice on the training regimen. The first time that this happened, Verus was so nervous that he stuttered over his words; after that performance, he was surprised when Tresias asked to see him again, and then again. These meetings quickly became a weekly tradition. They were formal at first—with Verus dutifully calling Tresias 'master' and standing rigidly at attention—but slowly they became more casual. They began to swap stories of their families and share exciting exploits of their former lives.

Tresias had once been a gladiator himself—although he never fought in the arena. He came from a wealthy family that owned several wool-dying factories across the country. As a boy, like all young men in Rome, he became obsessed with gladiatorial life and legacy. He would follow his favorite fighters around the city, buying every bit of merchandise that had the gladiator's name attached to it. When he was old enough, he ran away from his home and joined up with a gladiatorial *Ludi*. His family franticly looked for him until they found him just after he had taken the oath to serve as a gladiator. Before he could fight in a single combat, his father purchased him from the *Lanistas* and became his new owner. Since Tresias was now a slave, he was subject to all his father's commands. His father forbade him—under the penalty of death—to ever fight in the arena. By the time his father died, Tresias was too old to fight, so instead, he formed this gladiatorial *Ludi*.

On their last meeting Tresias, with a grin on his face, informed the Blacksmith that there would be a final gladiatorial test the next day and that Verus would be taking it—which was much sooner than he had anticipated. The *Lanista* continued to surprise Verus by telling him that three buyers were already extremely interested in him and, if he passed his test, he would quickly be sold to one of them.

This last bit of information sent a chill down his back; soon, instead of a wooden *rudis*, he would be using the permanence of a steel gladius. Training to fight was one thing, but actually facing a man to the death was something completely different. His stomach fluttered with nerves as he left Tresias' presence and headed down the stone halls. Everything about the *Ludi* had become so familiar that it became hard to imagine life without it.

The next day came quicker than the Blacksmith thought possible.

Five wooden platforms were erected in the middle of the circular sanded arena. There were dozens of contestants waiting in a big mob for the chance to prove themselves—all of them had many more weeks of experience than Verus. The Blacksmith was so nervous that he had to keep swallowing to prevent vomit from coming up. He kept tightening his hands into fists as he waited for his name to be called. He did not have to wait long, since he was first.

"Blacksmith. Go to *Palus* number one."

He was handed a wooden *rudis* and a square shield and sent up a few steps until he reached a wooden platform. Before him was another gladiator, armed like a Murmillo. He could not see the fighter's face because of the metal helmet, but he did recognize the fighter's stance. Before the combat could even begin, Verus had a good idea how it was going to end. The fighter was rocking back and forth, putting most his weight on his lead foot as he did. He was also holding his sword hand further back than normal—almost as if he was keeping it in reserve.

The Blacksmith smiled, took two deep breaths, and prepared himself for the fight to come.

A man with a long pole stood on the sandy floor below, looking at each fighter to see if they were ready. When they were both positioned perfectly the man whipped the pole out of the way and shouted, "Begin."

And begin they did.

Just as Verus had expected, the man went on the defensive, stepping back when Verus took the first two swings. Verus swung his sword quick and hard, but his opponent refused to open up his defenses; soon, the Murmillo was backed up against the other end of the *Palus*. Instead of going on the offensive, however, the man

211

continued to stand defensively, waiting for his moment to strike.

Verus lowered his shield just a little, tempting his opponent to swing. The man took the bait and swung as hard as he could, but the Blacksmith saw it coming long before his opponent could strike. Verus ducked under the swing and jabbed the wooden sword into the man's belly. While the Murmillo ducked with pain, Verus came up and struck the man in the helmet, knocking him completely off the *Palus*. The onlookers gave a cheer as Verus raised his hands in triumph.

It took him three months to train for this one moment, and now that it had come and gone, it all seemed a blur. His heart was pounding so forcefully he could feel a vein on the side of his head throbbing with excitement. He had won. Not only had he won, but he had defeated his opponent so easily that it left everyone—even the most stubborn *Doctores*—with a surprised look on their faces.

Verus still had his hands in the air, like he had just conquered Rome herself, when one of the *Doctores* came up to the side of the platform. "All right Blacksmith, put your arms down and get off the *Palus*. We've got many more fighters to test than just you."

Verus nodded quickly. "Sorry...I was..."

"Just get down from there."

"Yes...sorry..."

The Blacksmith had a long time to wait as the other men fought. Verus watched them all carefully, studying the way each fighter attacked and defended against their opponent. In almost every fight, Verus could pick out what was going to happen just by seeing how the two fighters stood. After several hours of testing, a hundred or so slaves had passed. They were lined up in the arena and ordered to stand at attention. Spiculus Aurelias climbed up on a *Palus* and yelled out to them.

"You men have been favored by Mars—favored by the Gods. Being a gladiator is a sacred right that has been passed down throughout the generations; this ritual is called a *Munus*, where we honor our dead ancestors with the blood of the living. Many people think that it is by the strength of our armies that Rome is protected, that it is by the whispering words of senators and traditionalists that we prosper. But I swear to you, that it is by the sacrifice and the honor that gladiators bring to the arena that honors the Gods the most. What we do in the space of a few moments of valor and death offers a greater protection than years of toil and labor by everyone else.

"The first gladiatorial combat took place in 264 BC and was staged by Decimus Junius Brutus in honor of his deceased father. Since then, the prosperity of Rome has been intimately connected with gladiatorial combat. The more we honor the Gods through our devotion—even to our death—the more prosperity Rome will have. For this reason, no matter if we are selected to die with honor or to live with dignity, we must face our fate as men—as guardians of the sacred *Munus*.

"You cannot falter in the arena and you cannot faint; if you lose, and you are selected to die, then you must kneel before your enemy and let him stab the killing blow that is to go down from your shoulder and pierce your heart. It is your fearlessness of death that brings honor to your life. Now all of you must take the oath, an oath that was first spoken by Mars himself and handed down through the generations."

The gladiators stiffened as they repeated in one loud voice the words they had been forced to memorize many weeks before:

I will endure to be burned, to be bound, to be beaten, and to be killed by the sword.

After this, Spiculus looked at them with a grim smile. "You are no longer men—but sons of Mars, born again with a rich blood that flows through your veins. You—my new brethren—are now gladiators."

* * *

That night as Verus dropped himself onto his straw mattress, he could not help but feel an ache in his heart. The little joy that he felt at the triumph of becoming a gladiator quickly gave way to a realization that this was not the end of his long struggle, but only the beginning. It had been more than six months since his home was destroyed—even longer since he had seen any of his family alive. He could only hope and pray that his son still walked among the living.

"He's a resourceful boy, one who loves adventure more than anything else; he's old enough to fend for himself for a time. Oh, great Jupiter, please protect my boy."

"Did you make it?" Priscus' voice came through the grate.

"Yes..."

"Was it as easy as I told you?"

"Yes..."

"Listen, lumber-miner, I was thinking about what you said a few months back about that philosopher—what was his name?"

"Plini."

"Yes—that is the one. Tell me how he came up with his conclusions."

Verus rubbed his teary eyes and cleared his throat. "Why would that matter to you, Gaul?"

"Tell me or I will rip this wall down and make you eat the pieces..."

Verus smiled. "Well, he watched nature. It was his belief that by observation of the world around us, he could discover natural principles about humans. He said that on the outset, nature seems balanced, but as he studied it closer, he realized that nature was really in opposition to itself. Then he gave the example of a coney and a wolf. While the coney looks to breed and eat, the wolf looks to eat the coney. Each of them has the same objective—that is to survive—but when one meets its objective, it cancels out the other. If the wolves were as effective at hunting as they would hope to be, they would all be able to catch their fill, but soon, the coneys would be so few, the wolves would not have food to eat. This opposition actually creates balance among the creatures."

The Gaul gave a small grunt and Verus continued.

"It is his belief that we, as humans, become balanced when we face adversity; it is only then that we appreciate the calm and the peace that follows. He said that we pray the most when we have the least. When we face adversity there are two reactions: Either we buy into our animal flesh and selfishly debase ourselves, or we choose a higher path that elevates us. Two people can go through the same experience but have drastically different results. He claimed that no matter how much wealth or power or even comforts a people have, they are not guaranteed happiness. Plini said that he had known kings and queens, dined with emperors and generals, but none of them,

214

despite everything they owned, were satisfied with life. He adamantly believed that joy does not come from our possessions."

The Gaul scoffed, "Then is there such a thing as happiness?"

"According to Plini, we are happy if we obey three principles: first, when we are freely charitable to others—which stops us from focusing on our personal flaws and shortcomings; second, if we are honest with our expectations of ourselves and others; and third, and most importantly, if we are appreciative of our relationships. Then we will find true joy—despite whatever we face."

Priscus laughed. "I can't imagine what kind of person would believe any of that."

Chapter 24
June 15, 70 AD
Priscus

The Trireme finally reached completion. It was exactly one hundred and twenty one feet long and sat eighteen feet wide. Priscus walked the length of the ship twice, scanning it for the littlest crack or imperfection, but there was none. Despite the inexperience of the builders, the ship was perfect, from its tight fitting boards to the dual rudders. While a crowd of onlookers gathered at water's edge, the gladiators ran around the ship, preparing the Trireme for its first sail. Tresias watched eagerly as the Gaul ordered the ship to be pushed into the water. Slaves on the ground started to push the boat forward, grunting with exertion. Soon half the boat was in the water.

"I will take it from here," said someone behind Priscus.

The Gaul turned around threateningly, but he was met by four swords. Before Priscus stood Valious Octor, who was wearing shining Legionnaire armor that seemed to have doubled the man's pride. Just behind him were four other gladiators armed with short swords and shields.

"I've studied for this," Priscus hissed. "I know the commands for the ship."

"I know infinitely more than you do about ships," Valious hissed. "I was hired for this very purpose. Despite your skill with the sword, I still have years more experience than you on the seas. Take an oar or I will have you tied to one."

The Gaul stood there for a moment, considering his options. He finally nodded and went over to the side of the ship, where he found an empty seat. The boat was full of slaves; most of them were kept below, while the gladiators were seated on the rows above.

216

Valious took the helm of the ship and cleared his arrogant voice. "I am the *Hypersesia* of this ship, and you will do as I command or be whipped for your disobedience. You've built a fine ship, but let's see if you can master its rowing technique. There are over 170 rowers on this Trireme and each of you has differing levels of strength. Those that try to outdo the others will bump oars and slow the ship down more than they will speed it up. The more you can row as one, the faster you will be; and in the maelstrom of a naval battle, all of our lives will depend on speed. It is easy to grasp the basics, but it is more than difficult to master them. The *Auletes* will set the pace—all you have to do is follow it. It will take some time getting used to the commands, but soon they will become as natural as taking a breath."

"Ready! Under oars!"

Slaves and gladiators alike slid the wood lengths out the small windows that were on either side.

"Down oars!" The wood lengths slapped against the water.

"Maximum crew. General speed."

Every oarsman began to paddle to the beat of a flute, which was played by a man called an *Auletes*. The speed was slow and steady, making it easy for the oarsman to keep in sync.

As the oars propelled the ship, Valious turned the rudders towards the other end of the lake. The ship glided across the water, making good time. After a long while, Valious yelled another command, "Continuous crew."

A third of the crew continued to row at a slower but steady pace. After some time, another third took over the rowing. This process continued until the entire crew had rested.

After a long time, Valious turned the ship around and shouted down to the slaves below, "Maximum crew. Quickened speed." Everyone ran to their oars, grabbing them in earnest; once in position, the *Auletes* began—this time the beat was faster. The ship cruised across the water, making a large wake as it headed back the way they had come.

After a while, with a grin on his face, Valious gave another command. "Battle speed."

The oarsmen were beginning to sweat—especially the slaves below who were not used to the strain. They glided on the water faster and faster, until they passed the spot where they had launched the ship.

"Ramming speed!" Valious yelled.

The *Auletes* blew even faster, sending the oarsmen into flurry. They were only able to keep at it for moments before the whole crew of slaves below broke rhythm and began paddling at all sorts of slower speeds. Still the gladiators rowed on together, making up for the weakness of the slaves by their unnatural strength. They pushed off with their legs and stretched their backs, whipping their oars into the water.

Valious drove them on and on, scolding them with his tongue when one of them slackened. Sweat poured freely from every gladiator face and cheek, dripping down to the slaves below. The ship went on and on until Valious raised a hand in the air. "Halt."

As soon as the *Auletes* stopped, the oarsman collapsed to their sides, sucking in breath as they did. The slaves below were especially winded; several of them filled the air with the foul smell of barley and vomit.

"It will take a few weeks of training before we are fast enough to ram a ship, a few weeks more before we are able to change fluidly between speeds. All of you did well. We will rest here for a moment, and afterwards we'll drill strategy."

While the men had been rowing, Valious and three of his assistants had been watching each gladiator carefully. As the men rested, the naval commander approached each one and gave a solid critique on what he did well and what he could have done better. After a brief rest, they were commanded to pick up their oars and row at general speed. While they rowed, they were taught how to pull their oars in quickly to prevent them from being smashed by an opposing ship. They also learned the commands and techniques of flanking the enemy.

They continued to drill these tactics for the next few weeks until each of the gladiators could command the ship on his own. They would set up targets in the water—small buoyant logs that were anchored by large rocks—that they rammed for practice.

Then they added a bridge to the front of the Trireme and padded themselves with armor. Another ship-like structure was built on the dock and the soldiers used it to stage mock-naval battles in which one army of gladiators in the Trireme would raid the other that was defending the dock.

Priscus mastered everything he did, and he, by himself, completely took over the dock several times—to the astonishment and jealously of everyone around him. The Gaul could think so quickly in the face of battle that his opponents could rarely react accordingly. He sent dozens of them flying to either side of the dock as he hacked at them with his wooden sword.

After one of these glorious bouts, Priscus had a grin on his face that refused to subside. He collapsed onto his straw mattress, giving off an obnoxious sound of triumph as he did. The lumber-miner was there—the Gaul could sense his apprehensiveness.

"What has your spirits so high?" Verus asked.

"Hah!" the Gaul laughed. "I just walloped a dozen of those hubristic gladiators as they were boarding my Trireme. Old Tresias was there and gave as loud applause as any when he saw it. If Plini would've been a gladiator, he would have added to his philosophy of happiness that knocking around a few gladiators is a great way to put a grin on one's face."

"That's good."

"What's wrong with you? Why are you so solemn?"

"I've been sold," Verus answered quickly, "to some *patrician* that saw me fighting the other day."

Priscus tightened his jaw and swore. "I've been here twice as long as you and you're the one getting out." The Gaul swore again and again.

Verus shook his head, "I can't believe you, Gaul. How could you be jealous of me?"

"You're getting out of here."

Verus closed his eyes and leaned his head back. "The road to freedom will be a long and bitter path for me."

"Why did you join up to be a gladiator if you're so dismayed by the life of one?"

"I was falsely accused of being a traitor and sentenced to a rock quarry to die; it was either fight for my freedom here, or slowly waste away out there. The only reason I'm here is so I can win my freedom and save my son."

"Your son? What about your wife? What about your family?

219

Why don't they protect your son until you come back?"

The Blacksmith sharply sucked in a large breath and rubbed his hands through his hair. "I lied to you, Gaul—I was lying to myself more than anyone else. They're dead, almost all of them. I like to think of them more alive than I do dead, but the cold truth is that they are gone."

"How?"

"I went to Rome to ask for grain, but I was fooled by Vittelian, who framed me so he could protect himself. By the time I got back, a Roman Century had already killed everything and everyone in my home village—not a creature was left alive. They looted and burned the town to the ground, leaving nothing but the bodies as evidence of the destruction."

Verus' words poured down Priscus' back like frozen water in the middle of summer. The Gaul opened his mouth to speak but no words would come out. Everything the lumber-miner said sounded so similar to the city that he himself had raided.

The Blacksmith shook his head. "I did not even have a chance to bury my wife."

"I'm sure she was buried..." Priscus murmured.

"I pray that they were..." Verus lowered his head in guilt. When he tried to speak again, he coughed on his words as tears collected in his eyes.

"Take it easy," the Gaul replied. "Breathe deep."

Verus cried hard for a moment. The tears dripped down and collected on his chin where they hung for a second before they fell down and soaked his tunic. He repetitively rubbed his hair back and forth, pulling some of it out as he did. Finally, he took a deep breath and regained himself. "My home is on a hill so I was hoping they would've had time to get away before the soldiers came after them— but they didn't. I found the bodies of all of my children except for one—one of them had escaped out the back window and ran for the forest. I ran into the woods, frantically looking for him, but I was caught by some Roman soldiers, who were convinced I was a traitor."

For the first time in years, a shock came over Priscus that seemed to paralyze his lungs. His eyes began to fill with tears. He dabbed at them with his hand, feeling ashamed that they were even there. Priscus shook his head. "*It's not the same family—this is not the same man. It's not the same boy."*

A thick hand suddenly thudded on Verus' door, making both the Gaul and the Blacksmith jump. There was a deep muffled voice on the other side of it. "Blacksmith, are you ready to go?"

"Blacksmith?" Priscus asked. "You're a blacksmith?"

Verus stood. "Yes, I lied about that too; I didn't know if I could trust you."

Another shock spiraled through the Gaul's body. *"A blacksmith?"* Then Priscus asked the question that he would later regret. "Are you from Pinacale?"

"Yes," Verus replied quickly. "How did you know that?"

"Come on," the guard said at Verus' door. "Your new master is waiting."

"Wait," Verus said to the guard. He then turned his attention back to the Gaul. "How did you know I was from Pinacale? How do you even know about Pinacale?"

Priscus' silence made Verus' blood run cold.

"Do you know anything about the villa on the hill? about a small boy who escaped into the woods? Where is my son?"

Large tears collected in Priscus' eyes but they did not fall. The Gaul opened his mouth to answer, but he couldn't—he didn't know what to say. For the first time in his life, the Gaul was afraid to speak.

More guards came to the door. "Blacksmith—you must come with us."

"Tell me Gaul: What do you know about my son!"

The guards opened the door and rushed in on Verus, grabbing at him as he wildly fought them off. "Tell me! What do you know! What do you know!" One of the guards grabbed him around the waist and lifted him up, while a few other guards snatched Verus' legs and arms. They forced him through his cell door, where they were joined by more soldiers who had heard the noise. Between all of them, they were able to hold the Blacksmith tight and drag him away.

Verus yelled out as loudly as his voice was able. "I've seen you before Gaul and I know who you are; there is no place you can hide where I will not find you! Where is my son!"

Chapter 25
June 20, 70 AD
Verus

For five days Verus silently bumped in a wagon with a sack over his head. No one spoke to him—no one even treated him like he was alive. Twice a day, the sack was removed and he was given food and drink, which he ate quickly and silently. His new Master had small dark eyes that peered out from a large, fat head. He never looked Verus directly in the face; instead, he would glance to either side of him, like he was a piece of meat that he was considering purchasing from the market.

Verus' new Master had an entourage of at least twenty heavily armed men. The warriors carried weapons that were as diverse as their garb: while some had short swords and square shields, others carried clubs and wore pants, and still others dressed completely in black and had a wide array of twisted weapons. Most, however, were armed like gladiators.

The cart had six other gladiators that had been purchased from the *Ludi*—Verus recognized only one of them. The men were so tightly packed in the wagon that their arms and feet were constantly rubbing up against each other, which increased the heat in the already stifling wagon until it was almost too much to bear.

On the third day of traveling, the heat became so forceful that a few of the men passed out. Still the sullen group pushed on and on until, finally, they reached the walls of Rome. There was a moment of pause at the gate before they were ushered in through the huge wall. Verus could not help but feel that he was leaving one prison just to enter another. He thought about escape, he even planned it out in his head, but between the chains around his hands and the Master's heavily armed guards, it seemed to be an impossibility.

The wagon passed through the walls of a huge estate, which was like a venerable fortress itself. The new gladiators were unloaded at a servant's entrance and shuffled through a series of doors and down some steps. One of the gladiators tried to speak, but the lead guard whipped the man in the mouth just as he opened it.

Three things were quickly becoming clear to Verus: One, his new Master was from the house of *Brutii* and, consequently, was very wealthy; two, he had a taste for the exotic and extreme; and three, what little mercy his new Master might've had when he was young, left him long ago. Everything Verus passed—from the heavy shackles to the blood-splattered walls—seemed to be a bad *auspice*. Whoever this man was, he was certainly not one to tolerate disobedience.

The Blacksmith was locked away in a small cell that had a thick layer of dry hay and some blankets. Weaving between the fodder like a field mouse, Verus comfortably slept through the night. The next morning he was well fed with vegetables and meat—a mix that he had not tasted for some time. Then he was taken into the forum of the *Domus* and trained with the rest of the Master's servants. He joined a group of nearly sixty gladiators. They ran laps and drilled with the sword, lifted weights, and bathed in the private baths of the *Domus*. It all seemed so similar to the *Ludi* that Verus barely felt that he had left it; this new opinion, however, quickly changed.

The training was drastically easier. Instead of sweating as they worked, the slaves often took breaks to sit down and drink wine; a few of them became so inebriated that they could barely stand. After an hour or so, the formal mask of training faded away completely and Verus found that there were no *"Doctores"* that watched him, no instructors that whipped him when he slacked off. The little formal instruction they did receive covered techniques and concepts that seemed like blatant cheating. Verus learned how to stab the ground, hold the sand on his blade, and then whip it in another man's face in such a way that it did not seem obvious to the crowd. They also learned how to fake a wound to draw the opponent in and then attack when the man's guard was down. Each tactic Verus learned seemed more deceiving than the last.

After most of the men were sitting down and sucking up as

much wine as they could, the newly purchased gladiators just stood there, waiting in vain for more instructions to come. They finally ended up breaking themselves up in pairs and drilling on their own.

From the shade of the *Domus*, the other experienced gladiators taunted the newcomers:

"Why are you wasting your breath training out there when there is a mix of wine and meat over here?"

"What are you preparing for? combat? battle? You fools don't know anything about gladiatorial matches—how do you think you know how to prepare for one?"

"Come join us and drink with men who have already spilt blood in the arena. You can spend all day drilling with wood swords, but I assure you that the best way to prepare for a match is resting with us."

After another hour of training, one by one the new gladiators began to drift out of the sun and towards the wine and shade. As they walked away they would always assure their partner that they just needed a drink and that they would be back in just a moment. Those who left the sandy arena, however, never seemed to make it back. Verus kept losing his partners to the taunts of the other men until finally, it was just him and one other.

"What is your name?"

"Verus. And yours?"

"Quintus."

Verus wiped the sweat from his brow and looked disdainfully at the men that rested in the shade of the *Domus*. "You can take a break if you want, but I will be here training all day, everyday—in the heat of the sun or the snowflakes of the winter—until I win my freedom."

Quintus laughed. "Already you assume that you can outlast me in your training. But, just like you, I have come to win freedom and fortune. Cheap wine might fill the bellies of some men, but it does not satiate me."

Verus smirked. "Where are you from?"

"Here in Rome. I was born to misfortune and fed misery my whole life, which is something that will soon change. Do you have more questions or can we get back to our training?"

Verus shook his head and the two men paired off.

Quintus was trained as Dimachaerus—a fighter that used two swords instead of one. It was a very different fighting style than what the Blacksmith was accustomed to. Quintus constantly used his speed and the two swords to go on the offensive. After several mock-duels, Verus decided to try to fight with two swords instead of his big bulky shield. His left hand was accustomed to wielding a sword, but his right hand felt so awkward that he found himself only able to do basic defensive postures.

This training regimen went on for the next several weeks. After a while, Verus found himself more apt with two swords. Their mock fights became more and more intense, and Verus, despite himself, could not help but feel that Quintus was competing with him. Verus was simply the better fighter, and he proved it with his versatility of weapons and fighting stances. After almost two months of training at the *Domus*, Verus began to best Quintus with two swords. The first few times it happened, Quintus shook it off like it was nothing, convincing himself that it was just luck, but after Verus won consistently for a week thereafter, Quintus started harboring a bitterness that would seep out on occasion.

Whenever Verus asked Quintus about the sudden mood swings, the squat man would adamantly assure the Blacksmith that everything was normal, that he was always that way. But Verus had been studying facial expression and body language long enough to know that Quintus' anger was anything but normal.

Quintus was not the only one to notice Verus' skill in the arena; the Master also began to take more interest in the Blacksmith. As the gladiators trained, the fat man would watch from a balcony high above and praise Verus with as many words as the inebriated man could string together. The more experienced fighters did not take to it, nor were they nearly as convinced that Verus was as "grand" as the Master believed. Verus found that as he walked down the halls after training or when he was in the bathing house, the other gladiators would bump his shoulder, or hide his equipment, or throw rocks at him. More and more of the men began to stare at him with narrowed eyes and blank expressions, almost as if they hated him more than anything else. Even men that Verus did not know by name—men that he had never talked to—turned hostile.

Quintus soon abandoned Verus completely and joined the

other gladiators who lazily lounged in the *Domus*. Still, the Blacksmith persisted in his training and went on drilling his sword technique from the moment the sun rose until long after it set.

After two months of training at the *Domus*, Verus was given the chance to prove himself. He, along with five others, were chosen by the Master and sent to an arena outside Rome where they would make their gladiatorial debut.

In the heat of the day, the fighters had to wait in small rooms that were beneath the arena for their turn to fight. Verus was selected to be a special fighter who would come at the end and, consequently, had the entire day to listen to the men fighting above. The Blacksmith sat in silence—as neither of the two men on either side of him would talk. He thought long and hard of the battle that was to come.

After most of the day had wasted away, a voice called from above. "Verus, get ready. It's your fight now."

Verus stood quickly, put his breastplate on, slammed his helmet on his head, picked up his shield and gladius, and entered the arena. Despite the sun having long set, the arena was full of people and laughter. They enthusiastically got to their feet and cheered as Verus and his opponent entered the arena. The sound was so loud that it carried for miles. The two gladiators were ushered to the center of a circle of fires where a third man waited to mediate the bout. The fires twisted violently and rose high into the air, sending a light so bright that it illuminated the fighters in the middle.

Everything was so surreal, from the firelight to the opponent that now stared at him. Verus took two deep breaths and focused his gaze on his opponent. The *Summa Rudis* came to the middle as the cheers began to die. He looked at the two fighters for a moment longer before shouting, "Begin!"

The combat went swiftly. The opponent was experienced but nervous. Instead of fighting cautiously the fighter went in quickly for the kill. Verus pulled back and blocked the attacks, keeping his sword hand back so it could swiftly come forward when it was needed. It was not long before the Blacksmith was able to shift to the left and open his opponent up. He stabbed down and pierced the man's leg with his blade; blood splashed up his sword and splattered against his shield.

The man fell to the ground in a sudden heap, his leg dripping with blood. The fight was over just as quickly as it had begun. Verus' opponent threw his sword to the side and pointed towards the sponsor of the games—the sign that a gladiator had had enough.

Verus stepped closer to the man and stood over his opponent. The Blacksmith put his sword point at the top of the man's shoulder—ready to stab between the neck and the collar bone if the sponsor made the sign of death. But instead, the sponsor made a rising gesture with his hands. Some of the crowd cheered while others hissed. It wasn't until the *Summa Rudis* raised Verus' arm in the air that the Blacksmith realized the full impact of what had just happened. His first match had ended in a victory. He would now be known by the title *Tirones*—a title that meant that he was worthy to be part of the *familia gladiatorial*. A title that meant that he was truly a gladiator.

* * *

"Here is to my new champion, Verus!" the Master yelled at the top of his lungs. The rest of the people in the room repeated the gesture, raising their glasses high in the air before they drained them.

The Blacksmith nodded gracefully, giving a slight smile as he did. All around him were the rich and wealthy that lived in the *Domus,* along with several guests and friends of the Master. Verus had seen a few of them before—but that was only a glimpse here and there. Now, instead of him envying their freedom, everyone around him envied his skill with the sword. Verus was seated just to the left of his Master, while all the other gladiators were scattered across the room.

Young girls of all shapes and sizes would sneak up behind Verus with small towels and try to collect the Blacksmith's sweat, since it was rumored that the best aphrodisiac was the sweat of a triumphant gladiator. The Blacksmith took the abuse rather well, laughing all the while as the girls attacked him with the small towels. Verus was dished large portions of various meats and mushrooms, fruits and vegetables. Every kind of food he had ever wanted, or even ever heard about, was right before him on the table.

The feasting and loud laughter went long into the night, turning wilder as time passed. After most of the food had been greedily gorged or tossed aside, the Master clapped his hands and a group of entertainers came out from the cracks in the walls, laughing and playing music. There were jugglers and fire breathers, midgets dressed up like gladiators and wild animals dragged out by *Doctores*.

After more hours of entertainment, the air filled with the sound of the slow and mysterious cadence of the Egyptians. Six dancers came out and swooned with the music—much to the delight of the Master. The girls breathed and sighed, shaking their bodies in sinful arcs that made the rest of the men grab at them when they came too close. Slyly the girls slipped away from the grasps of the men and continued their dance. Their faces were heavily painted while their bodies were only lightly dressed.

Verus looked down, pretending to be more interested in the food before him than the dancing women.

The tempo of the music quickened as a group of slaves threw a mysterious liquid on the fire that turned the bottom of the room into a thick cloud of smoke. From out of the smoke emerged one of the most beautiful, shapely women that any of the gladiators had seen.

Her eyes were as sharp and dark as the blackest night, while her skin was as smooth and gentle as a wave. She danced wildly before the men, staying just out of their reach as she spun and twirled her body. She was joined by the other dancers, their motions complementing her moves perfectly.

Verus continued to look down at his food, that is, until his Master saw him.

"What are you doing, boy?" the Master bellowed. "Look at the treat I have prepared for you this night."

"Thank you Master," Verus whispered.

"You don't understand," the Master laughed. "The one in the middle is yours for the night. Go and take her—here and now." The music stopped just as the Master finished his sentence.

A shocked rifled through the Blacksmith's body. "Take her?"

The master laughed. "Yes, go and take her. The crowd around you is eager to see if you are as good a lover as you are a fighter."

"I can't."

228

"Everyone around you would love to be in your place, boy. I command it. Go. Now."

"I am forbidden."

"I am your Master; I will tell you what is forbidden."

Verus stood and clenched his jaw. "You are my Master and I will serve you well until you set me free but, before you, I must honor my own conscience. This woman who dances before me is not my wife, nor am I her husband."

"She is for the night."

"My Lord," Verus said as he lowered his head. "I am grateful for the gesture, but I cannot betray my heart, for the Gods have given me to another."

"Are you married?"

The Blacksmith hesitated. "Yes, I was…she died several months ago…"

"Then you're a free man."

"This woman is not my wife, and I would be spurning the Gods if I behaved like she was."

"Nonsense. Every Roman has behaved this way since the beginning of Rome."

Everyone in the room, including the entertainers, were watching Verus and the Master closely now.

The Blacksmith stood and stepped out from behind the table. "Master, I must ask you for your leave. I am tired from fighting and I fear I bore you with my speech. I thank you for your gift." As he talked, he walked through the center of the room towards the doors that were on the other side.

The Master turned red-faced and clenched his jaw. "You will not leave my presence until you have explained yourself! I have given you a gift that has been in the tradition of Rome since Romulus first started our great city. Explain why you will not accept it."

"Please…I am tired…please allow me to retire tonight."

"TELL ME! Why will you not accept this Roman tradition?"

Verus turned around slowly, shaking his head as he did. "It was not so from the beginning."

The Master laughed. "What do you know? What do any of my slaves know of our history?"

Verus straightened up and clenched his jaw. "After the city

was established by Romulus, the Etruscans took control of Rome and subjected her Citizens to the rule of a tyrant. The Etruscans were open to everything erotic—from their sensual art to the banquets they held to the slaves they kept around them. The Romans, however, distinguished themselves by being the opposite of the Etruscans: While their rulers were immoral and lazy, the Romans were moral and industrious. Rome, in essence, was founded on the principles of abstinence before marriage and fidelity after."

The Master stood and swore. "LIES! Where is your proof?"

Verus swallowed as he circled the room. "We have all heard the stories of Rome, heard how the city won its independence from the Etruscan tyrants. It was not a man that started the rebellion—but a woman. One night, after a long week of banquets and parties held in Rome, a group of Etruscan princes leaving the city were engaged in a debate over whose wife was the icon of perfection. To settle the debate, they decided to disguise themselves and sneak back into the city to spy on their wives that were left behind. They went from banquet to banquet, each one of them finding their wife passed out from wine or with other men. They finally came to the house of Collantinus and peered through a window. There was a beautiful Roman woman named Lucretia, who, instead of wasting away with wine and drink, was hard at work sewing. An Etruscan prince named Tarquin was so infuriated by what he saw that he left the group of princes and snuck back to the house of Collantinus. He broke into Lucretia's home and, under knife point, raped her while everyone else was away. The next morning, rather than living with her disgrace, Lucretia ended her life. The people of Rome were infuriated. Lucretia's husband and a man named Brutus quickly organized an army. They rebelled against everything Etruscan, killing all the magistrates and soldiers that governed the city. Rome gained its unity and strength to win independence because of their morality; the Etruscans, however, were eventually enslaved because of their immorality."

The hall was silent—only the heavy breath of the Master could be heard. "No one divides my house with lectures on morality. Who are you to speak to me about morality; you are nothing but a common slave. Remove him from my sight and whip him until he passes out. You, boy, will live to regret what you have said this night."

Chapter 26

August 1, 70 AD

Priscus

"Priscus, please have a seat."

The large Gaul stood there, his eyes unflinching.

"Take a seat or I will have your legs cut off so you will be forced to sit."

Priscus took a deep breath before he resentfully sat down on the plush couch behind him.

Tresias shook his head as he pulled out another chair and sat down. "Never, in all my years, have I seen a student of mine kill so many fellow gladiators."

"They were trying to kill me."

Tresias shook his head. "Yes, they were, and anyone would have defended themselves like you did; but, they say that once you killed the first one, the other two retreated."

"They did."

"But then you chased them down, drowning one of them in the pool and hanging the other with his own tunic."

Priscus nodded.

"Why? Why would you go after them if they were already running?"

Priscus gave a loud sigh. "Is that why you called me in here? To find out why I killed two men who were seeking to kill me? If I didn't kill them, they would still be out there, plotting my death as we speak."

"I would have punished them so harshly they would not have tried it again."

"And now you don't have to."

Tresias rubbed his hands through his hair. "Oh, Priscus. If

231

only you knew how many people within these walls want to kill you; everyone from the slaves to the cooks to the gladiators wants your head on a platter, with a fat apple stuck in your mouth for decoration. How many assassination attempts is that on your life—three? I myself don't know if I should praise you or slit your throat while you sleep."

The Gaul remained silent.

"It is not supposed to be like this," Tresias said as he rubbed his eyes. "The *familia gladiatorial* is an elite brotherhood that is unified through their hardship and pain. We are the only social class that is truly equal because, usually, a gladiator's birth and rank does not give him privilege above the rest. As gladiators we are separate from society—we are apart from it. We are not buried with the rest of the soldiers and Citizens, nor do we strive to fit in with them. We are buried with our own in graveyards set apart from the cities. The highest honor of a gladiator is the respect a fellow fighter pays to another, not in the skill of their sword."

"I come here to win—not to honor those who I kill."

"You've missed the whole point of this conversation. You, my friend, will not win if a mob of people come at you and split your skull. Every day my *Doctores* come to me, begging for permission to kill you. And, I've almost granted it too. You're making a mockery of everything a gladiator stands for."

Priscus did not speak.

Tresias shook his head and continued, "I've sold you."

"Sold me? But my training is not complete."

"It's as complete as it is going to get," Tresias replied quickly. "I've sold you to a good master—one who will make sure you are treated fairly. He is a very old friend of mine. His skill was legendary, as is yours. When I first met him, he was just like you: brutal and merciless."

"When do I leave?"

"Right now," Tresias replied, "and not a moment later. I fear that your life will not last long after you killed those three gladiators. You might not have known them, but they were all *Doctores*; and their students—all of them—have taken an oath to kill you or die in the attempt."

"Put them before me and I will kill them all."

232

Tresias laughed. "I know you would—that is why I have to get you out of here. You would be saving your life, but you would be costing me a fortune. Listen, I have trained you the best I know how and you still stand as a good candidate for a Sea King of Rome, but I can no longer afford to keep you, nor can I afford to lose any more gladiators to your hands. Horace, he is yours now; please take him as swiftly as you can."

From the shadows of the room another man walked into Priscus' sight. It was a man just as old as Tresias, but twice as bald. The figure had more scars than Priscus had ever seen on another man. His movement was quick and precise, like he was twenty years younger. "So you're the Gaul? You're the one that keeps old Tresias up at night with worry. We better go before the other *Doctores* get wind that you're leaving."

* * *

Horace led Priscus down a flight of stairs and through a passageway that the Gaul had never seen before. They exited out the back, where a small wagon was waiting. Before Horace could say anything, Priscus stuck out his hands, ready to be tied before he entered the wagon.

Horace looked at the Gaul. "You're used to being carted around, aren't you?"

The Gaul did not respond.

Horace looked at the Gaul with his two piercing blue eyes. "Listen, Priscus. My rules are simple: the more disciplined you are, the less you will have to be disciplined. I need a warrior, a champion to win fights in the arena. Your freedom will be given to you in degrees; the more you obey, the fewer rules you'll have, until one day you will be as free as me or anyone else in this world. Now put your hands down—I am not going to tie you up."

"What if I try to escape?"

Horace gave a knowing smile. "And where will you go? What will you fight for then? You and I both know that cords will not hold you forever, neither will cell bars or stone. If you wanted your freedom you would eventually slit my throat and take it, as I have no doubt you have done in the past; but something else compels you to stay here, something that is a lot stronger than the cords I could put around your hands. Now take the reins of the horse, I'm going to take a nap in the back. Tresias was so worried that you were going to be killed that he had me come as fast as I could. It took me four days of rough riding to get here."

"Yes, master…"

"I hated calling my owner 'master' when I was a gladiator as I am sure you do too. My name is Horace. Don't consider me your master but, rather, your business partner—for neither one of us makes money without the other."

Priscus nodded and took the seat in the front of the wagon. He awkwardly sat there for a moment before he finally asked, "Where are we going?"

"To Rome. Follow the signs and we should be there in a few days."

Priscus was surprised to discover that Horace was the only one that came to collect him. The Gaul thought that after hearing all sorts of gruesome stories about Priscus, his new master would have certainly brought a small escort for protection. Not only had Horace come alone, he actually fell asleep in the back of the wagon while they traveled. Freedom was just on either side of the wagon for Priscus—all he had to do was jump.

For the next few days, they rode on in silence. But after a while, the tedious quiet began to aggravate Priscus more than conversation. "Were you a good gladiator?"

Horace shifted abruptly, almost as if the sound had startled him. "A good gladiator? Hah. I consider anyone that is an old gladiator a good one."

"Were you a killer?"

"You are a blunt one, aren't you?" Horace replied. "Yes, I killed—even when I did not have to."

"Were you ever defeated?"

"Yes."

"How many times?"

"Thrice."

"And you lived?"

234

Horace stretched out his arms in the air and cracked his back. "The sponsor did not want me killed. And you, Gaul, how many times have you been defeated?"

Priscus laughed. "Never."

"What about that time the *Doctore* knocked you in the water?"

Priscus tightened up.

Horace laughed. "Don't think for a second that I did not find out all I could about you before I came up here. Everything Tresias knew about you, I also know."

Priscus narrowed his eyes but did not speak.

After a few days they finally arrived in Rome. Priscus was amazed by the fantastic arches and stone buildings all around him. Despite the surprise he felt as he looked at each one, he kept his awe to himself. There were, however, two times when the Gaul forgot to maintain his tough demeanor: once when they passed the temple of Jupiter, the other time when they drove past the construction site for Vespasian's new Colosseum, which was so covered with slaves that it looked more like a mound of men than a structure.

Finally, they drove into Horace's arena.

Priscus raised his eyebrows ever so slightly. "Is this all yours?"

"Yes."

They passed through the gate and headed for the stables that were to the left. Horace jumped from the wagon and handed the reins to a servant that was walking by. "Bartemous, it is good to see you this day. Can you stable these horses for me?"

"Yes, sir."

Horace gestured towards the Gaul. "Come, follow me; I want you to meet my family."

"Your family?"

"Yes," Horace replied.

"They live here with you?"

"Yes."

Horace and Priscus walked down one of the long halls, passing several doors as they went. They finally came to a thick set of double doors that had a crack of light underneath and the sound of a few people laughing inside.

Horace knocked on the door, which instantly seemed to silence the voices.

"Come in."

Horace winked at Priscus before the two gladiators stepped through the door.

"Surprise!"

The old gladiator did his best to act startled but he was never a good actor. "What's this?"

Behind the door was a host of people, all standing there with grins as wide as their faces. The room was as tall as it was wide but, despite its massive size, it seemed wholly inadequate for the number of people that were in it. All kinds of individuals attacked Horace with generous grins and hearty handshakes. At least two or three of the guests gave Horace a friendly punch in the arm as they reminisced about some old story or tale.

Priscus had a look of disdain and confusion on his face. He took four large steps backwards until his back was against the wall—his eyes darting nervously around the room as he did. As the crowd continued to trap Horace with acclamation, a woman approached the Gaul.

"You must be Priscus."

The Gaul remained deathly silent.

"Now I know it is you," the lady replied. "Horace said that you aren't much for idle conversation."

Priscus tightened his jaw.

"My name is Elisia, and I'm Horace's wife." The woman was certainly older, but not nearly as old as Horace, who seemed to have long passed the shining moments of youth. Despite her age, she had honest features that were strikingly beautiful, especially when she smiled—which was about as often as she talked.

Elisia continued to speak. "This is my son Primus."

A man a few years younger than Priscus took two large steps towards the Gaul and extended out his hand in friendship. The man had the strong eyes of his father but the roundish chin of his mother. "Thank you Mother for the introduction, but you don't need to introduce this man to me, for I already know who he is—you must be Priscus the Gaul. You are an impressive sight. If half the stories I hear about you are true, then you have come to the right place."

"Well don't be rude, Primus," his mother chided. "Offer him some wine and food. Horace always forgets to eat when he travels and I doubt that Priscus ate much on the road."

"I *am* hungry," Priscus growled.

"Come with me," Primus said with a wink which was much like Horace's.

The Gaul was ushered to an empty table where he promptly sat down. In front of him were all kinds of meats and vegetables, large baskets of bread and fruit. Before Primus could speak another word, the Gaul had put a little bit of everything on a plate and was eagerly stuffing his mouth as if the food would disappear within moments.

"I know it's not a gladiator's diet," Primus jeered, "but that can wait until tomorrow."

An effeminate voice interrupted. "Who is this?"

Primus glanced over his shoulder and rolled his eyes as he saw his sister. "You can't tell, Arria? This is Priscus of Gaul."

The Gaul looked up from his plate, a piece of meat still hanging from his lip. When his eyes met hers, she blushed and he swallowed. He suddenly felt ashamed of the sweat on his back and the dirt on his face. He grabbed desperately for a nearby towel which he used to scrub at his cheeks. She was still young—very young—but she had a beauty about her that held Priscus' gaze.

With her cheeks still red, Arria spoke just loudly enough for the Gaul to hear. "My father has told us all about you. And I must say, you match his description perfectly, from the way you keep your dark hair to the scars across your arms to your dark, large eyes."

"Pay no mind to her," Primus muttered. "She is twelve, and you know how they are at that age; she gets all woozy just seeing a gladiator…"

Arria slapped Primus across the head. "Primus, you're the one that watches the gladiators all day, chasing them around like a little boy."

"Please, let us men eat in peace," Primus replied over his shoulder.

Arria gave a small, mocking laugh and left.

After a while, Horace stood on a large bench and quieted down the crowd. "Friends and family, old business partners and new clients, I want to introduce to you the reason I've been gone the last few days, the reason I was forced to travel on my birthday. Priscus— please stand up." He waited a moment for the Gaul to find his feet. "I've personally witnessed this fighter, seen how he attacks each opponent; there is not a gladiator who could stand toe-to-toe with him in the *Ludi*, and I am sure that there are not any that can best him in Rome. Allow me to introduce Priscus of Gaul, the newest member into our *familial Ludi*."

Chapter 27

January 2, 80 AD
Verus

The Master was true to his word.

Verus was moved to a larger, cleaner cell, where he could stretch out fully and pace around in the sun. He also had a large window at one end that gratefully let the light in and allowed Verus to overlook the courtyard. This gesture, however, as kind as it seemed, was to keep Verus in the best of health so that the Master could lengthen the Blacksmith's suffering. The Blacksmith was fed by a slave who dropped food into a tray that was outside of his cell. Verus had to grab two chains from either side of his cell to unlock and open a latch, which left just barely enough room for Verus to stick his head out and eat like a dog.

Several times a week Verus was harshly beaten for no apparent reason besides "to toughen him up." After these long and exaggerated beatings, the Master always would send in the best doctors to mend up his wounds. The torturers were careful never to hit or whip Verus in the face or groin—since it would damage his appeal to the crowd—but he was whipped everywhere else.

For the pure amusement of the Master, several times Verus was tied down and whipped by an array of odd people: sometimes he was beaten by a couple of midgets, other times he was hit by a group that was dressed like Egyptian Gods, and still other times he found himself beaten by a group of women.

After months of these beatings, Verus found that he could completely ignore the pain. He was not sure if it was his body adjusting to the strain or his mind simply becoming stronger, but either way, they no longer caused him the wrenching pain that the Master so enjoyed to watch. Instead of twisting about while he was

239

whipped, Verus would stare out the window, peacefully watching the clouds go by.

This infuriated the Master even more, who now more than ever, wanted the Blacksmith to beg for mercy. While most gladiators fought only three to six matches a year, the Master had Verus fighting matches every month—sometimes twice a month. And no matter how experienced the Blacksmith was, the Master always found someone with more experience to be his opponent.

After his first victory, Verus became a *Provocatores Tenth Palus*. In his next match however, he fought a *Thraex Ninth Palus*. The battle was longer and more even than Verus' first match, but it finally ended with Verus slicing the man across the arm. His opponent dropped his sword and sued the sponsor for quarter, which was given.

Verus was then raised to a *Provocatores Ninth Palus*, so, the next month, his Master had him fight a *Murmillo Eigth Palus*. This combat was quick and decisive; Verus took a cut on the arm, but kept on fighting until he had stabbed the man through the foot.

The Blacksmith then fought a *Hoplomachus*, which he finished by stabbing the man through the leg; then a *Dimachaerus*, who he knocked out with the butt of sword; then a *Samnite;* then a *Provocatores;* then two *Secutores* at the same time; then two *Thraex* who both smelled of garlic; then four *Damnatis*—all armed with clubs and shields; then a *Laqueriarius*, then a *Retiarius;* then two *Murmillos* at once; then a combination of three *Damnatis* and a *Thraex*. He was then forced to fight as a *Bestiarii* and was pitted against four lions; then a rhino; then a pack of wild dogs; then an elephant. His next task was to fight as a horse-riding *Andabatae*, which proved difficult for him.

The battles went on and on, but still that freedom which he so desperately fought for, eluded him like sand thrown to the wind. Verus became immensely popular among the people, who—much to the Master's disdain—would buy up any piece of merchandise with Verus' name on it. On paper, Verus had become an extremely wealthy man—more wealthy than several of the *patricians* that came to watch him fight—but the Master prevented Verus from touching the money by placing it in a separate account that only a Citizen could access. Without his Citizenship, Verus was as powerless as a newborn babe. On several occasions the Master even tried to spend Verus' prize money but was prevented by the mob of fans and a well-spoken orator who denounced such an act as a sin to the Gods.

During the years that slowly passed, Verus had only two clear thoughts: Find the Gaul that seemed to know something about his son and, if the Gods were willing, win his freedom. He would often drift in thought, pondering on what he would say when he finally caught up to the Gaul: Sometimes he would imagine facing the Gaul in the arena; other times he would dream that after winning his freedom, he would search for the brute. After a few months of searching, Verus would find the warrior in a gladiatorial *Ludi*. He would watch him for a bit, correcting any mistakes he made in his form, and then benevolently purchase the Gaul and immediately grant his freedom—if the Gaul could adequately answer his questions.

The more popularity and wealth Verus earned, the more jealous and fearful the Master became. Each time Verus crushed his opponent the Master's ambivalence towards Verus grew. The fat man was constantly stacking the odds against the Blacksmith, trying to kill him in the arena through the host of opponents he sent against him. Oftentimes, the Master would stack the odds against Verus so much that the sponsor would cancel the fight outright.

Despite his long list of victories on his belt, Verus had never killed anyone—not completely anyway. A few of his opponents died from wounds far after the fight, but Verus had never been the one to strike the death blow. He became known for his mercy just as much as the Master was known for his brutality. Whenever the sponsor ordered the execution of one of Verus' opponents, the Blacksmith would throw down his sword and simply walk away. This would have been the death of him had it not been for his enormous popularity with the crowd.

Every time Verus disobeyed the sponsor, it was a blow to the ego of his Master—who afterwards would severely punish the Blacksmith. The more Verus refused to deal the final death blow the more diverse and intricate became the Master's methods of torture. One day, after he had refused to kill his opponent, Verus was tied to an angry nest of fire ants that bit his body until it was swollen with venom. Another time, he was tied onto the side of a mountain during a winter storm, which made him so cold he was shaking for days.

Other times he was put into pits filled with spiders and crawling insects, or left for days in the dark, or hung upside down until blood dripped from his nose.

The only friend Verus had was a slave named Terstius. The boy was short and skinny, being fed little and forced to do a lot. The slave had been put in sole charge of cleaning Verus' cell and feeding him during the day. The Blacksmith never ate all of his food; instead, he always left a good portion for the slave, who would hungrily eat it up. The two of them would spend long hours talking about the world around them. Terstius did not have a last name, or at least not that he could remember. His earliest memories were of living on the street begging for coin. He eventually was so starved that he sold himself into slavery so he could avoid the inevitable death that awaited street urchins. He knew nothing of his past or his family, nor anything of dignity or honor, fame or fortune.

"Good morning," Terstius said one day to Verus.

"And to you the same," the Blacksmith replied. "How is the Master this morning?"

"He's gone—took another trip to the *Ludi* in Nepet."

Verus shook his head. "The fool would not have to keep buying gladiators if he would just train them properly; I think he enjoys watching them die more than watching them live."

The young boy grabbed up a bundle of straw from the cell floor, "That's true except I don't think he intends on using these *gladiators* for normal bouts."

"What will he be using them for?"

"What? Are you saying you haven't heard?"

Verus gave a small laugh—it sounded weak and bitter. "How can I hear about the world around me when you're the only person I ever have a full conversation with?"

"Yes, you're right," the slave said. "I'm sorry. Sometimes I don't think before I speak; Master beats me all the time for it."

Verus gave a more genuine smile, "No need to apologize good Terstius. I'm sure you did not mean any offense."

"No sir, I didn't. I feel lucky enough to be the one in charge of cleaning your cell and giving you food. Every other slave I meet in the market is completely jealous of me—once I tell them that I watch over you. You and the Gaul are the most popular fighters."

Verus lifted his head slightly. "The Gaul?"

"Yes. They say he's as brutal as he is large; I think I saw him once but I'm not sure."

"How big is he?"

"He's huge—or so they say—and scarred too, almost as much as you."

"What class of fighter is he?"

"A *Murmillo*."

Verus suddenly took in a sharp breath. "Is he merciless?"

"Yes. He's killed dozens of fighters in the arena even when he doesn't have to. But don't worry. I don't think you will ever have to fight him."

"Why?"

"He's been selected as one of the Sea Kings of Rome. The Emperor has built a huge lake off the river Tiber, and he is going to stage a naval combat or something. Everyone is talking about it, including the Master. In fact, that is why the Master went up to Nepet—to purchase a few gladiators that he can personally send into the naval battle."

"I need to talk to the Gaul."

"How are you going to do that?"

Verus started nodding repetitively the more he thought about it. "If I can join the Naumachia—I will see him face-to-face."

"The Master won't let you fight in that."

Verus clenched his powerful jaw. "Why not?"

"Because you're not a killer—or so I heard him say the other day; you might be the best with the sword, but you don't have the stomach to finish your opponent. These naval battles are huge. A fighter has to deal out a death blow with every swing if he hopes to survive."

Verus narrowed his eyes and nodded. "So, the Master wants a killer."

* * *

The Master came back from his journey to Nepet with a

larger than normal contingent of newly purchased gladiators. To celebrate his return, there was a large feast where all the gladiators dined on meats and exotic fruits. As expected, Verus remained in his cell, where he waited for the call he knew would come. Towards the middle of the night, Terstius finally ran up to Verus, shouting out as he did.

"The Master has summoned you."

Verus stood up slowly—his mind ready to do what was needed. The young boy led the Blacksmith through a series of halls until they reached a locked door.

Terstius hit the door. "Open up. I have Verus with me."

The guards on the other side obeyed quickly, letting both of them pass through. From here on, Verus was escorted by four guards who gingerly placed their hands on the hilts of their swords. They walked through a long, arched hallway, which was filled with the bodies of large stuffed bears, wild-looking crocodiles, and brilliantly colored tigers. Verus recognized the features and faces of most of the animals since he had been the one to kill them. They went up some stairs, headed back the other way for a bit and finally reached the banquet room.

Verus knew the room well, from the Egyptian columns to the exotic painting that covered the walls. A thick smoke already covered the ground and parted as they entered. The appearance of Verus suddenly changed the dynamics of the room; the musicians stopped playing, almost on cue, and the dancers stopped moving. Even the *patricians* along the table ceased their idle talk and their glutinous gorging.

"Verus…" the Master said with an evil smile.

"Master."

"Come to the center of the room—I know that is where you most like to be."

The Blacksmith quickly obeyed.

"Did you miss me?"

"Yes, Master."

"Liar," the Master said lazily. "I've brought back some real gladiators from Nepet…"

Verus stayed stone silent.

"Hopefully these ones know how to kill."

Again Verus did not speak.

The Master shook his head. "He's too much a fool to understand that I am taunting him. Bring out the entertainment."

Verus went wide-eyed and spun around just as three opponents charged him: Two of them were slaves, armed with swords and shields, while the third was a gladiator dressed in full gear, from his helmet down to the greaves. The Blacksmith armed himself with the sandal of his right foot, which looked pitifully weak compared to the weapons that now faced him. Despite being heavily armed and protected, the slaves were hesitant to step forward.

Verus charged in, throwing his sandal in the face of one of them, which made the man blink. The Blacksmith moved to the slave's right and, using the slave's own shield as a barrier, got behind his opponent. Before the other two attackers could aid their companion, Verus snapped the poor slave's neck and threw him to the side.

The Master arched his eyebrows.

Verus armed himself with the shield and sword of the convulsing slave and faced the other opponents. He attacked the other slave, cutting him once across the leg and then another time across the shoulder. The slave fell to his knees in pain. As quickly as he fell, the slave raised his hand, suing for the mercy from the Master, but before a response could be given, Verus sliced the slave's hand clean from his body.

The crowd cheered loudly as the hand flew through the air and landed on a nearby table. Without even a moment of hesitation, the Blacksmith finished the man with another horrific swing.

With blood dripping down his face, Verus faced the last gladiator. They circled for a few moments before the gladiator attacked. The Blacksmith ducked and sliced outwards, cutting the other man's leg guard. The armor absorbed most of the attack, but the swing took with it a portion of the man's leg, sending him limping to one side. Verus pulled back and let the man recover.

The opponent threw down his shield and grabbed another sword from the side of a nearby guard. Verus mimicked his opponent, pitching his shield to one side, but before he could pick up another sword, his opponent rushed at him, swinging so wildly that Verus had to step back in defense. Verus ducked and dodged as best he could, but without another weapon or shield in his hand, he could not keep his opponent's attacks at bay. Verus retreated through the room, glancing madly around him for some weapon he could use. Soon, he found himself cornered, trapped by the opponent in front of him and the crowd of people behind him. The Blacksmith took a slice to the arm and another to the side. Still Verus kept his feet, knowing that if he sued for quarter that the Master would not grant it.

With Verus wounded, his opponent became emboldened. The Blacksmith waited for the next attack. As quickly as he could, he ducked underneath it, punched the leg of the gladiator, and stood up, slicing his opponent on the inside of the other leg as he did. This sent a shock of pain that pitched the gladiator to the side.

Verus ran around his opponent, sidestepping until he could pick up another sword. Now that Verus had two swords in his hands, his bleeding opponent was not nearly as eager to attack. Verus went on the offensive, swinging so quickly that the gladiator could do nothing more than step back defensively.

The crowd roared its approval, cheering far louder than they ever had before.

The Blacksmith sliced off the better portion of a few fingers from his opponent's left hand, forcing him to drop one of his swords. The fight went on but it was only moments before Verus sliced the man in the other arm. The opponent, unable to hold a sword in either hand, fell to his knees and pointed to the Master for mercy. In a last effort to save himself, he also knocked his helmet off his head, revealing the pale face of Quintus—Verus' training partner from long ago.

"It's me," Quintus whispered. "It's Quintus, your old friend."

Verus ignored him and stepped closer. Without waiting for any sign from his Master, the Blacksmith lifted up his sword and plunged his blade into Quintus' shoulder, piercing his heart and killing him almost instantly. As Verus pulled the bloody weapon from the lifeless body, the crowd reeled back in horror.

Chapter 28
June 2, 76 AD
Priscus

"Horace? Horace?" Priscus said as he went from room to room, looking for his master.

It was a clear summer day, one that was so pleasant that even the most dismal of individuals had a hard time finding fault with it. The Gaul had just retired from his training, his body still glistening with sweat.

"Horace?"

It was not until Priscus reached one of the far back rooms that a voice finally answered.

"He's not here."

Priscus scanned the room to see who had said it, but no one appeared.

"Who's there?"

Suddenly a woman appeared, a smile stuck to her face. "It's me, Arria. I was just looking for a bracelet I mislaid."

"Oh," Priscus replied. "Where is your father?"

The young girl tossed her hair back. "You should know better than me; he talks to you more about business than anyone else."

"Can you tell him I was looking for him when you see him?"

"Yes I can."

"Thank you," the Gaul said as he turned to leave.

"Wait."

"Yes?"

"You are always rushing from one place to another; I see you almost as much as the stars in the sky, yet I know so little about you. Are you always so silent?"

The Gaul did not answer.

"See," the girl teased, "you can't even answer me that."

"Life is busy."

Arria batted her eyes. "Life is also pleasant—if you make time for it."

"I have to get back to training—excuse me," Again Priscus went to leave, but again he was interrupted.

"I will not excuse you," Arria said with even a more playful voice. "Come sit down."

"I prefer to stand."

Arria stood up. "How about a walk then?"

Priscus took in a deep breath.

"Oh, it won't be so bad. Walk me to the garden upstairs."

The Gaul nodded.

"Thank you, Priscus. Even though there are thousands of gladiators here running around all day, it gets boring for a girl that is not allowed to do much besides read the works of dead Greek philosophers."

There was a long pause as they exited the room together and headed down a long hallway that led to the gardens above.

The girl continued. "Tell me something about yourself, something about your past." Before Priscus could answer, the girl interrupted. "I mean, Father trusts you, and yet I know nothing about you. Where are you from? Well, actually I already know that: You're from Gaul, right? What brings you down here? Actually, I already know that too. You joined a Roman Legion that was later sent down here, is that correct? I saw some of the Legions of the north marching through the city when Vespasian became Emperor; they say that only the fiercest warriors are sent to Gaul, is that true?"

The girl finally paused long enough for Priscus to answer but, instead, he only shrugged his shoulders.

"Oh, here I am, talking too much. My mother says that when I'm around someone that is as quiet as you that I can't help but fill the silence with my voice—which to me, does not seem a nice thing to say, especially to a daughter who is so educated about the world as I. I've learned it all from private Greek tutors who teach my brother and me. My brother is good at most things but he hates philosophy—which is something I simply enjoy."

Priscus smiled.

"Oh, I'm speaking too much again. Well, it's mostly your fault—your constant silence makes me nervous."

"I like to hear you talk; it keeps my thoughts from wandering."

"And where do your thoughts wander if they can?"

The Gaul looked down. "About my life...about my future—and my past."

"And what have you decided?"

"Things are different, now, completely different than they used to be."

"Well," Arria said as she tilted her head forward, "things look good for your future—I can tell. Have you not beaten every opponent that you've come across?"

"Yes," Priscus said. "But how do you know that?"

"Oh, Priscus, my brother is your biggest fan, and even though I am not allowed to see you fight, it doesn't mean my brother does not recount every detail." They finally reached the garden and the young girl gestured to a nearby bench. "Please, sit down with me."

The Gaul hesitated for a few awkward moments before he sat. "I've never been here before; I didn't know there was a garden on the top of the *Ludi.*"

"My mother insisted on it; she said she would not live here if Horace did not put it in."

"It's nice."

Arria looked around and breathed in the air. "It is, isn't it? Now, Priscus, if I promise to let you speak, will you promise to answer my questions?"

"Ask your questions and I will give you my best answers."

"Why are you a gladiator? I mean, you seem so simple and silent—like a man who has spent his whole life in the field. Father says that you are different in the arena, but I have a hard time imagining that. How can one man be a fighter in the arena and yet be so calm and complacent out of it? Oh, I'm not letting you answer am I? You should just interrupt me when I start speaking too much."

Priscus smiled again. They both sat there silence, staring out into the distance. Finally, Arria spoke.

"Well, why are you a gladiator?"

"Some men sign up to be fighters, but I was forced to it."

"But Father says you are the best fighter he has ever seen. How can you be forced to do something and yet excel at it so much?"

"These are some hard questions for me to answer."

Arria laughed. "I'm so sorry, Priscus! How about I give you some easier ones? Tell me, do you remember Gaul?"

Priscus squinted his eyes as he tried to recall images of the past. "It was a long time ago, but I can remember the color of the grass and the scent of the wind."

"Did you have family there?"

"Yes. My father died when I was young and so did all my brothers. Not long after that, an invading army of Celts came in and finished my mother. I was captured and forced to be a slave."

Arria touched the Gaul's shoulder. "I'm sorry..."

"It was a long time ago; I can barely remember my mother, or my father..."

"I'm not very good at asking questions, am I?"

Priscus shook his head and laughed. "No, you're not ..."

Arria smiled nervously, unsure if that was meant as a jest.

Finally, Priscus broke the tension. "Tell me something beautiful."

"Like what?"

"Tell me something different than what I have to see every day; recite something—anything that takes my thoughts away from this place. You spoke of philosophy before: Tell me something that you believe in."

"Have you listened to a philosopher before?"

"Not exactly," Priscus admitted. "I once had a...friend...of sorts...who told me about the rantings of a man named Plini."

"Oh, I do love the words of Plini."

"You know him?"

"Yes, I love to read his words; but in truth I can't quote him, nor can I remember much of what I read. How about some poetry?"

Priscus closed his eyes and put his head down. "Please..."

"Well," Arria said with a smile, "don't get your hopes too high. I usually only memorize lines that make me laugh—not ones that make me think. Here are some lines from Horace—not my father, but the man that my father was named after." She cleared her throat:

> *More infrequent come the repeated vollies*
> *Riotous young men rattle off bolted shutters,*
> *they no longer rob you of sleep, and that door*
> *keeps to its threshold,*

> *Which delighted once in the swing of ready*
> *hinges. Less and less are you hearing lately:*
> *"While I languish long through the darkness, are you,*
> *Lydia, sleeping?"*

> *Your turn's coming soon as a withered hag who'll*
> *weep at lovers' sneers in some barren alley,*
> *Thracian north winds grown to bacchantic fury*
> *under dim moonlight,*

> *When the searing flame of your love and longing,*
> *which incites the mares with tormenting madness,*
> *rages ceaselessly round an ulcered liver,*
> *not without anguish,*

> *That the swaggering youths find their verdant ivy*
> *more enticing pleasure than dusky myrtle,*
> *but consign all shriveled up leaves to winter's*
> *crony the east wind.*

Priscus laughed long and deep, his voice echoing through the garden. Arria could not help but laugh as well.

After awhile, Arria hit him in the shoulder. "Why do you mock me? Did you not like it?"

"Oh, Arria. I loved it—I loved it even more to hear it from your angelic voice—but it was just not what I expected. I thought I was about to hear the soft sounds of ethereal philosophy, not the groaning of an old woman."

Arria laughed again. "I told you: I don't memorize things that make me think—only those that make me laugh."

Chapter 29
January 2, 80 AD
Verus

"Leave us! All of you—except you, Verus!"

The people in the room looked around with smiles on their faces—almost as if this was some joke.

"Leave us or I will have each of you flogged until the floor is painted with your blood!"

The slaves obeyed quickly, pushing each other as they crowded around the exits; the *patricians* took a bit longer, but before too long, the room was empty except for Verus and the Master.

Why did you kill when you could have maimed?"

"I killed because that is what I am now—a killer."

"Lies! You've never obeyed me in the past, nor am I sure you will ever obey me again in the future."

Verus tightened his jaw but did not respond.

"What is it that you want?"

Still the Blacksmith did not answer.

"You want to be flogged again? Answer me or I will flail you myself."

Verus narrowed his eyes. "I want my freedom. I've served you twice as long as what a normal gladiator should; and I've brought you more fame and fortune than all of your other fighters combined. I myself could pay for my freedom if you would let me have my coin—the coin that I earned by spilling the blood of others in the arena."

"So that is what motivated you to kill—the prospect of your freedom."

"Master, oh great leader of the Brutii, I am your servant, sold to you years in the past, and I will continue to serve you, even if it means I have to kill to do so, but I must be fighting towards something. Promise me my freedom and I will promise you more Denarii than you could fit in this room."

The Master laughed. "No gladiator has ever earned his master that much gold, nor have they ever had the time to. It would take you two lifetimes to fill this room with the sweat of your labor. How do you plan to make me wealthy?"

"The Naumachia."

The Master arched his eyebrows and shifted in his seat. "How do you plan on entering?"

"With your permission, I will compete for the position of one of the Sea Kings—"

"Now you're just being foolish. You do not know how to command a ship, much less a navy."

"No, I do not, but this I will promise you: If you give me the chance, I will master the navigation of a boat; I will learn how to command a ship."

"There is no time."

Hot anger flashed through Verus' body. "There is time! I will learn if you will let me be taught."

"Verus—you insipid dog—I admire your boldness, but I do not like your newfound brashness. This Naumachia will be held in just a few weeks. I barely have time to submit a few of my own gladiators, much less train them on naval warfare."

"Use your influence to place me on the lead ship, where the action will most assuredly be. When the opposing Sea King comes and meets our ship, I will be there to slice off his head. You know—as well as the whole of Rome—that no man has been able to stand against me in the arena; I've defeated them all—from charioteers to wild beasts, from opponents that wielded swords as well as tridents—and I will bring you wealth by killing the Sea King. I will stack the dead high, fighting with the strength of Mars and the luck of Fortuna. Put me on a ship and I will earn my freedom."

"Do you even know who the opposing Sea King is?"

"Yes—Priscus the Gaul. I know him because we were trained at the same *Ludi*."

"Then you also know that no man has been able to stand against him. And, unlike you, instead of granting mercy, he strikes his opponents down before the audience can even decide if they want him to be left alive."

"I will kill him just as easily as I killed Quintus tonight."

The Master sat there, scratching his head. After long moments and a few drafts of wine, he finally spoke. "I will get you placed on the lead ship—this should be no problem. But, in return, I want you to unleash your sword and kill every slave or soldier that you come across."

"And what about my freedom?"

"Bring me the head of the Sea King—and I will grant you your freedom."

Chapter 30

February 14, 80 AD
Priscus

A lone servant walked into the great room of the gladiatorial *Ludi*. The servant was thin and nimble, which enabled him to sneak past the host of guests and entertainers that had swarmed the tables with excitement. The servant ducked past a juggler and squeezed past a poet, but then accidentally bumped a minstrel and tipped over a tray of food. With a crash, the tray splattered the remains of meat and soup onto a nearby wall. Finally, with an exhausting breath, the servant leaned over and whispered into the Gaul's ear.

"The lady of the house requests your presence."

Priscus put down the leg of meat that he was chewing on and looked around him at the rows of gladiators that were eating their fill. "Doesn't the lady know that we are in the middle of our banquet? We go to battle tomorrow—some of us for the last time. She must be asking for someone else, not me."

"What is it?" asked Horace with a wide smile.

"The lady of the house requests my presence," Priscus replied. "I can't leave our men before the banquet is done—it is a bad *auspice*. Why don't you go talk to your wife instead?"

"I don't think it is my wife that is requesting your presence," Horace said with a smile. "My wife retired a long time ago—I think it is my daughter."

"Arria?"

"Yes," Horace said as he shook his head. "She has been up every night for a week. Go speak to her. It will ease her worries as well as her father's."

"There's a lot of money at stake," Priscus agreed.

"I don't think it is the money she is worried about losing; go see her before it gets too late."

"What about the banquet? I can't leave my men on the eve of battle."

Horace gave a loud laugh. "They are my men, not yours, and I will still be here with them. Go see her—that is an order."

Priscus took a deep breath as he sat there, thinking about what he should do. Finally, with sudden impatience, he stood up and tossed his leg of meat back onto the table. "I will be back shortly."

"Thank you," Horace whispered.

Priscus set off towards the other door in the hall, pushing through the host of servants with little finesse. As he walked by, gladiators from all around hailed him.

"Priscus—our great leader!"

"Where you off to?"

"Tomorrow we drink the blood of the Athenians—right Priscus!"

Priscus nodded to all of them but did not spend much time as he passed. He made it through the noisy hall and out one of the side doors. He went quickly, walking twice as fast as he normally did. Before he could span the whole distance, however, a voice from the shadows reached his ears.

"Priscus."

The Gaul turned around to see the partially hidden figure of Arria.

Priscus sighed.

"Please don't be mad," Arria quickly began. "It was I that summoned you, not my mother."

"I know it was you, child."

The girl stepped from the darkness and into the light. "I am not a child anymore—nor was I when you first met me. I am more than twenty years old and yet you still treat me like a little girl."

Priscus remained silent.

"Walk with me."

"I can't stay long."

Arria scoffed. "You don't even know what I have to tell you before you have already planned your escape."

"My men are in the banquet hall, waiting for my return. I know how superstitious warriors get on the eve of a battle, and I know that they will be looking for any excuse to point out a bad omen."

"Walk with me," Arria said as she tugged on his arm.

"Where are we going?"

"To the gardens?"

"Fine."

The two walked together in the dismal light of the night; between the moonlight above and a few weak torches they were able to find their footing. In the silence their steps sounded large and forebodingly permanent.

They climbed the stairs to the top of the *Ludi*, where they could see the whole of Rome. Torchlight was everywhere in the distance, which weakened the presence of the stars.

"Isn't it beautiful?"

"Arria—I really need to get back to the banquet."

The young woman sat down, flipping her hair as she did. "Please, sit down with me and wait awhile."

With a sigh he finally obeyed. "What is it that you want? What is so important this night that you could not wait until tomorrow?"

"You might be dead tomorrow," Arria said.

"Yes, that is true, but all of us must die sometime—whether it is by the choice of Saturn or the hand of Mars."

"Oh, don't mock me by talking about the Roman Gods—you don't even believe in them."

"Why did you call me up here?"

"Because...I...well I don't know. I...like you."

"And I like you as well as your whole family; never have I felt more comfortable, nor more welcome."

"Then why must you fight tomorrow?"

Priscus pulled his head back, almost as if he did not understand the question. "I fight for wealth and fame tomorrow; I fight for your father."

"And what if you go to your death?"

"Then I will meet my death head on—with a grin on my face and a sword in my hand."

"And then you would leave all those who care about you behind—to mourn and weep at your loss while you pass to the underworld in your glory."

"What's wrong?" Priscus asked. "That is the way life is."

Arria suddenly burst with rage. "I don't want to lose you! I don't want to have to bury your body tomorrow…" Her face suddenly turned from anger to tears. She reached out for the Gaul, grabbing him around the shoulders.

Priscus sat there, awkwardly patting Arria on the back. "I'm not a good man, Arria; I am not worthy of your affection."

Arria sobbed for a moment longer before she regained control of her emotions. "You are a great man—one of the kindest I've ever met."

The Gaul shook his head and folded his arms. "No. You've sorely misjudged me—"

"I've known you for years, Priscus; I know who you really are."

There was a long pause as they both stared out over the horizon. Finally, with some hesitation, the Gaul spoke again. "I've done horrible things in my past—I've ruined hundreds of lives."

"As a gladiator?" Arria asked. "Your opponents in the arena will kill you just as easily as you kill them; you're not a horrible person for taking on the holy responsibility of the sacred *Munus.*"

"It's not my life as a gladiator that troubles me…it is the life I lived before."

"What happened before?"

"I killed…many people, slaughtering whole tribes at my whim, but I never felt the pains of regret or guilt that so easily burdened other people because I did it all for Rome. Everything I destroyed was by the command of another; every city I conquered was for Rome—all except one."

"What city was that?"

"A city that I was ordered to detain but, instead, I destroyed. There was a man who lived there. He had a family and a small farm, positioned on a hill. I…I…killed the family of this man and then, by the curse of *Tiwaz*, I was forced to listen to him reminisce over sweet memories of them …"

"Who was this man?"

"I'm not sure—I only know the sound of his voice. He loved his children, he cherished his wife, and I, Priscus the Gaul, took it all away from him. I've never had peace in my life, never been happy—these emotions were only fables to me—but somehow, despite the madness of this world, that man had found it…and I robbed him of it. He *was* happy. I'm not worthy of your friendship, nor am I worthy to live a decent life. There is only one thing left for a man like me to do: fight as hard as I can for as long as I am able. One day, I pray that a man will be brave enough to kill me—one day, I pray that it will all end."

Arria's eyes filled with fresh tears. "How can you say that? You've changed from what you once were…"

The Gaul stepped up to a large planter that was littered with a few old, weathered tomatoes. He grabbed one of the dried red spheres and squeezed it in his hand, revealing the seeds inside. "Look at the seeds of this tomato. If I planted these seeds, hoping to get some other plant than a tomato, I would be sadly disappointed as the plant matured."

"I don't understand."

"Can a seed become something different than it already is?" The Gaul stood and started to leave. "No one wishes they could change more than I, but I, more than anyone else, know that I cannot change. Goodbye, Arria."

Chapter 31
February 15, 80 AD
Verus

Verus approached a large man in the middle of the ship. "Are you in command?"

"You've only been on this ship for a few moments and already you're asking me questions," the man replied. "You better be as good with the sword as they said you are. My name is Sextus and I am the Sea King of the Athenians." The man had a wide jaw and dark thick hair that was shaved on either side and tied in the back. Everything about the man, from his sharp eyes down to his steady hands, suggested a long line of military experience. He pulled back his head and gave the Blacksmith a scrutinizing look. "So you're Verus—the one that is to be my second. Tell me, what do you know of naval command?"

"Nothing."

"Have you ever fought on a ship before?"

"No."

"Then what good are you—"

Verus stepped forward and grabbed the man around the shoulders, shoving him into the mast that was behind them. "I am not here to tell you how to steer the ship, nor to prove myself to you. I am here to kill any man that stands before me—including you, you senseless dog."

Sextus laughed, a sound which echoed across the still water. After another few moments of laughter, he shoved back, forcing Verus to let go of his grip. "It is good to see that someone is as bloodthirsty as I! I am glad to see that they sent me a warrior to be my second in command instead of a poet."

"You won't be so bloodthirsty when you learn what you

face."

"Boy, I do not fear the armies that sit across from us in the lake, nor do I fear their Sea King, Priscus the Gaul."

Verus' neck was throbbing. "I am no boy and neither is the Gaul. He is as merciless as he is large. Not only is he brilliant at commanding the soldiers around him, he is also a master at the sword. If we have any hope of winning this fight, we will need to throw him off guard—catch him by surprise."

Sextus scoffed and walked away. "What do you know?"

Verus drew his sword. His voice became so lethal, so bitter, that everyone around him looked up. "You will listen to me or I will end your command even before it begins."

The other man spun around. "I give you credit for your bravery, but don't prove yourself a fool."

"I trained with Priscus at the same *Ludi*; I was in the cell next to his! I know how he thinks."

"Do you now?" Sextus hissed.

Verus sheathed his sword. "What are your plans?"

The captain turned and began to walk down the ship, checking everything to make sure it was ready. As he did, he hissed back to Verus. "We are going to charge straight down the middle, where the Gaul is sure to be."

"He's not a witless brute—as you think—but a man who is as brilliant at strategy as he is with the sword. If you charge straight in, you doom yourself to be rammed to pieces by the ships that will encircle you."

"He's a Gaul," Sextus scoffed. "The only strategy that he knows is to do a full-out charge. We will gain the advantage over him by concentrating all of our forces on a single point, where we will break through their lines and flank them."

"I swear to you that the Gaul will not be in the middle of the ships, nor is he planning to charge. Trust me—I know this man."

"Then point him out when we ram into him—I'm going to be the one who kills him."

Verus swore and shook his head. "So be it Sextus, but know this: The blood of every Athenian that dies today will be on your conscience—you hubristic swine."

* * *

The sun reached its zenith as the last ship pulled into place. The two naval armies stared at each other in the distance: One was dressed and armed like Athenians, with their blue flags, circular shields, and solid helmets, while the other was dressed like those of Syracuse, which had square shields and carried green flags. Historically, the Athenians were supposed to lose, but the Emperor played to the crowd's sense of justice and put exactly the same number of men on both sides.

The men tightened their grips on their weapons, readying themselves for the imminent battle. Verus closed his eyes and looked down, focusing his mind on the task that was before him. Thousands of men on either side now stared at each other, summing up their opponents, but as Verus looked over at them, only one face mattered to him—Priscus the Gaul. It had been years since the Blacksmith had seen him but, despite all that time, he was sure he could pick him out at any distance. *"I need to find him before the battle turns fierce. Find him. Find the Gaul. Find the brute and make him talk."*

From the deck of the ship, Verus could see all types of Roman *patricians* running along the shore, waving the green colors of Syracuse or the blue colors of Athens. The crowd looked like a flock of birds that fluttered on the ground but never took off. In some areas, benches had been erected that rose impressively from the ground. In the middle of the shore line, the Emperor had a private box of stone that rose up into the sky; from the balconies of the Emperor's box, a number of purple banners whipped majestically in the wind. The Emperor emerged, waving his hand in the air. Verus could barely make out the small man in the distance. After long moments of cheering, the crowd quieted down as the Emperor began to speak. Despite all of the gladiators straining to hear, they could just barely make out the muffled sound of the Emperor's voice. On and on he droned, filling the air with a constant run of words.

As the Emperor finished, a host of trumpets sounded, which was the signal for the gladiators to take the oath. The gladiators spoke in one solid voice that carried across the water and lifted up through the sky:

We who are about to die salute you.

Sextus had been right—Priscus' flagship was positioned in the middle, where it glared out like an open invitation to the opposing army. Verus shook his head—almost as if he did not believe it. Only two thoughts pounded through his head: "*Find out what Priscus knows, and then, chop off his head.*"

The Athenians made the first move.

Sextus, with a grin on his face, waved his hands in the air, signaling all of his ships to move forward. Like a massive group of cattle, and with oars slapping in the water, the ships slowly obeyed the command and began moving across towards the enemy. The lead ships went faster at first, allowing the other ships to fall into formation behind; soon, the Athenians formed a long column of ships that went straight for the middle lines of the Syracusians.

Whether it was out of fear, or hesitation, or by some other odd force, the Syracusians did not move—they didn't even ready their oars.

Verus shook his head. "This is not right."

They passed the Emperor's box, the crowd cheering them on.

This only encouraged Sextus. The Sea King leapt up to the front of the ship, drawing his sword out as he did. "Now is the time to strike! They're too disorganized to move. Battle speed! BATTLE SPEED!"

The *Auletes* picked up the beat—the ship lurched forward. The oarsmen heaved and pulled, grunting with the exertion. Every heart was pounding as they drew closer to the enemy.

Still, the Syracusians did not move—they did not even prepare their archers.

Verus swore and shook his head.

They were only a hundred yards away now. The Athenians began yelling so wildly that the sound far surpassed the noise from the crowd on the shore. After a few moments, the Athenian Sea King ordered that his archers move to the bow of the ship, where they fired their first volley of arrows; the Syracusians returned fire, hitting a rower in the back.

When they were only eighty yards away, the Syracusians

suddenly stuck out their oars and began to row. Their boat moved slowly forward at first, like a piece of driftwood in a stagnant pond.

Sextus' eyes were gleaming with fury. "RAMMING SPEED! Now we have them! SEND THEM TO THE DEPTHS BELOW!"

The slaves picked up their pace, but so did their opponents. The Syracusians rowed faster, trying to match the speed of their opponents. The two ships rocked steadily as they headed straight for each other—their bronze rams cutting through the water.

They were only fifty yards away now.

The Athenians unsheathed their swords.

Forty yards away.

A marine to Verus' right took an arrow in the arm.

Thirty yards.

Suddenly, Sextus turned the ship to the right and shouted out for all his men to hear. "Port side oars! Port side oars!" As quickly as he said it, the slaves began to pull in their oars, bringing them in just as the ships began to pass each other. The sides of the ships rubbed together, screeching and grinding loudly as they did. Pieces of wood exploded, fluttering through the sky like wounded birds as the oars of the Syracusians' ship splintered.

The soldiers around Verus cheered wildly. The Blacksmith looked back at the ship they had just struck: The vessel had lost all of its portside oars; it was now just sitting there, drifting in the water.

Sextus ran around the ship, screaming orders. "Turn the ship around. Let's not keep them waiting! BATTLE SPEED!"

The portside oars were dropped back in the water, where they matched the tune of the *Auletes*. It was an agonizing long wait as their boat slowly turned around. All the Athenian soldiers moved up to the bow of the ship, where a bridge was mounted onto the mast. With their swords drawn, they began to chant and beat on their shields in rhythm.

After the ship had completely turned around, Sextus screamed out above the noise, "RAMMING SPEED!" They drew in closer and closer to their enemy, which now braced for impact.

Long tense moments passed before a loud cracked split the air as the brass ram punctured through the stern of the Syracusian ship. Water gushed into the ship and on the slaves below.

"RELEASE the bridge," Verus shouted.

Someone cut the restraining cord for the bridge, sending it falling down on the boat below. Without a moment of hesitation, the Blacksmith charged in, waving his short sword. He quickly spanned the distance over the water and met the enemy forces head on. A spear came from nowhere, aimed at his head, but Verus was able to duck at the last moment.

He crouched behind his round shield and lunged forward with his sword, stabbing a man through the head. Then, as he ducked under the swing of one of his opponents, he kicked one of the Syracusians in the shoulder and broke the nose of another with his shield. One of the Athenians behind the Blacksmith tried to squeeze by but a spear to the throat sent him pitching over the side.

The Blacksmith went in ruthlessly, stabbing a man through the shoulder, another he butted with the hilt of his sword, and a third he cut across the soft part of the belly. Blood dripped across the deck just as freely as the water seeped in from below. Finally, after stabbing another opponent in the chest and a fifth one in the gut, Verus was able to force himself onto the deck of the Syracusian ship. The battle turned fierce as more Athenians crowded onto the damaged vessel. Verus led the charge, brutally slashing and hacking as he went, sending bleeding bodies overboard into the wine-colored water below.

Suddenly, a man to Verus' left lunged forward and stabbed deep into his round shield. The Blacksmith pulled back, but the spear would not come loose; using his speed, Verus quickly dropped his shield and ran forward, slicing off the head of his opponent.

The Blacksmith killed another, and then another. He picked up the spear from a fallen foe and used it to pierce a man's thigh. With blood dripping down his face, he pushed on and on, killing every slave or soldier he came across. The Blacksmith left a trail of broken bodies and bloody faces wherever he went.

"Where is Priscus! WHERE IS THE GAUL!" The Blacksmith stabbed another man through the leg, sending him wheeling to the side in pain. The Syracusian screamed out loud and fell to the ground; he tried to shuffle away but Verus caught him. The Blacksmith lifted the trembling man in the air with his thick, scarred forearms. "Where is Priscus!"

"Priscus?"

"Where is the Gaul!"

"The Gaul?"

Verus had no patience today. He stabbed the man through the throat and tossed him overboard. "Where is Priscus!"

But the large Gaul was not there, nor were any of the stronger soldiers.

At the end of the ship, the Blacksmith jumped below the deck, where it was already half full of water. "Priscus!"

Still there was no response.

"I knew it—I knew he would switch the flags of the ships."

Verus went to the very front of the ship and looked out across the torrential lake, scanning for the ship of the Gaul. The scene that greeted him was full of fire and blood, chaos and pain: there were bodies, weighted down by armor, thrashing in the water below; in every direction there were men with spears and arrows in their backs writhing in pain; to the right of him were four ships latched together as if they had been one—soldiers from all four ran in every direction, trying to defend their ships while attacking their opponents; directly in front of him was a large ship that had almost completely caught fire. The smell in the air was a mix of charcoal and steam that wafted up and drifted into the screaming fans on the shore.

"Verus…Verus…" said a soldier from behind.

The Blacksmith arched his eyebrows and turned around. Behind him were five or so Athenian soldiers—their swords bloodily dripping as they looked at him.

"Sextus has left us."

Verus had not been the only one to realize Priscus was not on the ship. While Verus had pushed the enemy back with his sword and shield, Sextus had recalled most the men and pulled up the bridge, freeing up the Athenian ship. Instead of waiting for Verus to finish up with the enemy, the Sea King had rowed off towards Priscus' large boat.

Now instead of facing the Gaul, Verus found himself knee deep in a sinking ship.

Chapter 32

February 15, 80 AD
Priscus

The Gaul's grin spread from ear to ear as he watched the large Athenian ships barrel down the middle of the lake. Instead of placing his best fighters in the slow ships in the center of his lines, where they would seemingly be the safest, Priscus put them in the fastest ships on the outside of the battle formation, where they could easily flank the enemy.

Priscus took a deep breath. His thoughts were everywhere except where he was. He had been thinking about Arria, about the features of her face in the dim moonlight. He was not sure what she saw in him—perhaps it was his skill in the arena, or the esteem he received from the other fighters—but for some reason, her eyes seemed so soft when she looked at him. And in those moments that they did, he felt more special than he really was. He wanted to tell her more than he did last night, tell her about his plans for the future, but good reason prevented it. He might, after all, end up with an arrow in his back or a sword in his belly. The Gaul shook his head. "*All I have to do is do what I've done hundreds of times before. If I can just win the day— just win...*"

The Gaul stood beside one of his men, tightening his jaw. "Maximum crew; general speed."

"Yes, sir."

The oars arched out and splashed in the water, moving the boat slowly at first. The ship took its time as it began to glide toward the Athenian's flank. The calm water was cut before the ship, making a white wake that followed closely behind.

"Sir, our right flank is engaging."

"Those fools," Priscus whispered. "They should've waited

until those Athenians tired themselves out; now they will be losing the advantage that they would've had."

A thunderous crash rippled the still water as two opposing ships hit each other head on.

Priscus laughed. "The Sea King went right for the center, right where I knew he would. The prideful worm—I hope he is alive long enough for me to finish him myself."

The Athenians, with their blue colored flags and round shields, seemed fed by the sudden noise—thrilled by it. They broke from their column formation and headed off towards the nearest opposing ship they could see, driven by the thrill of the hunt. The battle turned chaotic as both sides were now in range: arrows flew haphazardly through the air, followed by large balls of flame that were launched by catapults.

A small Bireme turned towards Priscus' ship, pointing its ambitious ram towards the mast. The Gaul laughed as the smaller ship went into ramming speed long before it was even close. The slaves worked hard inside the Bireme, pitching their oars into the water as quickly as they could.

Priscus held up a hand, waiting for the enemy to come in range. "Hold...hold..." Finally, when the Bireme was close enough, the Gaul gestured forward with his hands, and a small catapult loaded with a burning ball was released. The first few balls of flame bounced off harmlessly across the deck, but the third struck the mast. Immediately the Athenian captain ordered a dozen slaves to climb up the mast and cut the sail free; but with the wind fanning the flames, the fire spread too quickly. Within moments, the mast was cracking with flames, sending sparks of ash and debris on the slaves below.

Priscus slowly turned his ship around until his ram was pointing toward the Bireme. "BATTLE SPEED!"

The captain of the Bireme suddenly realized the danger he was in. Using every curse word he knew, he encouraged his men on, all the while the fire above continued to spread.

Priscus ran to the head of the ship where he could clearly see the watery battlefield. "RAMMING SPEED!" The boat lurched forward as the oarsmen rowed together, sending the ship straight towards the desperate Bireme.

The little Athenian ship was fast, which was evident as they manned their oars, but Priscus' ship proved faster. Before the little vessel could escape, Priscus' Quinquereme hit the ship in the aft, gouging out a hole as wide as a man's chest. With the ship taking water, it became almost completely immobile.

As the two ships broke apart and drifted away, Priscus narrowed his eyes. "Leave the ship to burn. Maximum crew. General speed." The Gaul walked back and forth along the deck, studying the naval battle with his keen eyes. Finally, he pointed to the far left. "Steer us to that Athenian vessel."

The ship pitched to the left, sailing over a few floating bodies as it did. The oarsman rowed on until the ship crossed the lake and drew close to an Athenian Trireme, which picked up speed as their Quinquereme approached. The two ships paired off and came at each other at full speed—each one daring the other to flinch.

The moments grew tense as both ships pitched up and down in the now choppy water. Just before impact, Priscus jerked on the rudder, veering to the right, while at the same time, ordered his slaves to take in oars. The opposing captain foresaw this and did the same. The ships came in close, slowly scraping sides as they drifted by. Both sides shot arrows and threw spears. As the boats were almost free of each other, Priscus lit a clay pot of oil and threw it onto the stern of the enemy ship, which sent up a wall of flames that instantly spilled out across the wood planks. A dozen or so men were caught in the burning oil; they thrashed and rolled in pain as they fought to put out the flames.

The Gaul narrowed his eyes. "Marines! Prepare to board!"

The Quinquereme slowly turned and twisted in the water, circling the burning ship until they were completely turned around. The Athenian captain yelled at his men to row, but between the burning boards above and terrified slaves below, the ship barely moved.

"Keep firing the catapult!" Priscus barked as he picked up a javelin. "They are frightened by the fire and disoriented by the flames. Now is our time to strike. Now is the time we earn our glory! Push forward and slaughter them all!"

The Gaul looked at the faces around him: He recognized most of them, from young Bassa—who on his first day of training stabbed his own foot—to the older man nicknamed "Tithinus." He looked to his right where Postumus stood, a poet turned warrior, and Canaeus, a man who always talked about becoming a doctor; and Primus and Tertius, two brothers who joined up together. Then there was Postumuian, Quintillian, Gaiuso, Aulus, and Decimus. On his left side there were Cnaeus, Tiber, Caiufus, Isiaha—who prayed more times a day than most men eat—and Primulian. He looked around him, seeing the fear in the eyes of his men. There were dozens of others that Priscus did not know, nor would he ever. Most had little experience in battle, the rest had none.

The Athenians had manned their oars again and were madly trying to escape Priscus' ship, but they had lost all of their momentum. Within moments, the Quinquereme reached the Athenian ship and released the bridge, sending it stabbing down into the enemy's deck. One brave Athenian tried to catch the bridge so he could throw it to the side, but failed as his body was crushed under the hefty blades.

"Bring me back the captain's head!" Priscus yelled.

With a scream that seemed to ripple the water below, the Gaul's men went in quickly, making a mess of everyone they met. Priscus watched the men with a smile on his face and a sense of pride in his eyes—almost like a father who is watching his son take his first few steps.

After a half-dozen casualties on either side, Priscus' soldiers were able to force themselves onboard past the edge of the bridge. The fighting turned more desperate for the Athenians, who now had the enemy to their front and the heat of the flames at their rear.

One Athenian, however, was more skilled than the rest and pushed the attackers back towards the bridge. Before long, three Syracusian soldiers lay dead at his feet and two more were wounded. The rest of the attackers hesitated before the soldier, unsure how to best approach.

Suddenly, a long javelin came from the side, spearing the Athenian through the neck, instantly dropping him to the floor. The throw had been perfect in form and strength, so exacting that its victim did not realize it was coming until it was too late. Priscus picked up another javelin and threw it with his might, hitting another warrior in the face, and then another. After he was out of javelins, the Gaul drew his sword and, with a shout that startled even his own men, Priscus dove into the combat, issuing death with each stroke of his sword. He ducked under one attack and sliced the legs of an Athenian; he then came up and knocked another over the edge of the boat.

Out of the corner of his eye, Priscus saw that young Bassa was in trouble. With a mighty heave, the Gaul threw his sword through the air, sending it into the back of a large Athenian. Before Priscus could see if this saved Bassa's life or not, the Gaul found himself attacked by three soldiers at once. Using his large shield as a ram, Priscus butted one in the head and kicked another; while he was grabbing for another sword at his side, however, the third soldier sliced Priscus across the thick part of his leg. The Gaul flinched but did not fall. He narrowed his eyes and lunged forward, grabbing the man around the throat and flipping him around. His body became a shield for the Gaul as a set of Athenians charged in and mistakenly stabbed their own comrade. As the man drooped with death, Priscus hefted him like a sack of grain and threw the body at his attackers.

With the Gaul in the lead, there was no man that could stand before them. Soon, the rest of the Athenians were either forced into the flames behind or stabbed by the Syracusian blades in front.

Priscus raised up his hands in the air, screaming with as much force as his massive lungs could muster. The rest of the soldiers joined in, mixing their voices with the wild cries of the enthusiastic crowd on the shore. Their moment of triumph was short-lived, however.

A panicked soldier suddenly grabbed Priscus' attention. "Sir, there is a ship coming straight for us! It's the Sea King of Athens, and he's almost upon us!"

Chapter 33

February 15, 80 AD
Verus

"What do we do?" asked one of the men.

"Silence," Verus hissed. "Let me think."

"We're going to have to swim for it. We're doomed if we stay on this sinking ship."

Verus scratched his head and scanned his surroundings again. *"If we jump in the water there will be no way of catching up to the Gaul—no way of hunting him down."* The Blacksmith turned around, sheathing his sword as he did. "This battle is still ours for the taking. If we cower beneath the waves, we may save our lives, but we will lose this battle. And what will befall the slaves that fought and lost? Will the Emperor spare our heads? The answer is a simple 'no'—he won't spare us if we are soaked in water and not in blood. All of you should remember one thing: You must fight this battle like it is your last, for if you don't, it most assuredly will be."

A larger, more resentful soldier stepped forward. "What do we do then?"

Verus looked around and then pointed. "There! The mast. Find what weapons you can to cut at it."

"You can't be serious," the other man continued. "You expect us to make a boat out of it?" The rest of the soldiers looked at Verus and then the other man, almost as if they were deciding who to follow.

"No," Verus replied sharply, "a bridge. I am still second to the Sea King; I am still in command here. Either you help me, or you will die."

"Like hell I will—"

Before the man could utter another word, he was interrupted

by Verus' sword, which pierced clear through the man's neck. Instantly, the body collapsed to the floor—its blood mixing with the water below.

"NOW!" Verus seethed. "Is there anyone else who disagrees with me?" The Blacksmith waited, but no one answered. "Good. There should be a few tools on the ship to cut away burning wood. Find me something to chop the mast down!"

Instantly the other men's demeanors changed. The five of them went about the ship quickly, looking for something substantial enough to cut down the mast. A few moments later, at one end of the ship, one of the Athenian soldiers held his hand up high and shouted, "I found an ax!" The man came running as quickly as he could towards the center of the ship. "It was tucked away in a box towards the bow."

Verus took the ax and with all his strength, swung it into the base of the mast. He struck it again. And again. The Blacksmith swung until sweat was pouring down his brow and chin.

After a while one of the soldiers spoke, "Sir, do you want me to take a turn..."

The Blacksmith was so focused that he could not hear the soldier next to him, nor the screams of pain and terror in the battle around him. His whole future seemed so dependent on whether he could cut the wood quickly enough that everything else slipped into the background. Even though the wood was soft, the mast was thick, making it more than difficult.

Despite it all, before long, Verus had a cut a deep wedge into the side of the mast. The Blacksmith handed the tool to one of the soldiers behind him. "Now, strike quickly on the other side at a downward angle until nothing but a thin piece of wood holds it all together."

"What are you going to do?" asked the soldier who took the ax.

"I am going to climb the mast and wait for another ship to pass by. When one of them gets close enough, I want one of you to hit the mast with the ax, while the rest of you pull it down with the ropes that are tied to it."

"I don't understand."

Verus narrowed his eyes. "We are going to make a bridge with

273

the mast of the ship. When another ship comes close enough, I want all of you to bring it down until it bridges the gap of water between us."

"Why are you going to climb up it then?"

"Because someone has to catch them off guard. If they see us running at them along the mast, they can just as easily knock us off. I need to be on the top of the mast when it falls so I can fight them off long enough for the rest of you to come aboard."

"What if our ship sinks before another ship comes by?"

"Just pray that it doesn't," Verus said as he studied the mast above him. "I can't swim very well and I doubt that any of you can."

"You're the craziest man I've ever met."

The Blacksmith did not respond; instead, after a short sigh, he began climbing up the mast. Using a thick piece of rope that was tied to the highest cross section, it only took him moments to reach the first part in the mast, moments longer to reach the top. From there, he could see the entire battlefield—which stretched out into a bloody and fiery mess in every direction. He looked towards the shore, where a large contingent of the crowd was waving at him. He waved back stupidly—almost as if he was about to perform some stunt for their entertainment.

Then he waited.

The air seemed cooler at the top of the mast, where it began to blow in earnest. Two times, enemy ships passed on both sides of the sinking ship, but both times they were too far. Verus was starting to doubt the whole idea, when finally, a small enemy ship slipped around their port side. The boat was running from a much larger and faster Athenian ship, which it avoided by taking sharp turns around the other boats that were locked in battle.

Verus swallowed. *"This is it."*

The small Syracusian boat had already been part of battle, which was evident by the blood stains and wounded bodies that dotted the floor, but the vessel itself seemed to be wholly intact. Twenty slaves rowed at a maddening pace, whipped by the fear of the larger ship that came at them from behind.

The Syracusian soldiers were so panicked they didn't see the man clinging to the top of the mast of the sinking ship that they were passing, nor did they see the other five soldiers that were knee deep in water and waiting to bring the mast down.

"NOW!"

One of the Athenian soldiers burst from his cover and began hacking like mad at the mast, while the rest of them tugged and pulled on the ropes that had previously secured the sails. It was a tense few seconds as the slaves in the Syracuse ship suddenly realized the danger they were in: While some of them tried to paddle in reverse, most kept doggedly paddling forward. The ship paused in the middle with indecision as the two forces thrashed the water on either side.

Suddenly, the mast snapped and shook; it teetered for a second before it came crashing down into the middle of the smaller vessel. The little boat bowed and rocked with the weight of the mast, making large waves that rippled out to either side. The whole thing happened so quickly that Verus had little time to prepare himself, even less time to leap away from danger. His body crashed towards the bottom of the small boat like a sack of rocks. His armored head hit one of the slaves in the shoulder while his feet smacked another across the face.

Whether it was the distraction of the mast or the fact that Athenians started running across it towards them, the Syracusians did not seem to notice Verus. He laid there for a moment, hugging the hilt of his sword.

"They're coming across!" yelled a Syracusian. "They're..."

Like smoke from a damp fire, Verus rose from the bottom of the boat—his helmet bristling with the blood of his opponents. He threw his sword into the chest of the man who was screaming. The body crashed to the floor, quivering with his last few moments of life.

An attacker charged at the Blacksmith but he was too quick; before the defender could swing his weapon, Verus hit him in the nose and sent him into the water. He recovered his gladius and paired off with another man, who had fear racing through his eyes; Verus stabbed this man in the leg, as well as the next man. From all over the ship, warriors rushed towards the Blacksmith, swinging their swords in a desperate fury.

The Blacksmith ducked and sliced the inside of one of his opponent's legs, and then, as he turned to the right, chopped another soldier's hand clean off his arm. As the bloody fist fell into the water, the other Athenians arrived, screaming as they leaped from the mast onto their opponents. One of the unlucky soldiers happened to land onto an upheld spear, which pierced his heart and sent him sliding to the ground.

The battle was fierce as both sides fought on. As the blood turned the deck red, Verus finished the captain with the butt of an oar. What was left of the enemy's courage suddenly broke.

As the captain's eyes glazed off into the distance, Verus turned around, seething with blood lust as he did. "KEEP THE SLAVES ABOARD AND KEEP THEM ALIVE!" The Blacksmith knocked one of the skinny slaves in the mouth, which accentuated his point perfectly. Try as they might, however, the remaining four Athenians could only keep a few of the slaves from leaping overboard, but this did not matter. Of the dozens of slaves that jumped in the water, only a precious few knew how to swim. The rest thrashed around, clawing at the side of the boat as they fought each other for air.

"PULL THEM IN!" Verus ordered as he threw a rope toward the thrashing slaves below. They were only able to rescue half of them, however, as an Athenian Trireme maneuvered around and, with all oars whipping into the water, headed straight for them.

"Verus! The Athenians are coming to rescue us!"

The Blacksmith turned around, shaking his head as he did. He watched the large Athenian boat for a moment, watched how they picked up their speed instead of slowing down. "No, they've come to ram. They think we're Syracusians." With this, Verus stepped up to the front of the ship. "All of you get behind an oar and row for your lives!"

"What about the rest of the slaves?"

"ROW!" Verus yelled. "Leave the rest behind! Those Athenians behind us will not rest until we are dead. You slaves once served Syracuse, but now you serve Athens; your side may have changed, but your lives are just as precarious as they were before. NOW, row if you want to live! Row before we all die!"

The boat became alive with movement. Everyone, including the Athenians, picked up the closest oars and shoved them into the water. They picked up speed quickly, but the large juggernaut proved faster. Verus took to the rudder, steering his ship straight into the confusion of the battle. Arrows whistled by; large spots of oily water were burning; bodies fell from above and bounced across the deck of their boat as they paddled. There were dozens of burning ships all around, sending a thick smell that permeated the air. Suddenly, just in front of them, two large ships collided with so much force that it sent a wave crashing into Verus' little vessel.

The Blacksmith turned the ship sharply to the right, screaming wildly as he did. "PULL YOUR OARS IN!" Moments later, their ship hit a bigger one, which sent it pitching to the right. The two ships squealed as their sides scraped. Verus' ship hit every oar that was in front of them, snapping them like twigs. From the neighboring ship, the sound of battle rang out in a mix of metal and screams. A man from above took an arrow to the chest and fell down right in front of Verus. They drifted on, constantly scraping the side of the enemy ship. More bodies fell on their vessel; more arrows whipped through the air.

They finally cleared the ship and stuck out their oars again. Verus turned hard to the left. A whistling sound came towards them. A moment later, the mast exploded into shards of wood. The large mast teetered for a second before it snapped in two.

"Cut it free!" Verus ordered. "Push the mast overboard!"

Their ship drifted slightly to the right while the mast trailed in the water behind. The slaves worked quickly on the mast, hacking at it until it was set adrift a few moments later.

The wind picked up, clearing the air around them. In the distance, Verus could see it: Priscus' flagship was several hundred yards in front of him, just waiting for Verus to come.

The Blacksmith narrowed his blood-filled eyes. "ROW! ROW!"

They found themselves free from the mess of combat. Now, instead of dozens of ships locked in battle all around them, they found fresh air and open waters. Verus could see that Sextus' ship was just in front of them, traveling as fast as it was able towards Priscus.

The Blacksmith encouraged the slaves on, using the most colorful language he could think of. Faster and faster the ship traveled. To the right of Priscus' and Sextus' ships was another

Athenian ship that was almost entirely consumed with flames.

Verus turned his rudder towards the burning hulk.

"Where are you going?" asked one of the Athenians. "We should regroup with the Sea King to reinforce his numbers; it is the only way we can beat Priscus."

Verus clenched his jaw. "I am going to flank Priscus' ship by boarding on the aft of his boat!"

"How will you do that? Our ship is not equipped with a bridge, nor is it as tall as Priscus' Quinquereme."

"I will go through that burning ship that is on the right; Priscus' bridge is still latched onto it, and it should be easy to break through the burning boards."

"You are mad…"

Verus did not answer. Instead he kept his course—his eyes fixed on a point in front of him.

The slaves in the boat were lathered in sweat but still they rowed on. Verus walked back and forth, waving his sword threateningly at anyone who slacked. Before they were even close to the burning hulk, Verus could feel the heat that wafted towards them.

He steered the ship to the farthest point of the wounded boat, where the fire was the weakest. The Blacksmith sheathed his swords and whipped his shield onto his back; he then grabbed a bloody cloak, soaked it with water, and threw it over his shoulders.

Before he could jump out to the other boat, one of the Athenians grabbed him by the shoulder. "May the Gods grant you good luck." Then the man handed him an ax. "Take this; you might need it."

Verus nodded. Without another word, the Blacksmith pulled himself through one of the rowing holes and into the burning ship.

All around him, flames voraciously engulfed the ship. He pulled himself into the middle of the boat, where a good amount of water had already flooded in. With the flames above and the water below, Verus began to crawl towards the other end of the vessel. Every once in a while, he had to pull himself out of the water to pass the supporting beams that crossed the floor; each time he did, the flames cooked his cloak with so much heat that it sizzled when he dove back into the water. The heat had a strong smell, like olive oil that had been cooked too long.

Towards the other end of the boat, the heat and flames became more intense. He tried to hold his breath as long as he could, but soon he was forced to the surface for air. His eyebrows singed as he pulled his head out of the water and took a deep breath.

Finally, he reached the far end of the ship, where he was sure Priscus' bridge would be. When he went up for a breath of air, however, the flames burned his lips so badly, he was forced back under the water. The Blacksmith tried to surface again; this time, he was able to take a slight breath but nothing that would sustain him for long. Panic started to well up in his chest, but he refused to let it set in.

He closed his eyes and gripped the wood handle of the ax. He stayed there for a few moments, thinking of everything that had led him to this point. He could see his Master's disapproving glare, which shifted and turned until it transformed into the face of the Gaul, whose looming image stood just before him, laughing at how pathetic he seemed. Suddenly, his eyes snapped open, and he exploded out of the burning wreckage.

Several dozen slaves on Priscus' ship turned towards the sudden noise just in time to see Verus shooting out of the fiery depths below, his eyes blazing red like some vengeful God. Thousands of burning embers were kicked loose, twisting through the air as they spread out and were picked up by the wind. The Blacksmith's helmet was smoking, as was the cloak draped around his neck. The slaves just sat there, staring with open mouths. Verus, however, did not wait, nor did he give the slaves much time to react.

Verus threw his ax and split an oarsman's skull. He then drew his sword and charged at the slaves. Within moments, four of them lay dead, two of them wounded. Verus pushed through the throng of unarmed slaves, cutting any of them that were in his way.

Then suddenly, like the light from the sun that breaks the clouds on a rainy day, Verus could see Priscus only twenty feet in front of him. The Blacksmith leaped to the side of the ship and stood on the railing where he could have a clear view. "PRISCUS!"

The Gaul turned around, surprised to hear his name.

Verus pointed his sword at Priscus. "You wretched beast. No more will you plague men with your foul presence, nor will you curse them with your brutality. I have come to remove your head and cut out your heart. There is no man that is able to stand before me, no soul that I have not been able to beat. By the power of the Gods—"

Suddenly, from out of Verus' field of vision, a broken oar hit him in the side of the helmet, sending him pitching overboard. He found himself falling for a moment before he crashed head first into the cold water. Verus flailed wildly, kicking and fighting with all his strength. He shrugged off his helmet and shoes. Next to go were his cloak and shield, followed by his breastplate.

With this weight gone, he was now able to struggle to the surface, where he grabbed one of the oar holes for support. From up above, the battle raged on. Soon dozens of bloody bodies joined Verus' side as they were tossed overboard.

Verus swam on and on, using the side of the ship for support. He reached the rear rudders, which were cranked heavily to one side as if the ship had been trying to turn. He breathed deeply and raised the sword that was still in his left hand. With a spiteful grimace, he hacked one of the rudders until it broke in two. He then did the same to the rudder on the opposite side. With the ship now immobile, the Blacksmith began to climb up toward the deck where he knew he would find the contemptible Gaul. He was halfway up when a Syracusian happened to look down over the railing.

The man let out such a bellow that his voice lifted high above the combat. "The Athenians are climbing up the ship; they're trying to flank us!"

Within moments, a few more men from above appeared, armed with bows and spears. Verus blocked a spear that was thrust for his head, and then another that came for his neck, but then a third nicked the top of the shoulder. The wound was not deep, but instantly it sent a trickle of blood down the Blacksmith's back. Verus climbed on, fighting with all the will that was still left in him. Another spear point came at him, but Verus was too quick; he dropped his sword and grabbed on to the shaft of wood. He tried to pull it out of his opponent's hands but to no avail. They struggled for a moment longer before another man appeared with a bow in his hand. Verus watched as an arrow was notched and aimed for the space between his eyes.

With no option left, the Blacksmith screamed as he let go and fell back into the water. When he emerged, he found himself the target for more archers. He grabbed the wood rudder, which was still floating by, and ducked behind it just as the arrows were released. They thudded against the wood, a few of them sticking. Using whatever strength he had left, Verus kicked away from the ship as quickly as he could. It was a long painful swim, but soon, the Blacksmith was far enough away that the archers could not reach him.

Through heavy breaths, Verus shook his head and swore as he stared at the Quinquereme in the distance. The Blacksmith could feel the heavy presence of the Gaul but, like the stonewall that had separated them in the *Ludi*, he could not get to him.

He had failed.

Chapter 34

February 15, 80 AD
Priscus

"You men there—come with me," Priscus yelled as he ran back over the bridge and onto his own ship.

Across the water, with its golden ram cutting through the waves, the massive Quinquereme of the Athenian Sea King came straight for them. At the head of the ship was the Sea King himself, his face grinning broadly as his boat streamed towards Priscus. In his eyes, which shined like the very beams of the sun, burned a surreal determination.

"REVERSE OARS!" the Gaul shouted. "Reverse oars; battle speed! Raise the bridge."

"There is no time," Postumus yelled. "He will ram us in moments!"

Priscus studied the situation, gauging all of his possible alternatives. "Slaves! Gather everything that you can and drop it down below—right where the ram is sure to hit. And all of you marines—pick up an oar and follow me!"

The men each grabbed an oar and followed the Gaul, who in turn went to the spot where the Sea King was coming. The Athenian ship was so close now that it was easy to distinguish each face that bobbed up and down.

Priscus grabbed an oar and pointed it towards the oncoming boat. "Position your oars towards the enemy. As the boat gets closer, we should be able to slow it down by catching it with our oars." The men obeyed quickly, pointing their oars like javelins towards the enemy boat.

The Gaul tightened his jaw. "Hold strong. Hold strong."

Tense moments passed as both sides stared each other down.

The ship came closer and closer until it was only yards away. The marines shoved their oars into their opponent's boat, pushing it back as best they could. The tactic slowed the boat, but it could not stop it. The next moment, the ram struck the ship, pitching it to one side.

Priscus drew his sword and lifted up his shield. "Testudo! Testudo! Archers fire at will!"

The warriors fell in behind Priscus and immediately made a wall of shields that faced towards the enemy ship. The next moment, the Athenian bridge came down, its long spikes stabbing into the deck of Priscus' boat. Standing on the other side of the bridge, with his chest puffed out, stood the Sea King of Athens. He was gripping a large circular shield in one hand and a spear in the other. The air became deathly silent.

"MY NAME IS SEXTUS! Where is the Sea King of Syracuse!"

Priscus stepped forward through the wall of shields and pointed his bloody sword towards the Athenian commander, but before he could speak someone else filled the silence.

"PRISCUS!"

The Gaul turned towards the voice—so did Sextus. Across the ship, only twenty feet away, stood a short but stocky, wild-eyed man, whose helmet and shield were charred black with flame. His clothing was soaked with water and spotted with ash and blood; he did not have the colors of Athens, nor the colors of Syracuse. It seemed that the very mouth of Hades had spit the man out of a bed of fire and planted him on the ship.

Standing on the rim of the vessel, he pointed his sword towards Priscus. "You wretched beast. No more will you plague men with your foul presence, nor will you curse them with your brutality. I have come to remove your head and cut out your heart. There is no man that is able to stand before me, no soul that I have not been able to beat. By the power of the Gods—"

But before the man could finish, a group of slaves from Priscus' ship attacked him with shards of wood and knocked him off the ship.

Priscus turned his head back towards Sextus, who began to speak but was quickly interrupted by the Gaul.

"Words are for the weak."

283

With this, Priscus ran towards the Sea King. The two clashed swords for only a moment before Sextus retreated behind a crowd of soldiers. With a horrific yell, Sextus sent his men charging forward. The Gaul stood there on the bridge, hacking and slashing at the soldiers that came at him. He had already sent two of them to their watery grave when the rest of Priscus' soldiers reinforced him from behind. The two sides clashed together with such force that it had the spectators screaming with excitement.

Bodies from both sides were stabbed and thrown overboard, where they sank beneath the waves like lifeless rocks. Priscus pushed on and on with his large shield; by his efforts alone, the Athenians were forced to retreat to their ship. Priscus' marines fanned out and swarmed in. Arrows flew in every direction, catching unsuspecting soldiers. A few of the Athenian defenders climbed up the mast with bows and started shooting. Six Syracuse soldiers lay bleeding on the deck before any of the attackers knew where the shafts were coming from.

Priscus stepped back from the line of battle, gritted his teeth, and picked up a lance from a body below; with a loud grunt, he threw it with all his might. The throw was so strong that the spear went through armor and flesh alike, killing an archer almost instantly. The limp man fell down on the soldiers below, convulsing with his last few moments of life.

Arrows came at the Gaul but they were deflected by his large shield. The Gaul grabbed up another lance. Just then, another arrow struck his shield—landing only a thumb's length to the left of his right eye.

Priscus growled and took several more lances from a soldier standing close by. He threw the first lance, hitting a man through the neck, and then another, which skewered a man through the thigh. One after another, Priscus brought all of the archers down from their roosts. The Syracuse soldiers were now able to drive their opponents farther back.

As they pushed their opponents past the mast, a small Athenian ship reinforced the enemy. Although they were few in number, they were certainly more skilled. The Athenians suddenly gained courage at the presence of these new men and pushed forward, stabbing all that stood in their way. One after another the

Syracuse soldiers were chopped down. They were driven further back towards the front of the ship when finally, Priscus—having dispatched the archers—joined the throng.

The Gaul ferociously elbowed past his own men until he was in the thick of battle. He lowered himself behind his shield and pushed forward, forcing the man in front of him back a few feet. This simple maneuver opened the defense of the soldiers to either side; Priscus lunged forward and stabbed one of them through the belly and slashed another across the face. He then swung to the right and left, killing two men in quick succession.

The Athenians withdrew a half step and reformed their shield line. The Gaul pushed on. He grabbed one of the shields of the defenders and, using his incredible strength, pulled it down and away from the defender's grip. The Gaul stabbed his opponent in the chest before the man had time to raise his sword. Two more men fell before the Gaul, then a third.

The Athenians were pushed farther and farther back. Sextus rallied his soldiers again and sent them in, crashing against their enemies with their shields. Men from both sides were wounded and cut down. Sextus charged in, attacking the right flank of the Syracuse soldiers. The man was as skilled as he was daring. He ducked behind his shield and pushed forward. He then dropped to his knees and sliced the calves of two men that were before him. As he stood up, he put his foot on the railing of the ship and leaped up into the air, which gave him just the right angle to stab down into the shoulder of one of the men below.

More men fell before Sextus—killed by his brutal sword.

With Priscus killing Athenians on the right, and Sextus killing Syracusians on the left, both of the shield lines broke. The combat spread across the ship like spilled wine. Priscus pursued the Athenian Sea King, shoving past friend and foe alike. He finally reached Sextus just as he was pulling his sword out of the lifeless body of a man named Decimus.

The two men paired off and flipped their weapons warningly at each other.

"So, it is down to you and me now—"

Priscus interrupted the man and lunged forward, stabbing so quickly that Sextus barely had time to defend himself. The Gaul pushed the attack, driving past men that fought all around them. Soon the two warriors were near the bow of the ship, where the bridge was situated. Priscus pushed Sextus back until they were both on the bridge, fighting for their lives. Once there, Sextus threw his shield angrily and drew another sword.

"Come and claim your glory!" Sextus yelled.

The Gaul silently stepped forward and attacked. Sextus counterattacked with just as much force, which took chunks out of the Gaul's shield. Priscus stepped back for a moment, luring his opponent into a sense of confidence. As the Athenian changed position and began to shift along the edge of the bridge to the other side, Priscus charged forward, using his shield as a ram. Sextus took the shield square in the chest and fell backwards over the edge of the bridge. With a tremendous splash the Sea King disappeared under the water.

Without wasting a moment, Priscus ran to a dead body that had been skewered by a javelin. With a quick tug, he freed the weapon and returned to the bridge. Raising it high in the air, Priscus waited.

Moments later the Sea King appeared, gasping for air. Priscus threw the weapon hard, hitting the man through the open mouth. Sextus choked and thrashed in the water until his body disappeared beneath the waves—the long shaft of the spear was the last thing to vanish. With Sextus gone, the remaining Athenians retreated and leaped over the edge of the ship.

Priscus raised his hands in triumph. "Soldiers! Return to the ship; we have more men to kill this day." The men responded quickly, running back over the bridge to their own ship. Priscus counted the men as they went—totaling up the day's casualties as he did.

"More than half gone."

The Gaul returned to his own ship. "Cut the Athenian bridge free! Reverse oars; maximum crew; general speed."

As the bridge was pushed free and the oars dipped into the water, Priscus tried turning the ship, but it would not move. "Something is wrong with the rudders."

Aulus, one of Priscus' most trusted soldiers, walked to the rear of the ship and peered over the edge. "It's been cut to pieces."

Priscus swore and shook his head.

"Sir, it does not matter now," Aulus whispered as he patted the Gaul on his shoulder. "Look across the watery field of battle— it's all but over. There is nothing left to fight."

Chapter 35

February 16, 80 AD
Verus

Long hours after the Naumachia, the *patricians* were still debating which side had won. The argument soon turned so confrontational that two of the leading Citizens of Rome armed themselves with swords and came at each other. With a raised hand, the Emperor stopped the conflict by declaring that both sides shared the victory.

The Emperor then declared with his loud voice, "Priscus the Gaul did gain the upper hand in the beginning with his strategy, but the Athenians quickly adapted by attacking everything that they could see."

Despite the Emperor's words, the argument continued on for days. There were, however, two points both sides agreed upon: Priscus of Syracuse was certainly the best commander, but Verus of Athens proved the most resourceful and best fighter. With Sextus dead, Verus was proclaimed one of the Sea Kings of Rome—one of the champions of Naumachia.

This sudden fame only fueled the hatred between the Blacksmith and his Master, since Verus—not his Master—was constantly being invited to dine with dozens of powerful *patricians*, including the Emperor himself. The Master always refused to let Verus go, claiming that the Blacksmith's wounds were still too fresh for him to be moved.

Instead of dining on exotic meats and spices with Emperors, Verus was locked in his cell and given nothing but coarse food and stale drink. In the midst of all the excitement, Terstius became twice as talkative as before. The youth talked incessantly about all the gossip he heard about the Blacksmith: about how the Emperor proclaimed him the champion of the Naumachia; about how all the women were dying to see his face again; and about how people were speculating if Verus would fight in Vespasian's Colosseum, which would be completed in only a few weeks.

"What's wrong?" Terstius finally asked. "You're one of the most popular gladiators in the whole world. Most people would be thrilled just to talk to you. Why do you sit there in silence?"

Verus rubbed his face with his hands and shook his head. "The Master will never set me free."

"I bet the Emperor will—if you ever get to dine with him."

"But the Master will never permit it," Verus said as he took another bite of his food.

Terstius wanted to disagree, he wanted to argue, but he knew that his words would be hollow if he tried. They both sat there in silence, waiting for the mood to change. Verus slowly drank the wine that was beside him and turned the cup in his hand once he finished.

"You need to impress him more—" Terstius said.

Verus laughed. "How? Have I not beaten everyone and everything before me? Was I not proclaimed one of the champions of the Naumachia?"

"All I know is," Tertius whispered, "Priscus will soon be granted his freedom—or so the people say."

This news sent a shock through Verus' body; he tightened his jaw and lowered his head.

"Why does that surprise you?" Terstius asked.

"He received the same honors as me, the same prestige and wealth from the Naumachia, and he—of all people—will be set free before me?"

"He's never been defeated in combat—"

"Nor have I!"

Terstius looked down, almost as if he was preparing himself to be hit across the cheek.

Verus shook his head and took in a deep breath. "I'm sorry Terstius; I did not mean to frighten you. It's just that I have always tried to live honorably, always respected the Gods and others alike. I've been charitable to all those around me and honest with everyone I've met. But look at me. I am in the same situation that I've been in since I was sold as a gladiator."

"They say that when Priscus wins his freedom he will retire from being a gladiator completely."

"What about the Colosseum? Doesn't the Gaul want to test his skill in Vespasian's new death Arena?"

"Vespasian is dead; he died several months ago."

Verus furled his eyebrows. "He's dead? I just saw him at the Naumachia not two days ago."

"Don't you ever hear anything?"

Verus rolled his eyes, "How can I? You're the only one that I talk to."

"You must have seen Titus. He is the new Emperor."

"Titus...yes...I've met him. He has a strong sense of fairness and justice in him. I'm sure that he would set me free if I could meet him face-to-face—"

"But the Master will never allow that."

Verus' mind was starting to put together the outline of a plan. "Well, if Titus commanded me to fight, then the Master could not stop it from happening. After that, I would just have to impress Titus."

"How are you going to convince Titus to personally select you to fight?"

"I am one of the Sea Kings of Rome."

"Still the Master will try everything in his power to prevent you from fighting; he won't let you march around and build up support amongst the mobs of Rome."

Verus rubbed the back of his neck for a moment, which seemed to soothe his thoughts. "Like any new arena, I am sure that Titus will select two of the best fighters to inaugurate it with their blood. If I use the mob of Rome to heighten my reputation, then they will be clamoring for me to fight in the arena."

"How will you do that?"

"With your help."

"But I am only a slave..."

"All I need you to do is send a few letters for me."

"To who?"

Verus stood up and paced the room. "First, we need to send a letter to Tresias—he is an old friend of mine. He is the owner of one of the most famous *Ludi* schools in the north; both Priscus and I trained there. We need to get the school to say that I am the best warrior that they have ever trained."

"The Gaul won't be too happy about that."

"Exactly," Verus said as he whipped around. "Nothing builds hype like conflict. The more I can enrage the Gaul, the more conflict I can create. I need to send a letter to the Gaul that insults everything that he is."

"You're going pick a fight with Priscus?"

Verus nodded slowly, almost as if the thought was just becoming clear. "An old friend once taught me that the best way to impress someone is to pick a fight with someone else. Since we are both Sea Kings of Rome, the conflict will be easy to build. Imagine it: Two undefeated Sea Kings of Rome—the champions of the Naumachia—selected to inaugurate Titus' Colosseum with their blood. Both of us will enter into the arena, but only one of us will leave it alive."

Tertius swallowed. "What if you're the person that ends up dead?"

Verus narrowed his eyes and lowered his voice. "I would rather die fighting for my freedom out there than live out my life as a slave here."

"Yes, sir."

"I need to publish the letters that Priscus and I exchange— that will liven up the mob."

"How will you do that?"

"There is an orator—the one that defended me when the Master was trying to steal my money. If you go to him, offering money upon winning my freedom, I am sure he will be able to publish the letters. After the letters are out there, I will need to make sure the Emperor is reading them."

"Who do you know that stands close to the Emperor?"

"I did know a man—a long time ago," Verus said as he strained his memory. "He was a *patrician* that was ousted from power when Vittelian ruled. I don't know where he is now, or if he is even alive, but he was a Vespasian supporter long before the Emperor came into power. If he survived the reign of Vittelian, I am sure that Vespasian would have reinstated him."

"What is his name?"

"Plini the Elder."

"He died."

"How do you know that?"

"He died a month after the Emperor—everyone knows about that."

Verus stepped forward. "What happened?"

"He was killed by the eruption of Mount Vesuvius, which destroyed the city of Pompeii and Herculaneum. The cities just seemed to disappear under the destruction—almost like the earth swallowed them."

"And Plini was there?"

"Yes."

Verus hit the wall and leaned his forehead against it. "If only I had tried to contact him sooner..."

"His adopted son is still alive."

Verus turned around. "Adopted son? What is his name?"

"Plini the Younger."

Verus repeated the name.

"Yes, that's him."

"Do you think he holds the same sympathies as his father?"

Terstius shrugged his shoulders. "It's worth trying."

"Yes," Verus nodded. "If this young Plini is as connected as his adopted father was, then surely he has a portion of the Emperor's ear. We will have to write a letter to him immediately, explaining the whole situation."

Tertius nodded solemnly, but then asked, "Can you write?"

"A little."

"Who will we get to write these letters?"

"If the Master is as cruel as he is brutal, I am sure that he has made many enemies in his house. Bring to me the most educated and refined person that is here—I'm sure he hates the Master as much as I. Go now with haste. We have a fight to pick."

Chapter 36

February 17, 80 AD
Priscus

It was a nice clear day—one in which someone in love finds the most pleasurable. Priscus, however, was not as pleased as was the young girl who sat next to him. The Gaul handed her a loose piece of paper and asked her to read it:

VERUS! VERUS! was the name the crowd cheered at the close of the Naumachia—and no wonder they did. After killing everyone aboard a Quinquereme, and finding himself stranded upon the sinking ship, the quick-thinking and resourceful man brought the mast down upon another ship of Syracuse. With the mast acting like a bridge, Verus led four other men and took over a ship that was occupied by twenty armed soldiers. But, seizing control of two ships was not the end of this man's fight. He then went straight for the Sea King of Syracuse, charging through the thickest part of the battle until he could reach the cowardly King. Verus finally found Priscus the Gaul—who was a long ways from the fierceness of the conflict. While Verus sent his men to the side to reinforce another Athenian ship, Verus climbed through the burning remains of another vessel so that he could flank Priscus. Like a demon from the underworld, Verus exploded from the burning ship and leaped onto Priscus' ship, killing slaves and soldiers all along his way. After having his fill of blood, the mighty Verus dove into the water and chopped the rudders of the Priscus' ship, which permanently disabled the vessel.

As Arria finished, Priscus narrowed his eyes and tightened his jaw. "Here, read this one."

With some hesitation, Arria began:

Priscus the Gaul has been known for his fierceness all of his fighting career, but, at his supposed apex, he completely failed to win the hearts of the spectators. He fought away from the thickness of the battle and only picked on smaller ships that he could easily beat. He might have been a force to fear in the arena, but he was far from fearless on the sea…

Arria suddenly stopped and looked up. "Why does it matter what they write? You have enough money to buy your freedom."

"It's not right," Priscus replied coolly. "I am the only reason the Syracusians fought so well; I was the one that predicted Sextus' plan and prevented it; I alone was the one that killed the Athenian Sea King." The Gaul handed her another sheet of paper, "Here read this one."

Arria frowned. "Why worry about all these things? You know what you've done. Why should it matter how badly others misjudge your deeds?"

"Please," Priscus said as he tried to restrain his temper. "Please read."

Tresias, the owner of the Gladiatorial *Ludi* of the north, has declared Verus the best warrior that they have ever trained. Tresias said that, "neither man nor beast has ever been more feared or more respected in the arena. Verus was a true warrior from the moment that he came into the *Ludi*. Everyone feared him—including all of the *Doctores*. He beat them all back with his fierce attacks and relentless persistence. I not only trained Verus, but also Priscus too—the large Gaul from the north. The Gaul certainly has skill, but if these two were paired together, I would put my money on Verus—who, in my opinion, is superior in skill. While Priscus may have the advantage of size,

Verus more than makes up for it with everything else..."

"Enough!" Priscus yelled as he stood and walked to the edge of the garden. He put his thick hands on the waist-high banister in front of him and stared out at the buildings of Rome. Every face that he saw in the distance was another face he wished he could punch.

Arria gently touched his shoulder. "What's wrong?"

Priscus clenched his jaw and waited a moment before he replied. "I fought so hard and so long—no one could ever defeat me—and now, right when I achieve my greatest victory, everyone waters it down like I did nothing. As a Sea King of Rome, I led Syracuse to victory. There is no question in my mind who won the battle: we did. After everything, we still had an entire Quinquereme still ready for battle."

"The rudder was chopped off." Arria said, correcting him.

"We could've substituted it with something else—it would have been an easy fix—but the Emperor had already called an end to the conflict. Have you ever had something that you wanted so badly that you would do anything to get it, but for some reason—even the simplest reason—you can never have it?"

Arria eyed the Gaul deeply, putting more weight on the next word then the Gaul expected. "Yes..."

"I want to end my career as a gladiator at the peak of success—not on the climb to it."

"My father says that he is going to give you a wooden sword—whether you want it or not."

Priscus gave a slight laugh. "Your father won't set me free— trust me on that. He of all people knows what it is like to want something more than what you have. Of course, he will offer me the wooden sword, but when I won't take it, I am sure he won't force it upon me. You will see."

Arria closed her eyes and shook her head slightly. "Can you not see what is right before you? You're wealthy now, and completely famous; you've got the respect of your master and...of his daughter."

Priscus nodded. "Yes. Which is not something that I would have ever expected—nor do I feel I deserve—but how can I give my heart to my new life, when it is tainted by the old? If I retire now, right when I am so close, I will never have the...peace that would befit...the life of a future family."

"Oh," Arria said as she poked him in the side. "Is there a family in your future?"

The Gaul did not answer.

"So, then, what do you plan to do?"

"I have to write back and defend myself; whoever is responsible for these reports is simply mistaken."

"Are you sure that will help?"

"Can you help me write the letter?"

Chapter 37

February 18, 80 AD
Verus

"Here," Terstius said as he ran into the cell out of breath. "This is being posted all over the city."

"What does it say?" Verus asked.

"You know I can't read."

Verus sighed. "Then how do you know it is about me?"

"Because..." Terstius replied, "I've never seen something copied so rapidly and spread throughout Rome so quickly."

"See if you can get the Master's daughter again to read it to us."

Terstius swallowed. "Are you sure we can trust her?"

Verus leaned closer into the bars. "We have no time to find out. The Colosseum is being inaugurated in just a few weeks."

"Right," the small boy agreed. "I will be back as fast as I can."

Verus paced his small cell as quickly as he could. It was exactly four paces wide and five long. He was able to walk up and down the small room at least ten times before a young girl appeared. She was short and skinny.

"Oh, Verus," she said with a light voice. "Do you need my help again?"

Verus handed her the letter. "Please, Sandina, could you read this to me?"

She winked at Verus before she read the letter in a dramatic voice:

Verus is no champion of the Naumachia, nor is he worthy to be compared to Priscus the Gaul. In his attempt to kill Priscus, he was knocked free of the boat; not by any great warrior either, but by a slave, who was armed with an oar. Priscus ruled the seas just as he has ruled the arena for years. He is the consummate warrior, having never lost to a single challenger. Even when he was wounded—when most gladiators would sue for peace—the large man fought on and on, until he snatched victory from the jaws of defeat. He fought in Gaul and northern Italy, where he trained with the best men and instructed the most talented soldiers. When Priscus was at the gladiatorial *Ludi*, as every man there can testify, he was so feared that even the instructors would not fight him in practice. Priscus is not just a gladiator, but a legend, whose talent with the sword is as great as the man he is.

Verus laughed. "Excellent!"

Sandina looked down. "Excellent? I don't know if you were listening very well, but he had nothing good to say about you."

The Blacksmith stepped closer to the Master's daughter and gave her a handsome smile. "Can you write something else for me?"

With a flirtatious grin, she nodded ever so slightly.

Priscus was once a brute, a man hardened by the life of a gladiator, but what once was fierce in him has quickly died off. Gladiators that are as strong as he claims to be, do not retire in the middle of their prime. Priscus is only twenty-nine, but he acts like he is forty-five.

—Verus—

Verus had this letter copied and posted throughout Rome. A day later, Priscus had a rebuttal. The letter was initially a private one, but after he received it, Verus quickly sent it to an orator, who had it reprinted several hundred times and spread throughout Rome.

Verus,

This is a dangerous road that you journey down, so I am

surprised you included your name as well as your insults. You are a brave man to be so open with your opinions, but do not mistake bravery for skill—for many brave men have fallen before with the skill of my sword. I order you to cease these slights at me. If you were so grand how come I did not ever hear your name in the halls of the gladiatorial *Ludi* where we studied together? You, however, knew mine—knew how I ripped open the eye of one of the *Doctores* and blinded him for life. So I give you this warning as one who is part of the *familial gladiatorial*: Do not cross swords with me.

—Priscus—

Priscus' letter had just the opposite effect that he was hoping. Verus seemed encouraged by it, thrilled to bait the large warrior. The Blacksmith replied with another letter, which he had published and spread throughout Rome. The insults were so specific, so railing, that Priscus was sure that he must have known this gladiator from the Ludi. But, despite how long or how much he thought about it, he could not picture who Verus was. He had never learned any names of the other fighters—they seemed so unimportant to him then—but now, somehow, this one fighter knew so much more about him than almost anyone.

The Gaul sent another private letter back, insulting Verus with as much disdain as could be printed on a piece of papyrus. The insults were so scathing that they seemed to melt into the words of each pages. Verus had the letter replicated and distributed among the populous—this time he had several thousand copies printed.

Plini the Younger had been more than willing to help Verus—especially after discovering Verus was from Pinacale. Each day as Titus ate breakfast, Plini would come in with the gossip that was flying between Priscus and Verus. After a few weeks of this heated exchange, the letters became so obscene that before Plini would read them, Titus would have the women leave the room. Everything funneled down to one single moment when Titus, who was enthralled by the mad exchange of insults between the two gladiators, sent out an official letter that was posted throughout

Rome:

Titus Flavius, the Emperor of the entire world and the second of the Fluvial Dynasty, has just announced the completion of the magnificent Flavian Amphitheatre. This magnificent edifice of eternal fame is capable of holding over 90,000 individuals—50,000 of them in seats. This freestanding circular monument covers over 24,000 meters and is equipped with the most advanced *hypogeum* in the world. These networks of tunnels will provide a level of entertainment that the world has never known before.

The magnificent Titus has announced 30 days of games to be part of the inauguration of this new Colosseum. The Emperor is keeping much of the details of the event to a select few, but he has made it known that on the first day of the Colosseum being open, Rome's greatest two Sea Kings will be selected to inaugurate it with their blood. Priscus the mighty Gaul—the undefeated warrior of the north, shall face the quick and powerful Verus—who is known as the merciful Blacksmith. While one of them will be the champion of the arena, the other will honor the Gods with his blood.

Chapter 38

February 28, 80 AD
Priscus

"Blacksmith?" Priscus asked as Arria finished the royal proclamation.

"It says 'Verus the Blacksmith'," Arria repeated.

A shock whipped through the Gaul's body, which squeezed his stomach until he felt dizzy.

Arria put her soft hand on the Gaul's back, "What is wrong?"

"I...I..." was all the Gaul could say.

"What's wrong?"

Priscus shook his head. "I need some time to think."

"Do you know this man?"

The Gaul did not answer.

"How do you know him?"

"Our...paths have crossed."

"Is he a friend?"

"I can't fight this man."

"This is an imperial proclamation. You have to fight him."

Priscus threw his hands up in the air. "I need to talk to him. Do you know where he stays?"

"Maybe Father does, but—"

Before she could finish, Priscus left. He ran hard and quick until he found Horace, but the old man was just as unsure of where Verus stayed as was his daughter. The Gaul scoured the whole city, bribing everyone he met for information on the Blacksmith. The information was as mixed and confusing as were the people that provided it. After three days, he finally found out that Verus was kept by the house of Brutii, but after presenting himself several times at the door, Priscus was turned away like he was a fool.

Finally, after six days of fruitless attempts to reach Verus, a Centurion provided the most useful information of all.

"Doesn't matter where he stayed all the nights before," the man said as he chewed on a blade of grass, "Verus will be locked up in the Colosseum tonight."

"In the Colosseum?" Priscus echoed. "Is he there now? Why will he be there? Shouldn't he be at a banquet with his master?"

"No, he's not there now, nor will he be there until sunset. Most masters have their gladiators at banquet the night before, but not the man from the Brutii. I've heard that the master of the Brutii is as fierce as he is wicked; and he's not happy that Verus is fighting tomorrow. I imagine it will be a cold lonely night for the Blacksmith."

After hearing this, the large Gaul ran back to his room where he paced around for several hours, thinking about what the Centurion had said. At times he would lie down next to the wall and close his eyes, pretending to be somewhere else.

"What do I do?" he asked the wall. "What do I do!"

After some time, there came a knock at the door.

The Gaul rose slowly to his feet. "Who's there?"

"It's Arria."

"Come in."

The young woman held an oil lamp in her hands which sent shadows scurrying across the room.

"Are you all right?"

"Yes."

"I can tell when you lie, you know."

"Yes, you can," Priscus said. "I know you can."

"What's wrong?"

"I have to go right now…"

"Where? The banquet is about to begin."

"I won't be there tonight."

"What can I do for you? How can I ease the tension in your heart? Are you scared about tomorrow?"

"Arria, I love you. I have loved you since our first conversation, but I have never deserved you. Even after all this time, I still feel guilty for saying what I am saying to you now." He stepped forward and put an awkward hand on her cheek. "No, Arria, I do not fear death—nor do I fear what tomorrow may bring. But I do fear my past, fear that it will one day force you and me apart."

She pulled him close, hugging his chest with her cheek. "Oh, Priscus, please do not die tomorrow. Please...I love you too..." She tried to talk on, but her voice would not let her.

"If the Gods will it, I will happily be your husband in the years to come. But, I must do something tonight..."

"Is it dangerous?"

"No, I will be fine."

She began to cry. "Please don't die..."

Priscus let her cry for long moments after. The tears came as quickly as they could, running down her smooth cheeks until they pooled just below her chin.

The Gaul pushed her away. "I'm sorry..."

She tried to protest but her lips lost their strength. Before she could speak again, Priscus was gone.

The Gaul traveled quickly through the streets of Rome, passing drunken travelers and Citizens as he went. The whole city was alive with fires and music, which carried haunting tunes that drifted through the night and echoed through the alleys. When he reached the Colosseum he was stopped by a set of guards, but after showing his passport and explaining that he was preparing for the games the next day, they ushered him through.

The building was the most impressive structure Priscus had ever seen—or it would have been had he looked at it. The whole thing was surrounded by arches that were decorated with various statues of Gods. The halls were wide and expansive, almost bigger than the roads outside. The structure was complex as well as large; so complex in fact, that Priscus kept losing his way. When he did get lost, however, there would always be a slave that would provide ample instructions that enabled him to continue on. All around him were the carved figures of past heroes and heroines, titans and Gods. The sculptures were so finely crafted that in the darkness Priscus first thought they were real people. Eventually, he found himself stepping down a large series of stairs.

He had to take the steps slowly because it was so sparsely lit by torches. Suddenly, Priscus stopped in his tracks and grabbed for the sword at his side—someone was looking straight at him from above. Through the flickering light, Priscus narrowed his eyes. It took a few moments, but finally he realized that it was only a large statue of Pluto.

This part of the Colosseum seemed completely deserted. Each of the Gaul's steps echoed throughout the halls and disappeared into the distance. As he walked down the last few steps, he could see rooms scattered out to his left and right. He stepped on and on, straining to see in the dim light. At one point it became so dark that the Gaul could not see the path in front of him. He doubled back and picked up a torch from a wall bracket and continued on. Eventually, the light from all other torches disappeared completely. He found himself entering the most miserable part of the whole arena, where a thick smell of mildew and water hit his nose. Priscus ducked under another set of doors and entered into an even more narrow set of rooms. To his left and right were all empty cells. It was not until the last cell that the Gaul found any trace of prisoners. There was a half-eaten dish of food on the floor with a cup of wine beside it. The food appeared to have been recently abandoned.

The Gaul studied the darkness of the cell. "Verus of Pinacale."

A man from the far corner emerged. "Priscus the Gaul."

"It is you," Priscus answered. "I can tell by your voice."

"Who did you expect?"

The Gaul did not answer.

Verus stepped closer to this new intruder. "I've been looking for you for years, Priscus the Gaul, and finally, after waiting all this time, you come to me. You're exactly how I remember—from the scars down your arms to the rigid jaw that sticks out from your face. Many years ago you and I trained at the same *Ludi*; we were almost in the same cell. Remember, Gaul?"

Priscus swallowed.

The Blacksmith suddenly stepped closer—his expression had changed. "What do you know about the destruction of Pinacale?"

"I came down to talk to you about the fight that is to come— to persuade you to change your mind."

Verus stepped away from the bars and walked around his cell. "To persuade me?"

"Things have changed—"

"What are you talking about? What has changed?"

"I don't want to fight you tomorrow."

Verus laughed and shook his head.

This time the Gaul stepped forward. "I've fallen in love with a woman who is as decent and pleasant as she is pretty."

Verus laughed again, a cold, bitter laugh that echoed long after it ended. "I thought that one woman would never satisfy you. You told me that having just one woman ties men down and makes them useless."

Priscus whispered. "One day, if the Gods bless me, I will ask her father for permission to marry her."

The Blacksmith narrowed his eyes. "Marriage? You said only fools marry. Why do you blather on about these things? None of this matters to me. You are a fool."

"I am a fool—a damned fool. But you are even more of a fool if you don't forfeit the match tomorrow."

"Forfeit? After what it took to get here, are you mad? For over ten years now I have been whipped and beaten, forced to kill and destroy all those around me. I've broken every big bone in my body, from the ones in my legs up to the ones in my arms. My body has been wracked by more torture devices than you could imagine. Twice I was chained to a nest of fire ants that tore at my flesh for days on end; four times I was hung upside down until the blood from my body dripped from my nose and eyes; thrice I was thrown into a pit of snakes and kept there for days; twice I was chained to the side of mountain in the bitter cold of winter. I've been beaten within an inch of my life so many times that my body hardly has feeling in it anymore. Whereas most gladiators fight three or four matches a year, I found myself in more than twenty. And now, Gaul, after all that—when my freedom is as close to me as the shirt on my back—you ask me to forfeit?"

Priscus narrowed his eyes. "If you fight me tomorrow—you...will die."

"What compels you to come talk to me: is it fear?"

"I don't want more blood on my hands. I want a new life—one where I can have a family."

"LIES! I saw the way you fought during the Naumachia, the way you brutally killed everyone around you. Your sword and face were speckled with the blood of every opponent who stood before you. If you didn't want more blood on your hands then why did you not buy your freedom after the Naumachia? Why did you blatantly refuse your freedom when your master offered you a wooden sword?"

Priscus lowered his head and his voice. "I did not know it was you who was writing those letters; I did not know it was you who was challenging me."

"Why would that matter? What do you know that you won't tell me?" Verus' whole demeanor changed; he rushed forward and grabbed his cell bars. "What do you know about Pinacale!"

Priscus looked down and to his left, scratching the brow of his head.

"TELL ME! I saved your worthless life in the *Ludi*. You owe me an answer."

The Gaul's eyes began to well up with familiar tears. "I did it. I did it all…"

Verus leaned closer. "Did what?"

Priscus stepped away, turning his back to Verus. "I was the Centurion who ordered the destruction of Pinacale. I had been sent to detain and capture but, instead, I tortured and killed. I am responsible for it, for it all…"

Verus stood there, rocking back and forth on the balls of his feet. "What do you mean? What are you saying? Were you part of the Century that attacked Pinacale?"

Priscus locked eyes with Verus. "I was not only part of the Century—I was the one that commanded it—"

"You killed everyone?" Verus hissed. "—you worthless dog! That is what you could not tell me in the *Ludi?* Do you know what that did to me?"

"Yes…in part…and that is why I beg you to forfeit. I do not want to take more from you than what I already have. Please, Verus, I beg you—. Cut off a toe or a finger, fake an illness or a disease; do whatever it takes to forfeit."

"I still have a son out there that I need to find. If I don't win this, my Master will never set me free, nor do I think he will ever let me fight again. I must have my freedom so I can find my child. And if tomorrow you are the last wall that blocks me from him, then I will tear you down and split your body from limb to limb."

"It's been ten years, Verus, what if your son is already gone..."

"My son is the only thing that has kept me going!" the Blacksmith hissed. "A hundred years could pass by and still no one—not even the Gods themselves—would be able to persuade me to abandon my son."

Priscus shook his head.

Verus continued. "How is it that you think your sacrifice is greater than mine? How is it that your new love for this woman of yours is more important than the love a father has for his son? I saw him take his first step; I heard him utter his first words. Your death might break the heart of your woman, but without me, who will find and protect my son. Can't you see—my life has more value than yours."

Priscus turned his back to the Blacksmith. Somewhere in the distance a pipe was leaking a few drops of water. The Gaul shook his head and turned back around. "He's dead."

"What do you mean by that? You don't know anything about him."

"I do," Priscus whispered. "I know that your house is built away from the city—on top of a little hill. There are three houses there that have small gardens in the back..."

"Stop," Verus whispered. "Just stop. You don't know anything about..."

"I remember the face of your wife as she fought to protect your children. The oldest one—he must have been six or seven—jumped out a back window and ran towards the woods..."

"STOP!"

"Verus, I am so sorry for what I have done to you—"

Verus narrowed his eyes, which were welling up with water. "Tomorrow, in front of all of Rome, I Verus of Pinacale shall finish you off. I...will...kill you. Go and tell your woman 'goodbye' this night because she will be burying you by tomorrow."

Priscus shook his head—tears now sliding down his cheeks, "I beg you to forfeit the fight. Please..."

"And why don't you do the same? Why don't you forfeit the match!"

"I can't now—not when I have come this far," Priscus replied. "Your little letters damaged my reputation along with the security I had for the future. How can I go against the will of Titus and refuse to fight? I have never refused to fight, nor have I ever feared anyone that has been pitted against me. You've tarnished my name—you've forced me to fight."

"You puffed-up wretch," Verus grabbed the bars of his cell, almost like he was going to tear them apart. "How can you ask me to quit when you would not do the same?"

"I WILL KILL YOU!" Priscus roared. "That is how tomorrow will end—with your body being dragged off by Charon." The Gaul straightened up to his full height. "Don't you understand me? There is no coming back from the place where you will be sent."

Verus wiped the tears from his face. "Not only have you just taken the last thing that might have given me any fear of death, you have also sinned before the Gods, killing an entire town of innocent people. For the crimes you have committed, for the wife and children you took from me, for all the people you have crossed—Priscus the Gaul—tomorrow, I will send you to hell."

Priscus shook his head. "So be it."

Chapter 39

March 1, 80 AD
Verus and Priscus

Before dawn the Colosseum was an anthill of activity. Gladiators of all kinds and types paced the crowded sub-levels, drilling with swords and shields. Verus watched as a group of chained lions passed by, followed by a set of entertainers who were dressed like miniature gladiators.

The Blacksmith was finally released from his cell and sent off to a food line, which was serving a hearty mix of vegetables, beans, and barley. The Blacksmith ate everything that was handed to him, including some flatbread that had long since gone stale. He had no desire for food, no desire to do anything but fight, but he knew he would need all of his strength. After his meal, he was guided to the upper levels of the arena where he could hear the chants and cheers from the crowd above. Collectively, they sounded like an ocean tide that waxed and waned as various *patricians* appeared.

Just after dawn, the arena filled with applause that ruptured throughout the building and echoed far into the distance. Titus, the Emperor of the world, had appeared, bringing with him an entourage of powerful generals and senators. The Emperor was wearing a flowing purple robe that seemed more alive than the man that wore it. Upon his head sat a golden crown of olive leaves, which bounced twice as the chubby man took his seat. The seat itself was something to marvel at, having been carved from a solid piece of marble and then ornately decorated with pillows. Around the Emperor stood the *Praetorian* Guard, a mix of fierce looking warriors armed with the finest weapons and armor.

After a while large trumpets silenced the crowd. Titus stood and raised his hands in the air. He gave a speech that was so forceful, so stirring that the crowd was on its feet most of the time, cheering as loudly as it possibly could. On and on the noise went until all of Rome must have heard it.

After Titus' speech, several Jews were rushed out into the center, where they had to wait while trapdoors from below revealed their fate. Suddenly, almost as if the Gods had willed it, the men were surrounded by multiple lions. The crowd cheered enthusiastically, yelling with all the force they could muster.

The noise was so loud, however, that the starving lions crumpled to the floor in fear. After long moments of watching the wild beasts frozen to the ground, the crowd began to laugh and hiss. One lion in particular drew more laughter than the rest as it began to play with the tail of another.

With a red face, Titus ordered men to prod and poke the lions into action, but to no avail. With the spectacle turning into a disaster, the Emperor summoned the beast master who was in charge of training the lions. The crowd cursed and hissed as a wizened old man entered into the arena. The man knelt down on the ground in front of the Emperor and waited. Tense moments passed as Titus looked out to the crowd, asking them to decide the beast master's fate. The answer was death. In another moment, the old man was ceremoniously executed.

This, at least, had the crowd cheering again. The Jews were rushed out of the arena and were replaced by a group of *Bestiarii* that skillfully attacked the lions. A few of the beasts turned more violent as they were backed against the wall, but after a short time, the creatures were systematically killed.

The entertainment went on and on: a group of elephants was pitted against a few hunters; a host of crocodiles fought a set of gladiators dressed like Egyptians; a wave of leopards were sent against men that were armed with nothing more than daggers.

Soon the sun reached the highest point in the day. While everyone was buying or eating a meal, Titus kept the entertainment going by holding mass executions of criminals. He hanged some, burned others, and had others whipped to death.

After the executions, when the sun had gone down a little more, Titus sent out gladiators en masse. Most of the men were criminals, condemned to die, but instead of being executed, they chose to fight. Now, with little gladiatorial training, they paired up with a fighter across from them and hacked at each other until one of them sued for peace.

Titus, who was still disappointed about the failure of the animals that morning, decided to let the people choose the fate of the fighters in the middle. The crowd was as eager as it was hungry for blood. The crowd ordered the execution of almost every man that sued for mercy. The Emperor found himself making the death sign so often that he usually just kept holding his hands in place. The more the red blood mixed with the sand below, the more the crowd seemed intoxicated by its smell.

After three of these massive battles, gladiators were brought out in single pairs. These gladiators were more famous and renowned for their skill, having proven themselves several times in the arenas around Rome. Fight after fight left another gladiator wounded and bleeding on the ground. Each time one fell, the crowd cried out for death.

Verus' heart skipped with the realization that his turn was quickly approaching.

The Blacksmith had never seen an arena where so many gladiators were killed one after another. Usually only one out of ten fights ended with death; now, it seemed, only the victor would survive.

Verus left the side of the arena and entered into the armor room. By order of Titus, Verus was to be armed and armored as a *Provocatores,* while Priscus would be armored like a *Murmillo.* A Colosseum slave gave Verus one of the most ornate breastplates the Blacksmith had ever seen. It was a golden crescent-shaped metal that had a layer of sheepskin on the inside that made it fit comfortably around his chest; it was strong and sturdy but still allowed a great amount of flexibility and movement. Three slaves helped Verus don his armor. While one boy secured and fastened a long greave on his left leg, another one attached a *manica* to his left arm. The third boy put on a flat brimmed helmet that had two large plumes of feathers coming out on either side. After the slaves finished, the Blacksmith then fastened two additional swords to his waist and grabbed a third for his left hand.

He went into a holding room that was mostly empty. To his

left and right sat gladiators that prayed fervently to the Gods for protection. As the sun sank lower and lower, more and more gladiators were called out of the holding room and sent into the arena. Only half of them came back alive. The rest of them were dragged off by a man dressed up like the immortal Charon, who not only had the job of clearing the arena of bodies, but also of finishing them off with a square spike.

Soon, Verus was the only one left in the holding room.

The Blacksmith looked down at his calloused hands. He closed his eyes and tried to picture his wife and children, but their faces seemed like hazy ghosts that eluded him. It was like trying to focus on something that was just too distant to see.

Verus lowered his head, shaking it with practiced impatience. *"What do I do? What do I do? Oh, great God—if there is a God—bless me with a clear mind and conscience for what I am about to do. Priscus took from me my past, and now, I will take from him his future."*

From somewhere in the arena, an orator shouted loud enough for the whole crowd to hear:

"This man fought in the Naumachia and brought the Athenians to victory. He was later crowned as one of the Sea Kings of Rome. He has fought three times as long as most gladiators and has battled four times as many opponents. This man has trained in all manner of combat, ranging from Provocatores to Bestiarii, from Dimachaerus to Hoplomachus. Tonight he comes before you as a Provocatores Primus Palus, which is the highest rank any gladiator can receive. This man will stun you with his technique, he will surprise you with his speed and, if you are his opponent, he will kill you before you realize you are dead. He is undefeated and unbeatable. Here is VERUS FLAMINUS the merciful Blacksmith of Pinacale!"

The crowd roared twice as loud as it ever did before. Verus entered the arena through two heavily barred gates which were held open by a couple of slaves. Flowers were thrown almost as if he was a *Consul* who was returning from conquest. He ignored the crowd and scanned the arena around him, looking for his enemy. After long moments of cheering, the orator tried to quiet the crowd. It was not until a set of trumpets were blown that the mob finally was subdued.

"BRUTAL AND FIERCE, this man was born into a land where power and brute strength rule. During the Naumachia, this man destroyed three Athenian ships and personally killed the Sea King of Athens. He has never been defeated in the arena, nor on any field of battle. This man is as brutal as he is large, as ruthless as he is intimidating. This night, he comes before you as a MURMILLO Primus Palus. He will amaze you with his power; he will captivate you with his strength. Presenting, PRISCUS THE GAUL, the most merciless fighter in the arena."

Suddenly, a group of low drums began as Priscus was slowly raised from the lower levels of the arena floor. The crowd went wild as they saw the Gaul emerge from the ground. He was heavily armed with the most brilliant weapons and armor that anyone there had ever seen.

Priscus stared at his opponent through the narrow slits of his helmet. Despite the cool draft from below, a steady stream of sweat was already dripping down the Gaul's back and shoulders. As the lift reached the top and the crowd around him thundered with applause, Priscus could not help but shake his head. *"Why did he not forfeit? Who is this fool to stand before me, wielding his sword like he has some chance at winning?"* Then the image of a boy rose like smoke to his memory. It was Trontian, his old friend who had been captured by the Celts. The memory was foggy at best, but as he focused his thoughts, the boy's face became clear. It was this same boy that he was later forced to fight—the same boy he was forced to kill. *"Curse you. Why did you have to die? Why?"* The Gaul took two large breaths before he stepped off the platform and onto the sandy arena.

The two champions approached each other from opposite sides of the arena—the crowd cheering them on with every step. When they both reached the middle, they were joined by a *Summa Rudis* who was dressed in black and held a long stick.

The *Summa Rudis* glanced at both fighters in turn, speaking only loud enough for them to hear. "This fight will be to the death. If you sue for peace, I doubt you will receive it; the crowd is as blood-hungry this afternoon as they were this morning." The *Summa Rudis* took a step back, shouting as he did.

"BEGIN!"

This simple word lit the crowd with fire and sent the whole

stadium to their feet. The arena was evenly divided: half of them were cheering for the merciful Verus, while the rest were cheering for the fearless Priscus.

Verus stood there for a moment, studying the narrow eyes of his opponent. There was no sense of emotion in Priscus' frame, no sense of fear. As he looked at the Gaul, Verus felt a flood of emotions break loose within him.

"Now you die!"

The first contact of their swords was so powerful, so tremendous, that it sent a ringing through the arena that reached everyone's ears. The Blacksmith took the offensive and attacked so quickly that Priscus had to duck behind his shield for defense. Swing after swing came at the Gaul with such precision that the large man was forced to take several steps back.

As the Blacksmith ran forward, the Gaul sidestepped and circled around his opponent. This time it was the Gaul that went on the offensive. He ducked down and swung for the legs, but he found his attack was easily blocked. As the attack was deflected, he charged forward with his shield, using it as a ram. Verus lowered his weight behind his own shield and met the Gaul head on. They were stopped in the middle, both struggling to force the other one to retreat. After a few moments the Gaul muscled his opponent back. Verus leaped to the side and let the Gaul charge past, kicking him in the leg.

The fighters walked back to the middle where they circled each other again.

Verus did not hesitate for even a moment. He lunged forward, swinging his sword with precision. Then, in a rapid twirl of body and blades, the Blacksmith suddenly changed his weapons. He ducked low, slipped his right arm through his shield strap, and grabbed a sword from the waist. One moment Verus was armed with a sword and shield; the next, he had his shield on his back with two swords in his hands. It all happened so fast that anyone who happened to blink missed the change completely.

The Blacksmith pushed the attack, slicing large chunks out of the Gaul's shield. Priscus stumbled as he retreated. As he was recovering, Verus swung one of his blades and sliced the top of Priscus' finned helmet. The armor squealed as the blade cut through the metal.

The Blacksmith swung for the legs while simultaneously sheathing his second sword and pulling out his shield. Again, the change was so quick that most of the audience missed it.

With a growl and a grin on his face, Priscus took to the offensive, attacking with so much force that Verus had to back away. Just as Verus was counterattacking, the Gaul smashed his shield into his opponent's face.

The blow stunned Verus for only a moment, but that was all the Gaul needed. Priscus charged again, swinging his sword with so much strength that each strike dented his opponent's shield and knocked him back. The Blacksmith tried to circle around, but the Gaul sidestepped and cut him off. Back and back Priscus drove his opponent until they were at the edge of the arena. Suddenly, the Gaul charged forward with his shield, ramming Verus' body against the stone wall.

The fighting turned desperate as the Blacksmith struggled to break free. Priscus stabbed up, but his sword was deflected by Verus' arm guard, which he then used to hit his opponent. The two twisted and turned, struggling to overpower the other. Verus' strength was no match for his opponent, however, and he quickly found himself losing control. In wild desperation, the Blacksmith began kicking viciously into Priscus' unprotected side.

The Gaul freed his sword and stabbed towards his opponent's head. The attack was mostly deflected by the Blacksmith's shield but the tip of the blade sliced into Verus' helmet. He felt a sharp pain just above his eye, where the blade cut into his flesh.

In a frantic move, Verus brought his head forward and butted the Gaul in the head, which provided just enough of a distraction for him to escape. Once away, Verus rushed back in, slamming his opponent against the wall. They exchanged a series of quick attacks that did not give either one an advantage over the other.

Using the wall behind him, Priscus suddenly leaped into the air and swung his wicked sword. The blade sliced the Blacksmith's back, leaving a large cut in its wake. The wound split wide but was not deep. The crowd gasped as the cut bled freely down Verus' back.

As the two began to circle each other again, Priscus whispered to his opponent, "Beg for mercy—I will grant it."

Verus laughed. "If that is the best you can do, then *you* should

315

sue for mercy." The Blacksmith did not wait for a response. He charged in, swinging his blade. Again he twisted around suddenly, lashed his shield to his back, and drew out a second sword. With two blades in his hands, he drove the Gaul back towards the center of the arena. The Blacksmith's swords seemed to come from everywhere, hacking and slicing deep chunks into everything they hit.

As they reached the center, Verus lowered himself down, stabbed the sand below, and flicked it at his opponent's face. To the crowd it seemed Verus had just taken another swing, but instead, Priscus had taken a full face of sand. Instantly the Gaul was blinded in one eye. He haphazardly swung at his opponent but hit nothing but air. The battle turned intense as Verus rushed in, attacking with all the force he could muster.

A lucky swing from the Gaul's shield knocked Verus in the head. There was a pause in the conflict as the Blacksmith recovered from the blow and the Gaul removed his helmet. Priscus' long black hair whipped in the wind. Quickly as he could, the large man rubbed the dirt out of his eyes and returned his gaze at his opponent, who was now grinning.

Priscus shook his head. "You can't win. You can't beat me— no one ever has, no one ever will." The words of the Gaul, however, were not quite convincing. New beads of sweat began to form on the titan's brow. For the first time, Priscus found himself at a disadvantage; for the first time, Priscus began to think of what could be lost. Arria's face flashed ever so briefly through his mind. He squinted his eyes tighter around the image of his opponent in front of him, which helped him to refocus. *"He can't win—he can't."* The Gaul spun around suddenly, taking his shield up in one arm, and with a mighty breath of air, threw it like a discus at his opponent. Before the shield reached its target, the Gaul drew another sword from his side and ran forward.

With two blades in both hands the fighters met each other at a run. They exchanged blow for blow, shifting to either side as they did. No matter how much force either of the men charged with, no matter what skills and techniques they employed, neither one could gain an advantage over the other.

From somewhere in the crowd, a small group of voices began to lift up throughout the arena. "Missio! Missio!" But neither the Emperor nor the two men in the middle could hear them. On and on the two men fought. They came at each other with such fantastical skill and speed that the members of the audience would jump back when one of the fighters lunged forward, almost as if they were in the fight themselves. With each terrific swing, the crowd cheered so loudly that the noise echoed for miles.

Verus spun around and blocked an attack with the shield that was strapped to his back. While the Gaul was stabbing down, the Blacksmith rolled and sliced up, cutting the right leg of Priscus.

The Gaul roared and stepped back, covering the wound with one of his large hands. The blood from both opponents now dripped down and mixed into the dirt below, turning the sand into a brownish hue.

A wicked grin spread across Verus' face. "Why don't you sue for reprieve, now?"

The Gaul took a second longer to recover before he came at the Blacksmith. Priscus threw everything into his attacks now. For a few moments they were stuck in a stalemate but then, slowly, Verus started to be driven back. As the Blacksmith turned to deflect one of the attacks with the shield on his back, Priscus swung straight for the shoulder strap and cut the shield free. The shield gave a large thud as it fell to the ground.

Verus turned around quickly, shoving his right foot under the fallen shield as he did; as Priscus came forward, the Blacksmith kicked his leg out and sent the shield into the face of his opponent. The hard metal and wood hit the Gaul in the forehead, instantly opening a large gash that bled freely.

Neither of the two fighters noticed it now, but more in the crowd were chanting together, "Missio! Missio!"

"Surrender!" Priscus yelled. "I do not want any more of your blood on my hands—nor do I want your death."

"Then *you* surrender," Verus replied. "You kneel down and let the crowd choose your fate!"

"You prideful fool!" Priscus yelled back. "I have a life to live after this one—"

"A life with your woman? Is she watching you now? Does she see you broken and bleeding? One day—a long time ago—my wife looked upon you charging through Pinacale with as much

317

apprehension as your woman now looks at you. You can't escape what you have done, nor can you cover it up."

Priscus swallowed. A nauseating feeling trickled down from his shoulders and spread down his back. The emotion finally rested in the pit of his stomach, where it burned like a potter's fire. "I can't change what I did—"

"That's the same thing I will say to your woman after I've killed you."

The two men shouted as they ran at each other. They exchanged hit for hit, striking so fiercely that the sounds of their blades carried up and out of the Colosseum. Verus took to the offense and began pushing the large Gaul back across the dirt. As the conflict continued, so did the accumulation of wounds: Verus took a cut in the side and one across the arm, while Priscus was sliced across the shoulder and shin. They were both covered in blood and sweat— worn down from the long conflict—but still neither one would yield.

Using his speed, Verus threw one of his swords at his enemy; the blade twirled for a second before it stabbed into the foot of the Gaul, sending him pitching to one side. As the Blacksmith went in to finish the kill, Priscus threw his own sword. The blade flipped sideways past Verus' defenses, hitting him in the breastplate. The armor caught most of it, but part of the blade stabbed Verus' shoulder.

The Blacksmith gasped and stepped back as he pulled the blade from his body. He dropped the sword and what was left of the crescent-shaped breastplate. The fighters stood there a moment, trying to recover from the pain that spidered throughout their bodies.

Verus drew another sword from his side but quickly found that his left arm had no strength. He switched hands and charged. The Gaul was rooted to the spot, unable to move because of the bloody mess that Verus' sword had made with his foot. They fought on.

The entire crowd was chanting it now, "Missio! Missio!"

Finally, Verus was able to knock Priscus' sword free from his hand. The blade skidded a few feet away where it sunk beneath the sand. Just as the Blacksmith hit the weapon away, however, the Gaul leaped forward and tackled Verus.

They struggled on, punching at each other with their fists.

After several moments of bitter fighting, Priscus was able to pin the Blacksmith down and pull out a dagger from his side. Verus raised up his left hand in defense, but it was so weakened that it could barely hold its own weight, let alone the weight of the dagger that was coming at him.

Priscus' face turned into an ugly grimace as an inner voice drove him on. *"Kill him. Finish him off. The pain ends when you end his life. Finish him! It all ends when you end his life. Win your freedom—win the heart of Arria."* But these thoughts lasted only half a moment before something else took their place. *"There is no joy without charity. There is no charity in ending his life…"*

Verus knew his life was over; he knew that everything would end in the next moment. So as that moment passed, he was surprised to find himself still alive.

Priscus held the dagger above the Blacksmith, pretending to be fighting with him, but Verus soon realized it was all a ploy. The Blacksmith did not have the strength to fend off the blade, but Priscus did not have the courage to finish it. Instead, the large Gaul punched Verus in the face; in return Verus punched the Gaul across the chin. They continued to exchange punch for punch until finally the Blacksmith was able to free himself and stand.

The audience was cheering so loudly now that not even the trumpets that were roaring through the stadium could be heard. Everyone—whether it was man or woman, elder or child, *patrician* or *publican*—was on their feet, cheering with a voice so loud that it shook the very foundation of the Colosseum. "MISSIO! MISSIO!"

Still the two opponents came at each other—raising a fist in the air as they did—but before they could complete their final swings, a long stick was placed between them.

"Halt!" said the *Summa Rudis*. "Stand apart!"

For the first time that day, Titus stood and smiled as he looked at the crowd.

With one large voice, the crowd chanted together, "Missio! Missio!" On and on the crowd yelled, screaming so persistently that it was long moments before the Emperor could silence them.

Titus raised his hands in the air dramatically, yelling at the top of his lungs. "My friends and family, brothers and sisters, we have just witnessed a bout that must have been arranged by the GODS.

Never in all my time have I seen two men come against each other with such skill or bravery. Neither one faltered or fainted when they were wounded, nor backed away when they faced their doom. Despite all their wounds, they came at each other with fire in their eyes and courage in their hearts. During this contest of life, I found them both equal to stave off death. At the end of the battle, I found not a winner nor a loser, but an equal division of talent. What will you have me do with them!"

"Missio! Missio!" the mob replied. "Missio! Missio!"

With a smile that spread across his face, Titus raised his hands high in the air. "Then as you have decreed, so it will be. These two men were equals to fight, and so, as equals they yield! For the first time in the history of Rome—since the first fight that took place between Remus and Romulus—I declare both of these gladiators victorious."

With this the crowd roared with applause.

Whether it was because of the loss of blood or the noise all around them, the two opponents were confused. From the base of the Emperor's box, a troop of *Praetorian* Guards marched out—each one carrying weapons at their side.

Titus disappeared down a set of stairs and reappeared moments later at the floor of the arena. His flowing cape whipped out behind him as he walked on, revealing a golden breastplate beneath his toga. At his side was a majestic sword that bounced gently in its ornate sheath, which was etched with such an intricate design it seemed more like a work of art than a weapon. Each step the Emperor took thudded with so much confidence and power that the men all around him looked down and away from the gaze of his eyes.

As Titus approached the two fighters, they both began to kneel, but as they did, the Emperor pulled them back up. "You are more than gladiators this day—more than men. Most days it is good that men pay homage to the Emperor, but on rare occasions, it is the duty of the Emperor to pay homage to a few men. For you two have shown me more bravery in the last few moments than I have seen throughout all the years of my life. For that—I, the Emperor of all the world, salute you." The Emperor pounded his chest and inclined his head ever so slightly. The crowd cheered wildly as Titus turned around and walked away.

A man dressed in a thick, heavy toga put something into each of the gladiators' hands. It took them both awhile before they realized what it was, but as they did, a shock rippled through their hearts.

Each of them held a wooden sword, wrapped with olive leaves. Despite the swords' plain appearance, the weapons were more than just training swords—more than simple tokens given by the Emperor. They now—as the whole Colosseum was still roaring with applause—held in their bloody hands the symbols of their freedom.

Chapter 40

March 1, 80 AD
Verus and Priscus

After they left the arena, both fighters collapsed in exhaustion. Men swarmed in on them, carrying an array of clean clothes and medical tools. With the match over and the rush of the fight gone, the two fighters were suddenly overcome by pain.

Priscus stood up on his one good leg. "Leave us! All of you." The Gaul's words echoed throughout the holding cell. The men all around them were at first confused—almost as if they had a hard time figuring out what exactly was being said. With the wooden sword still in hand, the Gaul pointed towards a door on the far end. "OUT!"

The men obeyed this time, mumbling to each other as they went. One of them accidentally tripped over Priscus' foot, which sent the Gaul reeling to one side in pain.

Verus passed Priscus as he headed for the door.

"Wait," Priscus yelled. "Verus...wait...."

Verus gritted his teeth and turned around. "I have no more business with you...Gaul."

"What will you do now?" Priscus asked.

The Blacksmith looked deep into the eyes of his opponent, his face twitching with emotion. "What I do now is my concern—not yours."

Priscus lowered his voice. "Please, sit down for a moment. Please..."

"Either one of us could die from these wounds," Verus replied. "The longer we wait to have these cuts looked at, the greater the chance they will bring about our death."

"I could have killed you in the arena."

"And I could have let you die in the gladiatorial *Ludi*, remember?"

Priscus leaned forward and put greater emphasis on his next words. "Verus... please... listen to me. I've never asked anyone for anything, nor have I ever expected much from anyone. But I must ask you for something—something I might not deserve. Forgive me. I am sorry—truly sorry for what I did to you."

The Blacksmith turned around and stared at the wall in front of him. His sight stretched beyond the walls of the Colosseum, beyond the city of Rome; he was looking at something that was far—very far—in the distance. "I am done with you Gaul—done being a gladiator. You do whatever you want. I will not pursue you, nor do I care whether you live or die—in sparing my life you've earned that much—but granting you forgiveness is something that I will never do." Verus turned towards the door again.

Priscus' voice took on a weaker tone. "At least tell me what you will do now. Where you are going?"

"My life is not my own—nor shall it be till I've paid a debt that has long since been due."

Verus left the room and found the healers waiting in the hall. The Blacksmith looked at them for a moment, almost as if he did not understand why they were there.

"The Gaul needs help," Verus whispered. "Attend to his wounds."

These few words sent the healers in a rush of movement. They grabbed their awkward-looking totes and hurried towards the Gaul.

Two of them stepped towards Verus, but the Blacksmith shook them off. "I'm fine."

One of them laughed and shook his head. "No, you're not." As the Blacksmith teetered on his feet, one of the healers took him by the left arm while another took him by the right. Between the two of them, they were able to half-carry, half-drag Verus to a secluded room. It was quiet—almost unsettlingly quiet. The air had a pleasant warmth that radiated from several oil lanterns that were attached to the wall. The flickering light revealed a mostly barren, sandy room. It seems that the builders of the room had not yet decided what purpose the room might fulfill, but the few blood splashes on the floor seem to indicate that healers, at least for now, had taken to using it.

"Leave me with him," one healer said to the other.

"Are you sure?"

"He'll be fine; his wounds are not mortal."

Verus nodded, appreciative of the silence. While the healer began cleaning the wounds, Verus' mind drifted to thoughts he did not care to have.

"I can't believe he is gone—my son is gone. He was the only thing in this world I had left—my one reason to stay alive. It was the hope of seeing him once again that kept me fighting through every bitter match. I needed him to be alive as much he needed me to stay alive. What use is a Father if he does not have a Son?"

The young healer continued in his task as he began to speak. "I've never seen a gladiatorial combat like that—I don't believe anyone else has either. It was truly an amazing spectacle."

"It's just as spectacular as forcing two caged animals to fight each other to the death. I've been trained to be cruel and brutal—to kill without hesitation. There is nothing stunning about slicing up a man. We die for the entertainment of the crowd—this match was the same as the thousands of fights before it."

"No, not this match, this match was different. Anyone with a sharp pair of eyes and a keen intellect could tell that there was much more taking place than gladiatorial combat. Neither one of you fought for glory or wealth. When the Emperor handed you your freedom, you would have thought he had given you a bowl of rotten porridge, judging by the look on your face. You fought for something more. The Gaul was impressive, yes, and I hear he always is, but you were something else entirely. You fought with a fire in your eyes that would not be quenched; the more he advanced upon you, the more passionate you became. You had no fear of death, no hesitation in the face of pain."

Verus looked up at the healer, almost as if seeing him for the first time. The man had a sharp beard and eyes that were slanted—much like his own. A large, purple scar dripped down from the man's left ear to his chin where it ended in an abrupt point. He had a wide chest and thick branches for arms. His body was so large that he did not seem fit to be a healer, nor any trade that required light movement and a steady hand. His voice was smooth and persistent, like a wind in an open meadow. His eyes were blue; his hair was blond. His garb was not that of a common healer, nor that of a wealthy Equite, but of someone connected to the royal family. His clothing suggested prestige and power, which contrasted sharply with his humble expression.

"Verus of Pinacale," the healer asked, "I've wanted to ask you for the longest time, what have you been fighting for? What has kept you alive all these years?"

Verus stared at the healer's eyes, afraid to blink lest he find himself waking from a dream. "The hope of seeing my son alive." The Blacksmith narrowed his eyes and paused, his lips forming a question that he was afraid to ask. "Tell me healer, what is your name? What do people call you?"

"I am known as Plini the Younger, the adopted son of Plini the Elder, but when I was young, my real father called me Gaius."

A shock rippled through Verus' body like nothing he had ever before experienced. His breath completely left him and did not return for several moments. His thick hands reached out for his son, pulling him into a warm embrace. Both father and son shed tears.

Only a few times in his life had Verus ever been overwhelmed with joy: Once when he first met his wife, another time when they were married; and yet again with the birth of each of their children. There were maybe a dozen other moments that he could remember that still brought a smile to his face, but this one brief moment far surpassed them all. It was as if a dam in his heart had broken and ten years of emotions that he could not afford to have as a gladiator had suddenly come pouring out.

They laughed. And then cried some more.

Verus studied his son before he spoke again, "My son, my dear, blessed son. You're alive."

Epilogue

<hr>

March 1, 80 AD
Verus and Plini

"How did you survive?" Verus Asked.

Gaius pointed to the scar on his face. "This thing is ugly now, but it was much worse when it was first inflicted upon me. The soldier that gave it to me left me to die. I don't know how long I was out, but when I woke up I heard Plini the Elder's voice and went to it. Somewhere along the way, I passed out. Plini later told me that he carried me to his horse and then to a nearby village, where he had been staying for the previous two weeks. There he mended my wounds and concealed my identity, afraid that whoever wanted me dead in the first place might be looking to finish the job. Plini raised me up as a son and eventually formally adopted me. When I grew into manhood, I began a long search for my true father. Plini had then confessed to me that it was rumored that you had died in the stone quarry. I refused to believe it; I refused to believe that stone and chains could break my father."

"But what led you here?"

"It was rumored that slaves from the stone quarry were often sold as gladiators to the various schools—even though that was illegal. I continued my search at the surrounding gladiatorial schools. Records of gladiators were sparse, mostly consisting of nicknames or a summation of one's abilities. I did come across the title of Blacksmith many times, but when I further investigated the matter it was never you. It was not until you gained notoriety in the Naumachia that I discovered your whereabouts. Your fame had made you more than just a commodity, however, and I found myself at the end of a long list of possible buyers. Your Master, as every one of those buyers quickly found out, would not sell you to anyone for any price.

"That is when you contacted me. It took all of my restraint not to write back and tell you who I was. If you were to gain your freedom, I knew that you would have to win it. And the only person that could grant the freedom of such a high profile gladiator would be the Emperor. I had to call in all of my political favors to orchestrate the tension between you and the Gaul that would ensure the Emperor handpicked your match.

"Last night was the hardest night of my life. I debated with myself whether I should come and see you, whether I should tell you who I am. But I decided against it. I had heard of the Gaul and I knew of his extraordinary skill with the sword. I decided that if you were to win your fight, you would have to have nothing else on your mind."

Verus rubbed his hands over his eyes and looked again at his son. "The Gaul was the one that gave you that scar—he was the one that ordered the attack on Pinacale."

"I figured just as much, judging by the way you pushed the attack in the arena."

"But he is a different man now than he was then. He should've finished me off in arena but he hesitated."

"What stopped him?"

"I don't know," Verus said as he shook his head. "But, none of that matters now that you are here."

Gaius nodded as he returned to his task of attending to Verus' wounds. As he dabbed at the various cuts, occasionally eliciting a pained expression from Verus' face, the Blacksmith stared off into the distance, his mind occupied with distant thoughts.

Finally, Verus broke the silence. "Plini once said that it is in the face of opposition that we find joy. I've spent the last ten years of my life fighting to find you, and here you are—almost as if I never had control over whether I found you or not. I've seen the very worst that humanity has to offer. I was forced to fight and kill at the whim of an insane man."

"Then, was Plini right?"

"Plini said that our relationships are the core of our happiness, and those relationships are forged by charity. I don't know how clearly you remember, but when you were young, Gaius, you were extremely sick. We could not afford treatment. A man named Tulias took pity on us and charitably agreed to attend to you for a much reduced price. It was while you were being treated that I formed a friendship with Plini the Elder. I'm sure that friendship was taken into account when Plini the Elder took you in and gave you his name, adopting you into his house. Later, as the adopted son of Plini, it was you who orchestrated this fight that led to my freedom—and to this reunion.

"But more than that, it was the mere hope that you were alive that kept my will to live intact. I would not let myself believe that you were dead—I couldn't in order to stay alive. If I think about it now, it made much more logical sense that you had died, either that day or in the weeks that followed. But it was that one hope that allowed me to wade through ten years of hell and not be consumed by it."

"What do you think it means?"

"It means, my son, that Plini the Elder was right."

Made in the USA
Monee, IL
24 January 2024

52264056R00192